THE LAST CHAMPION

THE LAST CHAMPION

Book Four of the Last War Series

Peter Bostrom

www.authorpeterbostrom.com

Summary: Admiral Jack Mattis has defeated Spectre, humanity's nemesis. But he had to destroy the USS Midway to do it. Now, one of his pilots has gone missing, terrorists have kidnapped a dozen infants, his own grandson is sick with a mysterious disease that no doctor can diagnose, and no one can put all the puzzle pieces together. Finally, Mattis finds an actual mutant human from the future in a derelict ship who has come back to kill Spectre himself. Because humanity's nemesis is not dead. And this time he will stop at nothing to carry out his apocalyptic plan of galactic domination. And only one champion can stop him. Or die trying.

Text set in Garamond

Cover art by Tom Edwards

http://tomedwardsdesign.com

ISBN-13: 978-1719545846
ISBN-10: 1719545847

Printed in the United States of America

For my three favorite admirals: Kirk, Ackbar, and Adama

Prologue

Pediatrics Ward
Edgewater Clinic
World of New Kentucky
Tiberius Sector

It was times like this that Keeley Dunn wished she hadn't dropped out of medical school.

She surveyed the orange-green pile of vomit with a disdainful, tired eye. This was her life now; moving from pile of puke to pile of puke, taking care of it while the doctors and nurses did the *real* work. Why did babies puke so much? Who knew.

The PA chimed. "All medical staff to the Doctor's Lounge," said a man's voice. Someone she didn't recognize. Must be new.

Fortunately, janitors were mostly exempt from boring staff meetings. Keeley stared glumly at today's special gift. It was an interesting one; it had chunks of mushed up pear mixed through it, last night's dinner come back for a cameo. Keeley dipped her mop into the bucket and sloshed it over the sticky mess. As usual, the hospital grade cleaning supplies did their job, but they always required elbow grease. She dejectedly dragged the mop back and forth, absorbing the technicolor barf into it, then wringing it out in the bucket. Then she did it again. And again. And again.

Only three more years of this, and then my student loans are repaid! She slashed her mop angrily across the smooth floor. *All that money spent for a degree I didn't even finish. Unfortunately, ninety-two percent of a medical degree is functionally equivalent to zero percent of a medical degree.* More angry cleaning. *But hey! At least they let me keep my sorority jacket. Nothing like a permanent reminder of that time I completely ruined my life and fucked up completely. Go Fight'n Wildcats!*

It was silly to be so angry over something so completely in her control, but she couldn't help it. Everything had gone so *well*, her grades had been perfect, and then... and then she found she simply couldn't concentrate. Information went into her brain and just as quickly left it. Nothing stuck. Even her day-to-day memory started to fade; she couldn't remember what she had for breakfast, what her lecturer's name was, or what exactly metformin was supposed to treat.

Type two diabetes. It was type two diabetes. Which she knew now, of course, because that was the first thing she'd looked up when she got home. If only she'd known that during that exam. More mopping. Stupid brain... at least, no matter how bad it got, she would never forget *that*.

Doctors moved past her, ignoring her as they usually did, but at least they paid attention to her *wet floor* signs. Minutes ticked away, and the pile of sick got smaller and wetter, until finally it vanished. Her task complete, Keeley and her bucket trundled toward the Doctor's Lounge. Might as well eavesdrop on all the stuff they assumed the lowly janitor couldn't understand.

Squeak, squeak, squeak. The wheel on her bucket whined in protest as she pulled it across the smooth floor, toward the lavish, expensive suite the doctors had all to themselves. She leaned up against the wall, ears open, waiting for whatever boring talk they were about to have to begin.

Instead of the murmur of the crowd and the chatter of voices, however, Keeley heard the faint dripping of water on carpet.

Drip, drip, drip.

Another leak. Dammit; if it wasn't the seals in the roof, it was the air processing condensers. Things here were *always* on the fritz. Repairing or replacing either was a filthy, but fortunately simple, job—and, silver lining, it would give her access to the doctor's lounge. Keeley put her hand to the handle and pushed open the door. Strange, really, normally the doctors were ready to complain the *moment* something stopped working at all—

The doctor's lounge was covered in blood.

Bodies were splayed out on the carpet and slouched over the expensive leather couches, their throats slashed and arteries opened. The tiled kitchen area more resembled a slaughterhouse than a place where medical technicians could get a cup of coffee.

A balaclava-clad man stood, partially hidden behind a potted plant, standing amongst the gore. He was right in the middle of turning over a body with his foot, the rest of him clad in a strange uniform; clearly military, but with no flags or

3

insignias Keeley recognised.

Keeley dropped her mop with a clatter, the bucket rolling in front of her.

The man's eyes snapped up and met hers. For a brief moment, nothing was said, and both remained motionless. The dripping sound continued, unabated. Water from his storm-soaked clothes.

He went for the bloody knife at his hip. Keeley wanted to run, wanted to shout or do *something*, but instead found herself frozen to the spot.

The man advanced on her, reversing his grip on the knife, Fixing her with a cold, even stare. His arm went up to plunge the knife into her. His foot hit the bucket and he went sprawling, the blade's edge fiercely slicing Keeley's cheek open and grazing her shoulder before clattering to the floor.

Pain. Pain in her face and arm. The shock of it broke the strange spell of the moment, and she turned and ran.

Keeley's feet pumped on the waxed floor, skidding and nearly tripping the rest of her. Behind her, the man clambered up to his feet, growling quietly as he leapt into pursuit.

Her voice found its way to her throat. "Help!" she shouted, squeaky and weak initially, but soon her fear gave her strength. "Help! Help me!"

If anyone heard, they gave no sign. Keeley sprinted through the hospital, desperately looking for someone. Anyone. They couldn't have all been at the meeting. They couldn't all be…

She skidded around a corner and darted around another, eyes fixated over her shoulder. Bracing herself, she shoulder-charged into the double doors that opened to the nursery.

There was always a guard at the nursery. They would be able to help her. The guard, Alexander, he had a gun. A gun was better than a knife.

"Help me!" she shouted.

Into an empty room.

Every crib vacant. Not a single child in sight. Alexander lay face down in the corner, his body surrounded by an ominous red pool. The only sounds were the humming of the atmospheric regulator and the gentle rustle of palm fronds on the skylight.

And no way out.

Through the skylight, a huge freighter passed overhead, slowing down, multiple ropes descending from it. More soldiers slid down the ropes, and inside its open cargo port, she could see dozens of incubators; cradles full of the children. The hospital's patients. She could even see their faces.

Keeley sunk down to her knees, closing her eyes and waiting for the knife to end her—for the madman to come and cut her down like all the rest. And, as she waited, a wide, genuine smile formed itself on her face despite it all.

At that moment, right up until the man's knife sunk between her shoulder blades, she was the most qualified doctor in the building.

And then she wasn't.

CHAPTER ONE

Meadows Country Park
Peterborough
Great Britain
Earth

July 4th, three months after the loss of the USS Midway

Admiral Jack Mattis slid himself onto a cold bench on the side of the trail through the woods and stared glumly into the morning fog. He had hoped that a trip across the Pacific would be enough to hide him from the world's gaze. He wasn't *that* famous. Only the guy who blew up a celebrated warship to save the human race. No biggie.

Or so he thought. Instead, as anyone with half a mind might have realized, eyes followed him everywhere.

Hey, aren't you Admiral Jack Mattis?

Oi mate, how was the space battle? Is it true Admiral Yim is dead?

How many aliens did you kill? Oh, wait, they're "future-humans" now, aren't they?

The first dozen times he had to answer those questions, they were merely tiring. By the hundredth time, he was completely exhausted. And by what felt like the ten-thousandth time… well. At least long walks through Meadows Country Park had proved to be marginally effective at taking his mind away from the destruction of his ship.

Marginally. Every time he closed his eyes, it seemed, he saw the ship's reactor blossoming in space, its bulkheads busting and superstructure evaporating into clouds of superheated metal and gas. How quickly, with seemingly only the throw of a switch, the mighty warship—his home and, probably, his only true love—had turned from something into nothing. For thirty years he'd served upon her, and then, after a few years of "retirement", another two more. Now she was gone. He felt as though a piece of him had died.

Alas, USS Midway, I barely knew you.

Still, not even a nightly ritual of a half bottle of scotch and a walk through an English wood had been enough to keep the doubts at bay. Maybe he shouldn't have tricked Spectre like that, maybe there had been another way… maybe, maybe, maybe.

Maybe he could have saved Friendship Station.

Maybe he could have saved Captain Malmsteen.

Maybe he could have saved Commander Pitt.

Maybe he could have saved Captain Salt.

Maybe he could have saved Ganymede.

Maybe.

The fog began to lift. Like ghosts, trees appeared from the mist, at first shadowy outlines and then branches and trunks and leaves.

And a person. A woman in a Royal Navy uniform, mud from the trail on her boots, walking toward his bench with calm, deliberate ease.

"About time you showed up," called Mattis, barely having to raise his voice at all in the quiet English wood.

Captain Pippa Spears stepped through the mud and, wearing a warm smile despite her customary stick-straight posture, sat down beside him. "Happy Treason To The Crown Day, Admiral Mattis. How's the Fourth of July finding you?"

"Not exactly feeling patriotic at the moment," he said, grimacing slightly. "It's hard to feel good about the upcoming Senate committee hearings. And, you know, add in a possible court-martial on top of that…" he closed his eyes and blew out his breath in a foggy cone. "A lot of people still believe the captain should go down with the ship."

Spears folded her hands in her lap. "You should talk to Admiral Fischer," she said, her clipped British tone polite and polished as always. "She might be able to help you. As a character witness if nothing else."

He didn't trust her. He didn't trust *anyone* these days. Mattis merely grunted.

"As you wish," said Spears.

They sat there in silence for a moment. "So," asked Mattis, eventually, "how are you doing, Pippa?"

"Oh, not too bad," she said, offhandedly. "Upholding the will of the Crown and all. Not with the various colonies everywhere, scattered to the star systems. Little pockets of England. Just like old times. It's true once more that the sun never sets on the British Empire."

"Because even God doesn't trust Englishmen in the dark."

She laughed pleasantly. "Allegations bold and scandalous, Admiral Mattis, but well received. Always have time for honest banter, I say." She considered a moment. "Command continues to be a bit of this and that. The Royal Navy is screaming for officers in command positions, so I'm losing my XO. The poor boy's going to get his own heavy frigate. Bit rough, given his age, but I'm sure he'll do a bang up job. And youth is something you grow out of."

Truer words were never spoken. "If you're lucky." Mattis shifted on the bench, turning to her. "Anyway. Last I heard, the *Caernarvon* was assigned to deep space patrol out of the solar system, until they get Goalkeeper back online after the latest SNAFU. How did you find the time to meet me?"

Spears only smiled knowingly. "Officially, our long range targeting radar needs tuning. Unofficially, we had that thing dinged into shape weeks ago, but when the legendary Admiral Mattis calls you asking for a meeting, you don't turn him down."

Mattis managed a slight, forced smile. "Legendary my ass. To be totally honest with you, Captain, I'm starting to find Earth a little tiresome. A few too many politicians for my taste, and far too little to do. Not even administrative work. I'm sitting around here rotting in the, ahem, lovely English weather. Never thought I'd be clamoring for the opportunity to sail a desk." His smile widened a little, becoming a shade more genuine. "Still. Coming all this way to pick up a Colonial? Britannia's generosity knows no bounds, after all."

"I wasn't sure if you had anything or not," said Spears, "but I know that if you did, you'd want to show it to me in person."

Damn straight he did. Or rather, he wanted to share his misgivings with her. He lacked *proof*, but Modi was working nonstop on that as they spoke. And when Modi set his mind to something, he tended to come out on top. "Come on," he said, standing up with a groan. "Let's go get a beer."

"In sunny England," said Spears, standing as well, "we call them *pints*. And let's get one each, please."

They left the park in companionable silence, emerging from the misty forest right on the edge of a bustling metropolis. Mattis let Spears lead the way, straight toward a classical-style English pub entitled *Drunken Pigkeeper & Touchy Leech Tavern*, complete with thatched roof and small plaque.

Established 2055

Why did they name them such unworldly titles? "Age before beauty," said Spears, grinning cheekily and pushing open the door. A bell chimed as she did so.

Mattis stepped through and into the pub, his nose immediately attacked by the sweet, almost fruity scent of beer, expensive timbers and, as was typical for these kinds of establishments, the inescapable aroma of body sweat.

Despite the early hour the pub had a dozen or so patrons, dejectedly cradling booze or grumbling to each other in low voices about the most trivial of matters.

"Seems like a happy place," he said, sliding onto a stool at a booth.

Spears sat opposite him. "There's a reason they call it drowning your sorrows. Someone who's drinking alone at 0950 is not a person whose life is going in the right direction."

Suppose I'll fit right in, then. Mattis squashed that thought as quickly as it appeared. Spending the rest of his days staring at the bottom of a stein just didn't sit right with him. "No question," he said, folding his hands.

Spears went to the bar, chatted with the surly looking barkeep—an ugly, squat man whose eyes seemed too big for his head—and then returned with two tall glasses of a dark brown, almost black liquid, placing one in front of him and taking one for herself.

"To the *Midway*," she said, holding up her glass.

"To the *Midway*," he echoed. "May her bones rest amongst the stars for all eternity." Mattis took a swig from his glass, the taste bitter but surprisingly palatable, the aftertaste smooth and almost pleasant. English beer turned out to be pretty good.

They sat in silence for a moment.

"You know… the old girl had four hundred and eighty days before her major refit. Even though she was outdated in many ways, she could have had another hundred years of service in her."

"The good always die young," said Spears, nodding sympathetically. "Because life is cruel and without that cruelty, victory has no meaning. You won the day, Jack. Never forget that. Spectre is dead because of you. And humanity saved because of it."

At what cost, though? And was it worth it? "Thanks," said Mattis, almost meaning it. "I thought you'd assumed I'd gone crazy."

"You are American," said Spears, dryly. "You are crazy and always have been. Fortunately for you, I find crazy to be quite endearing."

Mattis smiled grimly. "The last Brit I knew ran her ship without core containment, irradiated herself and her crew without a single word of complaint, damn near cooked herself alive… then rammed her ship into the enemy to save us."

Spears only gave a very slight incline of her head. "Keep Calm and Carry On. Our way since the war. I knew Captain Salt, mostly by reputation and sharing a table at staff dinners. She was a top shelf Captain and I can only hope to be half the officer she was."

"Live twice as long and I'll call it even."

The edge of Spears's mouth turned down. "When did you get so grim, Jack?"

He shrugged helplessly.

"So," asked Spears, an edge of forced joyfulness to her voice, as though determined to cheer him up. "The *other* lady in your life. How are you and Miss Ramirez working out?"

The answer to that was that they were not and Mattis hadn't seen her in long enough that whatever spark their reunion had kicked up had probably died right back down again. "It's complicated," he said.

"Ooo." Spears sipped at her drink. "Ouch."

"It's fine," said Mattis.

"I hate that word. *Fine*. It means the opposite of its literal meaning; it means things are not fine, but they are tolerable."

"It's… tolerable," admitted Mattis. "We kind of knew long ago it would never work. I've got my work, and she's got hers, and they often collide in unpleasant ways."

Spears tilted her head again, an old habit of hers that he was starting to get reacquainted with. "I saw her on the news this morning," she said. "Running another story. Apparently the Forgotten raided a nursery on New Kentucky and stole a bunch of infants. The galaxy's in uproar about it."

Stole infants? Mattis scowled darkly, but in confusion. He had crossed swords with the Forgotten—and, in fact, much as he didn't like to admit it, had more in common with their causes than he would ever admit publicly—but regardless of their... armed disagreement... he would never have pegged them for literal kidnappers. All they cared about was making sure that veterans of the Sino-American war got the help and care they needed... what possible gain was there for them to do something like that?

"That doesn't sound like them—"

But before he could voice his concerns, the bell on the door chimed again as it swung open, followed by a loud clatter and the shattering of breaking glass. Commander Oliver Modi stood in the doorway, a stack of portable computers in his arms, one of which had slid off the pile and broken into two pieces.

"Admiral Mattis," said Modi, completely and utterly oblivious to every eye in the bar being locked onto him, peering over the massive stack of computing equipment, a genuine excitement in his eyes. "I found a lead you might be very interested in."

CHAPTER TWO

Garden Lobby near Chuck and Elroy's Apartment
Georgetown, MD
Earth

"Sorry," said the receptionist on the other end of the line. "The test results were quite clear. There's just nothing to indicate anything wrong."

Chuck Mattis fumed as he paced the brown grass of Georgetown's only public park, shaking his head, phone pressed up tightly against his ear. "That just can't be right," he said, echoing a variation of the same set of phrases he'd been saying to doctors all over the county. All over the country. All over the planet. "Jack's heart has an issue. A congenital issue. He has sporadic cyanosis, usually when we take him out of hospital, and when we're feeding him he gets all exhausted, like he's too tired to cry. He sleeps too long and too easily, and sometimes he doesn't cry when he should, like he's just tuckered out even though he hasn't done anything. There's something wrong. I promise you."

"We couldn't replicate those symptoms," said the receptionist, her voice masked in professional patience. "I know it's difficult for you at this time, but—"

Chuck rolled his eyes at the wall, and then focused back on the call. "Fine," he said, a little more snippy than intended. "No worries. Thank you for your time."

"Thank you for choosing Pacific Medical," said the receptionist, promptly closing the link.

Chuck sighed and put the phone against his forehead in frustration. Angel of Mercy, Seattle Pediatrics, Boston General, Presbyterian Hospital, Beijing Medical Centre, and now Pacific Medical. None of them had been able to find *anything*....

Maybe he could call someone else. Maybe he could try more places in India...there was a lot of promising medical technology being developed there. It might be an idea. A potential. He scratched his chin, ready to start searching, but before he could, his phone flashed.

A news alert. He skimmed it over, instantly sick to his stomach. An entire nursery of babies kidnapped on New Kentucky. Every parent's worst nightmare. Who the hell would kidnap a bunch of infants? Immediately, his irrational parent's brain went into overdrive, and he was half tempted to run home and make sure Jack was safely in his crib. He nearly jumped when his phone started buzzing.

An incoming transmission from Elroy.

"Hey," he said, a tired, worn edge to his voice. "How's it going?"

The phone line crackled for just a moment, and Chuck *thought* he heard something, a voice on the other end, then it went dead.

A glitch with the phone company? A faulty connection?

Or something worse.

A thousand panicked thoughts flew through his head all at once. He redialed. A robotic, recorded voice answered.

"An error occurred with your connection. Please try again later."

Dammit.

He knew it was impossible that whoever stole those babies had also stolen his son, putting a bullet in Elroy's head in the process. It wasn't rational.

But the mess of his frustrations and despair and stress all conspired against him, and Chuck knew he had to get home *now* and see for himself. He jammed his phone into his pocket, ran the five blocks back to his apartment building, and dashed inside the lobby to the elevator, hammering the button up to his floor. Slowly, painfully slowly, the elevator began to hum and move.

Slowly.

The wait suddenly became unbearable. He felt like banging on the doors. Anything to speed the thing up…

Then it arrived, the doors silently parting. The quick ride up to the apartment felt like an eternity. Then he was there.

With shaking hands, he slid the keycard over the lock and ran inside.

"Hey," he called, "I rang, but—"

The living room was empty.

Chuck's stomach rose up into his throat. He ran to the nursery and burst through the door.

Jack was not in his crib.

No....

"Sorry," said Elroy, stepping out from the kitchen, waggling his phone, its screen an ominous black. "I think my talky-thingie is busted."

Relief. "Hah," said Chuck, managing a little smile. Elroy sometimes had weird names for technology. Real cute. His hands slowly stopped their tremble. Everything was okay.... "Where's Jack?"

Elroy thumbed back to the kitchen. "In his high chair. He won't eat, but he won't sleep either and won't let me leave his sight. So I figured he could help me with dishes." Elroy ducked his head back into the kitchen and Chuck joined him. Sure enough, there Jack was. Pale and lethargic, slumped over in his high chair. "No luck with the hospital?" asked Elroy, sliding his hands around him from behind, giving a little squeeze.

Chuck melted back against him, sighing and tilting his head back. "No. Again."

Elroy sighed, resting up against his back. "We'll find something. I know it."

Chuck knew it too. It just... was elusive. And he was impatient. "I know. I just... I just..."

"Maybe try your friend again," said Elroy. "Smith. You said he could help you."

He didn't know if Smith could, but if *anyone* could it was the enigmatic CIA officer who he'd met in... unusual circumstances. That was to say, breaking into the same place at the same time. His old boss, Senator Pitt's office. Since then they had teamed up to help investigate threats to humanity. Smith had proven himself extremely resourceful, and he had a prosthetic eye that was technology Chuck thought only existed in science fiction movies. The man had ... connections.

And now he wouldn't pick up his phone. Which was ironic, because Chuck had told *him* never to call him again.

"Okay," said Chuck, reluctantly taking out his communicator. He tapped the key to dial Smith.

Again, no response.

From the kitchen Jack began to cry. There was... *something* about it, some subdued, pained edge to the normally shrill and loud cry that instantly caused alarm for them both. Without a word, Chuck and Elroy went together.

Jack's breathing was shallow, his lips tinged blue. Chuck picked him up, and as he did so, Jack seemed to recover, squirming and breathing normally.

"Shit," said Elroy, his tone a mixture of relief and concern. "What... what was that?"

"I don't know," said Chuck, frustration building within him. "But I think we're running out of options."

Elroy rubbed his face roughly, obviously as concerned as he was. "Yeah." He sucked in breath. "There's gotta be some option we haven't tried yet. Some idea. Some...*person*. Anything." The desperation in his voice grew. "There's *got to be*, Chuck."

He felt the same way, but didn't have anything in mind. Couldn't see any other option.

Chuck sighed, tapping a few keys on his communicator. "Okay. Well, lemme see if I can get hold of Smith again. I'll keep calling until I get an answer—he's gotta pick up *sometime*."

CHAPTER THREE

Studio
GBC News
Earth

"...So our top story again tonight: nearly thirty infants are believed missing after a raid on a New Kentucky nursery. Interpol is investigating and we at the studio are hoping and praying for their safe return." Ramirez carefully followed the TelePrompter scroll to the end of her segment. "Thank you for sharing the galaxy's news with us at GBC News. I'm Martha Ramirez. Thank you and good night."

She waited, smiling into the camera, as nothing happened. Of course, behind the scenes, the production crew were adding in the visual effects, music, and flashy logos, but in the studio where Ramirez was recording, everything was a professional, almost deathly, quiet. Still, they would be recording her, so she continued to smile, her face frozen.

Then the red light flicked off, signaled the recording was

done, and finally Ramirez let her face relax. The studio broke into polite clapping.

"That's a wrap," said her director, Chelsey. Not a smart woman, but when it came to making the news run on time, she knew what she was doing. "Good work, Martha."

Martha smiled her acknowledgement, pushed back her chair, and headed out toward her dressing room. She exchanged the mandatory courtesies with the crew, beelining to her dressing room door and sliding inside.

Then, only then, did she relax. With a sigh she pulled the pins out of her hair, opened up her collar, and slid into her makeup chair, kicking off her heels as she did so. Okay… okay.

Her communicator vibrated. It had been doing so all broadcast; she had pointedly ignored it, but the subtle vibration reminded her that anyone might be on the other end. It could be a rival network coming to poach her away for a ridiculous salary. It could be a fan wanting to let her know that her show had made their day.

It could be Jack Mattis.

Jack Mattis with a scoop, she firmly reminded herself. *Admiral Jack Mattis. One of your contacts as a reporter. A professional lead who gives you inside information on the unique threat that humanity faces. Someone who is really helping your career take hold, and definitely not someone you want calling you for… other reasons.*

It helped to tell herself these things. Not much, but it helped.

So with cautious calm, Ramirez pulled her communicator out from her hip pocket and flicked it open. It was an unknown number and had actually come in before the presentation was supposed to air.

UNKNWN NMBR: Do not run the New Kentucky infant story. Replace now or disaster beyond your wildest imaginations will be visited upon you. Tell nobody of this. You have been warned.

Damn. She groaned softly. The worst kind of fan…the crazy one. Frustrated, she hit delete. It had already run anyway. No sense crying over milk, spilt or otherwise. She blocked the number for good measure, adding it to a long and growing list of 'special fans'.

Ramirez gently leaned back in her chair, closing her eyes a moment. Dammit… this industry. Full of perverts and crazies on both sides of the screen. She rubbed her aching forehead, sighing.

A knock on the door, frantic and pounding, nearly made her jump out of her skin. It stopped abruptly—locked door knob jiggling violently—before starting up again, more intense than ever. Ramirez emitted a strangled shriek and nearly collapsed backwards in her chair.

The pounding came again, even more insistent. Gathering her wits, she took a deep breath and snatched up her purse. Within, she carefully withdrew the snubnose 10mm pistol within and clicked the safety off.

"Who's there?" she called, far more timidly than she meant to, cradling the pistol in both hands.

No answer. More pounding. A crazed fan? How the hell did they get past security? Grateful she was out of her heels, Ramirez crept forward, hiding the weapon behind her back and, cautiously, opened the door with her left hand.

It took her a moment to recognise who stood on the other

side, disheveled, his face the color and shape of a ripe tomato. He'd been crying for hours. Or days.

"Oh my God…." She muttered.

Senator Pitt. A disgraced US Senator who hadn't been heard of for nearly a year.

"Uhh…" Ramirez stammered slightly, relaxing her grip on the pistol. "Senator Pitt…? How can I help you?"

"You have to convince him," said Senator Pitt, a thick crack in his voice. "You have to convince Admiral Mattis. You're the only one who can."

CHAPTER FOUR

Drunken Pigkeeper & Touchy Leech Tavern
Peterborough
Great Britain
Earth

It was *extremely* unlike the stoic, implacable, almost humorless Modi to be so excited. Mattis scooted over to make room. His chief engineer slid into the booth next to him with a complete lack of ceremony, dumping the portable computers on the fine hardwood surface of the table.

"Okay," said Mattis, taking in the stock of still-buzzing computer equipment. "What are we looking at, Modi?"

"Just a parallel cluster of nearly sixty-four thousand premium supercomputer processor chips working on a singular Z-Space translation problem," he said, prying open the lid of one of the machines to reveal a crude old-fashioned LCD display. A series of numbers flew past, far too fast for Mattis to read. "This is the sixty-sixth permutation."

"This is England," said Spears, politely. "So I'm going to need your solution in English, please."

Modi turned the device toward Mattis. "See this?"

Mattis stared at the screen impassively. "All I see are a lot of numbers moving really fast."

"Yes," said Modi, as though that were the point.

Mattis, taking a slow, patient breath, looked directly at Modi. "Commander, please explain to me the meaning behind the numbers and why the good Captain Spears and I should care about them."

Modi turned the screen back toward himself. "Very well. These," he said, jabbing a finger at the thing in triumph, "are Z-Space coordinates. More specifically, they are coordinates *and a vector.*"

"Okay," said Mattis, cautiously. "A vector toward what?"

"Toward a gravitational eddy," said Modi, snapping his fingers energetically. "Do you remember the Battle of Earth?"

"Do I... remember?" Did he remember the battle where Commander Jeremy Pitt had been killed? Did he remember the battle where humans from the future came to destroy Earth, fought with the automated defense network Goalkeeper, and nearly extinguished their species? "Yes. Vividly."

"You might recall," said Modi, "that one of the damaged future-human ships escaped from the battle. It was intact, largely undamaged, and it hasn't been located yet."

Mattis hadn't forgotten. Plenty of people were asking questions about that, but few had come up with answers. "Right," he said. "What do those numbers have to do with anything?"

Modi preened slightly. "Lynch said I was... and I quote...

'nuttier than squirrel shit' when I brought this up, but ever since Z-Space translation has been discovered, tracking a ship which has translated has proved to be almost impossible. We were able to do it before the battle because we could detect radiation from the translation engine of their flagship; they fixed that defect, obviously, and this ship wasn't equipped with the same model of engine, apparently…."

"I'm sensing there's a *but* here," said Mattis, impatience starting to creep in. "If we could skip to that, please, I'd be very grateful."

Spears, for her part, seemed to be patiently enjoying herself, waiting with hands folded primly in her lap.

"Right," said Modi. "Well, the conclusion is… the smaller ships have a weakness too. It's much harder to exploit, since it involves recreating the state of the Z-Space field at the time of the jump and cross-referencing it with the gravitational wave effects of a ship leaving real space, but from there you can calculate a trajectory."

He considered a moment, resting his chin in his hands. "So this will find the missing ship for us?"

"Oh God no," said Modi, shaking his head emphatically. "Not even close. It will only tell us where the ship went, not where it is."

Of course. Typical Modi. "I understand," said Mattis, grimacing a bit. "How confident are you in this?"

"Quite," said Modi, turning to Spears. "And it's good you're here, Captain. The HMS *Caernarvon* is a heavy frigate, so it's not quite as powerful as the *Midway*, but certainly capable. Capable enough to seek out this ship and engage it on our terms."

Spears sat impassively, a picture of stoicism in the face of an indirect insult to her ship. She narrowed her eyes. "You're being quite presumptive there, Commander Modi," she said. "My ship is currently under orders to conduct a deep space patrol out past the Tiberius sector. We can't just go traipsing off on some jolly lark all based on a wild hunch."

"Of course, of course," said Modi, waving his hand dismissively. "I understand that. But we don't *need* to do very much at all in fact. All we need to do is go to where the Z-Space gravitational eddies terminate and—"

Spears didn't seem convinced. "We have our orders, Commander. I can't divert a ten-thousand ton frigate based on what I heard in a pub. Plus, we don't know what to do when and if we do find it."

Modi gave Mattis a lopsided smile. "We tend to play these kinds of things by ear," he said. Which was true enough. "Where do the Z-Space eddies terminate?"

Modi rubbed his hands together. "Well, it just so happens it's out in the direction of the Tiberius sector anyway…."

Spears sighed, as if she knew there was no point in arguing. She leaned forward, her chin in her hands, weighing the considerations. "If it would only require a *small* detour," she said, almost to herself as much as to the other two. "And we could probably disguise it as some kind of navigational… thing. I'll have to talk to Blackwood, poor dear, and make her work out the details. But it's a start."

"It's a start," echoed Mattis. "To finding the missing ship. And unraveling this mystery of what the hell those future-humans were up to, and what Spectre had to do with it."

And a start was better than nothing. "What do you say,

Captain Spears?" asked Mattis.

"Well," she said, upending her remaining beer in one smooth motion, then blotting her mouth lightly with a napkin. "Since it's not a big detour… let's fire the old girl up."

CHAPTER FIVE

Hangar Bay III
Chrysalis

Harry Reardon ran up the ramp of the *Aerostar*, firing his pistol behind him wildly. "Sammy! Close the ramp! Close the ramp! Now now now now *now now now now now!*"

Bullets screamed into the hull beside him, wailing as they bounced around the inside of the cargo bay. He threw himself flat, hands over his head, as his former business partners— security consultants from Jovian Logistics and Supply— emptied their magazines into the hull and insides of his ship. Fortunately, it was well armored and small arms wouldn't hurt it.

Less so, himself. Slowly, agonisingly so, the loading ramp of the *Aerostar* began to raise. Up. Up. Up.

"Sammy!" Reardon almost shouted into the radio. "Do something! Fire the guns!"

"We're out of ammo for them, bro," said Sammy. Oh yeah.

PETER BOSTROM

That had been a thing. Because he hadn't bought any more ammo for them. Because they hadn't been able to sell *the box*. The box currently sitting in their cargo bay. Because the box had a frickin' mutant and several hundred pounds of explosives in it. "I'm closing up as fast as it'll go."

It needed to go faster. A round skipped off the deck barely an inch from his head. Finally, the ramp sealed shut and everything went quiet except for the ringing in his ears.

"Sammy," groaned Reardon, dragging himself to his feet. "We need to get the hell out of here."

The deck pitched as the *Aerostar* lifted off, turned toward the yawning mouth of the hangar bay, and got the hell out of Chrysalis into open space.

Reardon made his way up to the cockpit, sliding into the pilot's seat with a huff. "Chrysalis—come for the history, stay because the police won't release your body until cause of death is determined." He grinned across to Sammy, and the spot where his wheelchair rested in lieu of a proper seat. "Spoiler alert: it's homicide."

"It's always homicide," said Sammy, smiling right back. Although, Reardon noted, with seemingly a lot less enthusiasm than normal. "So I'm guessing the deal went south."

"The deal didn't even *begin*." Reardon put his feet up on the console. "Serious. They didn't even give me the package. It was like the moment I walked in, they took one look at me and yanked out their guns." He twisted in his seat, showing Sammy the fresh bullet hole in his jacket, sticking a finger through and wiggling it against the bulletproof vest below. "Didn't even give me the courtesy of a warning shot. All smiles, and then the shooting started. Ugh. This is starting to happen far too

29

frequently."

"We do seem to get betrayed a lot," said Sammy, tapping at keys on the console idly with one hand, his other playing with the settings on his wheelchair.

Reardon frowned. "You okay?"

"Yeah."

Any time Sammy fiddled with his wheelchair he was usually nervous or wanted to say something. "You *sure* you're okay? Because there's something in your tone which suggests that you are not, in fact, okay."

"I'm okay." Sammy wouldn't look at him. Fiddle, fiddle went his hand on the chair's settings.

A familiar song and dance. Reardon waited, just a few seconds, then tried again. "Okay, so. What's bothering you?"

"It's the mutant," mumbled Sammy. "I mean, it's not our fault that she's here, but… we still have to take care of her. And I don't think she's getting better."

The mutant—they hadn't given it a name yet, at Reardon's insistence, and he also firmly considered it an *it* rather than a *she*—was obviously not doing too well. Reardon's best working theory was that opening the box too soon had hurt it in some way, and although it could move and kind of talk, it obviously wasn't well.

"Okay," said Reardon, as the *Aerostar* drifted further away from Chrysalis, "so what do you want me to do about it?"

"Well… well, uh, when you were busy getting shot at, I went ahead and took *another* look at the logs of the ship while Smith was on board."

Oh boy, here we go.

"I know you kept telling me to purge the logs, but

sometimes it's important to keep this kind of data, you know?"

It was really *not* important to keep potentially incriminating evidence around their ship, but Sammy just couldn't help himself. "Okay," said Reardon, an edge of exhaustion creeping into his voice. "But we've been over this. There isn't anything there. His phone signals were encrypted, and who knows how many relays it jumped through before it connected."

"Seventeen," Sammy said, matter-of-fact. "That's what I figured out."

Oh. Well. "Okay," said Reardon. "What does that mean?"

"Well, it means that fortunately, this time, I managed to figure out that the contact he kept calling was…" Sammy touched a screen in the cockpit. "This number."

Just a normal phone number, nothing special about it. "Who's is it?"

Sammy's eyes rolled. "Scroll down. Name's underneath."

"Oh. Interesting." Reardon stood up and made for the exit. "I gotta piss. Think you can get us to Earth by the time I get back?"

Sammy grinned. "Consider us already there."

CHAPTER SIX

Location unknown
Chrysalis

Lieutenant Patricia "Guano" Corrick struggled to open her eyes. All she could see was sky blue through the thin cracks of her eyelids. Where was Doctor Brooks?

"You know," came his familiar voice, words drifting from somewhere at once near and far away, like a nearby speaker. "Sometimes drugs open your mind, and while it's open a lot of weird shit gets in there."

A strange distortion twisted his words, making them difficult to follow. She tried to talk, but her mouth had something in it. Like a tube she could bite down on.

"Don't talk," said Brooks. "Just relax and wake up. Open your eyes."

Relax. People telling her to relax always made her stressed; it was like thinking of elephants when someone tells you not to think about elephants. You can't avoid thinking about them.

But, finally, she was able to pry her eyes open. Guano found herself in a tank, roughly two meters wide and ten high, like some kind of glowing blue cigar. A long white, clear tube, full of seemingly nothing protruded from her mouth, snaking upwards toward the top of the vessel. Guano was wearing a bright orange jumpsuit, like a prisoner. She otherwise appeared to be inside a hexagonal room full of computers.

Through the glass, she could see—warped and distorted like a fun house mirror—Doctor Brooks, staring intently at her. His dark skin was distinctly lighter than last time she'd seen him, and his eyes were sunken, hollow pits, dead and lifeless. His hair seemed to be falling out in clumps, as though he were dying from some kind of horrible radiation, and he had a shiny chrome pistol strapped to his hip.

"How do you feel?" he asked, raising a hand and, with palpable reluctance, tapping on the glass, as one might try to startle a fish.

She couldn't talk, so she shrugged helplessly. Cold. Wet. Weirded out being in an elongated aquarium.

Brooks gestured to a keyboard, down almost out of sight. She pulled it up, fingers awkwardly finding the keys.

Hello? She typed. The viscous liquid made the effort difficult. *Where am I?*

"Oh, you're inside a little device which will heal you," said Doctor Brooks, something strange, something off, about his voice that disquieted her in a way she struggled to comprehend. "Don't worry. We'll have you out of there in just two more days."

Two more days? Guano's fingers stabbed at the keys. *How long have I been here?*

33

"A few months," said Brooks, nodding thoughtfully. "Unfortunately, we had to keep you under for a while. Don't worry, you'll be fine."

A few months? Drugs? Memories flooded back to her. Memories… *You drugged me.*

"I needed to sedate you," said Brooks, lying through his stupid lying teeth. She could just *tell*. "You were disorientated. You had a concussion when you landed, along with some damage to your lungs. The system restored you."

Oh, there was no way she believed that. *Did you clone me or something?* She typed angrily, fingers sloshing through the fluid.

"No," said Brooks, smiling in that weird, faux-friendly way he had. "The cloning tanks may look similar, but they function quite differently. This one is restorative. "

She had been joking, in her just-woken-up brain-dead way, but Brooks acting like this sparked a distinct possibility. He could make a clone of her if he wanted.

Some part of Guano began to realize that Brooks was not who he appeared to be. Hadn't been from the start, most likely. Then the memory dragged itself out of her addled brain, like a person dragging themselves out of thick mud. Spectre…

Spectre.

Brooks was Spectre.

How? Did he have control over two bodies? Were there more of him?

Guano didn't really know what to type, so she simply hit *k* and shoved the keyboard away angrily.

"Oh, don't be like that." Brooks emitted a wet, sickly cough that he barely managed to cover with his hand. "Patricia, you have to understand. Things are different now. The galaxy is changing. You have the opportunity to be on the ground floor of something very special indeed." He smiled broadly. "You know what I'm saying is true; there are people arriving from the future. The *future*. Traveling back to your time. They aren't doing it for no reason. They have a goal. They have a plan. And they want you, and others, to be a part of that plan."

Guano simply stared at him, glaring through the glass. She fumbled awkwardly for the keyboard, pulled it back in front of her and typed, *You know I'm not going to work for you, right?*

Brooks said nothing, just staring at her through the glass, a huge smile on his stupid face.

Her blood boiled. The smile was the worst thing. So much worse than the unspoken promise of breaking her; so much worse than anything else. She stabbed her fingers at the keyboard. *Patricia Corrick. Lieutenant. United States Navy. Serial number 429114939.*

Brook's smile remained unchanged. "You can play that little game with me," he said, "but you'll work with me eventually."

Patricia Corrick. Lieutenant. United States Navy. Serial number 429114939.

"Very well." Brooks coughed again, wetly and roughly. "You'll play the game eventually. I know you will."

No, that wouldn't happen. Guano glared at him and then, pointedly, took hold of the tube in her mouth. She began pulling, short little tugs at first, advancing to violent yanks. Something dislodged in her throat, a long thin tube that probably went down to her lungs.

Brook's confidence wavered. "Wait," he said, "stop struggling. It's dangerous to remove that."

She continued pulling. Something broke inside the mechanism that attached it to her mouth and water flooded in. She sealed her lips, holding her breath.

"Stop," commanded Brooks, eyes narrowing with anger. "Patricia, what are you doing?"

Guano didn't stop. She pulled the whole thing out of her throat, resisting the urge to choke. Water—or whatever the blue liquid she was floating in was—trickled into her mouth. It tasted strangely sweet, like sugar water, or liquid cotton candy.

Brooks slammed his fist onto a large red button. Alarms sounded. The liquid around her began to recede, draining away into some unseen mechanism. Guano kept holding her breath, folding her arms petulantly.

Slowly, painfully, the water drained past her head and, lungs burning, she exhaled and took in a breath. And then another, and another.

"Do you know how expensive that fluid is?" asked Brooks, bitterness in his voice. He moved right up to the glass. "Replacing it will be difficult. You don't know what you've done, Patricia. This place has limited resources, even for someone of my—"

Guano put her fist through the glass, catching the man by the throat. The whole tube shattered, transforming into long, translucent knives that slashed into her arm and tore up her weird orange jumpsuit, but she held fast.

"My name," she growled, her voice dark and low. "Is Guano."

She squeezed his neck until it snapped, wetly and loudly. Almost too easily, as though it were made of cardboard and not bone. Her fingernails tore into the skin of his neck like wet tissue paper.

Horrified, Guano tossed the body to the side, barely able to suppress a shudder of revulsion. Fear and pain must have given her strength.

Gingerly, she stepped out of the ruined tank, trying to avoid as much glass as she could. Strangely, her arm didn't seem to be bleeding as much as it should have been. The blood kind of seeped out of the long gashes on her arms, rather than gushed, as she might expect from wounds of that size. She was probably dehydrated.

Moving carefully over Brook's body, Guano crept toward the computers that lined the walls. They seemed to be mostly diagnostic equipment. Medical stuff.

A door—really, one of the walls of the hexagon she had woken up in—slid open, computers and all. She balled her fists, head snapping to the noise, ready to fight.

"Well well well," said a man who looked remarkably like Doctor Brooks—except … younger—casually stepping through the doorway as though the scene were the most normal thing in the world. "Thank you for taking care of the trash for me. I'd been meaning to get rid of that one for some time now. It was getting somewhat … haggard."

Guano's eyes flicked to the corpse at her feet, then to the identical—and yet, not sick—copy standing in front of her. She grabbed the pistol off the body, drew it up and squeezed the trigger.

The brand new Brooks didn't even flinch as the round went through his chest. He merely stared at her, slumping backward against the wall, and then down to the floor.

Guano, smoking weapon in hand, snatched up the two

spare magazines from Brook's pocket, then ran past his clone and into the corridor, away from the ruined tank and the twin bodies, toward the light.

CHAPTER SEVEN

Location unknown
Chrysalis

Guano ran, legs pumping as she surged down the corridor, following the four lines of light which—she hoped—marked an exit to the building. As she did, she passed a row of vats— vats which seemed ominously familiar. These ones had green fluid in them, and beyond, copies of Brooks. Copies of people she didn't recognise.

Lots of people.

Pushing herself, she reached the doorway, slamming her shoulder into it as hard as she could. Although she knew, on some level, that shoulder-charging a door was a pretty stupid idea that never worked in real life, the door smashed and popped off its hinges, daylight flooding in.

Or rather, the harsh, artificial lights of Chrysalis's industrial district flooded in, near where her escape pod had crash-landed. Tall buildings, three to five stories, lined the crowded alley, the whole street lit by garish fluorescents that seemed, to her darkness-accustomed eyes, much brighter than she remembered.

Everything was vaguely fuzzy, a slight blur around her vision, and she felt lightheaded. Adrenaline pushed all of that aside.

A hideous growl, low and threatening like that of a giant cat, echoed down the street. From one end of the cramped alleyway, a trio of horrible green mutant creatures—thick arms and broad shoulders making it difficult to even fit inside the cramped space—raised their weapons at her. Stolen human rifles, possibly, seeming far too small for their huge hands.

Guano leveled her pistol toward them and emptied the magazine, the staccato *crack* of the rounds echoing in the narrow alleyway. The wild, inaccurate fire caused the creatures to duck and cower in fear, but if she hit any, they showed no sign.

Her rounds depleted, Guano turned and sprinted down the alley, taking the first turn that presented itself, a split second before a round hissed past her head, followed by a ripple of automatic weapons fire.

A labyrinthine maze of tight alleyways and garbage-strewn gaps between buildings presented itself. Chrysalis was notably ungoverned, which had allowed structures to be built with an almost deliberate disregard for fundamental civic design philosophies; squat structures jutted out of the surface like teeth, and Guano had little time to make an informed decision.

Her fantasy roleplaying group when she was younger had always had a philosophy: always go left. So she took the leftmost passage, thumbing the magazine release on her stolen pistol and jamming in a fresh one, nearly dropping the spare.

Only one more mag, she thought, turning left again. *Better not waste it.*

Angry voices behind her heralded more gunshots and the stamping of booted feet. Guano passed a large pile of garbage, cardboard and plastics piled up to her shoulders that blocked half the already tight passage.

Perfect spot for an ambush. She stopped, crouching behind the garbage pile, pistol in both hands. Slowly, carefully, she nestled herself within the garbage, pulling cardboard sheets over her and trying, desperately, to ignore the smell.

Horrible beasts approached. Green, mottled skin and grotesque faces, like in the video broadcast to the galaxy a month ago from that rogue scientist. Cardboard rustled, moving, as they pushed past the trash pile. Curses followed. *Three, two….*

"I'm stuck," said one of them, its voice a low growl.

One. Guano leapt out of the trash pile, lining up her pistol to the leader of the hideous mutants. She put three shots in, center of mass, and the creature went down. Miss. Miss. Two more into the stunned creature behind it.

The third fired its weapon, a frantic burst that clipped Guano's left side. Her ribs cracked and she smelled blood. Pain flew up the side of her body, deep and burning, but she howled through the searing agony and put her last two rounds into the final mutant. It teetered for a second, then slumped against the wall, its rifle clattering to the ground.

Hands shaking, Guano replaced the magazine in her pistol, gritting her teeth and trying to banish the searing fire that burned on her side. *Damn it.* She imagined she should have a snappy one-liner for these kinds of situations, but nothing came to mind. Nothing except anger, revulsion, and adrenaline-fueled panic. Shoot. She needed to shoot.

She dropped the slide forward and put a round into the face of the first wounded mutant, then shot the last one twice to make sure. Clambering over some garbage, her ears ringing, she moved up to where the third mutant lay. It was no longer a threat. It was slumped up against the wall, bleeding from two holes in its chest, weapon laying useless at its feet.

Cautiously, Guano moved forward and, slowly and carefully, picked up the rifle and slung it over her shoulder. Then, she stared down at the wounded monster. It looked back up at her with a strange, humanlike intelligence that she found unsettling.

Her pistol twitched in her grip. She knew what she had to do. Finish the horrible creature like the others.

But something stayed her hand, and the distant sound of approaching sirens sealed the deal. Guano tucked the pistol in a pocket of her still-wet jumpsuit and, without looking back, walked out of the alleyway and into Chrysalis proper.

CHAPTER EIGHT

Alleyway outside Doctor Brooks's Lab
Chrysalis

The enemy was human.

Private First Class Kaden Franks's blood trickled from his wounds. Dying in some dirty alley on a foreign planetoid surrounded by the bodies of his squad. And he looked up at the horrible creature who had killed all of them with just a pistol, taken his rifle, and now seemed ready to finish him off, too.

His enemy had vaguely human skin, a human face and human eyes. Just … greenish and warped and … monstrous. It looked like a woman in an orange jumpsuit, but a woman who'd been ruined by whatever experiments had been run on her. She had a military bearing. Short hair. She also looked like she didn't *want* to shoot him.

And she didn't. She just walked off into the distance. In the feeble light he could almost swear he saw normal color

43

return to her skin. As if her monstrous appearance was something … temporary.

Franks breathed. Gently. The pain faded, replaced with lightheadedness. This is what it was like to die. Slowly, feebly, his hands found his radio.

"K2," he said, breathlessly. "Man down in section…" What section was this? "Eight."

"Roger," said K2. "We're en-route, one minute to your position. Hold tight K4."

No worries. K2 was a hell of an operator. What his real name was escaped him, but… K2, man. What a legend.

Time passed. How much he couldn't say, laying in the trash, the bodies of his squad cooling around him. He half expected the monster to come back, but she didn't.

Instead K2 arrived, medpack in hand.

"Hey buddy," he said, sliding in beside Franks and pressing the device to his chest. "I got you. Here."

His wounds began to hurt again. Hurt like they were being burned. Was it supposed to hurt? He kicked, feebly, but the device kept doing its work. It hurt, then itched, then…

Well. He knew he was still wounded. It just meant the injury was sutured and wouldn't bleed too much more. He'd need surgery, probably. And a bunch of other follow up work. He wasn't out of the woods yet, but it was something.

"So," said K2, with a grim smile. "The others?"

"They're dead," said Franks, shaking his head. "No need."

"Damn."

Franks shifted slightly, the ache in his chest returning. "Where do you think she's going?" he asked, trying to keep himself focused. "She can't go far. I hit her. Pretty sure."

"That's easy." K2's face lit up. "The only place it makes sense for her to go. Don't worry, we'll make sure she gets there."

That was good. His people hadn't died for nothing.

"Do you think she saw you as people?" asked K2, curiously. "Or monsters?"

Franks grimaced. "Monsters," he said. "People don't kill people like that."

"Eh," said K2, clearly unconvinced. "I've seen things you wouldn't believe. Just minutes ago I saw her put a bullet into an innocent scientist's chest." He rubbed his own chest. "Looked like it hurt."

"Either way," said Franks, looking at the bodies of his dead squad. "I think whatever they were doing to her, it's working."

CHAPTER NINE

HMS Caernarvon
Low Earth Orbit

It had been a long time since Mattis had stepped foot on a Royal Navy ship. They were smaller, in general, than American ships, but more compact; they fit a surprising amount into a slightly smaller package. Still, for someone as tall as Mattis was, walking through the cramped corridors was a bit of a drain.

"I hope you find the accommodations to your liking," said Spears, leading him toward a tall, narrow door labeled *State Room*. "These are the VIP quarters."

Mattis smiled. "Can't complain about that," he said. "On the *Midway* the state room was almost as good as the CO's quarters. Better, actually, in some ways."

The mention of his former ship cast a pallor over everything, and he regretted doing it. For what it was worth, Spears merely kept her polite, British smile. "I'm sure you'll settle in just fine."

With no luggage and only a few hours out of bed, Mattis had no desire to rest. "How long before the ship can be ready to commence Z-Space translation?"

Spears straightened up slightly, almost eagerly, as though anticipating the question. "I've had my XO, Commander Blackburn, prepare everything as we were coming up from atmo'. Haleigh's a peach, you'll love her."

It was always good to have the best staff. Speaking of —"What about Commander Lynch?"

"He's being bought up right now. Seems a bit frustrated that, allegedly, this is the second time you've interrupted his fishing—apparently he self-described as 'a mite ornery'—but he should be docking with the *Caernarvon* in about fifteen minutes."

It would be good to see Lynch again. "Promise him that, next time, he can fish as much as he wants. I won't interrupt him even if the world's ending."

"I'll relay that message," said Spears, gesturing for him to follow. "Let's see the ship translate, shall we?"

It felt odd to receive such a suggestion—and it was phrased kindly, in a way that suggested he could say no if he wanted to—after years of being the CO, but Mattis understood that, here, on this boat, Spears was in command. "Let's," he said, and followed her through the *Caernarvon*'s passageways, toward her armoured core.

"Captain on the bridge," said a smartly dressed young woman with shockingly white blond hair as the two of them entered.

"Thank you, Commander Blackburn," said Spears, moving to the command chair which, Mattis noted, was much farther aft than his old one had been. "What's the status of my girl?"

"She's ready to jump, Captain," said Blackburn. She tapped on a wrist-mounted computer for a moment. "All systems check in and all crew are aboard. Engineering has informed us we are good to go for Z-Space translation."

It was very strange not to have a direct line to the ship's engineering team, but that was something Mattis was going to have to get used to.

"Very good." Spears settled into the command chair. "Execute Z-Space translation."

Mattis moved to stand beside her on the left. Blackburn moved to her right.

The *Caernarvon*'s primary monitors were engulfed in a sea of bright, familiar, multi-hued lights as the ship transitioned into that strange, otherworldly place: Z-Space. It was just as it had been with the *Midway*. Otherwise, the ship seemed completely unaffected.

"Just a short jump, then," said Spears, nodding resolutely at the monitor. She seemed, if possible, more British since returning to her ship. Even her accent intensified. "Where's my bloody tea?"

A fresh-faced seaman stepped forward, cup and kettle in hand, and soon Spears, Blackburn, and Mattis held steaming cups in their hands.

"More of a coffee drinker, myself," said Mattis, lightly.

"Barbarian," said Spears, her tone playful, sipping at her drink.

"Actually, ma'am," said Blackburn, swirling her own cup idly, "I developed quite the habit while I was in Boston. Just one of those things, I suppose. Gold Coast Blend with a spot of milk. Lovely."

Spears clicked her tongue. "Heavens no. Can't stand the stuff, honestly." It sounded like a conversation they had had many times before. "Anyway. Admiral Mattis, while we're making our translation to where that Avenir ship was headed… how are you holding up?"

A difficult question to answer, but what grabbed his attention was the strange word. "Avenir, Captain?"

"French for 'future'," said Blackwood. "Apparently it's what all the kids are calling the future-humans these days. *Homo insequens* was apparently too much of a mouthful."

"Language marches on," said Mattis, sipping his tea. "Maybe one day you'll learn to drop all those silly *u*'s from your words and learn English properly."

"Not while I'm alive," said Spears, her tone chipper. "We invented this language and you yanks are bloody well not going to bastardize it any more than you already have."

Mattis couldn't help but smile. "Fair enough." He took another sip of his tea which, despite its strangeness, he had to accept was not actually that bad. "And… I'm doing well. I lost command of the *Midway* before; I'm somewhat used to being on board a ship I'm not in command of."

Spears nodded, sipping her tea gently. "And your crew? How are they faring?"

It was difficult to say with honesty. "Some of them are fine. Some of them aren't. Most are somewhere in between; Fleet Command is doing their best to keep the crew together as much as possible, and so most of the crew are being transferred to the USS *Stennis*, where they'll serve under Captain Flint. The *Stennis* was heavily damaged during the

Battle of Earth when their forward superstructure decompressed. They lost a lot of good people and have been screaming for replacements for some time. Fortunately the fact that they got damaged means they managed to snag the same upgrades to their engines the *Midway* had. Those Chinese ones. They're good."

"I know Captain Flint," said Spears, with a cautious edge. "He's a bit of a prick, but a good officer. They'll do well there."

Mattis hoped so. He'd met Flint a few times over the years, at formal dinners and other events, but most of what he knew was rumor. And that rumor was that he was an asshole. Most notably, he's heard that Flint and Admiral Fischer had, for many years now, maintained quite a bitter animosity the exact nature of which was difficult to pin down. Of course, hopefully baseless speculation abounded, mostly that they had been lovers at some point, which was as ridiculous as anything he'd ever heard. Leave it to the military to assume that everyone who hated each other had previously knocked boots.

"I'm sure," he said, somewhat guardedly. "As to what will happen to Modi, Lynch, and I, well, I'll probably be sailing a desk for the rest of my career, and they are *utterly* determined to follow me in doing so, so… here we are."

"I'll have the desk moved out of the state room," said Spears, smiling at him.

A moment of pleasant silence descended over everything.

"Captain," said Blackburn, her tone gathering energy. "We are arriving at the coordinates determined by Mister Modi."

Mattis almost gave the command but caught thankfully himself. He nearly jumped as a voice whispered in his ear, "Still not used to spectating on the bridgeHe turned to see ?"" Commander Lynch grinning at him.

"Translate the ship out of Z-Space," ordered Spears. "And sound General Quarters throughout the ship. We have no idea what the hell is out there."

"Aye aye, ma'am." Blackwood touched her wrist. That thing seemed useful, Mattis thought. He should get one. "Sounding General Quarters. Z-Space translation in thirty seconds."

The ship's bell, a different sound from the American one, sounded throughout the bridge. Mattis felt that old, familiar feeling like electricity through his veins. The feeling of action stations. Of sailing into an unknown situation where anything could happen. He smiled lopsidedly back at Lynch. "I could get used to being a spectator. Not having everyone looking at you for the solution. Kicking back and relaxing as everything goes to hell around you, and for once you're not responsible for getting everyone out of the frying pan." He lied. That was exactly what he wanted, but maybe saying the opposite out loud would make it true.

It didn't. But Lynch went along with it anyway. "I hear ya, Admiral. And speaking of going from frying pans to fires, you interrupted a perfectly good salmon smoke I was doin' up by Denali. Have you seen those Alaskan salmon? Bigger than Modi's brain," he held up his hands a shoulder's width apart. "Not quite as big as his ego though."

The seconds ticked away as the *Caernarvon* translated out of the unreality that was Z-Space and reappeared in the black, inky void.

"Report," said Spears.

"Nothing on radar," said Blackwood. "Pulsing again just to be sure. Squawking IFF on all channels, passive eyes are on. Thermals are searching for hot-spots."

One of the bridge officers clicked on the main monitor. Mattis recognized the place instantly; Pinegar System. The Gas Giant Lyx.

Or more correctly, what was left of it. The future-humans —or Avenir, he mentally corrected himself—had opened a rift in the system to the future, and in doing so, destroyed a gas giant and all its attendant moons. The *Midway* had barely escaped from the system in time.

Planets, it seemed, did not die quietly. The ship had exited Z-Space in the middle of the debris field, and now rocks small and large whizzed past the ship at an entirely alarming rate. Rarely in space was debris so close and so active.

"Evasive maneuvers," said Spears, firmly. "Helm, ensure we don't ding the paint, I'm rather fond of it."

The ship began to duck and weave, bobbing and rolling to avoid the rocks. Instantly, Mattis was grateful for the smaller British ship. It was more agile than the *Midway* due to its narrower frame, giving it a distinct advantage his larger ship wouldn't have had.

"Any sign of what we're looking for?" asked Spears, as calm as if she were asking about the weather.

"Aye ma'am," said Blackwood, pointing to the screen. "One of the larger debris pieces has a strong thermal signal. It's weak, but otherwise consistent with what we'd expect from an Avenir vessel. Magnetic signature matches the ship that was seen at Earth."

The screen flickered, zoomed, then showed the ship.

Spears leaned forward in her seat. "Lock weapons," she said. "Prepare to engage."

"Wait," said Mattis, peering at the ship. It had no lights, as expected, but it was buckled, warped, as though it had suffered some great calamity even before being slammed into the rock.

"Looks like it crashed," Mattis said. "The weak signal is probably the reactor core in standby mode. Look at the buckling on the forward hull… the whole thing nearly broke in two. Must have just gone right in. Nothing made of meat could have survived that."

"An astute observation, Admiral Mattis." Spears nodded to Blackwood. "Take a landing party down there. Send Eversman and a hand-picked team of Marines. Eyes peeled. I want to find out if there is anything alive left on that ship. And I want answers."

"Captain," asked Mattis, smiling lightly. "Admiral Fischer got on my case about playing heroic captain but, well, I'm not in command of this ship. Permission to lead the away team?"

Spears considered for a moment, then nodded firmly, her teasing smile returning to her face. "You have to do something around here to earn your keep. Permission granted, Mister Mattis. Good hunting."

CHAPTER TEN

Chuck and Elroy's Apartment
Georgetown, MD
Earth

Chuck waited as his phone tried to contact Smith again. His little device rang and rang. Did anybody in the galaxy pick up their phones anymore?

On a whim, he dialed again, but this time entered in the old diplomatic security code he had when on Senator Pitt's staff. It could often be used to bypass standard security systems. Surely they would have disabled it by now since—

Finally, a voice came through, thin, female and robotic.

"This is the Tiberius Sector's Z-Space relay switchboard, based on New Los Alamos, run by Tiberian Intertel, your trusted interstellar telecom provider. The number you have dialed is no longer in service. We value our customers, and want to make your interstellar communications experience as smooth as possible. If you believe you have reached this switchboard in error, please press one. If you are having a medical emergency, please hang up and dial nine-one-one. Para hablar en espanol, por favor oprima la tres. For all other inquiries, please—"

Well, shit. He switched off the connection. New Los Alamos was a world in the Tiberius sector, the most populated area of the galaxy besides Earth and its near neighbors, nestled inside the Tiberius Nebula—a dozen solar systems full of worlds, mostly colonized. Billions of people. If Smith was somewhere in there, he was in the wind. Gone.

"It's okay," Elroy soothed. "Don't worry about it. It's a long shot anyway. It doesn't matter."

That was true. Chuck slumped down in a chair, running his hands through his hair. "Okay. I guess that's true. I guess… we could try another hospital. More tests."

"That's the spirit," said Elroy. "The fact is that Jack is alive… that's the miracle of it all. Don't worry. We'll solve this, I promise. Together."

They sat in silence, enjoying a brief moment of quiet, exchanging smiles. Then a realization hit him.

"Wait," said Chuck. "That call. It failed to connect."

"Is that worse?" asked Elroy, curiously.

"Yes. Probably. I don't know. But it's… *different*. Before it just rang out. This time it said the phone was actually not in service."

Right on cue, Chuck's device rang. He jumped up, snatching it out of his pocket.

UNKNOWN NUMBER
CALLER ID MASK DETECTED

How odd. A caller ID mask? Only criminals and black-ops people did that. Black ops… it could be Smith! He connected the call. "Chuck Mattis speaking."

The speaker transmitted a strange noise, a faint whine as though some great power source was nearby, or perhaps the rushing air of a moving car. "Chuck!" said a strange, Indian-accented voice. "Heya buddy, how's it going?"

Chuck squinted. "Who—who is this? Where's John Smith? Who are you?"

The voice on the other end of the line snorted. "Kinda hoping you could tell us that, kid. My name's Reardon. Harry Reardon. I'm an associate of Smith."

Chuck nearly—very nearly—hung up, his finger hovering over the button. He recognized the name and couldn't afford to be associated with petty criminals—not after his recent brushes with the law. But he was doing it for Jack. "I don't know," he said, summoning his patience. "Smith won't pick up his phone, and the robolady on the other end said it was disconnected."

"Oh, I know that," said Reardon. The noise in the background—was he driving?—picked up. "We're looking for Smith too. Damn bastard won't answer our calls… we can't get hold of him."

"Then how did you get this number?"

Reardon snorted. "Well, Smith's some kind of secret agent or something. What you called was one of his dead drops… basically a number people dial to get in contact with him in an emergency. We've been monitoring it ever since we—" he coughed politely. "Discovered it. *Legally*, I might add. Totally legally."

Right. This was what he'd feared. Getting involved in illegal activity ... he did *not* want to get arrested again. "How coincidental." Chuck pinched the bridge of his nose. "Do you think he's dead?"

Another voice came on the line, distant as though speaking a yard or so away. It was a younger voice, but similarly Indian. "Nah. Smith can't die, he's way too cool for that."

"Shut the fuck up!" hissed Reardon, then returned his attention to Chuck. "Okay. Kid. We need to talk."

He stared at the wall in confusion. "But... we are talking. Right now."

"No," said Reardon, obviously annoyed. "I mean... *talk* talk. In private. Can..." there was a slight pause. "Can you just answer this: why were you calling Smith, anyway?"

Chuck chewed on his lower lip. "My son is sick," he said measuredly. "Smith knows a lot of people. I was hoping he might know someone who might have some answers for me."

"Apart from Smith himself?"

"Yeah." Chuck wasn't sure exactly how much to tell the strange voice at the other end of the line. "I think it's a genetic condition. Look, it's a long shot, but... I just want to help my son." His voice cracked. "He's just a baby."

"Oh man," said Reardon. "A kid? A baby? Harry, we have to help. We have to help!"

The two started to banter, but it sounded muffled, as if Reardon held a hand over the receiver. Chuck shrugged helplessly to Elroy. He shrugged back.

"Well if it's a *baby*," Reardon said, finally, "you might really be in luck. There's a guy I know. Well, know by reputation, more like. Steve Bratta. British geneticist. Fun guy. Not great at parties, though."

A geneticist? Bratta? Something tweaked in his memory. The news broadcast… the clip of the mutant attacking someone. On some planet. Was Bratta the guy that filmed that? Or was it someone else…? He couldn't remember.

"Oh yeah," said the third voice. "But isn't he Scottish? Not English…."

"That's the same thing," said Reardon.

A third voice whistled mournfully. "Oh, yeah, this is going to go *great*…"

Reardon spoke over the other guy. "Hey. Can you come up to the roof of your apartment block?"

Chuck blinked and said nothing, unsure if he was actually being addressed.

"Won't take a moment," said Reardon. "Just so we can talk."

"You're on the *roof*?" Chuck glanced at Elroy. "They're on the roof."

Elroy grimaced and lightly bounced Jack. "Well that ain't creepy as shit."

"We're … not on the roof," said Reardon, entirely unconvincingly.

This was madness, but, well, he was out of things to try. Sighing, Chuck walked to the apartment's front door, then to the fire escape leading up to the roof. Elroy followed, lightly cradling the gurgling, now seemingly perfectly fine Jack Mattis Junior.

As they climbed the stairs upward, the noise on the end of the line got worse. "If you're not up there… then is it because the signal's better on the roof?"

"Not quite," said Reardon.

A slight tremor grew in the concrete stairs. It intensified, a whine becoming a howl. Chuck pushed open the door that lead to the roof and immediately saw why.

A spaceship hovered about ten meters above the apartment complex, its engines emitting the noise Chuck could hear over the phone, but now magnified by a million. The ship was a light pink, reflecting the setting sun in every direction, creating a pseudo-disco-ball effect on the otherwise flat concrete of the roof of his apartment block.

"Holy shit!" Chuck balked. "You're…. you're hovering over my apartment!"

"That's breaking at least five laws," said Elroy, moving beside him, fingers in Jack's ears. Babies have sensitive hearing.

The loading ramp dropped and a tan-skinned Indian man wearing a leather jacket over a pink undershirt, slick-backed black hair, and a pair of aviator glasses stepped down—more like waddled down, like an overconfident peacock—and picked a toothpick out of his mouth.

"Harry Reardon," he said, "smuggler extraordinaire. And this is my ship, the *Aero*—" A wind whipped through his hair. The ship tilted slightly and Reardon nearly fell off, grasping hold of a support pole. "*Star.*" He turned and shouted over his shoulder. "Dammit Sammy, I nearly fell!"

"Sorry!" came a call from within.

Okay. This was okay. This was fine. "So," said Chuck, cautiously, "do you think we can look for them together? Smith and this… Steve Bratta?"

"That's what I was thinking. Or rather, I think Bratta can

help us find Smith. He's kinda brilliant," said Reardon, climbing back onto his feet and—with a little more caution than his previously flamboyant movements might have suggested—tapped his temple. "Anyway, I have a plan."

That was better than what Chuck had, which was nothing but desperation, a sick baby, and a vague sense of impending doom. "But we need to find Bratta first," he said. "My son's getting sicker. We need help. He worked at the lab that made those mutants. If that's related to whatever is wrong with Jack…."

"And *I* need to find Smith first. He's got the answer to my little … *cargo* problem. Once we deal with that, *then* we can find Bratta."

"Fine. Do you even know where Smith is?" asked Chuck, casual.

"I … uh … no." Reardon said, deflated.

Chuck smiled. "Well I do. So if you want to find him, take me to Bratta first."

The other man grumbled and swore under his breath. "Great. Fine," said Reardon. "Come aboard. Just give your little poopmaker to your hubby there aaaaand we can get going."

As tempting as it was to leave Jack behind—very tempting —Chuck was reluctant. He grimaced slightly. "We'll need to bring Jack with us," he said. "And Elroy has to come too. If we find Bratta, I want him to look at Jack right away and—"

"I can't," said Elroy, shaking his head. "I have work tomorrow. And since you've been out of a job since… well, since the *thing*, if I lose that job, we lose the apartment." He bounced the baby lightly. "Lemme keep Jack. Just come back here as soon as you find Bratta."

He really didn't want to go anywhere without his husband, but he was out of options. "I know you have work, but… what if Bratta wants to treat him right away? Maybe he should come."

Elroy seemed a lot less convinced. "This is a wild goose chase," he said, softly, even over the howl of the engines. "You don't have anything more than a name."

"It's better than nothing." A weak argument if ever there was one, but sheer desperation made the choice, the risk, seem easy. "It's Jack. If there's a chance this Bratta can help him … I *have* to go. And I've got to take Jack with me."

For a moment Elroy seemed unconvinced. Then, slowly, he nodded. "Right." Elroy handed over Jack with some palpable reluctance. "You just take care, okay? You be careful."

"Yeah," said Chuck, grinning a little. "You know me. I'll be fine." He turned back to Reardon. "Jack comes with me."

Reardon pulled a disgusted face and snapped off his sunglasses. "A baby? On my ship? Hell no!"

A speaker crackled. "Hell yes!" said the voice Chuck presumed to be Sammy. "Harry, he's *so cute!*"

"No," said Reardon.

"Yes," said Sammy, wobbling the ship ominously, forcing Reardon to grab hold of the hatch's edge.

Reardon seemed to consider for a moment, then sighed melodramatically, throwing his hands up in the air. "Fine! But don't let him puke or shit on anything, or out the airlock he goes."

"I'll pay for any damages," said Chuck, with absolutely no idea of how he was going to do that if it happened, given he was flat broke.

The ship began to descend, loading ramp extending a little further. It touched down on the roof of their apartment block, its engines whining.

Chuck held up Jack's little hand. "Wave bye-bye to da-da," he said. Then he smiled at Elroy. "We won't be long."

"You better not be," said Elroy, reaching up and wiping something out of his eye. "You better not be."

Chuck stepped onto the loading ramp beside Reardon. "Let's get going," he said.

"Fine." Reardon squinted down at the baby, then, almost as a side note, seemed to consider. "Also, little word of advice. Don't touch the mutant."

Chuck stared in confusion. "W-wait, the what?"

CHAPTER ELEVEN

The Warren
Chrysalis

Guano tucked her rifle against her body as she ran, keeping the muzzle low and the stock pressed up against her, ready to draw it up and engage. She tore through winding alleyway after alleyway, until—suddenly—she found herself out in a wide, open street full of people.

Panting and covered in sweat, she looked around, shifting her stance, ready to fire.

Nobody paid any attention to her. The crowd moved around her like water past a stone. Apparently, on the libertarian's paradise of Chrysalis, a blood-splattered woman wearing a prisoner's outfit and carrying a rifle was normal.

Fine. She slung the weapon and moved into the crowd, trying her absolute best to blend in. She still felt light-headed, as though she'd had a handful of small glasses of strong alcohol, and everything was edged in blur. Like she was seeing through a lens filter.

She'd been unconscious for weeks. Months, if Brooks— Or *Spectre*, more correctly, although that thought seemed to struggle to sink into her head—wasn't lying. Which she could never be certain of. What exact effect this would have on her eyes she was uncertain, but it could be her brain. He'd mentioned a concussion. He was also a lying sack of shit, though, so there was that.

Good God. Spectre. He … he was alive. But in a different fucking body. Or was she hallucinating?

Guano rubbed her eyes, hands covered in grime from hiding out in the trash pile. That damn thing had saved her. She should name it. Maybe … Cayden. Yeah. Cayden the trash pile. A stinky mass of refuse which had turned out to be kind of useful in the end.

It was a strange thought to be having. Naming piles of garbage. Guano clutched her rifle closer. If more of those mutants came, she'd be ready.

She followed the crowd, buffered occasionally by the people who pushed and shoved with seemingly no regard for her dizziness. Guano grabbed some passerby's shoulder, using it for a moment to steady herself.

"Hey," said the woman, peeling her hand off. "Fuck off, druggie."

So she did. Things got dizzier. Spinnier. Guano felt herself be turned around and around, and where she went, she had no idea. She wasn't unconscious but wasn't fully conscious either; and then, slowly, she realized.

It was the battle fugue. Or something like it. Changed. Altered. Whatever it was, it kept her mind focused, her presence centred.

And that was good. She'd tried to summon that feeling for months, to no avail. And now it came, readily.

Then, almost as though some force had guided her, Guano felt herself return. She was standing in a queue leading to a ticket booth on an interplanetary travel company. InterStat.

She felt like she had been sleepwalking and was only just now waking up. Her wallet was in her left hand, credit chip protruding and ready. In her right, she had a ticket printed out from the machine. It was for the New Kentucky route. She must have bought it while she was out. Why New Kentucky? She couldn't say. Maybe she'd heard it spoken of recently and it was the first place she thought of to escape to.

Her side hurt. She remembered, vaguely, that she'd been shot. Pulling back her collar, she risked a look down her shirt. The wound had closed and, despite the blood, barely seemed to be anything more than a congealed scab. It itched slightly but didn't hurt.

Maybe it was a residual effect of the tank.

"Next," said the attendant.

Guano stepped forward, blinking away the last remnants of the dizziness. "Uhh … yeah." She held out the ticket order clumsily. "I'd like to go… um, here."

The attendant looked at the order with a skeptical eye. "You okay, ma'am?" he asked, regarding her clothes and her weapon. "You look a little … ill."

"I'm fine." Guano took a breath to steady herself. "One ticket please, one way."

He assessed her with a sceptical eye. "You know that not all of the galaxy is as tolerant as we are here. You won't be able to be dressed like that where you're going…" his eyes fell to her rifle. "Or go carrying around that piece with you, all open like."

Chrysalis was known for its extreme lawlessness and liberty. A little *too* much of both for her tastes. "I know. I'll surrender it to customs when I get there. I just want to go home."

"Very well." The man swiped her credit stick. "Thank you for flying InterStat. Next."

CHAPTER TWELVE

Moon Debris
100m from the downed Avenir spacecraft
Pinegar System

Mattis clipped on his helmet and double-checked the seal. The loading ramp on the shuttle opened, and before them stretched a massive field of broken debris. Grey fragments of starship hull, wires, and the metal girders that composed a ship's skeleton lay splashed out on the rock's surface like the bones of some dead beast. Below the metal debris lay a field of broken stones, sharp and jagged, like the infinite teeth of a monster waiting to chew them up as soon as they stepped off.

"Damn," said Lynch beside him, blowing a low whistle. "And I thought the surface of that Dark Side place was messed up. You seeing this, Captain Spears?"

The Dark Side, a rogue world with a private gambling establishment, had been destroyed by the future-humans. Lynch had been one of the first ones on the surface. For him to make that comparison was sobering.

"I am receiving your helmet cams," said Spears, bringing Mattis back to the moment.

He glanced at Lynch out of the side of his helmet. "You going to be okay here?"

"Sure," said Lynch, stepping down the ramp. "Second time's a charm. There's much less gravity this time, so be careful."

Mattis followed him, then stepped in front and took the lead. A full squad of Marines followed behind. As their boots hit the ground and touched the metal, it crumbled instantly, and turned to powder that floated up into the void before, slowly, sinking back down. The sharp rocks beneath them similarly disintegrated.

Weird.

Modi lingered behind, waving some kind of scanning device around. "Radiation levels are extremely high in this location," he said, as though discussing incoming rain. "Our suits will protect us for twenty-six minutes, but I would imagine that, after that point, the damage will be done."

Twenty-six minutes. It sounded like a lot of time but Mattis knew it wasn't. Not really. Everything could change in that time. "Okay," he said, "let's make sure we get in, find what we need, and get out. Modi, is the radiation coming from that ship?" If so, the closer they got, the worse their suits would be affected.

"No," said Modi, an element of wonder in his voice as he jogged to catch up.. "It seems as though the radiation is naturally occurring in this area. It is coming from the stones beneath our feet. Some process as yet understood. I would enjoy, greatly, if we could stay and study it—"

"That's not up to me," said Mattis, well aware that Captain Spears would be listening in on their communications. "Besides. This place is dangerous enough as it is, and we're not on a scientific mission. We'll make full notes in our logs and pass them along to Fleet Command. If they send someone out here, good. If not … well. I'm sure this place will be around long enough for you to come back some day."

"Some day," agreed Modi, a distinct edge of regret in his tone. "When all the fighting is done and the last peace is achieved… when heroes and champions are no longer needed."

"Feeling poetic, Modi?" asked Lynch. Mattis couldn't see his face. "That's unlike you."

"Something about this place brings out the wordsmith in me. The starkness of a ruined world, jagged and toothy, contrasting with the ruined ship." Modi's voice turned somber. "I projected the course of this moon fragment over the next ten thousand years; it will drift through space uninterrupted until it finally falls into this system's star. If nothing is done … well, we're the only ones to know about this ship. Left to its own devices, it will drift, never corroding, never weakening, until fire consumes it. Until then, the only damage to it will be our footprints; the only things to come of it what we take with us."

"Then let's take a lot," said Mattis, nodding resolutely. "I plan on living a good long time, but ten thousand years is stretching it."

They walked in silence toward the ruined ship, the only light provided by the shuttle behind them and the lamps on their suits. As they touched the ship debris and stone alike, both instantly and silently crumbled. The only noise they could hear was the hissing of the suit's CO2 scrubbers.

Finally, the hull of the alien ship loomed up before them. There didn't seem to be an obvious way inside, but they had brought enough high explosives and cutting fluid to render that a concern trivial .

"You know," said Lynch, casually reaching out and brushing his hand against the brittle black metal, "this is probably the closest any human has ever come to one of these things."

"Not strictly true," said Modi. "During the Battle of Friendship Station, several of the *Midway*'s strike crafts crashed into the surface of one of their ships."

Lynch's voice soured. "You know, I preferred you as a poet."

"We're wasting air," reminded Mattis. "Lynch. Get us inside the hull."

He watched as Lynch took out the cutting fluid, but then —as though struck with a strange impulse—reached out and knocked on the hull with his gauntlet. The metal crumbled as he touched it. "Look," he said, peeling back thick slices of it with his hands. "It's brittle, just like the rest of it."

"Weakened by the radiation," said Modi, moving beside him and assisting Lynch, the two of them peeling back the hull like the rind of an orange. "This must be how they construct their armour. Layer upon layer… the damage has weakened the fasteners, along with the metal itself. Made so brittle that the extreme temperature swings from exposure to this system's sun has—"

A thought occurred to him. Something that made his eyes widen. "You know," said Mattis, interrupting Modi and talking as much to himself as he was to the others, "if we could find a way to generate this radiation…"

Modi shrugged. "It's only neutron radiation, Admiral. Nothing exotic—"

"We could weaponise it," said Spears, energetically. "Mattis, that's perfect. I love it."

"Maybe we should come back," suggested Modi, peeling back another layer.

He was beginning to think they should. "That, again, is up to Captain Spears," said Mattis, although he hoped, somehow, that suggesting it might influence her in the affirmative. "Perhaps when our mission is complete?"

"Perhaps," said Spears with a hint of promise.

Modi and Lynch peeled back another layer of the hull, and the outermost layer of the ship's insides was exposed. A layer of piping and tubing, along with what seemed like three dimensional circuit-boards. "We're past the outer layers," said Mattis, peering at the exposed circuitry—or what he presumed to be circuitry. "It looks like the ship has some kind of distributed processing network on the inside of its hull… as though they completely lined the inside of the outer hull with computing equipment."

"Why would they do that?" asked Lynch, presumably to Modi.

"It might be for redundancy purposes," said Modi, thoughtfully. "Our ships keep our computer cores lodged deep within for protection, but there is a *lot* of hardware here. What I can see here alone is more than the *Midway* ever had in her whole server banks. It's possible, almost likely, that they are doing it as a redundancy measure; a penetrating hit may take out some systems, but there are still many more remaining that can take up the slack. And in the event that a vast amount of computing power is needed, well, then it is available."

Vast amount of computing power… "Modi, you were using all those piles of laptops to track where this ship went, yes?"

"No," said Modi. "Those machines were merely providing the front-end required to run it. The actual work was being done on a server-farm in Canberra, Australia. The effort required was … substantial."

Mattis nodded thoughtfully. "Is it possible that the enemy is doing the same thing?" he asked. "Using huge amounts of computing power to track our ships? Predict our movements?"

"It's possible, but any supposition toward the exact purpose of such hardware is merely speculation."

Speculation was all they had, but they *also* had a profound lack of time. "Cut through this barrier," said Mattis. "But take a sample of their computers. In fact, take a sample of *everything*. Whatever we can carry or drag back to the shuttle."

"Aye sir." Modi sprayed one of the removed sheets of metal with a red X, then did the same to a chunk of computing hardware, marking it for the Marines to carry back. Then, he and Lynch broke through the layer of computing hardware with remarkable ease, pushing it aside as though it were paper.

Now the insides of the ship were exposed. They had cut into the side of a long corridor strewn with debris, and right in front of them lay a crumpled form, almost completely unrecognisable, barely more than a lump of dust with a few humanoid features protruding.

"I'm guessing that's what's going to happen to us if we stay here too long?" asked Mattis, grimly.

Modi said nothing, which was all he needed to say.

The three of them slipped inside the ship, Marines following. Mattis took the lead, unslinging his rifle and awkwardly shouldering it. They crept through the ship, working deeper into its bowels. They found another body, this one far more complete; merely dessicated, ghoulish and hollow-eyed.

"The radiation seems to be significantly less the farther we get into the ship," said Modi, crouching beside the corpse and examining it. "This one died at roughly the same time, but obviously its condition is much better." As he touched the corpse, it floated off the ground before slowly sinking back down. "Gravity is much less, too."

Odd. "Modi, hypothesis?"

Modi turned toward him. "Hypothesis for abnormal gravity inside an Avenir ship?" He shrugged helplessly. "Weird technology gone amuck? An effect of the radiation? Maybe they just like it that way?"

All seemed equally likely to him. Mattis pointed down the corridor. "Into the ship," he said. "Whatever effect seems to be generating this—whatever vulnerability they might have toward this strange place—I want answers."

"Sixteen minutes," said Modi, cautiously. "We should be mindful that the effect might become less prominent the farther we get into the ship. Or stronger. Nobody can say. We are truly groping in the dark here."

"We're blind bulls in a very fragile china shop," said Lynch.

Right. Enough metaphors for now. Mattis lead the way deeper into the ship, moving past the occasional corpse or broken pile of debris. The hallway cracked and splintered like snakeskin, buckling on occasion, and they found more complete bodies that had been crushed by some immense force.

"Poor bastards came in hard," said Lynch, lightly touching one with his boot. It drifted up into the air, floating, bouncing idly off the ceiling.

There, on the roof, was a strange symbol. Two teeth biting into a planet. Mattis shone his shoulder lamp at it. "I wonder what this means?"

Nobody had any kind of answer.

"Sir?" asked Modi, an unusual energy in his voice. "I'm detecting a power source. Atmosphere."

Mattis squinted. "There's an air bubble on this ship? A section that didn't decompress?"

"An unlaunched escape pod," clarified Modi, moving over to a section of bulkhead that seemed heavier than the others. It had a small, reinforced door no greater than one meter wide next to a large purple button. "Behind here. It's small… one man, maybe. It's tiny but I'm sure that's what it is."

With such a tight opening, it was the only thing that would possibly fit. "Okay," said Mattis, "hand me the cutting fluid."

Lynch gave him a thick tube with a plunger on one end. He placed the extruder against the metal hull and squeezed the plunger. Liquid leaked out the tip, smoking as it came into contact with the metal, dissolving it far too easily.

At the other end of the tiny airlock was the escape pod. No bigger than a coffin, it was barely big enough to hold a person, and was sealed by a thick door with a small glass window.

A face stared out from it, head tilted at an odd angle. It almost looked like it was squinting curiously at the light from Mattis's lamp.

A mutant face.

Alive.

CHAPTER THIRTEEN

The Aerostar
Low Earth Orbit
Sol System

There was no way they had a mutant aboard.

"So," said Reardon, leading Chuck through the ship's cramped interior. "This is the *Aerostar*. Just a little note, kid; that's the name of the model, not this *particular* ship's name. Except it's one of a kind. So it's just the *Aerostar*. Not the USS *Aerostar*. Or HMS *Aerostar*. Or whatever. *Just* the *Aerostar*."

Chuck blinked in confusion. Ship naming conventions were strange to him. "Why?"

"It's that way because…" Reardon waved a hand dismissively. "Because of how it is."

"Ooookay."

They passed a series of small rooms. Reardon jerked his thumb at one. "Your place. Try not to make a mess."

"Okay."

He whistled as he walked. Even God hated a whistler. Chuck's ears ached. If this was going to be how the trip went…

A young-looking Indian kid in a wheelchair zoomed out of a door, using his grip on the frame to spin himself around and stop. "Hey, buddy!" he said, grinning like a half-moon. "Oh man, this is Admiral Mattis's kid, huh?"

Admiral Mattis's kid… he was more than that. "Yeah, I'm Chuck Mattis."

The kid wheeled up to him, extending a hand. "I'm Sammy Reardon."

Chuck took the hand and shook it firmly. "You're the mutant?" he asked, hesitantly.

The elder Reardon laughed. "Ha! He wishes," he said, reaching down and ruffling his brother's hair.

"Hey!" Sammy swatted his hand away. "Don't!"

Reardon shot little finger guns at Chuck. "Best brother in the galaxy right here."

"Okay," said Chuck, hoping his scepticism wouldn't come through *too* badly. And he needed to keep Reardon distracted. "So, uh, is there really a mutant—"

"Yeah, yeah." Reardon leaned up against a wall. "You'll see her soon. Not that she says much, still being in her box and all. But first, let's see the lead you were talking about. For Smith."

Uh oh. "Uhh…" Chuck gently bounced Jack. "I think I smell poop. How about I change him first?"

Reardon casually reached into his pocket, pulling aviator shades and putting them on. Chuck was significantly taller, so it seemed an almost laughable attempt to be a tough guy. "How about you gimme that lead, kid?" he said.

Sammy snorted dismissively. "You're twenty-two. You're like… five years younger than him." He grinned a bit. "Sorry, I looked up your arrest record. It had your date of birth."

"Thanks," said Chuck, grimacing. Permanent records sucked.

"The location," said Reardon, an almost genuinely threatening edge to his voice. "Where is Smith? Or the baby gets tossed out the airlock."

Chuck's chest tightened at the idea, but Sammy just laughed some more.

"My bro's kidding," he said, casually reaching over and punching Reardon in the side. "He won't do that."

Reardon crouched beside his brother, hissing and speaking in a faint whisper that Chuck was still able to hear. "Hey, what did I tell you about not undermining me when I'm intimidating people?"

Sammy spoke in a normal voice. "You're not intimidating anyone, Harry." He looked up at Chuck. "But if you have info, that'd be real helpful."

"No,"he replied in his most imperious *Admiral Jack Mattis* voice—an attempt to let Reardon know that he wasn't someone he could intimidate with empty threats. "Not until Bratta has seen my kid. Where is he?"

Reardon opened his mouth to say something, then shut it and broke into an awkward, goofy smile.

Sammy thumbed in his brother's direction. "He doesn't know."

Shit.

"What? You're kidding me." *Unbelievable,* he thought. "Fine. Set me back down. I'll go find him on my—"

"Now hold up, Mr. Mattis," said Sammy. "It turns out that when I was hacking into Smith's comm logs, I came across another number. The metadata was encrypted, but that was no match for me, obviously, and it turns out it's Bratta's number. That is, I think."

Reardon swung around to face his brother. "Why the hell didn't you tell me that?"

"You were busy arguing with *him* over the phone," he said, pointing to Chuck.

"Well? And?" Reardon stretched his arms and palms out.

"It's active, but I think he hasn't paid his bill or something because it won't let me connect. I traced it to New Los Alamos. Quirky little world out in the Tiberius Nebula."

Chuck nearly laughed. How convenient. Smith was in that general location. Somewhere. "New Los Alamos is Nerd Heaven. By far the most technical world in the Tiberius sector, originally set up to study the nebula, and now… well, basically anything they can. Makes sense Bratta would be there," said Chuck. He eyed the two of them. In spite of Reardon's blustery persona, he could tell it was an act. The brothers were clearly not hardened criminals. At least, not the violent kind. "Ok. I'll tell you. Smith is also out in the Tiberius Nebula. Not necessarily New Los Alamos, but one of the other dozens of worlds out there."

Reardon looked surprised at how easily Chuck gave up the information. But he scowled suddenly. "Wait. How'd you come into possession of that information?"

"I … called him," said Chuck, simply.

"That's it?" Reardon raised an eyebrow. "We've been tapping Smith's line. That's how we knew to come get you—

but nobody's actually been in touch with him for ages."

"Well," he said slowly, "when I called Smith, I let it ring out. And when it did, the error message mentioned the Tiberius Sector." He figured he didn't need to tell them about his still-operational diplomatic security code.

Reardon stared at him. Then down at Sammy. "We called him too, right?"

"Yeah," Sammy shot back defensively. "But I didn't wait for it to ring out. Why would I?"

"Why *wouldn't* you?"

"Waste of time. I just put a trace on the wire, to track anyone who calls."

"Well obviously it wasn't working!"

"Well obviously you're a stupid idiot!" Sammy spun his wheelchair around to face Reardon. "If you weren't so stingy using the long-range communicator to download all those stupid romance flicks you watch, then *maybe* I would have been more comfortable letting it ring out like that!"

"Shut the hell up!" hissed Reardon, and then, adjusting his glasses, regained some measure of his composure. "Okay, then. New Los Alamos. Let's hit the road." He coughed. "And by road I mean Z-Space. And by hit, I mean plot and execute a translation into." He stormed out.

"Okay," said Sammy, then turned to Chuck, grinning a little. "So, want me to help you change the baby?"

"That would be good, actually," said Chuck, slightly confused. "But uh, wait, you… actually *want* to help me with this? You know there's poo, right?"

Sammy didn't appear to be distressed. "I just really like kids, so I wanna help. It's not a problem at all."

"Okay," said Chuck. "Can always use a hand."

"Just, uh," Sammy considered. "Do you wanna see the mutant? We don't know much about her, so … be careful."

Careful. Of having a mutant with a baby around. Chuck held Jack closer and managed a little nod. "Yeah," he said, as much to himself as anyone else. "I think I will."

CHAPTER FOURTEEN

InterStat Transport IS-221
High orbit of New Kentucky
Tiberius Sector

Guano jerked awake.

"—come to the Tiberius sector," said a calm, likely pre-recorded voice over the transport's intercom. "We have now completed our Z-Space translation and have arrived above New Kentucky. In a few short minutes we will begin our transition into the atmosphere and will be preparing for landing. As per United States quarantine guidelines, all fruit and vegetable matter must be submitted to quarantine and inspection. Thank you for flying InterStat. We understand you have a choice in carriers, and…"

She tuned out the rest of the boring garbage.

"That was quite impressive," said the guy sitting next to her, a gentle smile on his face. "You slept the whole way through. Thirteen hours and you were out like a light. Not a peep out of you the whole time. I almost considered calling the flight attendant."

Guano, for some reason, couldn't even bring herself to look at him. "I'm fine," she said, folding her arms and staring out the window.

"I like what you're doing, by the way," the guy said, seemingly determined to talk to her.

"Huh?"

"The costume," he said, gesturing to her blood-flecked orange jumpsuit. "A lot of people are protesting the media silence about the kidnappings, too. That's a really effective way of getting your message across." He nodded approvingly. "We're all prisoners of the mainstream media."

"Y-yeah," said Guano, fixing her eyes out the viewport as the beginnings of New Kentucky's atmosphere began to come into view. "Totally."

He kept trying to talk to her, but Guano stubbornly gave only short, one-word answers, waiting for the ship to drop into the atmosphere, until finally he gave up. When they landed, Guano waited until the plane was almost empty and then unclipped her belt and got up.

What was she even doing here? Why didn't she remember buying a ticket, and why had she slept the whole way?

She almost sat back down and considered flying back to Chrysalis to demand answers about what was happening to her, but she knew it was silly. Going back would be horribly dangerous, suicidal really, and she needed to rejoin her crew. Whoever was left after the battle.

At least that's what she told herself.

Walking as casually as she could, Guano disembarked the

spacecraft and strode into the terminal. The rifle and pistol she had traveled with had been surrendered to Customs and that was *not* an argument she wanted to have, so she decided to just let them keep 'em. Where she was going she didn't need guns.

Within fifteen minutes Guano was through decontamination and out into the cool, fresh air of New Kentucky. It reeked of sulphur, a product of the planet's regular volcanic eruptions, and on the horizon burned the ever-present glow of distant fires.

She breathed in deep, savoring the stink. What a shithole.

What was she even *doing* here?

Guano wandered out of the airport and down the long road that lead away from the airport. It seemed to stretch on forever, asphalt laid over basalt and igneous rock. The surface of the road was hot against her feet, but she kept going, putting one foot in front of the other until she came to the city center—a flat, urban area that felt more like an overgrown country town than the capital of a whole planet. Buildings sprang up from the ground in neat squares. The roads were well maintained and logically arrayed. A stark contrast to the chaos of Chrysalis.

And she walked.

CHAPTER FIFTEEN

The Aerostar
Low Earth Orbit
Sol System

There was a box with a mutant in it.

It seemed far too small to hold a person, let alone such an obviously huge creature as her. Chuck stared in bewilderment at the … *thing* stuck within. She—and Chuck was only calling it a *she* because that's what Reardon had called it—was a huge, hulking beast, over two meters tall and built like a linebacker. She had strange, mottled skin and muscles like bounded cords, which made her current posture—folded neatly into a too-small box—so much more perplexing.

Even more perplexing was that she seemed to be alive. She lay on her side, only one almost completely human eye visible, but it tracked Chuck keenly. A few small tubes and wires connected her to the inside walls of the box, but she was otherwise free to move.

But she didn't. She only watched.

"Hi," he said, unsure of what else to do.

The mutant said nothing. Just stared up at him with those eyes; so full of life and, seemingly, pain. It couldn't have been comfortable inside that box. How long had she been in there?

"See," said Sammy, a little ruefully. "She doesn't say much. Doesn't eat, doesn't drink. We think those tubes from the box feed her. We've tried everything and she won't move or react."

That seemed strange to him. Chuck moved over to the box, within touching range, but Sammy grabbed his shirt.

"Hey, don't get that close," he said, cautiously. "We don't know what it's capable of. We don't know anything about it."

Wordlessly, Chuck handed Jack to Sammy, who seemed delighted to hold him. That gave Chuck the momentary distraction he needed; he slid forward, crouching beside the box, hand just a few inches from the mutant's body.

"Hey," he said, gently. "It's time to wake up."

Surprisingly, her eye flicked at him, meeting his gaze. He held it, smiling.

"Whoa," said Sammy. "What the…"

Chuck ignored him. He moved his hand forward, touching her side. Her skin was cold and clammy, probably because of the temperature of the ship. Or was it maybe something else? *Something* pulled Chuck towards her, and he slowly rubbed her side.

She let out a contented sigh. At least, it sounded content to his ears.

"Just like a baby," said Chuck, almost to himself. "She's… basically a baby."

Sammy's eyes went wide. "I never really thought about

that," he said. "She's just so …*big*."

"A baby in a full grown mutant's body," said Chuck. And then he had it figured out. "There has to be some kind of way to get her out of here."

Sammy blinked. "Okay, I like kids, but we are not having a box baby in the cargo bay of my brother's ship. He'll kill me. Metaphorically. And maybe literally. Or maybe just literally-metaphorically. More on the literally side than the metaphorically side, but… still. It's bad." He ran his hands through his hair. "Harry always has a way of finding these things out."

"It's the only humane thing to do. Whatever she is, she's also clearly … human. You can't leave someone there like that, suffering," said Chuck, frowning and looking over the box. "There's gotta be some way to get her out. It must be—" There. A small red button. "Maybe this is it."

"Maybe it's the life support system. Or self-destruct. It's too risky, Chuck."

"If it is the life support system," said Chuck, considering, "maybe that's what wakes her up. You know. A shock to the system?"

"Or kills her. Or blows us up. Did I tell you about all the explosives lining the box walls?"

That was a distinct possibility. "Gotta be better than life in that box." Couldn't ask for more than that, going in her sleep…

Sammy's face was a sour mask. He tapped the frame of his wheelchair pointedly. "Yeah, I mean, what would *I* know about when life is worth living, huh?"

Good point. Chuck looked away for a moment and then,

before he could change his mind, pressed the button.

"Ooooh shit," whined Sammy, wheeling back.

For a moment nothing happened. Then, with a faint hiss, small wisps of smoke started to rise from the edges of the open box.

"Ooooh shit," echoed Chuck, standing cautiously. "Maybe that *was* the self-destruct."

More smoke rushed out of the edges of the box. Then, just as quickly as it had begun, it stopped.

And the mutant sat up.

CHAPTER SIXTEEN

The Aerostar
Low Earth Orbit
Sol System

It was alive.

Chuck stared in bewilderment at the creature he had just freed. Now that she was out, she—and Chuck was only calling it a *she* because that's what Sammy had called it. She had strange, mottled skin and muscles like bounded cords, and stood hunched in the cargo hold, her head almost reaching the ceiling.

"Whoa," said Sammy, his tone soft and awed. "You woke her up."

The thing glanced right at Sammy for a moment and, despite it all, looked quite frightened. Her hands hovered over the box.

"It's okay," said Sammy, behind him, his voice gentle. "Hey, giant mutant baby thing, this is Chuck Mattis."

"Chuck Mattis," she repeated in a grunt. Then, with a suspicious glare, she turned to look out the window. She held up her hands to the porthole in the cargo bay, fingers extended as though laying them over a keyboard.

It was such a strange gesture that, for a moment, he didn't know what to make of it. "Does…" Chuck considered the placement of her fingers. Her steady gaze out the window. "Does she think she's flying the ship?"

Sammy shrugged. "How the hell should I know."

It certainly seemed that way to Chuck as he watched the mutant's fingers fly across the invisible keyboard, typing meticulously.

"She needs a name," said Chuck. Only one seemed to be right. "How about… Lily?"

"Like the flower?" Sammy paused, considering. "It's … actually a nice name. A family member? Friend?"

"Nah. Back when Elroy and I were adopting, we considered Lily for a girl, Jack for a boy. Obviously, Jack got picked, so…"

Lily continued to stare out the porthole, fingers wiggling away. "Lily."

"It works," said Chuck, with a playful little smile.

Right. Okay. There was something else, too. Something he was missing. the way those fingers were moving. Chuck slowly realized that it was less like typing than grabbing. It as a motion he'd seen Jack do a hundred times. "I think she's hungry."

"I'd be hungry if I'd been sleeping in a box for a few months," admitted Sammy. "What do you think she eats?"

"I'll find out," promised Chuck. And he would. "But first, we should probably, you know, get back to work."

"Work. Right." Sammy tapped the side of his wheelchair and a screen folded out of the armrest. "Hang on," he said. "I'm just going to check my scripts." He typed for a few seconds, and strange computer code flew across the screen. "Mmm. Looks like the signal from Bratta's phone really did originate in New Los Alamos. I've even got the city. Hell, I've even got a cross street. Time to go check it out."

"Great," said Chuck, feeling the first thing approaching hope he'd felt since Jack had first gotten sick. "Let's get a move on, then."

Sammy eyed Chuck with a curious look. "You got any luggage?"

"Nope. Just me and the baby."

"No gun?"

Chuck blinked in surprise. "I live in Maryland," he said.

"You say it like there are no guns in Maryland." Sammy sighed, tapping the other side of his chair, withdrawing a pistol; it was chromed up and seemed loaded. "Take this one. I hate the color. Harry keeps saying..." His tone became sing-songy and sarcastic. "You just *gotta* get the chrome plating, Sammy. Nobody will respect you if you just have a *normal* gun, Sammy. Real men aren't afraid of having people *look at them*, Sammy. Blech." He fished out three magazines, then held the thing out. "Take it. I don't need it. There's a holster in the cargo bay."

Chuck hesitated. Was this some kind of test? Some kind of weird initiation? He cautiously took hold of the gun.

It'd been a while since he'd held a piece. Dad used to take him to the range, even as a kid. Some of his fondest memories were scrounging up spent brass and stacking it as high as he could. Chuck thumbed the magazine release, ejecting the device into his hand, then awkwardly racked the slide. A brass round was ejected, hitting the wall with a *tink* and rolling around on the deck.

"Damn," said Chuck, peering through the ejection port to make sure he could see the deck, then clicked the slide forward and eased the hammer down. "You kept the thing loaded?" He inspected the magazine. Standard twelve round box, full. "Dirty loaded, too."

"You know guns," said Sammy, nodding in agreement. "Harry says I have to keep it that way." His voice became mocking again. "Never know when you might need one more bullet, Sammy. Smuggling's a dirty job, you gotta give it a smuggler's load, Sammy."

"Right, well, I'd prefer to keep it clean if you don't mind. Prevents negligent discharges." He squatted, picked up the stray round, and put it in his pocket.

"Negligent discharges," echoed Lily.

They both turned to her in surprise. But that was all she said, and resumed grabbing hungrily at her imaginary keyboard.

Sammy tilted his head. "Sounds like a military term," he said.

"That's just how my Dad described accidental gunfire. They aren't accidents because they're preventable."

"Fair enough," said Sammy, then murmured to himself. "Okay. Fly us to New Los Alamos, got it. But not *too* fast—if I push the compressor too far, it blows. And if it blows, I don't want to have to pay to have our new friend buried. Especially when I'm dead."

"No explode," said Lily, tapping on her imaginary console

with her comically oversized fingers.

Great, thought Chuck, holding Jack nice and tight against his chest. *At least the mutant cares if I live or die...*

CHAPTER SEVENTEEN

Derelict Avenir vessel
Moon Debris
Pinegar System

There was a mutant alive in there.

Mattis took a moment to process it. One of the creatures who had brought so much ruin and devastation to them was, save for the airlock portal, almost within arm's reach. It wasn't moving. Wasn't doing anything but calmly watch him through the thick glass. Its face was mottled green, like a bloated corpse's, but its saggy, leathery flesh pulsated with life and it blinked, slowly and deliberately, staring at the away team that stood on the other side of the glass.

"Holy shit," said Lynch behind him. "Is that—"

Mattis thumbed his radio. "Captain Spears," he said, trying to keep his voice steady. "We have a survivor."

"A ... survivor?" Spears seemed to adjust her headset on the other end of the line. "Away team, please confirm. Are you saying there is someone alive on that ship?"

That's what being a survivor *means*, he itched to say. Instead he dutifully replied "Affirmative," still staring at the mutant creature, its face lit up by his shoulder lamp. "It's contained in an unused escape pod nestled inside the ship."

"An escape pod *on the inside?*" Her scepticism was justified. "As in, right at the very core of the ship?"

"That's correct," said Mattis. "We don't know enough about its layout to comment as to what it's doing here, but it's possible that it's for some kind of VIP. Hell, they keep their computers right on the outside of their ship… we have *no* idea why this could be."

"Very well," said Spears, resolutely. "Retrieve the survivor as a priority, Admiral Mattis. All other objectives are now secondary. This creature represents a profound opportunity I do not want to miss. I want to have words with … them."

Alright then. "Mister Lynch, time?"

Lynch consulted his instruments, including a glowing panel mounted on his suit's wrist. "Twenty-one minutes, sir. If we're going to do this, we better hurry."

Yes. "I need a no-B.S. assessment. Can you extract this pod before the radiation cooks us?"

Lynch's face was unreadable behind the visor of his space suit. He seemed to be staring down at the wrist device, tapping at it with his spare hand. "Probably," he said. "If I'm lying, I'm dying. Fifty-fifty chance."

Mattis had played much worse odds. "I'll take it," he said. "Extract the pod. Work with Modi." It had taken them five minutes to walk there. So five minutes to walk back. Which meant they had sixteen minutes. Not long.

"On it, sir," said Lynch. Immediately, he and Modi leapt into action, puzzling over the glass door .

"We'll need to re-compress this section of the ship," said Modi. "Just in case we nick the escape pod. Normally I wouldn't concern myself with planning to fail, but given the time pressure, best not to risk it." Modi pointed to a glowing panel on the wall. "See if you can interface with that thing right there."

Right. "I'll get on that," said Mattis, walking over. The system seemed still to be lit and connected to the ship's main systems. Writing flowed across the panel, written in a strange language but using stylized English and Chinese characters. From what Mattis could make out, which was little, it seemed to be a strange creole of various tongues mashed together. In a way, it reminded him of reverse Shakespearean text; words out of time, separated by hundreds of years of linguistic evolution.

He was reading from the future.

A word flashed by, somewhat recognizable.

ATMOSFEER

It was highlighted in red. He scrolled back, touching it. An outline of the derelict—or rather, what he presumed the derelict would look like had it not smashed into the piece of debris—floated onto the screen, mostly red except for one section in the middle highlighted in green.

Pinching the screen, Mattis zoomed with clumsy, stubby fingers, almost flying right past the green bit, which seemed to be the only intact section. The pod. A bunch of buttons flew up beside it.

Behind him, Modi pressed the cutting fluid extruder to the frame around the glass. "Sir," he said, "we're about ready to try cut it out."

"Wait a moment," said Mattis. He flicked through the controls, into the logs. "I see the problem. There was a fire in this room... the automatic fire suppression vented it to extinguish the flames." He tapped on a few keys. "Here."

The doors they had passed through to get there slid shut. Nothing happened for a moment, although on his screen, the red box Mattis was standing in slowly began to turn a sickly green. Faintly at first, but then rapidly growing in intensity, air rushed in, hissing as it filled up the room.

"Don't remove your helmets," said Mattis. "It's just a precaution."

"Ain't no way I'm removing my gear inside this rickety ship," said Lynch, jabbing a thumb up toward the ceiling. "Whole damn thing could come down on top of us at any moment."

That wasn't a bad point.

Modi began cutting away at the framework holding the pod. The fluid made a loud *snap-hiss* as it bit into the metal. The hull seemed stronger here, far less affected by the radiation, and the work was slow. Modi had to refill the cartridge three times before any real progress had been made, and the cut he'd performed was depressingly small. Less than a meter long, a quarter of the distance they needed.

The minutes ticked away. Mattis felt sweat starting to bead on his forehead even though he was cold, and air struggled to find its way into his throat. All the while, the mutant creature just stared at him, at Modi, and sometimes off into space, impassively ignoring them.

Three more changes. Another meter cut. "Time, Lynch," said Mattis, tapping his foot impatiently.

"Eight minutes remain," said Lynch.

Dammit. "We're not going to make it."

Modi replaced the cutting fluid magazine and continued to work. "Actually," he said, "it is likely that when this section starts to come away, the pod will be removable with some degree of manual force."

Six minutes. Four minutes. Two minutes. The sweating continued. Mattis found his hands trembling slightly inside the suit. He could practically *feel* the radiation seeping into his bones. This couldn't be good for his long term health…

Then, with a dull creak and groan, the pod came loose, tumbling into the chamber. It was followed by a much deeper, much more troubling rumble from somewhere else on the derelict.

"Okay," said Mattis as the rumble all around them intensified. "I'm sure everyone's feeling as shitty as I am, so grab this thing and make for the shuttle. We are *leaving.*"

"Spears to away team." Her voice carried a charge with it. "A ship is coming into sensor range."

Mattis moved beside Modi, grabbing hold of the pod. Utilising the low gravity still present in this part of the ship, he hoisted it along with the others and began making his way out. "What kind of ship?" He knew he wouldn't like the answer.

"Unknown," said Spears. "A big one."

He hated being right.

CHAPTER EIGHTEEN

Landing Pad 4
Fermion City Spaceport
Los Alamos v2.0
Tiberius Sector

Two hours later

New Los Alamos—a busy, crowded, technological world that Chuck had read about but never visited. It was the location of a former research facility which, apparently, had been converted into a trading post that had ballooned into a small city. The atmosphere was thin, a strange orange-red color, and it reeked of sulphur. A slightly crooked neon sign marked the place as *Los Alamos v2.0*. Something was burning some distance away, pumping even more pollution into the atmosphere.

Delightful.

Chuck stepped down the loading ramp of the *Aerostar* and

into the streets of Fermion City, the weight of his new pistol forcing him to resist the urge to plug his nose to keep out the smell. He'd strapped on the holster Sammy had mentioned; he resolved to keep his hand off the weapon unless necessary.

It'd been some time since he'd actually shot anything, after all.

Chuck adjusted his backpack, Jack strapped in and squealing inanely. Taking his son on a risky investigation mission didn't sit well, but it was better than leaving him on the ship with Lily.

"Hey," said Sammy, wheeling up to the top of the ramp behind him. "You can't be serious. No."

Chuck knew what he was talking about. "Jack will be safer with me," he said, cautiously. "Don't worry. I'll make sure he's okay."

"No no no," said Sammy, rolling down the ramp, his hands on the wheels to slow himself. "You cannot be serious. C'mon. Leave him with me."

Chuck shook his head. "That's not safe."

"I'll keep Lily in the cargo hold and lock the doors," he said. "It's much safer than out there. I promise. Good Lord, don't you smell that shit? You want him breathing that?"

The idea that his kid would be left on a ship with a mutant whose intentions none of them could know, and nothing more than a wheelchair-bound kid to keep her in her place was … less than comforting. "You absolutely sure you can handle it?"

Sammy touched a few keys on his wheelchair's screen. "The doors are locked and she isn't going anywhere." He turned the screen around to show the feed from the internal cameras. Lily was standing there, gazing out the porthole, seemingly unaware she was trapped. "Those doors are triple-reinforced composite. She'd need an anti-tank weapon to get out. Meanwhile, all that's between Jack and a bullet out there is, well, you."

All the reassurances in the world couldn't fully convince Chuck, but he knew Jack would statistically be safer on the ship. With palpable reluctance, he handed the backpack over.

Sammy extracted Jack and smiled like he'd just been handed a check for a million credits. "I'll take *great* care of him, don't worry."

Easier said than done. It felt strange to be leaving Jack with Sammy, but Chuck forced himself to think it was okay. The kid was kind and Jack seemed to like him. Plus, it made it easier to focus on his mission. Or so he told himself.

The only thing that mattered was to find out what was wrong with Jack, and to cure it—before it was too late.

Reardon had fitted Chuck with an earpiece, through which he was giving instructions. "Okay, so, you're on the main street now."

"Thanks," said Chuck, not even bothering to keep his sarcasm in check. "You're a big help to me, you know that?"

"You're welcome," said Reardon, without even a hint of irony. "So… basically, here's the thing. Lily's firmly secured inside the ship—can't have a big girl like her walking around somewhere like that, especially when we don't know her at all —and we can come to you if we need to get you out of there in a hurry. Sammy's going to do computer stuff; if Bratta turns on his phone, I'll make sure you know about it. And also take care of the little poop goblin."

Chuck ground his teeth. "That *poop goblin* is my son," he

said. A cloud of foul-smelling gas rolled over him, causing him to wrinkle his nose and fight the urge to gag. "And what about you?"

"I'm going to give you the benefit of my smuggler's wisdom," said Reardon. "Remotely. Where it doesn't smell like someone took a dump right there in front of me."

It was okay… it was okay. He just had to find Bratta. "How about you share a little bit of that so-called smuggler's wisdom and gimme a hint where I should be heading to find Bratta?"

"Well," said Reardon, crowing a little, like he was the font of sagacity and experience. "The thing with these missing person cases is… everyone always ends up at a bar. I've done a bit of bounty hunting work in my time—"

"You found a lost dog," said Sammy in the background. "Once. And it was hiding on the *Aerostar*."

"In my time," continued Reardon, slightly louder. "And the thing is: everyone always ends up at the bar. Ex-husband making you pay alimony you don't want to pay? Bar. Crazy wife trying to cut off your booze? Bar. No wife or husband? Bar. Always to the bar."

"He's actually right," said Sammy. "For once. If nothing else, it's a great place to catch some rumors, and on New Los Alamos, indoor locations have filtered air. Which means they're popular hangouts, especially for travelers not used to the atmosphere. Plus, I ran a few more scripts and managed to hack into the location monitor for his phone. Turns out, yeah. He's in the bar."

Reardon's voice broke heavy over the comm. "What? Why the hell didn't you lead with that?"

Chuck could practically hear Sammy grin. "Because I like hearing you make a fool of yourself, bro."

"Okay," said Chuck, hand subtly patting the pistol, just to make sure it was still there. "Where's the bar?"

Faint sounds of typing in the background. "There's just one in town," said Sammy. "The *Lone Star Bar*. Should be about a two-minute walk down the main street; look for a big neon sign of a white star. It should stand out in the atmosphere like a … well, like a giant …white … light."

Two minutes later, Chuck found himself inside a bar. It was as all bars were; dingy and dark, but the smell of it—fresh air, slightly synthetic as though passed through some kind of filter, was a profound relief for his nose.

A single man sat at the bar, awkwardly perched on a rickety stool. To the far side of the room slouched in a booth, a woman half-sat, half-lay down on the cushion, her hands wrapped around a large brown bottle.

Obviously she was not Bratta. But the male … Chuck took in the guy's appearance. He had an unruly inch-long beard and wore a massive ten-gallon white cowboy hat, completed by a faux-leather jacket. He sat at the bar, scotch in hand. The ice had melted, his drink untouched. A large suitcase sat by his feet. His skin was so pale, he might as well have been a ghoul.

It had to be him. Chuck vaguely remembered a description of him as "quirky".

"Mister Bratta?" he asked, cautiously, sliding into the seat beside him.

The guy practically jumped out of his skin, his reaction telling Chuck all he needed to know. "H-how did you find me?" he asked, his accent distinctly British.

Chuck almost told the truth, but thought better of it. "Doesn't matter," he said. "I'm Chuck Mattis. I need your help, Mr. Bratta." Chuck nodded to the man's pale hand and up at the cowboy hat. "Or, should I say… cowboy vampire who is most definitely *not* Bratta."

A pause. The man hesitated. Then, slowly, the words came out. "I'm… Bratta," he said, as though saying it, somehow, might make it untrue. "Yes."

Chuck smiled grimly. "You look like you're going to take me back into your lair and drink my blood. How long has it been since you saw the sun?"

Bratta grimaced and set his scotch glass down on the table. "Uhh… well, I don't go outside much. There's a UV lamp in the bathroom—they use it to find stains and things—and I walk past that sometimes. The, uh … air here doesn't agree with me."

Well. That explained a lot. "Why are you dressed this way?"

"I'm fitting in," said Bratta, an edge of offence creeping into his tone. "Most patrons of this pub are Americans. This is an American colony. The *Lone Star Bar* is an American-run institution."

Ten-gallon hat. Fake deerskin leather jacket. Calling a bar a pub. Definitely passing for American. "Anyway," said Chuck, trying to conceal his laughter. "Yeah. So … you're hiding out here, huh? Still worried about the Maxgainz folks tracking you down?" He supposed ever since the feds had shut down the rogue company, its owners would probably not think too kindly about the former employee who shot the video that led to their demise.

"That's right. Blending in like a ... like a true American patriot. And ... hiding. Yes. I suppose you could call it that. Why? Who's asking?"

Chuck held his hand up to formally greet him. "Like I said, Chuck Mattis. Charmed. You may have heard of my father— the guy that helped bring down the folks you're hiding from. Believe me, you've got nothing to worry about from me." The scientist looked relieved at that. "Well. On that note, how would you like to hide out somewhere less smelly? Maybe on a ship?"

The light in Bratta's eyes shone. "You have a ship? And ... you'd be willing to take me away from this place?" His voice became high-pitched and frantic. "Oh, thank God. I'm almost out of money, not even enough to buy a ticket offworld, and... and the *smell* of this place. No, no, I don't care if *they* catch me. I can't stay here another second."

Apparently he had reason to believe the Maxgainz folks were still active and holding a grudge. "That's right," said Chuck, tone soft, trying to calm him down. "Well, technically it's Reardon's ship."

That seemed to do it. Bratta snapped his fingers. "Oh! The *Aerostar*! I know her well."

Right. Okay. "Well," said Chuck, diplomatically. "There's only one catch. I need your help."

"Done." Bratta slid out of the chair, hoisting up his large suitcase. "I'm ready to get off this smelly rock as soon as you are."

Chuck smiled and beckoned him outside. "Right this way, cowboy."

Outside, the stench of the air returned. Chuck turned

toward the landing pad, frowning slightly as he spotted another column of smoke rising. This one seemingly emanated from the pad itself. "Reardon," he asked, touching his earpiece. "Mind telling me what's going on?"

"Get back to the ship!" Reardon almost shouted. "We're being shot at here!"

Nice of him to tell him. His son was on that ship. Chuck grabbed Bratta's shoulder. "We gotta run," he said. "Or there isn't going to be a ship to escape on."

CHAPTER NINETEEN

Edgewater
New Kentucky
Tiberius System

Guano's mouth felt like sandpaper. Walking through the heat of the grimy city of Edgewater, practically drinking the humid, sulfurous air, had turned her lips as dry as chalk. She needed a drink.

Why was she here?

Damned if she could remember. Everything was such a blur in her mind. She just knew this was the place to be.

And, God, her dry mouth…

Fortunately, fate presented a solution. A slightly askew neon sign labelled *The Hole* hung precariously, glaring, above a large set of old-style saloon doors. From within, raucous cheering and off-key singing drifted out, along with the scent of cheap alcohol and the promise of … company. Or something.

Guano pushed open the doors and stepped inside. The bar was full of women and men in uniform and was dark, dingy even, with thick clouds of smoke clinging to everything like a fog. Row after row of seats were aligned to thick oak tables, the corners occupied by booths. A fire burned on the far wall, and in front of it lay a thick bearskin rug. Viewscreens hung in the corner showed sports and news on repeat.

All eyes immediately fell upon her. The singing trailed off. She could have heard a pin drop with the force of a grenade.

"Guano?" asked a familiar voice. Major Muhammad "Roadie" Yousuf. The CAG and her boss. He stood off of a stool, cigar falling from his mouth in shock. "W-what the fuck?"

"No way," said Junior Lieutenant Deshawn "Flatline" Wiley, her gunner, from a nearby stool. "No way. No fucking *way*."

Seeing them snapped her back into a feeling of … normalcy, she supposed. She put her hands on her hips and grinned triumphantly. "Guess who's not dead, bitches."

Roadie approached her, eyes wide like saucers. He had his neck craned forward, skin pale as though he were looking at a ghost. "Is it… really you?"

"Who the fuck else would it be?" Guano laughed, reaching out and plucking another cigar from Roadie's chest pocket and planting it between her teeth. "Light me up, boss."

He didn't. He just stared at her. "But you're dead," he said, plaintively.

She chewed on the cigar, grinning like a wild cat. "Do I look dead to you, jackass?"

Roadie didn't look amused. Nor angry. Merely confused.

"The battle of Chrysalis," he said, with an ethereal edge. "We looked all over for your pod. Couldn't find it. We put a one hundred thousand dollar bounty out to the locals for any word… nobody answered it 'cept a bunch of local scammers trying to cash in with a salvaged pod from God knows where." Roadie's voice cracked. "We had a wake. We … gave up on finding your body. And here you are, just waltzing in on us like there's nothing wrong." He stared at her in utter bewilderment. "Where have you been?"

She almost told the truth. The full and complete truth, right there in the bar, with everyone listening. But the words snagged in her throat.

There had been multiple copies of Brooks. Multiple people in those tanks she'd seen. Guano didn't believe for a *second* that Brooks—or whoever he was—had laid everything on the table for her. There were bound to be other secrets. Other lies. Things she hadn't known and could be dangerous to voice. If she told them about Spectre, that might raise suspicions about her. And she wanted to fly, to get back into the saddle as soon as she could.

She wanted her life back.

So, she lied as well.

"In some guy's basement," she said, piecing together a series of what she *hoped* would be believable lies as quickly as she could. "I hit my head pretty hard when my pod landed. Some local drifters picked me up, brought me back to their ship. They, uhh … wanted to hold me for ransom, to try and extort the US government for a bounty or reward, but because I was unconscious, they didn't know my name. When I came to, I wouldn't tell 'em anything, either. Eventually I escaped, and I … made my way here."

Flatline stood up, his face a mask of wonder. "That's amazing," he said, awe painting every word. "We had huge issues with getting cooperation from the locals at Chrysalis; I totally get why those bastards would have wanted confirmation you were who we were looking for before they turned you over." He spat onto the ground. "What pieces of shit."

"Yeah," said Guano, grinning still. "They were arseholes."

"That explains what you're wearing," said Roadie, gesturing to her bloody prison garment. "We'll get you changed out of that when we take you back to the *Stennis*."

"Sounds good," said Guano. "*Stennis*? New ship, huh? They kept the whole Midway flight crew together? And what are you guys doing here?"

Roadie rolled his eyes as groans sprung up around the bar. "They merged our whole group with the *Stennis*'s flight group, which was new and tiny to begin with since the *Stennis* is new. And some kids here on New Kentucky got stolen," he said, acid dripping from his tongue. "And apparently the local police are *staggeringly* incompetent, so here we are."

Fair enough. She would have hated it too. "I'm itching to fly again." Suddenly some vague recollection of a conversation she'd overheard—some snippet—some brief side comment made somewhere recently—came back to her mind. Who'd said it? "Is it true that the *Stennis* got the same Chinese engines as the *Midway* had when she blew? I'd … heard that was … a thing."

Roadie laughed, obviously glad to no longer be talking about their work assignment. "Who the fuck cares about engines?"

She could sense that they had a lot of questions and, especially from Roadie, some suspicions that she wasn't telling the *whole* truth, but all of that was buried under a deep, profound joy that she had returned. All of the pilots and crew rushed forward, surging toward her, all yammering at once. They grabbed at her, asking her a torrent of questions she couldn't possibly answer in the time they gave her. They even hoisted her up and carried her like some kind of rock star.

"Guano! Guano! Guano!"

Finally, the crowd set her down. Flatline and Roadie grabbed her and she hugged them both with one arm each. "Hey, you motherfuckers know I wouldn't leave you. I wouldn't leave you."

"You better not," said Flatline, his voice wavering. "You better fucking *not.*"

And then they were all crying. All three of them. Standing in a bar on a backwards-ass planet, holding each other like family, crying like babies, surrounded by their coworkers.

Roadie broke it off first, giving her a firm slap on the back. "You're going to have one hell of a post-operation debrief paper to write when we're out of here," he said, reaching up and wiping his face with the back of his sleeve. "But for now, you useless AWOL piece of shit, let's get fucked up."

That sounded perfect.

Shots were passed around; small glasses of a translucent liquid that burned like acid as it went down and was, most likely, used to strip the grease off engines. Guano took one after the other after the other, slinging them back like they were water. Beer. More liquor. Ciders. A full spread of shots of a liquid that was as alcoholic as it was sugary. A bunch of stuff she didn't even recognize.

And then, eight or nine hours later, most of the flight crew had passed out on top of, or around, the various tables, stools, and furniture of the bar. Someone's boots protruded from under the rug. Guano slumped down into a booth. She could smell vomit and cigar smoke.

What a night. She settled onto the couch, stifling a loud, profound yawn. It was good to be back.

One of the viewscreens in the corner was showing the news. Some kind of breaking event. Guano drunkenly glanced at it. The sound was off, but text rolled across the bottom, holographically floating in front of her vision as she tried to fixate on it.

DISASTER: InterStat transport on Chrysalis to New Kentucky run explodes in upper atmosphere. Related to child abductions? US marshals report that…

InterStat Transport? The Chrysalis to New Kentucky run? That had been her ship.

The ship she'd come in had exploded almost the moment she got off it? Something about that nagged at her—almost screamed *"trouble!"* in the back of her mind—but she dismissed it. Boring. Guano shrugged her shoulders and looked for something else to drink.

"Hey," said Roadie, slumping onto the couch beside her, comfortably draping his arm around her shoulder. "You did good, Guano. I honestly didn't think you'd come back. Thought you were fucked."

"Proper fucked?" laughed Guano, leaning against him a little.

Roadie snorted. "Not for a long time," he said, letting out a loud, long burp. "You know why."

She did, but it didn't do to dwell on the past. Guano nestled up against Roadie. "You know, losing the ship… it was nothing like what I thought it would be."

"Things are rarely how you imagine them." Roadie paused. "Back when I was in high school, I smashed up my first car driving on a road that was all iced up. I thought a car crash would be a long, roaring fire and screaming. The thing that stuck out about it to me was the noise; a sharp crunch, nothing more. Deafeningly loud as the metal bent and twisted, but brief, followed by the most eerie noiseless aftermath. Just a big ole' nothing as I sat there, car upside down in a snowy Michigan ditch.

"I don't really remember the crash itself. Just how utterly quiet and peaceful it was. All I could hear was the gusts of wind through the shattered glass, and the gentle *thump-thump* of the windscreen wipers trying to clean nothing. If I wasn't bleeding so much and had been upside-down, I would've almost liked it."

Guano shuffled on the bench. "You grew up in Michigan?"

"I did." Roadie tilted his head back, looking up at the roof. "I loved the lakes. Sailing, boating, kayaking…"

"Those are all the same things." She grunted. "And I mean… I mean, the ocean is just a really big lake. I've been in the ocean. It's fine. It's okay, I guess."

Roadie looked at her oddly, went to say something, but his

communicator chirped. *Buzz buzz.* He fished it out, reading it. Then his eyed widened.

"What?" asked Guano, sitting up. She felt vaguely sick as she did so. *Don't puke, shithead.*

"We're being recalled," said Roadie, his tone picking up as he fought his obvious drunkenness. "The USS *Stennis* is recalling all leave, effective immediately. All hands are to return to the ship post-haste."

Huh. "What about me?" asked Guano, staring.

"Well, the order was for all former *Midway* pilots to report to the *Stennis*. We'll see what Captain Flint says about that when we drag you on board." He stood up, clapping his hands. "Come on pilots, move out!"

Groaning, the pilots around them resisted.

Guano, however, couldn't wait to get spaceborne again.

CHAPTER TWENTY

Main Street
Fermion City
Los Alamos v2.0
Tiberius Sector

Chuck drew his pistol and sprinted down the road, chambering a round with a soft *click-click*. Above the landing pad, a pair of sleek black fighters dove toward the *Aerostar*, strafing it with their guns. Sparks flew in all directions as rounds struck the hull, ricocheting off and flying all around. One whizzed past his ear.

Well, his little pea shooter wouldn't do anything against aircraft. And standing out in the open with all the stray rounds flying everywhere was a dangerous idea. The black fighters tore into the orange sky, engines roaring as they banked around for another pass at the pink ship.

Bratta, one hand on his massive cowboy hat and the other clutching his bag close to his chest, seemed somewhat more oblivious to the danger. "Is that the *Aerostar* over there?" he asked, squinting and leaning forward. "It looks kind of... more bullet-y than I recall."

Great. This was the scientist who was going to save his son. "That's right." Every father's instinct in him *screamed* abuse into his mind, saying that this was wrong. He'd been wrong.

A turret popped out of the top of the ship, spinning and facing one of the oncoming ships. It let loose a stream of bullets, the *crack-crack-crack* of automatic fire rippling through the air. The ship burst into flame, banking away from the city, leaving a long, thick black trail of smoke behind it, obviously out of the fight.

"Reardon," said Chuck, touching his ear. "Why didn't you tell me you were being shot at?"

"We ... forgot," he answered, and Chuck could almost hear the sheepish grin in his voice. "Hey, this is stressful, ok?"

"It's going to be a lot more stressful for you if Jack gets hurt over there," Chuck promised. He did his best—his absolute, genuine best—to avoid blowing his top. To avoid blaming himself. To be angry at Sammy for talking him out of bringing Jack with him. The more he thought about it the more he would get angry, so he decided not to think about it.

Tried very, very hard.

The remaining black ship strafed the *Aerostar* again and then flipped over, dodging a stream of return fire.

"Okay Bratta," said Chuck, taking in a deep breath. "When that bastard takes another pass, we're going to run to the ship, right?" He glanced to the suitcase. "Ditch the case."

Bratta snorted indignantly, clutching the suitcase closer. "I'm afraid I can't, Mister Mattis. This is my most recent project. I don't let it out of my sight. Plus, all my equipment is here."

He knew better than to argue at a time like this. "Okay. When we get a chance…"

The black fighter came in low, wings sharp and angled like a knife. It let off a stream of fire, then roared high into the sky.

"Now!"

Chuck sprinted across the open ground of the landing pad. It had been churned up by the strikes of the exploding cannon shells. He stumbled. Catching his balance, Chuck powered toward the open loading ramp.

Twenty meters. Ten meters. He could hear the howl of the black fighters' engines, coming back around to make another pass. Five meters. His feet thumped up the loading ramp. He turned back to Bratta.

The guy had fallen behind, waddling as he walked, carrying that big, heavy case. His hat fell off, tumbling as it rolled away. Bratta stopped and looked for it.

"Forget the fucking hat!" roared Chuck. "Get onto the ship! Now!"

His anger seemed to encourage him. Bratta waddled up the loading ramp just as the howling of the engines reached a crescendo; explosive rounds burst on the ground all around the ship, shrapnel screaming as it tore up the paintwork, and pieces whizzed around him, striking the inside of the cargo hold with a *plink*.

Fury boiled up within Chuck. "Hey—hey! Baby on board here!" he shouted out the loading ramp, as though the near-supersonic fighter kilometers away could hear him.

Bratta threw the suitcase onto the deck, panting and

wheezing in exhaustion. "The adults want to live too," he gasped.

Fair call. "This is Chuck," he said, touching his ear. "Sammy, we're aboard. Raise the loading ramp and let's get the hell out of here."

"Working on it," said Sammy over the line. The ramp began to raise and the ship finally lifted off.

There was a tense moment when Chuck felt a pronounced sense of helplessness. If the ships came back, there was nothing he could do. He needed to hold Jack Jack, just do something to protect his son.

Then Sammy sighed with relief into his ear. "Looks like the other fighter is breaking off too," he said, giving a halting, nervous laugh. "Guess we showed them."

Chuck wasn't so sure about that. "Who the hell were those guys?" He glared at Bratta. "Tell me what you know."

"Okay," said Bratta, standing up and dusting himself off. "Um. Well? Just this. They're terribly creepy guys. This is the second time they've tried to kill me. Jeannie would be quite proud of me, I must say." Chuck had no idea who this 'Jeannie' was. "But she's wrong. It turns out hiding in civilian areas *is* a good way to stay safe."

"Second time for us too," said Sammy over the line. "Someone out there must *really* hate us."

Wait. Chuck stared into nothing. "You guys have… encountered these things before? Fighters like that?"

"Yup. It's okay, they tend to just kind of shoot a bit then break off. Dunno why."

The only conclusion he could come to was that they didn't want either the *Aerostar* crew *or* Bratta dead, and were just sending some kind of warning. Possibly. It didn't make much sense.

"So," said Bratta, smiling nervously. "We've escaped, life and limb intact. Uhh, what was it you needed me to do again?"

"Save my son," said Chuck, firmly. He wasn't sure exactly how much to tell him. "He's got a strange illness nobody can even diagnose, let alone treat. And you're smart. So ... fix him."

Bratta stared a moment. "There are plenty of doctors in the galaxy," he protested, blinking rapidly. "Specialists in childhood diseases which, let me remind you, I am *not*." His posture became slightly defensive. "Are you a crazy person? Oh God, please tell me you're not a crazy person."

"It's more than a simple runny nose," said Chuck, anger rising again. "And I'm not a crazy person. It's…" He couldn't decide how much to say, so said everything. "It's something related to all this nonsense. Mutant research. MaxGainz. The kidnapped babies on New Kentucky too." He wasn't being paranoid either, no, definitely not. It was all—must be—connected. "Something ... different ... is wrong with him, and I think it's not something a regular old doc can handle. I can't rely on normal medical science. I'm out on a limb here. I need *you*."

Bratta squinted. "Do you have money? I could really use money. Not much. Just enough for food. And whatever supplies I need."

The one thing he *didn't* have. But feeding Bratta would be possible. Probably. Supplies… well, maybe. It would depend on what he needed. Elroy still had a credit card or two that weren't *totally* maxed out. "Sure," said Chuck, grinding his teeth a bit.

"Why not."

Seemingly convinced, Bratta nodded firmly. "Okay. I have my other research projects to pour time into—my automatic homing dart launcher is still too heavy and unwieldy—but I can dedicate some time to that."

"Good," said Chuck. "Make sure it happens." He considered a moment. "Also, don't talk to the mutant."

Bratta stammered a moment. "Wait, the—the *what?*"

CHAPTER TWENTY-ONE

Cockpit
The Aerostar
Upper Atmosphere of Los Alamos v2.0
Tiberius Sector

Chuck fetched Jack from Sammy in the cockpit. Sammy had set out a small, baby-sized collapsible bed in the rear of the cockpit—did he just carry that thing around with him at all times?—and Jack didn't seem upset at all. His kid gurgled happily as he picked him up, seemingly oblivious to the chaos which, mere minutes before, had reigned around their ship.

In the quiet, the only noise the gentle hum of the engines, he spent just a minute rocking Jack back and forth, admiring his playful little squeals and gurgles, while Sammy pretended not to be there. Fortunately, true to his word, the mutant had been kept in the cargo bay.

Eventually, Bratta called him down. With visceral reluctance, Chuck left Jack with Sammy and went down to the ship's open space. Lily stood in the corner, industrial shackles around her wrists. Seemed safe enough.

But Chuck felt a twinge of guilt at seeing her shackled. Despite her horrid appearance and mutations, Lily was still … human. Wasn't she?

"I've finished setting up my equipment," called Bratta as Chuck entered, no small amount of pride in his voice. It was obvious he was itching to do more science stuff.

"You sure this is going to be okay?" he asked, cautiously, eyeing the tableful of implements Bratta had pulled out from his suitcase. Computers, random tubes, boxes and wires; junk he had shoved into sorted piles. No sign of clothes or personal effects at all. No wonder it was so heavy. Had Bratta been wearing his cowboy costume *the whole time he'd been there?*

Best not think about it.

"Welcome back," said Reardon, stepping down the ramp into the cargo bay, a toothpick in his teeth and his stupid glasses on again. "Nice work recovering Bratta. All thanks to my tip, of course."

Chuck glared. "Yeah. Is the *Aerostar* damaged?"

"Nah. We gave her an armor upgrade lately. Worth every —" he mumbled, "*borrowed* penny."

Right. "Okay, well, just stay out of his way," said Chuck, turning a skeptical eye to the table full of equipment. So much trash…

"Okay," Bratta said, holding up a thick-looking needle to the overhead light and inspecting it. "First thing to do is to check his blood."

Blood. Always with the blood. "The hospitals did that," said Chuck, tired. "They always gave me the same bullshit."

Bratta bristled slightly, a strange sight in his outfit. "My medical opinion is the opposite of bullshit."

The opposite? Chuck stared.

"I mean, as a geneticist, I can probably analyse your son's blood with this equipment much better than those monkeys at a *general hospital* could."

Chuck wasn't exactly sure about that. "Okay," he said. "Go ahead."

With one swift movement, Bratta slid the needle into the baby's arm. Jack was so brave, he didn't even cry.

Reardon grabbed his forehead, his tan skin noticably paler.

"You okay?" asked Chuck, worried.

"Look, it's not…" Reardon shuddered, closing his eyes and looking away. "It's not the blood. It's the needles. Jeez…"

Bratta extracted a sample of blood, then injected it onto a small plate. One of the computers lit up, text scrolling. Bratta hunched over the screen, partially obscuring it, muttering something soft to himself as he read.

Silence. Chuck waited for the results.

More silence.

"Well," said Bratta, trying to lighten the obvious tension. "He's pregnant."

With the adrenaline of the battle still lingering in his veins, Chuck wasn't in a humorous mood. "Just tell me," he said, a little more sharply than he meant to.

More waiting.

"We need to make a phone call," said Bratta, a slight tremble in his voice. "I need to speak to John Smith. Sooner rather than later."

Smith. The same guy Reardon had been looking for. Huge

coincidence if it was the same John Smith… Chuck frowned. "What is it?" he asked.

"I'm afraid I don't know," said Bratta, looking over his shoulder, the corners of his lips turned down. "But there's *no* way this blood is normal."

CHAPTER TWENTY-TWO

Derelict Avenir vessel
Moon Debris
Pinegar System

Debris, powdered metal and sheets of bulkhead rained down from the roof of the corridor, bouncing off Mattis's helmet and thumping against his suit. Strips of metal, corroded almost into powder, plinked off the escape pod. The denizen trapped within didn't seem to react or complain in any way, even as the whole damn ship was collapsing around it.

But then again, having spent how many months in an escape pod, who knew how sane it was?

"Here!" said Lynch, panting as he ran up to the hole they'd peeled in the hull. "Exit here!"

Not a moment too soon. Mattis felt as though he was drowning in his space suit. Sweat was pouring off him like he was in a sauna, but his joints ached and his back felt strange. It had been a long time since he carried something as bulky as the pod. Even in the very low gravity, it still had mass and was difficult to move.

Mattis and the others sprinted out of the ship, Lynch guiding them urgently. The doomed vessel groaned, twisted, and the bulkheads collapsed in on themselves, becoming a massive debris pile on a debris-strewn moon.

The team ran towards the shuttle, which flashed its lights at them hurriedly.

"We know," said Mattis, breathlessly, into the radio. "We goddamn know, alright!"

His boots pounded silently on the broken, powdery terrain, the pod jostling between them all. The hundred or so meters between him and the shuttle seemed the longest dash of his life; his breath came as thin wheezings and his whole body ached in a deeply profound way.

Definitely something to blame on the radiation, old man. Not the fact that you're old as fuck and running around on a broken moon fragment hauling a massive lump of metal with a huge mutant inside it.

Closer. Closer. Mattis closed his eyes, focusing only on the effort of putting one boot in front of the other. He just had to get to the shuttle…

And then he was there. Practically falling over the damn loading ramp.

Modi, Mattis and Lynch—along with the Marines—pushed the pod up the loading ramp and unceremoniously jammed it inside the shuttle, the container stuck in at an awkward angle. But it fit. "We're aboard," he said. "Get us out of here."

The shuttle almost immediately began to move, jerking from off the surface of the debris with a painfully sharp motion that nearly sent them tumbling.

"Spears," he said into his radio. "What's the situation out there?"

"We're working on IDing that skunk," said Spears. "Stand by." There was a long pause as the shuttle, its engines whining with the strain, took them farther and farther away from the moon debris. Of course, that meant that it might be taking them closer and closer to an active firefight, but… Mattis put such thoughts out of his mind.

"Admiral," said Spears, relief in her voice. "It's the USS *Stennis*. They weren't expecting us here so they were running on stealth mode."

Dammit. Those Chinese engines were fast *and* quiet. Then again, that's exactly what he would do in that situation. Leverage the hardware he had. And the *Stennis* had no way of knowing there were friendlies in the area.

But what the hell was the *Stennis* doing here? Something deep in his gut told him that something was—off.

"Copy that," said Mattis, fighting the urge to say what he was *really* thinking. "We'll talk more when we get back to the ship."

"Actually," said Spears, "I have Captain Flint on the line. Given that you're a US admiral, he'd probably prefer to talk with you rather than me."

That was true enough. Mattis lumbered over to one of the shuttle's monitors. "Sure, put him through to the shuttle. I'll route it to this station."

The screen flickered to life in front of him. Seated in a command chair was a young, clean-cut man with racially ambiguous features and a completely shaved head. Even his eyebrows seemed to disappear into his face, giving him a slightly alien, unsettling look.

"Captain Flint," said Mattis, nodding respectfully, trying hard not to think *Captain Prick*. "Good to see you here."

"I'm afraid I can't say the same, sir," said Flint, adjusting his grip on his command chair. "My sensors are detecting heavy amounts of highly damaging radiation down there, and also, *you*. What in God's name are you doing down there?"

The way he spoke was some kind of strange mix of respect and contempt that Mattis couldn't help but scowl at. Fortunately, his spacesuit's visor would hide his expression. "Completing an important mission," he said. "Following up on a lead."

"Ahh yes, Mister Modi's pet project." Flint leaned forward in his chair slightly. "The *vast* amount of processor time Modi was consuming at the Canberra Naval Supercomputing Laboratory hasn't gone unnoticed and, frankly, his results aren't that difficult to interpret. My mission was to follow up on what he's learned and assist you in any way possible." He looked at someone off-camera, then back to the screen. "Mattis, it would probably do you well to return to the *Stennis* and turn over everything you have to me. As you're part of the *United States* Navy, what you're doing would seem to fall under our jurisdiction. Plus…" Flint nearly sneered at him, "shouldn't you be on Earth? *Sir*?"

For some reason—a little niggling feeling inside him that he couldn't quite give voice to—Mattis didn't trust Flint one bit, no matter what he said. Maybe it was him giving orders as though Mattis was his subordinate or, possibly, just his tone. "On behalf of Captain Spears," he said, well aware that she was listening in on the conversation, "I'd like to thank you for your offer of aid and welcome what support you can give us. However, this operation is being conducted under the auspices of Captain Spears and the Royal Navy. I'm just here for the ride." A little lie wouldn't hurt. "I'm familiar with the *Stennis's* capabilities, Captain, and the HMS *Caeravron's* facilities are better suited for our operations at this time. But, of course, we welcome you to join us and assist us in any way you can."

Military speak for *fuck you, I'm in charge here, bitch.*

"Admiral," said Flint, "perhaps you're not fully understanding the situation here—"

"Perhaps you're not understanding that *admirals* give orders to *captains.*" Now he was definitely being a dick. "You might be God aboard the *Stennis*, but right now, I'm not there."

Flint hesitated a litttle—just a little—then nodded his head reluctantly. "As you wish…" He stressed the word, "*Admiral.*"

Mattis extended a stubby finger and went to close the connection.

"Before you hang up," said Flint, looking back to the person off-camera once more. "I have someone here who wants to talk to you. Someone who made me an offer I couldn't refuse. And, truth be told, is the real reason I'm here and not on shore leave at New Kentucky."

Mattis shrugged a little. Then again, much more visibly, remembering that the suit would hide much of his expressions. "Who's that?"

With almost palpable reluctance, Martha Ramirez stepped into frame, moving to one side of the camera beside Flint, her hands folded in front of her. "Jack," she said, "we need to talk. Now. Or a lot of little kids are going to die."

CHAPTER TWENTY-THREE

Cargo Bay
The Aerostar
Upper Atmosphere of Los Alamos v2.0
Tiberius Sector

Chuck hesitated. "What's wrong with the blood?" he asked. "Specifically."

Such a sea of emotions. He felt intense relief that *someone*, at least, was *finally* acknowledging that something was wrong— but Bratta had only barely glanced at the results to see it. How had the hospitals missed it?

Or had they deliberately turned a blind eye?

Bratta closed his eyes for several moments, deep in thought. "Okay, this is complicated, but let me try and explain it in a way you might understand." He sighed and clapped his hands together. "Okay. Imagine a junkyard that has been neatly organized. Whitegoods to one side, metals to another, furniture to another. It's still pretty chaotic, but it makes *sense*, right? There exists a sense of order and structure to the junkyard, even if it's full of trash. Right?"

"Right."

"Well, imagine that a tornado whips through that junkyard. Distributes everything randomly. Totally randomly. Nobody has any control over it. That's basically your junk DNA. Yours, mine, everyone's. It's totally random. It doesn't do anything." Bratta pinched the bridge of his nose and inhaled. "I mean, look. It's a *lot* more complicated than that, because there are, in fact, some things that it does do and we're discovering more all the time, but… as Jeannie says, 'keep it simple, stupid'. So, it doesn't do much. With me so far, yes?"

"Sure," said Chuck, not entirely clear on which one of them was supposed to be 'stupid' in this case. "You're saying my son's DNA is all scrambled?"

"No," said Bratta, "I'm saying that it *isn't*. It's supposed to be, like all of ours. But *his* has been re-ordered and restructured and it's … neat. Clean. Everything isn't where it's supposed to be, no, but it's all clumped together." He cupped his hands, moving them over the table. "The whitegoods are *here*, now. But they're still whitegoods. The furniture has been restacked and re-ordered, and moved over to *here*, but it's still all furniture. It's been randomly reordered, true enough, but the *staggeringly impossible* odds of it happening in this way…" he gave a nervous laugh. "Well I mean it's many, many, many, many orders of magnitude more unlikely than a million to one."

It was a lot to take in. "So what are you telling me?"

"I'm telling you," said Bratta, "that the only organization who could do this is either a massive private bioengineering company—someone like MaxGainz—or... a government. Someone like a big bio corporation subcontracted to the CIA or DOD or something."

"And Smith," said Chuck, starting to piece the bits together. "Is a CIA officer. You think he might know what this is?"

Bratta hesitated a moment, obviously confused as to how Chuck knew that, but then he nodded in understanding. "Exactly. He won't know how to fix Chuck, but he might be able to give us a solid lead."

"Great." Chuck set Jack down gently, then threw his hands up in frustration. "Well, he's missing too, and frankly I don't think we'll just randomly stumble onto him like we did with you."

"Well, fortunately," said Bratta, brandishing a phone from his pocket. "I actually spoke to him just yesterday." He stammered a little. "I-I mean, I got a message from him yesterday, I didn't *speak* to him, exactly."

"He wrote you a message?"

"No," said Bratta, confused. "It was a bunch of images."

Chuck shook his head in annoyance. "Huh? Let's see."

Bratta fiddled with the device and handed it over.

It was just as Bratta said. A bunch of images. The first one was of a table, shot at about head height, with a magazine on it; some kind of picket fence enthusiast rag. The number 4 was carefully torn out of the price and placed in clear view. The next was a wall, the number 6 scratched into the paint. An image of a pen, laying straight on a table, an eraser underneath it, the whole shot framed as though taken with a shoulder mounted camera. A picture of a pile of trash, papers and plastic. There were many more.

"What am I looking at?" asked Chuck, scrolling through them. More images. One of a sickly green sky, seen through a window with thick glass. Another of a brown sea, stretching out to the horizon; the view was distorted, as though seen through a space suit. The "beach" at the bottom of the shot was littered with garbage, a man's hand barely in the frame.

"I have no idea," said Bratta, sighing. "They just look like… random snaps of some dump."

Chuck continued to flick through them. "They're all from head height," he said, curiously. "Like someone was holding a camera… but Smith didn't need one, because he has—"

"He has a prosthetic eye." Bratta's eyebrows shot to the roof. "Of course. That's what we're seeing! We're seeing what he sees!"

He scrolled through them faster, each image coming as a blur. And then something caught his eye.

An image of a finger drawing on a steamed up mirror. Drawing a bunch of numbers. The first few were 4-6-1…

"What's this?" asked Chuck, showing Bratta the screen. "These numbers."

He read for a moment. "Looks like planetary coordinates," he said, realization dawning. "Followed by latitude and longitude. He's telling us where he is." Bratta smiled. "You're not bad at this investigation thing."

"Thanks," said Chuck, genuinely. "Okay. So where are we going?"

Bratta typed on his computer for a moment. "Oh boy," he said, grimacing. "And here I thought New Los Alamos smelled bad…"

CHAPTER TWENTY-FOUR

Pilot's Ready Room
USS Stennis
Debris field
Pinegar System

Guano slumped in one of the huge beanbags strewn around the ready room, giving the cloth covered bag a firm pat of approval. "Damn," she said to Roadie, grinning like a jackal. "This is some serious comfort right here. Beanbags. Why didn't we think of that back on the *Midway*?"

Roadie sat opposite her, almost completely sinking into his own spongy seat. "Well, I guess we were too stupid back then, and now we know."

She snorted dismissively, leaning back and getting comfortable. It wasn't the *Midway*, but it was shocking familiar, as though ready rooms came in some kind of stock format. "You and I both know that's true. The kind of people who climb into metal tubes to go shoot other tubes in an age of nukes and drones are kind of dumb."

It was the sort of comment that would never have been allowed between pilots and non-pilots and would have absolutely been considered fighting words, but between Roadie and Guano, it was not just okay, it was their own language.

"Yeah," said Roadie, grinning cheekily. "Well, I'm glad you're here with me." His eyes lit up, as though remembering something. "Also… um, how did you go with the… thing?"

"The thing?" She stared blankly.

"The…" Roadie tapped his temple. "The *thing*. The thing that happens when you fly sometimes."

"Oh," said Guano, relaxing comfortably in the puffy seat. She wasn't sure where the words in her throat were coming from, but they seemed natural. Not really a lie. Just the truth spoken with a confidence she didn't quite understand. "I got that on lock now."

That seemed to pique Roadie's interest. "You serious?" he asked. "I mean, just like that?"

"Yeah," said Guano, conjuring back into her mind the story she'd told earlier. "While I was those guy's prisoner, I figured it out. It took some time, some alone time, you know, but I… I figured it out. I can basically turn it off and on at will now."

Roadie blew out a low whistle. "Damn girl," he said, "you gotta show me this."

Wordlessly, Guano squirmed out of the beanbag, made her way out of the ready room, and down the hall to the simulator room. Roadie followed her, equally silent but obviously curious. She climbed up the ladder leading to the simulated cockpit and jabbed a thumb behind her. "C'mon," she said to Roadie. "Wanna gun for me?"

"Hell no," he said, shaking his head. "This is about you."

Fair enough. No gunner then. She wouldn't need one. Guano scrolled through the various simulations available. There were many, but one caught her eye.

Encounter at the Concorde. The no-win situation. The one Brooks, that dickhead, had described as the Kobayashi Maru from ancient sci-fi.

She thumbed the power up switch. Time to win it.

Her virtualized ship appeared in space, surrounded by 'allies'. Eight fellow Warbirds; identical ships with identical layouts.

They were the real enemy in this simulation. Friends pretending to be enemies.

Carefully and deliberately, Guano took in a deep breath and let it out slowly. She felt the rush of energy fill her, and then nothing. Nothing but total calm. Tranquillity. No energy, no anger or passion, just cold, calculating piloting. Pure survival.

Guano set her course, falling into formation with the ships she knew would eventually betray her. As soon as they arrived at Objective Alpha, the Warbirds flickered and turned red, but Guano was ready. The moment the Warbirds turned toward her, she pulled the stick back into her gut. Cannon fire flew below her ship.

Easy. Guano kicked out her foot, jamming it on the rudder pedal and swinging her ship to the left. One of the Warbirds floated directly into her sights. She barely breathed on the trigger, firing a quarter-second burst that sailed into the cockpit of the simulated fighter, blasting the crew compartment into shreds and sending the ship tumbling listlessly through space.

One down, seven to go.

The chattering of guns—sounds played through the simulator's speakers to provide pilot situational awareness—gave her just enough warning to jerk the control stick to port, swinging her ship out of another devastating line of fire. She flipped around, flying backwards through space, painting the lead Warbird with her missile lock radar. It couldn't get good tone.

But that was okay. Heat seeking missiles had a maddog mode, where they would just fly out straight and hit the closest target that, hopefully, wasn't the ship that launched it. Use of this mode was highly discouraged because US spacecraft almost always traveled in groups, but she was alone out here.

Guano switched on maddog mode, then dumped two of her heat-seeking missiles without lock. "Fox two, fox two. Maddog, maddog."

The twin missiles streaked away from their railings. Just as she anticipated, they parted and flew in different directions, each spearing directly into a fighter, blowing it away. Guano fanned her rudder pedals, little puffs of gas maneuvering her reversing ship from side to side, fishtailing away from the inevitable return fire. It flew past her cockpit, missing the canopy by inches, but a miss was a miss.

Three down, five to go.

The other five, probably reacting to some hidden quirk in their programming, broke off their attacks and reformed their attack wing. Guano was more than okay with letting them go; she had a full complement of radar-guided missiles just itching for targets. She flipped her ship again, flying the same direction her nose was pointed, and burned away from them.

Perhaps the programming wasn't anticipating that; an aggressive push with close range missiles followed by a retreat to distance. The fighters circled aimlessly. Perfect targets for the radar-guided missiles. "Fox three, fox three," said Guano, squeezing off both missiles. Again, both found their targets, splashing a pair of simulated fighters to white hot balls of flaming debris and expanding gasses.

And then there were three.

The missile strike seemed to galvanize the remaining fighters into action. They turned toward her, cannons flashing bright twinkles against the black of space, vomiting glowing streams of fire straight toward her.

Easily avoided. Guano twisted her ship and opened the throttle, moving out of the way of the deadly streaks. Three computer opponents versus her. Easy meat. She tipped her nose up. The opposing ships immediately did the same. She tilted her nose down. The enemy ships did the same, too. Interesting. She had two more long range missiles left, and two heat seekers, but she wanted to keep them.

She didn't think she'd need them.

The enemy ships fired their missiles. The wailing of the missile lock alarm filled her ears. Completely on muscle memory, she tapped the countermeasures; flares, chaff, and electronic decoys. The enemy missiles lost lock. Easy peasy, lemon squeezy.

Wiggling her nose up and down, Guano cruised towards the three remaining enemy fighters. Bots were dumb. They kept trying to compute a lead on her ship but they didn't count on someone like her constantly changing their course to make them miss.

When they got close enough, Guano gave each fighter an intense burst from her guns, and that was that.

"Holy shit!" shouted Roadie from the sidelines. A small crowd of pilots had wandered down from the ready room and gathered around the entrance, watching her fight. "You... you killed them all?"

"Naw." Guano pointed up at the large screens. Eight red dots had appeared at the edge of her radar range. "There's another wave spawning. I'm pretty sure that they just keep sending you more fighters until you run out of fuel and ammunition."

Roadie smiled at her. "Alright, well, you proved your point. C'mon down here and we'll celebrate. Pretty sure nobody's even reached the second wave before."

She turned back to the screens. "I'm not finished."

The next wave—appearing from nowhere— swooped in, missiles screaming toward her. Guano dumped flares and chaff to decoy them and then, as though it were the easiest thing in the world, split them up one by one and cut them down. She tried to conserve her ammunition as much as possible, giving each ship only a short burst when she was sure she was going to hit, but two craft remained at the end, her missiles depleted and her guns empty.

Now things were getting interesting.

The two remaining fighters, seemingly possessed of infinite ammunition, dove down on her, and she jerked her fighter back and forth to avoid them. She kept dodging and they kept firing. Far more rounds than they should have. It almost seemed like two streams of constant fire were coming from each of them…

Something she could use to her advantage. Guano pulled back the stick, opened the throttle, and gained some distance between the two fighters, fishtailing her ship to spread them out. The distance between her and them grew. Then, when she was well out of range, she flipped over and burned hard, straight toward them.

The two spacecraft peeled away, one to port, one to starboard. She accelerated, her ship trailing an expanding silver stream behind it. The two hostiles turned back and opened up with their infinite ammo guns, shooting endlessly at her.

Ever so carefully, Guano thread the needle, flying between the two ships. Precisely between them. Both ships turned to fire at her and, instead, their lines of shooting crossed.

Both ships burst into white-hot fireballs that quickly faded.

"Holy *shit!*" shouted Roadie again. The gathered pilots and crew cheered like crazy.

A third wave appeared, predictably, but this time Guano was out of tricks. She took off her helmet and flicked off the simulator. With a sigh, she blew out a breath she hadn't realized she was holding, and with it came the battle fugue. She grinned impishly over the side at Roadie.

"Wow." Roadie and the others stood by with stunned expressions on their faces. "That… was sensational. Bravo zulu, pilot." Bravo zulu. 'Well done' in naval slang.

Guano climbed out of the cockpit and waggled her eyebrows. "See? I'm fucking fantastic."

"That you are," said Flatline. "You set a new record." A slight edge of bitterness crept into his voice. Or jealousy. "And all without a gunner, too."

She clambered down the ladder and grinned at him. "Next time," she promised. "I'll need you if I'm going to get beyond the second wave."

That seemed to mollify him slightly. "Okay." Flatline gave a playful little bow. "Anyway, I guess you're back to form. We should probably find you some quarters."

She smiled her appreciation.

Everyone seemed so pleased with her. So proud of her achievement. They showed her around the *Stennis*, they bought her a few drinks to 'cure whatever was left of her hangover', and finally, Flatline showed her to a spare set of quarters on the port side of the ship, right next to the reactor cooling network—a detail she wasn't quite sure why she knew, but it seemed important for some reason.

Guano slid into her rack, rolled over onto her side and stared at the bulkhead. She knew coolant fluid pulsed beneath it, almost like a heartbeat, keeping the ship's powerful reactor alive. A stray wire poked out from the panel, a tiny sliver exposed.

She reached out for the panel, gently pried it open, reached into her pocket, withdrew a small black device she didn't even remember carrying, slid it into the gap, then pushed the panel closed.

Within moments she was fast asleep and dreaming, the incident completely forgotten.

CHAPTER TWENTY-FIVE

Hangar Bay
USS Stennis
Debris field
Pinegar System

Mattis stepped off the shuttle and finally removed his helmet. Standing in the recently re-compressed hangar bay, a woman in a suit was waiting for him. His chest tightened as he took in her features. Olive skin, hair done up tight in a bun. It had to be Martha, flanked by a pair of Marines.

He hadn't been prepared to see her on the bridge, but he was *really* not ready to see her standing right there. Suddenly he felt twelve years old again; words struggled to find their way past his lips.

"It's good to see you too," said Ramirez, smiling a little.

"Yeah," said Mattis. He jostled his helmet under his arm. "So… uhh."

"Mmm."

Silence. "Every time we meet," said Mattis, managing a small smile, "there's always a little bit of awkwardness."

"And whose fault is that?" said Ramirez with a notable edge of bitterness, then seemed to catch herself, obviously embarrassed. "I'm … sorry."

"No worries," said Mattis, grimacing. "I know I should have called."

"You *definitely* should have called," said Ramirez, but she shook her head as though dispelling the thought from her mind. "Never mind. Look. The thing is, there's a real danger here that you need to deal with."

That was good. They could deal with their relationship— or lack thereof—later. Later… it was always later when it came to Ramirez. But this time, *this time*, he would make the time to talk to her about everything. As soon as they had the time.

"Okay." Mattis adjusted his grip on his helmet, turning to speak over his shoulder. "Move that pod into quarantine. We don't know anything about it and I don't want it fucking up the ship. Inform Captain Spears that our mission was successful, and leave it for her to follow up." Then he turned back to Ramirez. "Let's walk and talk."

"Very well," she said. "The main conference room is toward the stern, we can have a proper chat there."

They fell into step together, walking out of the hangar bay and into the ship proper. "Okay," said Mattis, firmly putting one boot in front of the other. He didn't want to wait until they got to the conference room "What's the deal with these missing kids?"

"Have you watched the news?" asked Ramirez. She seemed strangely okay with talking out in the open.

It was difficult for Mattis to say, especially given her prominent role in the show, so his answer came out as a guilty, "No."

"Well you should." Ramirez was obviously fighting the urge to let sarcasm and frustration into her voice. "We ran a program recently about some children that were stolen from a nearby world, New Kentucky."

Her words sparked a flash of memory. "Yes, you're right," he said, nodding firmly. "Spears mentioned the same thing." It was very bad news indeed. "Stolen kids, huh?"

"Straight out of their cribs," said Ramirez, disgusted. "The bastards killed every adult in the whole facility, then they lifted the kids offworld. A review of the security footage showed that the ship carried a Forgotten insignia. Which is why I need you—or at least, part of the reason why I need you." That last little bit, almost a confession, drew a little smile from him. "We know you've had experience with these people before."

"That's right," said Mattis, "and like I told Spears, this just isn't their MO. The Forgotten had a specific grudge against specific people, and yeah they were basically terrorists, but despite their violence they were otherwise… well. I wouldn't say they were good people, but they wouldn't massacre a facility of childminders and steal kids. It just doesn't sound like them at all."

She considered. "Well, regardless, I think that working on the assumption that it was them, for now, is probably best."

Despite his gut feeling misgivings, Mattis couldn't help but begrudgingly agree. "Sure."

Ramirez led them toward the main conference room and pushed open the door. "Just keep an open mind," she said, with something that seemed almost like caution or warning. "Okay," said Mattis, stepping inside.

The conference room was a long, low-ceilinged room with one far wall dedicated to a screen. In the center was a long oval table with a dozen chairs arranged around it. And at the end of the table was a man who stood up as they entered. His eyes were closed, but Mattis recognized him.

Senator Pitt.

Mattis's hands became fists at his side, acutely aware of the pistol strapped to his hip. "You bastard," he said, the words escaping as a faint hiss. "What the hell are you doing here?"

Senator Pitt opened his eyes. They were red and puffy, as though he'd been crying. "Hello, Jack."

"Fuck you." Mattis practically spat the words, setting his helmet down on the end of the table with a clatter. "I should ask Flint to throw you out an airlock. What are you doing here?"

"I'm here," said Senator Pitt, his tone weak, "not to fight with you. I'm here to ask you for help."

That was a stretch. A little of the anger left Mattis's body; the man seemed genuinely upset, and if this was some kind of trick or misdirection, it was a bloody good one. "What do you want?" he asked, skeptically.

"It's about Jeremy." Commander Jeremy Pitt. Senator Pitt's son.

"Okay," said Mattis, gently. The loss of his son had obviously affected him. That was understandable. "I'm sorry about that. You know I did my best. I didn't want anything to happen to him. You know that."

"You don't understand," said Senator Pitt. "He's … he's

alive."

The words hit him like a bombshell. They took a moment to process, as though the idea was just so ludicrous and insane that merely thinking about it was tantamount to believing it, which was crazy. "Pitt," said Mattis, with as much kindness as he could muster. From one parent to another. "Jeremy's— Jeremy's dead. I was at his funeral. I saw his body. He's gone."

Whatever reaction Mattis was expecting, it wasn't a broad, happy smile piercing through the mask of sadness. "I've learnt recently that's … not quite true." A strange, almost manic energy seemed to take over him. "My son never really died, Jack. Not really. He survived the explosion of the ship he was on. The president, President Schuyler, she wanted to keep it a secret given all the politics going on right now and the diplomatic situation with the Chinese. She even kept it from me." His words came out almost frantically fast. "He was very badly injured, and he was in a coma for some time. He nearly recuperated and was going to make his return, but then the Forgotten—they got hold of what was happening and kidnapped him and are going to use him for ransom. For extortion."

There was something about the whole story that seemed off, strange, as though it were full of half-truths and misdirections by omission, but there was also a palpable truth there as well—Pitt was not lying. That much was clear.

Just enough for Mattis to believe him. Sort of.

"Okay," said Mattis, nodding his head. It was strange to agree with Senator Pitt, but… if Ramirez trusted him, then he could, too. "What can I do for you, then?"

"Well," said Senator Pitt, taking a deep breath and slowing

his voice as though through deliberate effort. "I was the architect of the US—China peace deal. Something the Forgotten didn't exactly like. I'm worried that they're going to use this as leverage, to try and ruin the deal, somehow. Blackmail me into pulling out of the continuing talks."

That made sense. "And what about the missing kids?" asked Mattis. "How do they play into this?"

"That's the thing," said Ramirez. "We don't know that. Not yet. But if anyone can find out, it's you."

Mattis wasn't a detective. He shrugged helplessly. "How am I supposed to do that?"

Ramirez tapped on her wrist computer—did everyone have one of those these days? Everything old is new again. He felt so behind the times—and the wall-mounted display lit up. "Before I ran the story about the stolen kids, I received a text message telling me not to run it. Unfortunately, because I'm a dumbass who doesn't check her phone, I missed it and ran the program anyway. They *specifically* told me not to run it and *specifically* not to talk to you. I think that's what they're afraid of. They don't want you involved in this—probably because they saw what happened to Maxgainz when you got involved."

Something in the back of his mind made him wonder if that was bait, but he pushed it aside. It came from a place of regret and pain.

He'd done the right things in the battle where Pitt's son had died. He'd taken all the correct steps to assure victory, but it had not come without a price; a price the Pitt family had paid with the life of its eldest, and only, son.

Now there was a chance he could be alive. A slim chance. The word of a deranged father, most certainly, but … he wanted very badly for this slim chance to come true.

"Right. Well, it's good that you did exactly that." He turned to Senator Pitt, giving him a look which was as much a glare as anything else. "Any idea where to begin? Where they might be holding your son?"

"Of course," said Senator Pitt, turning to the monitor. "You think I came here empty handed?"

"Okay," said Mattis, eyeing the screen warily. "I'm listening. But be quick, Captain Flint wants to debrief—" he wasn't sure what to tell them. "A guest."

Ramirez was looking at him, trying to pry the secrets out of his gaze. He steadfastly avoided looking at her.

"Well, you see," said Senator Pitt, tapping a key and sending a slide up to the monitor. "There's a   supposedly abandoned supply station. I believe the Forgotten are using it as a base."

"Okay," said Mattis, cautiously. "What's the catch?"

Senator Pitt gave a strange smile. "It's like what they say… location, location, location. It's in the dead center of the Tiberius Nebula."

The busiest, and most populous non-Sol colony in the galaxy.

"So if we get there, and they bail, they can escape, blending right into the Tiberius Sector crowd.   Dozens of nearby worlds there. Disappear again," said Mattis.

Pitt nodded. "Exactly. If we don't surprise them …" he trailed off. "I can't lose my son again, Mattis."

CHAPTER TWENTY_SIX

Interrogation Room
USS Stennis
Debris field
Pinegar System

Mattis folded his hands behind him, standing beside Captain Flint in the interrogation room.

The *Stennis*'s Marines had cut the mutant creature out of the escape pod and dragged it to this small room, whose only notable feature was a table, two chairs, and a wall of bulletproof, one-way glass. Two hulking marines, their sleeves rolled up, stood by the magnetically sealed door. Next to each of their feet was a black, opaque bucket.

The mutant itself was shackled to the table. It stared impassively at Mattis. Mattis stared back.

"What were you doing on that ship?" asked Captain Flint, an edge of aggression in his voice. "Talk, freak."

Nothing. The creature just stared ahead blankly.

Flint nodded to one of the Marines. She picked up the bucket, walked over to the mutant, and upended it over its head. Water and blocks of ice splashed over the mutant's body, soaking it with freezing water.

It didn't react.

"Maybe we just need to get the mutants to *chill* out," said Flint, grinning.

Mattis didn't laugh. This was Flint's ship. He *could* order him to find out information another way, but giving orders on someone else's ship was a major faux pas. "It doesn't seem to mind the cold."

"Point," said Flint, nodding to the second marine. The second guy picked up his bucket and, just like the first, tipped it over the mutant.

Steam billowed out, and the water must have been scalding, but again the mutant didn't react.

"What do you think of that, hot stuff?" asked Flint, obviously enjoying himself.

Mattis had no stomach for this stuff. Never had, never would. Moral implications aside, torture rarely revealed information that was useful, as the subject would typically say *anything* to make the pain stop.

Yet this one wasn't saying anything at all.

"That's enough," said Mattis, shaking his head. "We're done here."

That seemed to annoy Flint. "You sure you don't want Sergeant Page to work the subject over a little first, Admiral?" he asked, idly nodding to the Marine.

"Very sure. We'll have to wait until it's ready."

Flint didn't seem happy about that, but nodded

compliantly. "Aye aye, Admiral."

With that, the two of them turned and left.

"Where to now?" asked Flint. "My ship is at your disposal, Admiral."

Might as well tell him. The Captain deserved to know. "Senator Pitt has informed me that there is an abandoned resupply station in the Vellini system. Smack dab in the middle of the Tiberius Nebula. It's called Jovian Anchor."

"Vellini System?" Flint nodded. "The *Stennis* was constructed there at the Vellini shipyards. Hell of a place to look for a missing man—Vellini itself is huge. A billion people at least."

The mention of *Stennis*'s construction at the Vellini Shipyards reminded him of his old love. "The *Midway* too. Was the first ship constructed there. But lucky for us, Jovian Anchor is not anywhere near the shipyards. It's orbiting a tiny planetoid way out on the fringe of the system. Like, Pluto-way-out. Called … Slingshot, I think. The station was abandoned years ago because Slingshot has an unstable orbit around its sun—in a few hundred years it's going to be ejected from the solar system, and with it, Jovian Anchor."

Flint snorted gruffly. "Heh. Slingshot indeed. Well that's an Army Corp of Engineers cosmic blunder if I ever heard one. How the hell did they not realize the rock was going to be slingshotted out of the system when they built the damn thing?"

"What else? The contractor in charge of the feasibility study turned out to be a one-man operation in his parent's basement in Baltimore. He was seventeen, and he did it as his senior thesis project on cybersecurity. Go figure. His mom was a congresswoman so he got away with it. Anyway, long story short—"

"Too late," quipped Flint, to Mattis's annoyance.

"Senator Pitt thinks a faction of the Forgotten has holed up there on Jovian Anchor, kidnapped his son, and is holding him for ransom."

"And you want to go in there and kick some ass, I presume."

Mattis shrugged. "More or less."

Flint nodded, then did a double take. "Wait, did you just say Senator Pitt's *son* is there? His *dead* son?"

"Turns out he's not quite as dead as everyone thought. Just a flesh wound, as they say."

Flint blew out a low whistle. "No wonder the Senator was eager to talk to you."

No wonder indeed.

"So," said Flint, turning to fully face him now. "Last time you showed up on a US warship unannounced you took command almost immediately. You're not here to do that to me, are you, Admiral?"

The *Midway* had been a special case. "Don't worry, Captain. I won't interfere with the operation of your ship."

That seemed to mollify him somewhat. "It's a mighty big relief to hear you say that, sir." Flint tilted his head to the side. "So begging your pardon, but what *do* you want? You can return to the *Caernarvon*, but I'm guessing it's not it."

Very true. It wasn't. "I want to see Jeremy—I mean, Commander Pitt—again, if such a thing is even possible. Honestly, something feels ... off about that whole thing. I swear he was dead. There's no way anyone could have survived the explosion of that ship. I want to see him for myself. In the flesh."

Flint clicked his tongue. "That might be a problem," he said, cautiously. "Admiral Fischer is asking about you. I got off the phone with her just before you arrived—she's ... well, she's a bit pissed, Jack. Seem's she's had enough of your *gallivanting*, as she called it."

Mattis snorted. He was enjoying having his feet on the ground too much after years of command, and the top brass would only get in the way if they had any involvement at all. "Did you tell her you'd bring me back?"

"Of course," said Flint. "And I will, no matter how many ranks you pull on me, Admiral." Mattis rolled his eyes—the other man's asshole reputation was starting to shine through.

"Well, don't. Not yet. In fact, pass along the bare minimum of information you possibly can. What I'm doing here is *very* important. Fate-of-the-human-race level stuff, Flint. Jeremy Pitt should be dead. And he's not. Given the recent context of all the shit we dealt with when Spectre and his Maxgainz mutant garbage were running rampant, it sounds a hair too suspicious to me. This is the kind of operation that doesn't need to involve the brass for now, okay?"

"For now," said Flint, not seeming convinced.

He wasn't sure he believed him, but had to accept it. "All I want *for now* is to see Pitt with my own eyes." Mattis had to offer Flint something to make sure he would cooperate. "And I know protocol dictates that I take command, but that's not why I'm here. To prove it, I'll be going over with the strike team. Totally out of your way."

Cautiously, Flint nodded. "Gallivanting indeed. Well, I

can't stop you, Admiral. *For now*. Right. I'll make sure there's a place for you. We have a spot open in the team that'll secure extraction, if you want?"

"I," said Mattis, smiling a little, "had a slightly different idea. I heard you brought over what was left of the *Midway*'s Rhino teams."

Flint's face changed in an instant. "Sir, you cannot be serious," he said. "You *do* know what the Rhino teams are like, don't you? Their IQ is a shoe size."

"I understand," said Mattis. "I know these particular folks. I'm sure I'll be fine."

Flint hesitated and then, slowly, nodded. "Okay. It's your choice, Admiral. I'll inform the team."

"Very well." Mattis grinned a little. "Hey, what can go wrong?"

"Famous last words."

Mattis turned to leave. "That's what I thought about Jeremy Pitt's last words. And look where we are now."

CHAPTER TWENTY-SEVEN

Cargo Bay
The Aerostar
Upper Atmosphere of Planet Vellini
Vellini System
Tiberius Sector

Chuck checked his pistol for what felt like the ten-thousandth time. He wasn't a soldier. He wasn't a Marine. He was just a guy who had been shooting with his Dad as a kid. He mentally ran through what to do. When shooting distance, align the rear sights to the front sights. Keep it steady. Squeeze, don't pull, the trigger.

When shooting up close, ignore all that and just pump as much lead into them as possible. Pistols were notoriously inaccurate, but when the target was yards away the only thing that mattered was firing as quickly as possible.

When shooting distance, align the rear sights…

The *Aerostar* shook as it descended through the strange

planet's atmosphere. Down it went, shaking slightly as it passed through a pocket of turbulence. They had no idea where they were going; they had executed the Z-Space translation into that area, then followed the planetary coordinates straight down.

Could be a trap.

Could be a dead end.

Could be a lot of things.

He'd never felt this before. The rush of adrenaline into his body, knowing that right at this moment he was dropping into what might well be a firefight. He could get shot. He could die. Elroy would be left with Jack—

No, Jack was on the ship, too. What would they do with him? He'd be okay, right? Right?

Regret began to crawl back into his mind. Fear. What was he thinking, bringing a *baby* on this crazy adventure? What if the ship's hull punctured? There was only a thin wall of metal between him and…*nothing*. Nothing that would kill him in seconds. And that was a fit adult human. How would a baby handle explosive decompression? What was he *thinking*?

"Hey," said Reardon next to him. "You're breathing like you're about to pass out."

He shook his head and forced himself to take slow, deep breaths. "Yeah. This is—this just isn't what I'm experienced at. I'm a political campaigner. I'm not a warrior."

Reardon seemed to digest that as the *Aerostar* continued to descend. "Wanna know a secret?" he asked, casually pulling the toothpick out of his mouth and slipping into his breast pocket. "Back before I was an 'entrepreneur,' I was a janitor. By night. By day I stacked cans in a factory. Working sixteen-hour days just to put food on the table. Eventually I figured out a better way… I learned to be a warrior, and it was easy, because *every* human is a warrior. We didn't evolve from apes to be weak. Only the strongest survived. No matter who they were. We're *all* strong. We're all heroes. You just gotta reach inside you and summon that energy too."

That made sense. A warrior was just a man. "Easier said than done," said Chuck. His hand was shaking.

"I know," said Reardon. His voice was smooth and calm. For all his silliness and bluster, Chuck realized in that moment that, despite it all, Reardon *actually* knew what he was talking about, or was good enough at faking it that it didn't matter.

Reardon's confidence gave him confidence. The confidence to put his fears and worries away. He was going to be fine. Jack was going to be fine.

"How do you do it?" asked Chuck, reaching up and wiping his brow. "Do … *this?* As a life?"

"Pretty simple," said Reardon, adjusting something on his belt. A brace of grenades. "Just don't die. Ever."

That simple, huh. "Okay," said Chuck, checking his pistol one last time. "Let's do this, then."

With a soft *clank*, the *Aerostar* came to rest on the surface of the planet they had picked out. Through a small porthole, a large structure made of prefabricated panels stood on a mountain of garbage. It was papers and plastics and even larger things; the skeletons of starships and partially completed constructions, all mired in garbage and puke-brown water that resembled stuff that came out of Jack.

The loading ramp pressurized to the airlock. Chuck drew his pistol, looking down the sights with hands that barely trembled at all. When shooting distance, align the rear sights to the front sights. Keep it steady…

With a faint hiss, the door slid open. A man stood on the other side, rifle in hands, a silhouette with all detail washed out by a powerful backlight.

Sammy powered up a small drone armed with a pair of submachine guns. Reardon raised up his gun. Chuck lined up his sights.

"Put the guns down, gentlemen," said Smith, stepping forward onto the loading ramp, orange prison garb glaring. There was blood splattered on his knuckles. "We have a lot to talk about."

CHAPTER TWENTY-EIGHT

Patricia "Guano" Corrick's Quarters
USS Stennis
Planetoid Slingshot
Vellini System
Tiberius Sector

Guano woke up feeling more rested and relaxed than she had in years.

She brushed her teeth. She fixed her hair. She got into her brand new uniform with her brand new *Stennis* shoulder patch: an anchor draped around the neck of a furious-looking turtle, encircled in the words *Unyielding and Unbroken*.

Neat.

The Z-Space journey from Pinegar to their currently classified location had taken some time—far too much time for her liking—but she was, at least, getting settled in nicely. With a surprising spring in her step, Guano stepped out of her quarters and wandered down toward the pilot's ready room, pushing open the door with her shoulder.

She was greeted with cheering and raucous shouts. Grinning like an idiot, Guano held up her hands to quiet the din.

"Well, well," said Roadie, casually waving a printout like a fan. "Look who it is. I submitted your sim score to the academy. Only one percent of tested pilots at the Top Gun naval academy were able to reach the second round. Literally nobody before you had ever reached the third round. So, Lieutenant Corrick, your name is *officially* in the history books… until some other chump breaks it."

"Oh," said Guano, unable to resist the urge to preen a little bit. Just a little. "I'm actually thinking I can get past wave three with a gunner. If nothing else, more ammunition."

Flatline, having seemingly recovered a chunk of his confidence, piped up. "You line 'em up for me, and I'll knock 'em down. Just keep it steady enough that I can shoot."

One of the other pilots, Frost, smiled a giant half moon at the both of them. "You guys are going to do great," she said.

She could definitely get used to being fawned over like this. Guano opened her mouth to say something wise and humble and funny, most of all humble, but then the red alert siren sounded.

"Damn," she said, There was no way the *Stennis* could have had a fighter ready in time. Everyone else ran to get suited up. Guano just stood around like a dumbass.

"Come on," said Roadie, obviously catching her dejected expression. "I got a surprise for you."

Curious, Guano followed him, jogging toward the changing rooms. The pilots and crew pulled on their flight suits; Guano jammed herself into a loaner about a size too small and too narrow around the shoulders. But it was airtight, which was all that mattered.

Then the pile of fighter jocks poured out into the hangar bay and, weighed down by heavy suits, awkwardly ran to their fighters. Guano, with no better idea, followed Roadie, Flatline in hot pursuit.

"This way," said Roadie over his radio. "Check it out."

Then she saw it. The fighter she was being led to. A Chinese-made J-88, long and thin like a cigar, with stubby wings bristling with weapons, painted in the standard US Navy grey and emblazoned with the US military insignia.

"A gift from our friends at the People's Liberation Army Naval Airforce," said Roadie, waving his hand with a flourish, a faint air of sarcasm painting his words. "A sign of our continued mutual trust and understanding in the face of a common enemy."

Guano's eyes nearly fell out. "You're shitting me," she said, stammering slightly. "I get to fly a J-88?"

"Correctamundo." Roadie rapped on the side of her helmet with his gloved knuckles. "I've had my best pilots and crew practicing in them for the last two weeks. They've been configured to use the same control scheme as the Warbirds, more or less, so you should feel right at home."

She couldn't help but rub her hands together gleefully. "All for me, all for me!"

"Hey," said Flatline, somewhat put out. "I'm here, too."

"All for *us*," corrected Guano. Without further ado, she put her foot to the ladder and climbed up to the cockpit. It was much smaller than in her old Warbirds; she threw a dejected glance to Flatline. "Are they serious?"

"Chinese are short," he said, swinging a leg into the gunner's seat and squirming until he fit. "Damn thing is a tight squeeze."

Well, she shouldn't really complain. "Are they really *that* short? I thought it was mostly a diet thing." Guano similarly swung herself into the cockpit and into the seat. Despite her misgivings, inside of the fighter's cockpit was surprisingly roomy, and she found her hands right over the controls.

"Huh." Guano touched the throttle, the flight stick, and the various glass screens in turn. Everything seemed comfortable and within reach. No worries. "Okay, I think I got the hang of this."

"You ready to go?" asked Flatline, swinging the J-88's turret around. It spun like a top, then settled pointing directly rearward. Damn, that thing could turn.

"Yeah." Guano thumbed the engine start and the ship beneath her. It didn't move at all. A bunch of lights flicked on on her console, but she couldn't *feel* the engines working. Must be a malfunction. She pressed it again and the computer whined. "Uhh… dead start?"

"It's on," said Flatline. "Just get ready to launch with the others."

Wow. Quiet. Absolutely no vibration or hum from the engines at all. Just the flashing of various displays.

The hangar bay doors slowly drifted apart, revealing space beyond.

Flatline thumped on the back of her chair. "You sure you're up to this?"

"Yeah!" She felt energized looking at that wide field of

stars. "We'll get our mission objectives en route, yeah?"

"Yup. And go gentle on the throttle, okay? She's fast."

The doors slid open. Roadie's ship, and the rest of Wing Alpha, drifted up and out the hangar bay door. Next was Beta Wing. Then Charlie, which was her. Guano lifted the ship off the deck, marveling at how light and feathery it seemed to be, then opened the throttle.

The J-88's engines roared to life, shaking the whole ship and causing her to jump so hard she nearly jerked the control stick to one side and speared into the hangar bay doors. She roared past Beta Wing, then slammed on the reverse thrust, letting the silver exhaust cloud of the J-88 wash over her. "Shit!"

"They're fast," said Flatline. A glance in the rearview mirror revealed his skin several shades lighter than it should have been. "I said to be fucking careful!"

Okay, okay. She pulled her ship back, sheepishly falling into formation with Wing Charlie. The J-88 was *really* snappy on the controls; a rocket with guns and brimming with missiles.

Her radio crackled and Roadie came in over the line. "Okay idiots, listen up. The *Stennis* has come out of Z-Space right next to a resupply and fueling station called Jovian Anchor. The best available intel we have is that the Forgotten, bunch 'o pricks, have been occupying this place for some time, as is their want-to-do. We're here to clear these parasites out. Be aware, we have been advised there is a distinct possibility that the Forgotten have acquired a limited number of Warbirds from places like Chrysalis, so ... be on your toes."

Warbirds? US-made heavy fighters? How the hell did a bunch of terrorists get hold of *them?*

"Oh man," said Flatline, groaning audibly down the line. "I guess it really *is* true."

The flight drifted to the side. Guano adjusted the ship's course to match. "What's true?"

"Ah, you wouldn't have known." Flatline coughed. "Well, there was a rumor going around that, in order to secure the use of the minefield at Chrysalis, Admiral Mattis traded a bunch of surplus Warbirds for ammo and other such things. Some people say it was only a single Warbird, some say it was more, but who knows really."

"Great," she said. "Just great." Right on cue, almost as though hearing their radio communications and reacting to them, her radar lit up with a single large contact—almost certainly the fuel station—and then a bunch of smaller ones. She counted six—wait—eight in total. "Bandits," she said, "two o'clock low."

Other pilots relayed the command. Guano tapped a few keys and brought up a relayed image of the ships, beamed in from the *Stennis*. They were Warbirds alright, sporting an ominous all-black paint job. They blended in with the inky black of space, almost invisible except for the stars they blocked out.

For some reason, she didn't think these were the Warbirds Mattis had traded for. They looked … different. Modified. More advanced than the ones she had flown, and the ones the *Midway* had fielded.

"Well," said Flatline, giving a short burst of the rear gun to warm it up and verify it was serviceable. "Looks like they definitely got more than one, either from us or from someone else. Good thing you've had a bunch of practice against

Warbirds, huh?"

Yeah. Good thing.

"All craft," said Roadie, "break formation and engage those bandits. Weapons free. This area is designated a free-fire zone, so any fighters here that are not squawking friendly, blow them to dust. Be advised, however: do not engage the station at this time. I don't need to tell you inbred morons that a *fuel station* blowing up this close to our strike craft would be one hell of a problem for us all."

"But," said his gunner, Frost, her chirpy voice at odds with her words. "Only for a little while!"

"Shut the fuck up," hissed Roadie, and then his CAG voice returned. "Call out your targets, break and engage. Good hunting."

Guano swung her ship to the side, opening the throttle once more and zooming away from the rest of Charlie wing. This time she was ready for the acceleration, although, as before, she was shocked at just how fast the ship moved.

The Chinese pilots she had raced back at Friendship Station must have been holding back.

Weaving her ship from side to side, Guano painted targets with her targeting radar. Four sprung up; one of them, frustratingly, flashing a friendly signal. As she watched, the green was overridden by red.

"Hey Guano," said Flatline, "now might be a good time to turn on that battle fugue thing, you know?"

She took a deep breath and focused, hoping she could deliver on her promise.

CHAPTER TWENTY-NINE

Breaching Pod
USS Stennis
Planetoid Slingshot
Vellini System
Tiberius Sector

Mattis adjusted the helmet of his regular ole' space suit, trying to find room to breathe, very glad he couldn't smell the other people crammed into the metal box with him.

"Okay," said Spears into his ear. "The *Caernarvon* and her fighters are going to engage the Forgotten cap-ship—how the hell did they get their paws on a cap-ship?—you and the Rhinos are to insert into Jovian Anchor and recover Pitt."

"Got it," said Mattis. He couldn't help but smile. It actually felt good to be on the front lines, actually *doing* something for a change. Even if it was smelly and cramped. *Gallivanting*, as Admiral Fischer called it. "We'll get in there, get him, and then signal for extraction."

He could practically hear Spears roll her eyes at the other end, but her tone carried with it the hint of approval. "We'll launch you when we're close to the station. Good hunting."

"Good hunting," said Mattis, then closed the link."

"Admiral, you want a Rhino suit?" asked Corporal Janice Sampson, eyeing him with a concerned eye.

Definitely not. He could barely breathe as it was, crammed into a breaching pod with the *Stennis's* Rhinos—elite boarding and counter-boarding Marines with specialist suits of armor— and Mattis was certain that one more suit would make it almost impossible to disembark at the other end.

Then again, Rhinos were not exactly known for their brainpower.

"I think I'm fine," he said, wiggling around until he could check his rifle. Definitely loaded. "As long as I have air, I'm okay. I wanna maintain my ability to manouver."

"Okay boss," said Sampson. She reached around and scratched her ass plate, something that seemed not only patently ridiculous to him because of the thick layers of composite armor that overlayed it, but also took up a little more of their extremely limited room. Her suit had extra lights and spotlights dotted all over it. Mattis vaguely recalled something in Lynch's report about her being afraid of the dark. "Your call."

Lynch raised a hand. "I'll take one if you don't mind. I like my skin and organs intact."

Mattis glanced at him sidelong. "Have you even ridden in a Rhino suit before?"

"No." Lynch eyed Sampson, who was still trying to scratch through her ass plate. He lowered his voice and mumbled in

Mattis's ear. "Can't be that hard, could it? Look who's riding them now."

With a gruff chuckle, he shook his head. "We'll be fine without. These fine people will soften them up for us, and we'll just need to mop up."

With a lurch, the pod launched, fired from the magnetically accelerated launch tubes that dotted the side of the *Stennis*. They were on their way, drifting through space toward their target.

The launch, or perhaps the brief conversation they'd shared, stirred up others in the cramped pod that reeked of gun oil and sweat.

"So hey," said one of the Rhinos, his chest emblazoned with the name Kluger. "Admiral. You sure you don't want a bigger gun?"

The other Rhinos had miniguns either slung over their shoulders or carried in their hands. They required battery packs on their backs for the motors, and a sizable ammunition cache which made their suits even bulkier. He was carrying the standard issue main battle rifle of the US Navy. "What's wrong with this one?"

"Well," said Kluger, hoisting his weapon, a massive tube with a heat shield on one end, the other connected to twin tanks of fuel. "Nothing, really, except overkill is fun. I mean, check this out. I call this one the Bob Rossinator. The fuel it uses kind of sticks to everything and makes really awesome, like, paintings I guess, on the target's skin. And when they burn, it leaves happy little splodges of blood everywhere. I thought I'd be using it in a second war with the Chinese and, but it never got to see service—apparently it sometimes misfires and explodes or something—so… really excited to finally get a chance to see it in action."

Lynch grinned. "Bob Rossinator. Love it."

Mattis resisted the urge to groan out loud. "I guess we'll see. Just make sure to point that thing away from me."

Sampson grinned at him through her visor. She twisted around in the cramped space, holding up a multibarreled rocket launcher, giving it a worryingly rough shake. "Hey Admiral, check this out. It's a heavily modified signaling device."

He recognised it at once. A M-449A. "That's an anti-tank rocket."

"Mmm hmm. Signaling device. You fire it, everyone's going to turn their heads and look. I call it… The Ambassador."

"I thought you called it a signaling device," said Kluger.

"Hell no. It's The Ambassador."

"You put the *ass* in amb*ass*ador."

She poked him with the tip of her missile launcher. "Hey, fuck you."

"You wish."

"*You* wish!"

Kluger grunted and shoved her. "That doesn't make any sense, idiot."

She shoved back. "*You* don't make any sense."

"Whatever," said Kluger. "You're just jealous of my big-ass flamethrower."

Sampson sneered. "Why's it an ass flamethrower, huh? Is it made of asses? What's with you and asses?"

Lynch looked at Mattis with eyes that said, *are you sure you want these fine folks along for the ride?* Mattis just nodded.

The two Rhinos continued bickering and pushing each other, each motion rocking the breaching pod back and forth. Almost on cue, the boarding pod shook violently as though impacting with some kind of weapons fire. Fortunately the front of it was heavily armored, essentially a giant drill to bore into the enemy station. Still, Mattis was suddenly, acutely aware that, despite the thing's armor, if it was breached—whatever went through it would also go through them.

There was a moment's brief silence.

"Oh, Admiral?" Sampson handed him a set of what looked suspiciously like earmuffs, but with extra padding. "You'll want these."

He narrowed his eyes skeptically. "I have earplugs," he said. "And an airtight spacesuit."

"I know. You're going to want these *over* your earplugs and *under* the helmet. Those miniguns are firing sixty, seventy rounds a second, each one of them a pretty heavy 12.7mm round. I mean, if you *want* to be deafened in seconds, that's totally fine, but I figure you'll probably want to preserve some of your hearing for retirement."

Mattis and Lynch reluctantly accepted the earmuffs. He popped off the helmet, put the earmuffs over his head, then reattached his helmet, sealing out almost all other noise. Strangely enough, voices came through just fine; better, even, as though the device was picking out the frequency used by human voices and amplifying it.

"Much better," said Kluger. He peered down at Mattis—not a thing that was easy to do at Mattis's height—with a little bit of pity. "You should really have a Rhino suit."

The more he saw of the suits and the people within them, the gladder he was to be out of one.

"So sir," said Kluger. "What's the mission?"

It was time to tell them. "Some of you may have heard," he said, "that Commander Jeremy Pitt was killed in action in the battle above Earth. There's a suggestion that this might not be true—that a militant faction of The Forgotten might be holding him . We're here to investigate this claim and, if possible, retrieve him—or whoever's pretending to be him."

There was a moment of silence.

"But… isn't he dead?" asked Sampson, her tone gilded with confusion.

"Some of you may have heard that," said Mattis again, trying to keep the annoyance out of his voice. "But it might not be true."

Her eyes widened. "We're saving a—a zombie?"

"No." He had to simplify it. "Look. Doesn't matter. Mission objective is: find all prisoners of the Forgotten and bring them here. We'll sort out the rest later."

"Aye aye, sir," said Sampson. That seemed simple enough for her. "Even zombies?"

"Even zombies," said Mattis.

"Even … Jesus Pitt?"

He shook his head. *Good Lord.*

"Even Jesus Pitt. If such a thing exists."

Lynch grinned. "Just watch out for vampire Pitt. You see that, you gun that shit down."

The pods computers chirped and the lighting flashed red.

"Okay," said Kluger, flicking a switch on his massive flamethrower and igniting a pilot light perilously close to

Mattis's face. "Let's rock and roll!"

"Just remember," said Mattis, keeping his head away from the fire as best he could. "We're here to retrieve prisoners, so —"

A faint hiss was all the further warning he got. The pod latched onto something, the whole device shuddering as it bored its way thorough the hull, then exploding devices blasted the way clear. Light flooded in from fluorescent flickering tubes and The Rhinos ran out, heavy metal feet thudding on the deck. Mattis let them clear the way.

"Contact left!" shouted Kluger, the pilot light of his flamethrower flaring. A gout of flame poured down the corridor, bathing the inside of the breaching pod with orange and red hues.

"Contact right!" shouted Sampson, adopting a firing stance, leveling her missile launcher to the right. Surely she couldn't be ready to fire that thing in here. Surely—

With a powerful roar that was painfully loud even through the earmuffs *and* the earplugs, all three barrels of her missile launcher fired in rapid succession below them, each one creating a powerful shockwave that Mattis felt in his bones. Almost immediately, three explosions reverberated through the pod, followed by the howl of escaping air and wailing alarms.

Rhinos.

"Spread out," ordered Mattis. "Search this complex. Find Jeremy Pitt."

Sampson and Kluger stomped off. The rest of the squad poured into the corridor. Mattis heard shouting, followed by a gunshot, and a metallic scream as the round bounced off Rhino armor. "Well that doesn't sound promising," said Lynch.

"Sir," said Sampson over comms. Another gunshot. Another ricochet. "They're shooting at us."

"Shoot back. If they're hostile and armed and engaging you, take them down. That's the ROE for this mission."

More shouting, then a staccato series of gunshots. One of the Rhinos opened up with their heavy minigun, the massive weapon making a sound like ripping cloth, and then pained screams errupted, instantly cut off ominously by bullet impacts.

They know this is a rescue mission, right?

Mattis shouldered his rifle and stepped through the threshold onto the station, Lynch close on his heels. The left-hand corridor had been burned black, scorched and seared, with small fires dotting the steel bulkheads and the deck. Eerily, it resembled a kind of surreal painting, just as Kluger had promised, tendrils of the fuel clinging to the metal and illuminating it in strange patterns. The right-hand corridor had completely blown out, and what was left of the air rushed out through a large hole in the side of the station.

A thick, heavy emergency bulkhead slid down over that section of corridor, sealing it off and preserving the remainder of the station's oxygen. At least that was something. And it made the decision of which corridor to take easier. They went left, stepping over burning piles of debris—or at least, what he *hoped* was debris—and made his way down the hallway, following the sound of weapons fire, heavy Rhino feet, and cries of alarm.

They avoided all the doorways that were on fire, blown out and breached, or riddled with bullets. Wherever the Rhinos went, they would do their job more or less, but Mattis wanted people alive. And without a suit, he could go places they couldn't.

Finally, they found a passageway that didn't look like it had recently been a shooting range. A long, narrow corridor which was probably some kind of service area. Almost too small for Rhinos.

"Sir?" came a voice from ahead. A Rhino, the name Cho on his chest and Lance Corporal's epaulets on his shoulders, stood there, minigun slung over his back, identical rifle to Mattis's in his hands. "That's a maintenance shaft. Nothing on thermal imagery, but there's hull integrity if you want to take a look. I'll make sure nobody surprises you from behind."

Something about the way the kid was speaking made him consider. "You don't think it's worth investigating?"

"On the contrary, sir, if I were hiding from Rhinos, that's where I'd be." He pulled up his visor. "Our current weapons and equipment layout displays a profound tactical deficiency."

Mattis smiled at him. "Well, Lance Corporal, if you don't mind me saying so, you're smarter than the others."

Cho smiled back. "I love the Marines, sir. But I have a broken back. The Rhino suit interacts directly with the nervous system. I don't carry the suit; the suit carries me, and I don't need legs when I'm not doing the walking. This is the only position I can actually continue to serve in."

"No wonder Captain Flint wanted to keep you around."

Cho nodded firmly and extended an armored hand. "Lance Corporal Ji-Hun Cho."

Mattis took the hand and shook it as firmly as he dared, given the strength in it. "Admiral Jack Mattis." He got the impression that Cho already knew who he was. "Okay. I'm going in. If anyone who isn't a Rhino or our target comes down this corridor, and they have a gun, light 'em up."

"I'll watch your back, sir. And if Kluger comes back, I'll make sure he doesn't flame that passage." He made a face. "I mean, I'll do my best. We're talking about a guy who read Animal Farm and decided that the moral of the story was that pigs are evil."

Lynch smiled grimly and turned to the small passage after Mattis. "Perhaps the biggest shock is that he can read."

Cho grinned. "Aye aye, sir."

They shouldered their rifles and stepped inside, leaving the noise of the battles behind them as they crept deeper into the bowels of the space station.

CHAPTER THIRTY

Cargo Bay
The Aerostar
Surface of Vellini
Tiberius System

Chuck lowered his pistol, exhaling a long, deep breath he didn't realize he had been holding. "Well," he said, holstering his weapon in what he hoped was a single, smooth motion. "That was the easiest rescue ever."

"Rescue?" Smith blinked in confusion. "I've been free for months. All I needed was a lift off-world. Overpowering the guards was easy enough, but jury-rigging a spaceship was somewhat harder."

"Then what was with the signals?" asked Chuck. "The subtle numbers in the mirror and whatnot?"

"That wasn't subtle. I mean... I wrote things down for you. In full view." Smith rolled his eyes. "I couldn't send a clearer message—something like, *Hey Reardon, come get me, I killed all those guys holding me, and I'm now sitting in that house they set up for me, totally defenseless to an orbital strike!* That'd just be dumb."

It didn't really make much sense to Chuck, but it was better than nothing. "Okay, well… you're getting rescued. Come aboard and let's do that talking thing you said."

"I thought you'd never ask," said Smith, stepping onto the loading ramp and into the *Aerostar*'s cargo hold with a loud, relieved sigh. "Thanks, though."

"No worries." Chuck stepped back, ushering Smith aboard. "So, okay. Talking."

"Right." Smith squatted on the metal deck. Reardon moved around near him, and Chuck filled in the third point of the triangle.

"So," said Chuck. "Talk away."

"Okay," he grimaced. "So, basically Harry, after we met last, I got ambushed almost as soon as we parted ways. Some ninja-dudes."

"Ninja-dudes," repeated Chuck, skeptically.

"Hey, my turn to talk." Smith waggled his finger. "You'll get your chance."

Fine. Chuck shut his mouth.

"So, yeah," said Smith, clicking his tongue. "You know, I never really bothered to ask. They claimed to be The Forgotten, but, well, honestly they seemed too professional. Too organized. And well-funded. But it turns out that great care must be taken when imprisoning CIA officers because we are tricksy, patient, violent people who are more than happy to collapse crying in despair in the corner and then, when their captors come in to interrogate them, break their necks, steal a gun, and shoot the rest of them. Who would've known, huh?"

Chuck's dad had told him about the Forgotten. They weren't ninjas—or at the very least, they weren't *all* ninjas—and it was pretty unlikely that all they were doing was guarding Smith just for fun.

"The Forgotten were on the news," said Reardon, snapping his fingers rapidly. "They said that they'd stolen a bunch of babies."

Smith's features hardened. "Hm," he began. "But you know what? It doesn't add up. Why would the Forgotten get involved in deep shit like this? They're about veterans' rights, not kidnapping kids and torturing CIA officers, and … more: they kept talking about the *harvest* they'd come into possession of, but I agot the impression it was some kind of genetics thing. They kept talking about DNA markers and the like. I didn't realize they were *kids*. Damn." He made a face. "They seemed pretty nonchalant about the whole thing. Like kidnapping a dozen infants was an average Tuesday for them. The Forgotten might be a lot of things, but they're not child-nappers. They're just veterans who feel, well, forgotten by the system. They aren't bad people at heart."

"Did you pick up anything else useful while they held you?" asked Chuck.

"Not really," said Smith. "If anything comes to mind I'll let you know."

Reardon coughed. "Also, Smith. Uhh. There are multiple Spectres now. At least we're *pretty* sure there are. We overheard some people talking. Through one of the cat-based-listening-devices."

That didn't seem to impress him. "You always put bugs on weird things," said Smith. "It never pays off. Not once. Not *ever.*"

"It did this time."

"That's bullshit."

"Nevertheless, this time I'm not shitting you."

A brief silence fell over everything as they digested that.

"Oh, Smith?" Chuck smiled lightly. "While you're aboard… don't talk to the mutant."

"The *what?* You have one of those things aboard?"

"Yeah," said Chuck. "Showed up in a cargo box that Reardon opened. Packed with explosives, too. But don't worry. She's harmless."

Reardon glared at him. "Pff. Harmless, you say. A *harmless,* freakishly strong mutant human. We have her locked up in the cargo hold just in case, no matter what this bleeding heart says," he thumbed at Chuck.

Smith glowered and didn't seem pleased at all, looking away for a moment. Then his eyes lit up as though remembering a forgotten detail. "There was one thing, actually," he said. "While I was being held by the Forgotten, now that you mention it. Right on the first day, I overheard an odd word mentioned. Phrase, more like it. *Operation Ad Infinitum.* It was only once, and the one who said it got socked pretty hard by the boss. I think they got more careful after that."

Wasn't much to go on. "That's all they said?" asked Chuck.

"Right. That and the *harvest,* which we now presume was them kidnapping a bunch of babies."

"Yeah," said Chuck, scowling. "Well … that solves that, I guess. At least a little. Though what they're harvesting them *for* is a mystery."

"Mmm." Smith adjusted himself, getting a bit more comfortable on the deck. "And we know the future-humans had been looking for Spectre. Hunting him, almost. And in return, Spectre was tinkering with brains. Something about radical surgical techniques designed to improve human potential."

"Right," said Reardon. "And I think everyone's calling the future-humans the Avenir now. Not sure why."

Chuck interjected, "French for 'future'. future-humans."

Silence, as they were reminded of the gravity, of the sheer urgency and near-unbelievability of the knowledge that a group of mutated humans from the future had come back to the present, multiple times, for … what?

"Anyone else got something to share?" asked Smith.

"Remember, dead Jeremy Pitt's still alive," said Reardon.

Oh yeah. Chuck had heard his father talk at length about Jeremy, but that was just another piece of the puzzle now. He held up his hand in a fist. "Okay, so. We've got baby abductions." He pulled out a finger each time he named something. "We've got mutants being transported in explosive-laden boxes. We've got 'Operation Ad Infinitum,' whatever the hell that is. We've got a formerly dead Commander Pitt. We've got this 'harvest'. Which may or may not be the kids. We have…" he thought for a moment. "The Avenir attacking the gene bank on Ganymede. So we know they're into genetics too. And they're after Spectre, too. And Spectre and brains and surgeries. And Jack being sick."

"Jack doesn't seem related," said Reardon. "He's just a kid."

Smith raised an eyebrow. "Who's Jack?"

"My son," said Chuck. "Infant. He's got a strange heart problem. Not one doc has been able to explain it, and Bratta thinks there's something fishy going on with his DNA. Given everything going on, that's too much of a coincidence for me. Sammy's taking care of him in the galley."

Smith blew out a low whistle. "You let a baby onto the *Aerostar*, Harry? You must be truly desperate."

"Shut the fuck up," hissed Reardon, reaching over to push Smith in the shoulder. "Okay. So. You know things. Where do we go next?"

"Well," said Smith, considering. "I can take a look at Jack, that's fine, but I have no idea what 'Ad Infinitum' is. I have no idea what the mutant-boxes are or why anyone would be shipping them around."

"I know the answer to that one, at least," said Reardon. "The crates thing. Jovian Logistics. They were putting self-destruct devices on ships, and they used them to blow up US Navy ships, including one at Chrysalis. In fact, I think the one I ended up with was destined for the *Midway*—Your father's old ship." Chuck expected him to make some kind of joke, a flippant remark, but his voice was somber and quiet. "Anyway, they run depots across, well, everywhere. They're one of the biggest military contractors out there."

"Jovian," said Smith, ominously. "That's one of Spectre's companies."

"You told us the last time you were here," said Reardon, clicking his tongue. "Seems like he had his hands in just about everything before he passed."

"Well, where's their headquarters?" asked Chuck. "Where do they operate out of?"

Smith pulled out a tablet, searching for a moment. "Looks like … oh! Well, that's convenient. They operate right here up in orbit. In a station adjacent to the Vellini Shipyards." He whistled. "Christchurch Corporate Business Park. Lots of corporate HQ's there. Lots of companies with a presence, which will help our disguises. Hell, even our old friends MaxGainz used to have an office in Christchurch Corporate." Smith scrolled through the data.

"Why would a criminal enterprise be run out of a shipyard?" asked Reardon.

"It's not just *a* shipyard. It's *the shipyards*. The US Navy's premier shipyards outside of the biggie orbiting Earth. And Jovian Logistics is a well-regarded company—at least, no one outside of myself and a few spooks at the CIA ever suspected it was a front company for part of Specter's operation."

"Well? What should we do?" said Chuck. "Bratta's working on Jack. But it sounds like these Jovian Logistics folks might have even more answers for us."

"Okay, well, in lieu of any other options…" Smith closed his tablet. "Let's go check out Christchurch Corporate. Whatever the spider at the center of this web is, I'm sure we'll find it there." He smiled. "Might even find a solution for your sick son, too. Or a lead, at least."

"If nothing else," said Reardon, "we might be able to beg, borrow, or steal access to some advanced lab equipment for Bratta to run more tests on."

"Christ, we don't have to beg," said Smith, half-joking. "We're not *veterans*, Harry."

Veterans. Veterans like his dad, practically begging not to be put out to pasture. Clinging on to his relevance. Unwilling to settle down, take off the hero hat and, well, just be a grandpa.

He put that thought out of his mind. "Okay," said Chuck. "Let's go pay them a visit."

CHAPTER THIRTY-ONE

Maintenance Adjunct D
Jovian Anchor station
Planetoid Slingshot
Vellini System
Tiberius Sector

Mattis and Lynch advanced carefully, their rifle stocks pressed close up against their shoulders, and the farther they got into the cramped passageway, the more certain they were it was abandoned. Water pooled from dripping pipes in the ceiling, the bulkheads were moldy and corroded, and spiderwebs hung in the corners. Nobody had been down here for months.

Or, at the very least, it was deliberately engineered to give that impression.

Carefully, Mattis advanced. The tunnel came to a three-way fork, branching off into the darkness. He swept all three passages with his rifle, but they seemed identical. Three passageways, no real options or maps, and alone.

The latter part slowly drifted back into his head. They could have asked for reinforcements, or at least told someone other than Cho where he was going. "Mattis to *Caernarvon*," he said into his radio, his voice much louder than he had anticipated. But static was his only answer. Must be too far deep inside the station, and probably interference from the reactor core, surrounded by metal and thick bulkheads. "Is anyone receiving me?"

Not even Cho answered. They were on their own.

Three passages, each seemingly alike. Mattis swept his foot over the ground, seeing which one was less dusty. Plenty of dust to the left, plenty to the middle. The right one had substantially less, and as his foot moved over the deck, it revealed something else, too.

The symbol of two teeth biting into a planet burned into the metal. The same symbol they saw on the ruined Avenir ship back in the Pinagar system.

Well, that made the decision easy. "This way," he said to Lynch. Clicking the safety off his rifle, he turned right, the corner swallowing the illumination from behind him, the only light coming from the torch from his rifle. He came to another fork, and searched around until he found the mark again. He followed that passage. "Almost like a bread crumb trail, of you ask me," grumbled Lynch. "Just watch out for an ambush."

The air began to grow warm, then hot. He must be getting closer to the reactor core. Water dripping down from the ceilings intensified; was this near the atmospheric and water processing plant? An industrial sector?

After a short while, the passage came to a dead end,

emblazoned with a crude rendition of the spray-painted symbol. Mattis reached out and carefully touched it. The bulkhead slid to one side, sinking away and out of sight.

Beyond was a large room done up like some kind of barracks or, possibly, cell. There were four sets of bunk beds, a large, long table with eight sets of plates, cutlery, and cup of water. Mattis stepped inside, shining his light on the table, then around the walls.

And on some woman's face, sleeping in one of the bunks. Her eyes opened as the light hit them.

"US Navy!" Mattis stepped forward. It seemed utterly surreal to him that someone could sleep through a Rhino attack, but he'd seen stranger things. "Hands where I can see them!"

Another woman rolled out of bed to his right, coming to the ground holding a twin-barreled shotgun with two huge drums of ammunition. For a split second, Mattis just stared like a dumb, stupid idiot. Where did she get *that?* Was she sleeping curled up next to it? Lynch yelled at him. "Admiral! Ambush!"

Then it hit him—they weren't sleeping. It was just an act to get whoever discovered them to lower their guard. Just like he had.

But he didn't have time to think about it. Mattis kicked over the table, knocking over the plates and cups, sending everything crashing to the deck. The shotgun blew two indentations in the table, the echos reverberating around the cramped room. Lynch ducked behind the door, and sprayed the inside of the room with suppressing fire from his assault rifle.

"We got an intruder!" the woman shouted, jamming the shotgun over the edge of the table and firing it blindly.

Mattis ducked to the side. His rifle had better penetrating power than a shotgun. He fired through the table, rounds flying through, leaving large holes. Satisfied, he emptied his magazine, each round blasting a thumb-sized hole in the sheet metal, shooting until the weapon went *click*.

Silence. Mattis changed magazines, then cautiously crept forward, peering over the table's edge. Blood was everywhere. No need to check. She was gone. "Clear!" he said.

A door opened at the far end of the barracks. Four people wearing various military uniforms and clad in hodgepodge composite armor ran in, weapons pointing at him. Mattis opened up, spraying the corridor with fire, his shots catching one of them in the neck. Lynch stayed in his cover behind the door and picked another one of them off with a shot to the head.

Yet, standing out in the open with no cover had its drawbacks. The remaining two Forgotten fired, the rounds plinking off his space suit, one of them digging into his shoulder. Fortunately, the suits were armored to protect against micrometeoroid strikes, but high velocity rounds were another thing.

Pain. Mattis ducked behind the ruined table. His helmet flashed up warnings of a breach, but while the wound hurt, the suit had absorbed much of the impact.

A spray of hostile gunfire through the table—somehow missing him completely—reminded him of the exact weakness he had, only moments ago, exploited. He leaned around the side, letting off a burst that sparked as it caught the shoulder pad of his attacker.

"US Navy!" he called, knowing it was futile. "Drop your weapons!"

His answer was another burst of fire through the feeble defense, reminding him that concealment was not cover. One of the shots hit his visor, sending spiderweb cracks all along the surface, the impact causing the whole suit to shudder around him and knock off the earmuffs, the sudden noise making him jump more than anything else. Air rushed in, and with it, the smell of the place; mold and sweat and gun smoke. His ears rang.

Another round struck his back, fortunately absorbed by the micrometeoroid plating. That the rounds had to travel through the steel plate helped. Everything helped. But it couldn't last. He could hear Lynch firing back from behind the door, but the Forgotten must have had decent cover themselves since they continued peppering him with rounds.

Fuck this. The table had stopped shotgun blasts, it would probably stop fragmentations. Mattis snatched a grenade off his belt and yanked out the pin. The lever flew wide. *Three, two, one...* he flung it over his shoulder.

"Grenade!" shouted one of the Forgotten, right as a thunderous detonation cut the words from his mouth.

Mattis, disoriented and with the ringing in his ears amplified, staggered to his feet. The blast had shredded the opposite side of the table almost as completely as it had shredded the four Forgotten and their combat armor. Well. The British *Caernarvon* had more powerful grenades than he was used to on the *Midway*. They didn't mess around.

"Mmm... 'splodey goodness," said Lynch with a smile as

he surveyed the carnage left by the grenade. "You ok?"

He nodded, holding a hand down to tell Lynch to shut the hell up since there might be more enemy combatants down the hall, and stepped over the shredded bits of the Forgotten corpses, ejecting his magazine with a clatter he barely heard. Replaced it with a click he barely heard. Next room.

It was some kind of prison cell, completely with little waiting area and floor-to-ceiling bars sealing off a whole section, presumably where the guards had been taking shifts. This far in, the gunfire was barely a distant rumble, hardly audible over the rattle of machinery and whine of air processors. There were no lights. Either they had been switched off or blown out.

"Anyone in there?" he called, probably a little too loudly, a profound ringing still in his ears.

"You aren't Forgotten," said a raspy voice from the shadows. He caught sight of two eyes on a grime-smeared face, hiding low in the corner. They studied him with an unsettling intensity and Mattis saw recognition in them.

"Hand up, and step out slowly."

There was a brief flash of *something* in those eyes. Anger. Confusion. Doubt. "Who are you?"

"It's Jack. Admiral Jack Mattis."

From the shadows emerged a man. Unshaven, disheveled, and wearing the tattered remains of an orange jumpsuit which had been, seemingly, cut apart and crudely sewn back together —or something unskilled hands had made themselves. Mattis wouldn't have recognized him if it weren't for the look in his eyes. A view straight into the man he used to know.

Lynch gasped. "Oh my God. That's Jeremy Pitt."

CHAPTER THIRTY-TWO

Patricia "Guano" Corrick's J-88
Space near Jovian Anchor
Planetoid Slingshot
Vellini System
Tiberius Sector

Guano closed her eyes, focused, and—with just a moment's pause—the battle fugue came back, strong and focused and clean. When she opened her eyes her vision was clear and sharp, the enemy ships practically drifting through space on entirely predictable paths.

A dozen thoughts flowed through her head.

Stay aggressive. Conserve fuel and ammunition. Use missiles sparingly, and remember, each ship only has twenty seconds of cannon fire aboard.

She throttled up, giving a gentle touch on her rudder to align her ship's nose to the first target, painting it with her targeting radar. There was something odd about it. Something wrong and false about the RCS return. Guano struggled to understand, falling back further into her fugue. What was it? What was causing her finger to hesitate over the firing trigger? It was a perfect shot.

Too perfect. And the maneuvering enemy fighters… also too perfect. Too sharp. Too precise. They were either the world's best acrobatics team, moving and flying in perfect sync, or they were drones.

The other ships in the flight loosed their missiles, a flaming barrage of thin projectiles screaming silently across space, her spacesuit helmet full of missile calls. *Fox two, fox two, fox two…*

No. Guano thumbed the radio key. "All craft, all craft, emergency traffic! RCS returns are ducks. I say again, they're decoys. We're looking at decoys."

"Guano, Roadie, interrogative." The voice of the CAG came over the line. "How do you know they're decoys?"

Shit. It was one thing to just say something, but proving it was another. *I had a feeling* just wasn't going to cut it. "Uhh…" She released the key, then pressed it again. "Stand by."

As she watched, the storm of missiles streaked towards their targets, winking out one by one as they connected with their targets and exploded. The radar return signals continued to come through strong, as though no damage were done at all.

"Dammit," said Roadie. "Weapons safe, all ships weapons safe. Hold position. Confirm targets are ducks."

The J-88's around her banked and weaved as they decelerated, stopping dead in space. Fortunately nobody collided with each other. The strike craft milled absently as, presumably, Roadie talked to the *Caernarvon* and the *Stennis*, asking for orders.

"We're RTB," said Roadie, finally. "Everyone return to your ships. Ground pounders will mop up on the station. Nothing for us to do here." He grumbled. "Now why the hell would they send out ducks? Don't they have pilots for these things?"

Whining and bitching and complaining filled the radio waves as his question went unanswered, but it died down pretty quickly. The flights split up, banking toward their ships.

"Well," Guano said, switching frequencies so only Roadie could hear her. "That went well."

He drifted his ship toward hers. "Any battle we didn't die in is a good one," he said, without any sarcasm. "I know we got tricked, but … eh. Everyone who went out came home. As a CAG, can't ask for more than that."

Guano nodded, even though the gesture was entirely lost on him. "Right."

Flatline spoke up. "That's true," he said. "Most people die in the most stupid, inane ways and for stupid, inane reasons. Like being too old and shitting themselves to death."

That was true enough. "Or," she said, "you know. Like Longjohn."

Longjohn had been one of their pilots who had died in the battle of Friendship Station. Mentioning his name caused a pallor to settle in over everything.

"I miss him," said Flatline.

A brief moment of silence over the line.

"Back in flight academy," said Roadie, a distant wistfulness coming over his voice, "they used to tell a story. During one pilot's early space flights—like, third or fourth, I think—a wasp got into the cockpit about halfway into the flight. No idea how it got into the ship, although it probably made its nest somewhere when the ship was in atmo'. No idea why it waited that long to come out and say hello. The fucker just buzzed around until the instructor, sitting in the gunner's seat, tried to swat it. It stung him. Instructor was allergic. Died right there in his seat. Damn nugget pilot had to fly all the way back to the mothership with their instructor's corpse right behind him."

"Gnarly," said Flatline, behind her. The same seat the dead guy would have been in.

Roadie's voice cracked slightly. "Yeah. Not sure if they dropped out or not, but eh. I would have." Silence for a bit, then his professional voice returned. "Hey Guano, nice spot on the ducks."

She smiled a bit. "Yeah. Thanks boss. You're not mad, are you?"

"Nah," said Roadie. "If you get mad at someone for being right, they'll second-guess themselves constantly. If you yell at them for telling the truth, they'll just lie next time."

Fair enough.

"Okay." Roadie cleared his throat. "ILS locked in, let's go home, pilots… refuel, re-arm, and get ready to get back out there at a moment's notice."

The flight drifted toward the *Stennis* and then, as they drew close, Guano aligned her nose to the hangar bay and let the computer do the landing. As they passed through, Guano touched one of the buttons on the console; she didn't quite understand what it did. The ship shuddered slightly as something flew off the bottom, latching hold of the hull. The device flashed a bright blue light then went dark.

"What was that?" asked Flatline.

"Nothing," said Guano, extending the landing struts and powering down the engines, aligning toward the landing strip and slowing the ship, steering with little puffs of gas. "Don't worry about it."

CHAPTER THIRTY-THREE

Cockpit
The Aerostar
Upper atmosphere, Vellini
Vellini System
Tiberius Sector

Chuck couldn't sleep.

After their little meeting in the cargo bay, he'd changed Jack, then Smith had suggested everyone get some shut-eye while the ship's computer flew them to their destination up in orbit. The others had filed off to their cramped little quarters —Reardon's snoring echoed throughout the ship like the bleating of a dying lamb—and Chuck had no doubts the disciplined, self-controlled Smith would sleep as well. But no matter how much Chuck lay on the bottom bunk of the cramped guest quarters thinking about Elroy, he couldn't get his eyes to close.

So he decided to pay Lily a visit.

The mutant had been shackled to the wall of the cargo bay ever since he'd let her out of her box. She was still there when Chuck arrived, staring out the porthole. Just like she always seemed to. What was she looking for?

He wasn't sure what had bought him to her, but a slight mania brought on by chronic lack of sleep, possibly, contributed. Even so, *something*—a father's instinct, perhaps?—called to him. "You hungry?" he asked, curiously.

No answer.

Chuck fished into his pocket, pulling out a protein bar. Instantly Lily's head turned to him.

Food. She wanted food. "Here you go," said Chuck, holding it out.

With startling speed, Lily dove forward, her hands outstretched for his neck. She stopped short, yanked back by the chain.

It wasn't his neck she was going for. It was the bar.

"This is for you, Lily," said Chuck, crouching down and sliding the bar across the metal floor toward her.

The mutant snatched it up and tore into the packaging with her teeth, scoffing down the tasteless hunk of compressed vegetable protein.

He stared until she was done. She looked at him expectantly. "No more," he said, turning out his pockets. "No more."

"More," she said, growling out the word.

Well. That was unexpected. Carefully, Chuck stepped back, peeked into the supply cupboard—it was almost all instant ramen, cereals, and dried junk food—and found a second bar.

"Here you go," he said, sliding it back to Lily. She ate that one too, with equal gusto, but at last didn't ask for more.

"So…" Chuck smiled at her. "I think we got off to a bad start. I'm Chuck. Hi, Lily."

"Hi, Lily," echoed the mutant, turning to stare, once again, out the porthole, her hands outstretched as though she were flying. "Hi, Lily."

Chuck sat there, waiting for the mutant to pick up the conversation, but she didn't. "So," he said, ever-so-casually drumming his fingers on his hip. "How's… stuff? How's the, uh… the *piloting* going?"

"Piloting going," said Lily. "Going."

He wasn't sure if that was her echoing him, or if she was saying that the 'ship' itself was going. "Okay."

"Okay," said Lily.

Chuck leaned back on his heels and closed his eyes a moment. "So, hey. I don't want to just, you know, stand here awkwardly. Do you mind if I just talk for a bit?"

"Little bit," said Lily.

That probably as close as he was going to get to a yes. "I met Elroy's parents for the first time a few weeks ago." He smiled slightly. "You know, it's kind of weird. They didn't come to the wedding. They haven't been a part of his life for, oh, about fifteen years, give or take. Which is an insane amount of time when you're young, but gets significantly less terrifyingly vast when you're older. And finally they decided that, since we had a grandson now, they were going to—you know, *finally*—be a part of his life again.

"So we arranged to go out to dinner. Elroy wanted to impress them. I know how fucked that sounds—*they* were the ones who abandoned *him* because of who he was, not the other way around—but… you know. He still loved them, I think, in his own way. So we went to this super expensive seafood place two blocks down from our apartment. We brought Jack. Everything was planned down to the last detail. We were going to meet them at seven sharp.

"We arrived at the place. Our table was this little round thing with four chairs and a bunch of candles in the middle. Elroy was fussing so much. *Is my tie straight? Are you sure this is the place, how bad is the traffic?* Ha. He had his eyes glued to his phone, and he just—he just kept worrying and worrying and I kept telling him that it was going to be okay.

"So we finally got there, took our table. They weren't there yet, but we were, like, an *hour* early, so it was okay. We just sat there, feeding Jack and snacking on fifty-dollar artisanal bread, and we waited. Seven o'clock came. Seven fifteen. Seven thirty. Seven forty-five. We kept saying *they'll be here, maybe they've just found the wrong place, maybe traffic is real bad.* Then they showed up.

"His dad, Jonathan, was drunk. I could smell the bourbon on his breath as he sat down. As he did so, this woman who… look. She was *extremely* pretty. My age, okay? And Elroy's only three years younger than me. There's no way his mother gave birth to him when she was a toddler.

"Elroy and Jonathan start to argue. He asks where his mother is. Jonathan explains, drunkenly spitting everywhere, that he got divorced a few years back and that this was his new girlfriend. She didn't speak English, and just sat there with this Stepford Smiler look on her face, like it was totally normal for a family to go out to dinner and immediately erupt into a shouting match.

"So Elroy's *actual* mother isn't anywhere to be seen. The fuck, right? Anyway, I basically tell him we're leaving, but Elroy wants to stay. He wants to patch it up with his dad, even if he thought it would be both of his parents. So we make small talk.

"Jonathan explains, proudly, that the woman—whose name was some African word with clicks in it I couldn't even pronounce if I tried—was a prostitute. A *fucking whore* as he said. I thought he was being rude, but no, he meant a literal, actual prostitute. They weren't dating. They were total strangers before tonight. Then we figured out why, because Elroy's mother showed up.

"They immediately started to have a screaming fight, of course. Like, full on screaming at each other. The prostitute saw the writing on the wall after a few minutes and booked it, zooming outta that place without even looking over her shoulder. I hope she got paid in advance. They were just, I don't know, just screaming over the top of each other. He blamed her for leaving. She blamed him for drinking. Everyone was staring, whispering to each other in hushed murmurs.

"But then Jack starts crying and, I don't even know, that seemed to calm them both down. They both pay attention to the baby for a bit and that gets them calm enough to sit down. Janet—that's Elroy's mother—tosses her purse into the middle of the table, knocking over a glass of water and some of the candles. I right everything before there's *too* much water spilled. No biggie.

"The waiter comes over and asks if we needed any help, I say we're fine, just an argument. I must have apologized a thousand times. Elroy was a saint. I don't know how he put up with it.

"We order the seafood platter. Janet tries to feed Jack an oyster. We try to tell her that he wasn't on solids yet, and she went crazy, shouting that she had raised four kids and knew what kids ate. That was the last straw; the waiter came back over and told us that we were being too loud and we'd have to leave. Janet stood up and started abusing him too, just shouting and hitting him. I was so ashamed. Then, well, then she leaned over and grabbed her purse. Her hair touched the candle and it lit up like a firework. She must have had some kind of hair spray, or product, or something, in there.

"She starts screaming. Elroy starts trying to put it out, hitting her with the menu, trying to smother her hair. Jonathan, he—he thinks that Elroy is attacking her. He starts to beat Elroy. I throw a jug of water over Janet's hair. A waiter comes and breaks up the fight. The cops come and arrest the pair of them, in front of everyone.

"We tipped like two hundred percent, and then we fled in shame into the night."

Chuck sat in silence, just reliving the story. He often tried to joke about it—saying things like, well, there's a reason *Mother-in-Law* is an anagram for *Woman Hitler*—but he just couldn't find the humor in it right at that moment. Not with Lily just sitting there.

"That's sad," said Lily. "People… they are mean."

Chuck opened his eyes. "What?" he asked, perplexed. "What did you say?"

"Say?"

"No, don't just copy me. You said it was sad. Did you understand what I was talking about?"

"Talking about," said Lily.

He sighed and slumped forward, half bending over. "What's up with you?" he asked, shaking his head.

The ship's computer beeped. It would soon dock at Christchurch Corporate Business Park station. "Okay," said Chuck, pushing himself up to his feet. "Try and pretend there isn't more to you, but I know. I know you were listening."

"I'm listening," said Lily.

Frowning skeptically, Chuck watched her for a second, then turned and went to wake up the others.

CHAPTER THIRTY-FOUR

Hidden Compartment
Jovian Anchor station
Planetoid Slingshot
Vellini System
Tiberius Sector

"Jeremy?" asked Mattis, staring wide eyed at the man and lowering his rifle. "Is that really you?"

"Is it really *you?*" asked Commander Pitt in response, glaring at him suspiciously. He leaned forward slightly, almost to the point of unbalancing, his face near the bars. "What are you doing here?"

"I'm saving you." Mattis looked around for some way to open the doors. "Key. Where's the key?"

Wordlessly, Commander Pitt pointed through the bars, through the doorway, to the barracks where scorched, shredded bodies lay splashed out on the ground, wisps of smoke still filling the room from the grenade blast.

Begrudgingly, Mattis went back into the barracks and began sifting through the bloody hunks of meat that were once the Forgotten who'd tried to kill him. The acrid stench of the gunfire mixed with the coppery smell of blood seeped in through the crack in his helmet, and soon his hands were coated in gory mess.

His fingers found something attached to the blasted remains of one of the bodies. At first he thought it was a spare magazine, but it was too thin. A key card. He pulled it out, wiped it off, then returned triumphantly to the prison cell.

"This it?" he said, holding the yellow thing up.

"Yes."

Mattis swiped it over the sensor and the bars, with the faint groan of stressed metal, slid into the floor.

It suddenly occurred to him that he was now only a step away from grabbing distance of a total stranger which could probably snap his neck before he could shoot. He stared at Pitt. Pitt stared at him.

"So," said Mattis, figuring that if the guy was going to kill him he would have done it by now. "Where to now?"

"Out," said Pitt, eyes falling to the door. "What happened out there?"

"Had to turn their internal organs into external organs." Mattis checked his rifle. "I didn't want to. But they didn't exactly give me much choice."

Another period of silence, broken only by distant reverberations of gunfire through the decks of the station.

The… *man*. Mattis struggled to think of it as Jeremy Pitt. It looked so alike; the last time Mattis had seen him he looked exactly as he did now. And if what the man's father said was true…

But what if it wasn't?

"Jeremy," said Mattis, unable to keep an edge of caution out of his voice. "How are you alive? What do you remember?"

Pitt's eyes seemed to flare with an inner light. "I don't know," he said. "I remember… going aboard the *Paul Revere*. I remember Ensign Sexton. I remember Ensign Ward. Lieutenant Haney. I remember their skill, their bravery. I remember Lieutenant Burnett, standing in the CIC, her hands folded behind her back like she was going to ride that ship all the way to Captain." His voice softened, some of the gravel draining out of it. "I honestly thought she would." Then it returned to normal. "We hit something. Rammed it. A ship. Big one. No—a rock. A big rock. We were trying to…" he smiled faintly. "Modi was trying to give me a physics lecture and I wasn't having a bit of it. Then—then we pushed the engines, we slowed the rock, we sent it back. We pushed it back to the ship that fired it. And then…" his voice trailed off.

"Then," said Mattis, "the port engine exploded. We detected a fire onboard. A surge in power. We requested the *Jianghu* assist, but they went radio silent after acknowledging the request. They just sat there watching. Escape pods went out, some of them, and then the ship blew into pieces."

"I…" Pitt obviously struggled. "I remember fire. I remember Burnett. She was dead. Something—some piece of metal, big as a car—it had come from somewhere, speared in from the upper decks, almost cut her in half. Ward… don't know. Haney, don't know. I thought I was dead too. I remember lying there, watching the pods escape. Watching them fly away like little angels taking the crew... *my* crew... away to safety. I wanted to get on board one. I wanted to save myself." He shook his head, firmly, as though trying to shake loose the memory. "I... I remember the fire spreading. Stealing the air from the room. We had our suits, of course, but there was something ... something else. I don't remember exactly. A presence in the room. Something *dark*. As though it were stealing the life away from all of us. It touched Burnett. It saw she couldn't be saved. Then it touched me too. Like a damn ghostly Grim Reaper. Maybe I was dreaming. But it put its finger on me, and then the next thing I remember was waking up on a surgical table in some dark place."

"You were saved from a burning ship," said Mattis, skeptically, "by the Grim Reaper?"

That brought a scowl to Pitt's face. "No. I was dying at the time. What I saw was just a shadow. I don't understand it any more than you do."

A burst of distant gunfire echoing through the metal of the space station reminded him that, although this was a very curious thing for Pitt to remember indeed, the questions he had would have to be answered later. "We have to get out of here," he said. "Follow me. We'll talk about this when we have time."

Wordlessly—his former XO seemed to not want to talk much—Pitt nodded toward the exit. Together, he and Mattis returned down the maintenance corridors, retracing the steps he had taken to get there.

As they passed by the symbol of the planet biting teeth, Pitt's eyes seemed drawn to it. "This mark," he said. "I know it."

Curious. "From where?"

"I don't remember."

Even more curious.

There was no more time for questions. His radio crackled into his ears as they got close. Waiting at the end of the narrow passage was Lance Corporal Cho, a small fire burning behind him.

"Sir," said Cho, who, to his credit, didn't stare at Pitt even a little, "we have to get out of here. The whole place is coming apart. The structural foundations of this place were damaged by…" He flicked his eyes to the side. Sampson stood there awkwardly, her still-smoking rocket launcher slung over her shoulder. "Someone."

Mattis touched his radio. "Mattis to HMS *Caernarvon*. Mission accomplished, we have the package. I say again: Commander Pitt is with me."

The radio crackled and in the background of the audio Mattis could hear the dull rumble of weapons impacts and bridge chatter. "This is *Caernarvon* actual," said Spears. "Standby."

A faint rumble spread throughout the station. Mattis did not want to wait around. "Recall the Rhinos," he said to Cho. "We are leaving." He touched his radio again. "Mattis to USS *Stennis*. Captain Flint, come in."

Flint came through clearly, his voice as drawl-y and painfully slow as he remembered. "This is *Stennis* actual. Go ahead."

"Looks like the *Caernarvon* is a little busy," said Mattis. He turned and headed toward the breaching pod. "Requesting extraction. Break." He took his hand off the talk key. "Cho, is the breaching pod okay?"

"Yes sir," said Cho, moving up beside him. "Just climb on in and break away from the station. One of the ships can pick us up, no problem."

Sounded like a plan. Mattis pressed the talk key again. "We'll be heading to the breaching pod and breaking contact. Wouldn't mind a lift."

There was a slight pause. "Technically," said Flint, "that would be Captain Spears's call. I'm not going to cross an angry lady Brit." His voice dripped with what Mattis could only interpret as pleasure at making him wait.

"It's *your* breaching pod," said Mattis, frustration building despite his efforts to calm it. The guy was being a total dick. Just leaving him here.

"I am aware. Retrieval, however, was to come when Spears was ready—it was part of the operational plan."

This much was true. But it was also a technicality. Dammit, the man was a prick. "Granted," said Mattis. "However, we cannot get through to Spears at this time." Right on cue, another ominous rumble—this one more significant and longer lasting than the previous—shook the station. "Things are getting unstable here in a big way. I'd rather not float home, Captain."

"Standby," said Flint. He kept walking. The breaching pod appeared. Most of the Rhinos were there when he arrived. All their eyes turned toward him, toward Pitt. Mattis tried to keep his mind on the job. He couldn't see any children there. That, in some way, vindicated his decision to use the Rhinos. He couldn't imagine Sampson with kids. "Mattis, we are good to extract you when you're ready."

That was good news. "Confirmed. We'll eject as soon as we've loaded. Mattis out." He waved toward the pod. "All aboard! Marines, we are leaving!"

Mattis anticipated that herding the Rhinos aboard would be like gathering up a bunch of cats, pulling all their tails, then throwing food in every corner of the room while detonating fireworks at the centre. Yet, despite their obvious misgivings and more than a little grumbling, most of them began filing back into the breaching pod.

"They're out of ammunition," said Cho, through the radio, using a private frequency. "They're like big ole' babies, all tuckered out and wanting their naps."

Depressingly accurate. Mattis watched as Kluger trudge through the threshold, the heat shield of his flamethrower snagging, nearly pulling him off his feet. "I just gotta ask; how do you handle it? I mean, I can respect them and their destructive potential, but you seem different. What gives? Why ride with the Rhinos?"

"They're fun." There was a genuineness to Cho's voice that made Mattis smile. "They really do mean well. They aren't bad people. They're just … well. You have to be ten percent smarter than the equipment you use. Fortunately, the stuff we issue to Rhinos is almost childproof. But they get results."

Mattis threw a sideways glance to Sampson. She was trying to fold down her rocket launcher but obviously missing a step. Finally, she just bashed the thing against a bulkhead, damaging the launch tube. Seemingly satisfied, she boarded as well, glancing at the dark corners of the ship as though worried there might be monsters there.

"Mmm hmm," he said.

Kluger leaned over to Sampson. "Hey. Is shooting people gay?"

"What?"

The guy shuffled uncomfortably. "I mean, you're putting things into other guys. That kind of does sound gay to me."

"Huh, good point," said Sampson, seeming to consider the thought with some gravity.

That the two of them were able to operate heavy weapons completely dumbfounded Mattis.

It took longer to load the pod than he would have liked. Pitt got in last, both eyes staring squarely at Mattis.

There was a brief period of silence as the pod's computers worked, then with a hiss and a groan, the pod disengaged. It moved away from the station and out into open space.

"Okay," said Mattis to Pitt, as the nebula came into view through one of the pod's portholes. "Mission complete." A wide smile came over his face. "It's good to have you back, Jeremy."

"It's good to be back," said Pitt.

Spears's voice pierced the quiet of the pod. "Mattis. I think we've figured out what the hell was going on here."

"What do you mean? Like, besides the Forgotten keeping Pitt here as ransom?"

"Like, why the warbirds defending this godforsaken station were ducks. Drones."

"They were drones? Remotely piloted?"

"Looks like. Turns out they were a distraction. Nothing more. While we were engaged with them and the Forgotten capital ship, a smaller ship escaped unnoticed from the station. We would have missed it had we not reviewed the footage just now."

A pit formed in Mattis's stomach.

"And? Any idea what was on it?"

Pitt broke in. "Kids."

Mattis's head snapped towards him. "What did you say?"

"I heard kids. Crying. When I was in that cell." Pitt closed his eyes and started shaking his head, as if simultaneously trying to remember and forget a dramatic memory. "Couldn't see anything going on. But the sound was unmistakable. There were some kids on that station. Young, too."

"You hear that, Spears?" said Mattis.

"Yes. The bastards. Look, Jack, from the footage we can pinpoint the second that the ship entered Z-Space, but it's going to take a while to triangulate a vector, given what little information we have. So I suggest—"

"Further into the system," said Pitt.

"What?" said Mattis and Spears simultaneously.

"From when I overheard them talking. My captors. They always kept me hooded, but I could hear them sometimes. They've got another base in this same system. Further in. Not all the way—not at Vellini itself. But ... maybe one of the gas giants. The magnetic fields on those are great places to hide things you don't want found."

"Jack, there are three gas giants in the Vellini system. Could be any one of them. And ..." she lowered her voice as if to keep Pitt from hearing, though they both knew he could, "are we ... sure ... about the source of this information?"

Mattis eyed Pitt, who nodded with understanding. "Of course we're not sure, Spears. But it's all we've got." The expression on Pitt's face—a mixture of relief and ... hope?—

told Mattis that Pitt knew he couldn't be trusted, not under the current circumstances, but that he was relieved his old commanding officer was trusting him and giving him the benefit of the doubt.

"Very well," said Spears. "Looks like of the three gas giants, only one actually has a powerful enough magnetic field to actually hide anything. Erebus. Though why anyone would build something there is beyond me. The strength of the planet's magnetic field does interesting things to the ionized nebula gas. It's like a maelstrom in there once you get close enough."

Pitt shrugged. "It's where I'd hide something. If I were the Forgotten and hiding a bunch of stolen kids?"

Mattis glanced again at the other man's eyes. He seemed so … earnest. That did seem like the old Jeremy Pitt.

"Ok. Spears? Captain Flint? Let's get to Erebus. Let's go bring these kids home, and call it a day."

CHAPTER THIRTY-FIVE

Guest Quarters 3
The Aerostar
Christchurch Corporate Business Park station
Vellini, High Orbit
Vellini System
Tiberius Sector

Bratta was enjoying far, far too relaxing a sleep when it ended abruptly with a banging on the door.

"Time to go," came Chuck's voice from the other side.

Already? "Okay, I'm up." Bratta yawned and stretched himself out, swinging his legs off his cramped bed and checked himself in the tiny mirror. Needed a shave. But that could come later. So could a shower. They had shower facilities on these ships, right?

Bratta cast a longing eye at his suitcase. Within was his new invention; his dart thrower. Firing little homing drones laced with a knockout poison, it was his current little pet project.

Except it kept exploding when he fired it. A minor bug. Only happened, like, a quarter of the time though.

No, it wasn't ready and he couldn't risk it. Instead, Bratta changed, threw some deodorant on, and then opened his suitcase. Inside was *another* of his little projects… cameras so tiny they could be worn on clothes and not seen with the naked eye, appearing to be little specks of dirt or grime. He picked a dozen of them out with tweezers, which would activate the adhesive, then stuck them all over his clothes, including one on the tip of his index finger.

Seeing Modi and his inventions on Chrysalis had been inspiring. Bratta was looking forward to seeing his own creations in action.

Satisfied, Bratta went down to the cargo bay where everyone was waiting.

"Hi," said Chuck, the nice young man whose baby was sick. Not just sick, but something else. Something that worried him. In his few weeks as an employee of Maxgainz, he'd worked on … interesting genetics problems, using samples his managers had provided him.

The kid's DNA had sections of striking similarity.

"Good morning," said Bratta, pushing the confusing thoughts out of his mind. "Ready to make a completely unsuspicious social call at the corporate offices of Jovian Logistics and Supply? I'm an old hand at this by now."

"It's actually evening planetside," said Smith.

Technically correct, the best kind of correct. "Good evening," said Bratta, apologetically.

Sammy wheeled down the ramp towards the cargo bay, hands on the wheels to brake himself. "Hey, guys."

Everyone said hi.

"Hey," said Reardon, his hair a mess as he sauntered down the ramp into the cargo bay. The guy looked like he hadn't slept much. "So what's the plan, nerds?"

Bratta frowned and pushed up his glasses. "Excuse me, I'll have you know I'm *extremely* skilled at infiltration," he said, snorting dismissively. "I'm a lot more than just an engineer, thank you very much."

"Oh, good." Reardon pulled out his aviators and slipped them on his face. "So I guess you'll be our point man on this operation, right?"

Stammering just a little, Bratta nodded his head. "F-fine. I will. No worries at all. Top form."

Smith caught his eye. "I'm going with you," he said, a firm edge to his tone that brooked no debate. "We have *no* idea what they're up to. Even if there are answers there about Jovian's connection to the missing kids and Chuck's son and Zombie Pitt and all the rest of the shit going down. To find them, you're going to need someone handy with a gun, especially if things go tits up. And I have multiple implants which should be useful, should the situation arise."

"And you're going to need fake documents," said Reardon, grinning like a hunting cat. "And there ain't nobody in the galaxy who's better at coming up with convincing fakes than me. Sammy can help."

"Help?" Sammy snorted. "Yeah. Help. You mean, do all the work while you take all the credit. Right?"

Reardon held his chest with both hands as if mortally wounded. "Bro. You cut me. You cut me deep."

Chuck coughed. "What about Lily?"

The mutant? Bratta frowned. "What about her?"

"I think I'm making progress with her," said Chuck. "Maybe she could have a part in the mission."

"No," said Reardon.

"Absolutely not," said Sammy.

"Definitely not," said Bratta.

Chuck folded his arms defiantly. Interesting. Even though the mutant woman had most likely had all traces of humanity stripped out of her by the creeps at Maxgainz, Admiral Mattis's son still thought of her as a person. Something that science said she most definitely *was not*. Her DNA was all wrong.

Sammy sighed. "Right, well, Chuck—Lily can stay here and watch the ship. And you watch her. I'll maintain communications and keep my fingers on the gun turrets in case we need them—and…" he looked to Chuck. "Maybe you can help me with that."

"Okay," said Chuck. He looked a little left out.

Reardon spat out his toothpick and put in another one. That seemed distinctly unsanitary on a spaceship. "A'right," he said, grinning from ear to ear. "Let's do this thing."

Weapons were handed out. Bratta had his shocksticks but he took a pistol reluctantly. Melee weapons were not his speciality. It was a shame his dart launcher wasn't ready. Next time… next time.

A fake, plastic-looking ID card was thrust into his hand with his picture on it. No name, just a barcode and a picture. That was okay. The data would be inside it. He squinted, examining the image of himself. His pictures never looked anything like him.

It would be fine, it would have to be.

Twenty minutes later, the *Aerostar* docked at the airlock to the shipyards, and Bratta and Smith lined up at the hatch, ready to depart.

The loading ramp lowered. Smith confidently strode down it, his steps measured, relaxed and even, just like he owned the place. Like he was mildly frustrated that he was late for some meeting, and that his boss was going to yell at him for it. The perfect employee.

Bratta took one step forward and stumbled, nearly falling flat on his face. Half jogging, he stumbled down the loading ramp.

Smith glared at him but, fortunately, said nothing.

Two private security guards stood at the other side of the airlock, rifles held comfortably in their hands, wearing black uniforms with military-style helmets. No insignia or markings to be seen. Concerning.

"Identification," said the guard.

Smith handed his over, practically oozing frustration and boredom.

The guard swiped it through a reader. "Thank you, Mister Kade. Welcome aboard."

Kade. Kade was a strange name… Bratta didn't recognize the origin.

"Identification," demanded the guard, watching him carefully.

Fumbling slightly, Bratta turned over his card. Upside down. He rightened it sheepishly.

The guard scanned it. "Welcome aboard, Mister…" He hesitated, squinted, peering closely at the card. "I'm sorry, how do I pronounce this?"

Bratta's chest tightened. The card didn't have his fake name written on it, he had no idea what word the guy was even looking at.

Think, think…

"Just pronounce it like it's spelled," he said, doing his best to appear offended. "C'mon, it can't be that hard."

The guard, obviously not wanting to be seen as racially insensitive, hesitated. "Uhh… Purushottam-Narasimhan."

Of course Reardon's documents would be Indian names. Of course they would be.

"Close enough," said Bratta, taking the card and, with a huff, stepped past the guard and into the airlock, which began its cycle. As the atmosphere moved from the docking port to the inside of the station, Bratta breathed deeply. That could have gone *really* wrong.

"What the hell were you thinking?" he angrily whispered, knowing that Reardon would hear him.

"It's easy," said Reardon. "Purushottam-Narasimhan. Like you said. It's pronounced just like it's spelled."

"Do I look Indian to you?" Bratta sighed. "I guess I could be adopted…"

The airlock completed its cycle and the doors opened, letting them in. Smith stepped onto the crowded, spacious mezzanine, and Bratta followed.

"Okay," said Smith, looking over his shoulder at him. "Where now?"

There were guards and people everywhere—workers and janitorial services and food servers heading to their noon shifts. Dozens of doors led off the central mezzanine of the station's center and Bratta couldn't help but feel his eyes be drawn to a door nearby with a symbol on it. Teeth biting into a planet. "There," he said. "Or somewhere like it."

"Roger," said Smith, heading in, Bratta close on his heels.

If I die here, Jeannie will kill me...

CHAPTER THIRTY-SIX

Patricia "Guano" Corrick's J-88
USS Stennis
Gas Giant Erebus
Vellini System
Tiberius Sector

Land. Refuel. Check systems. Re-arm. Have a too-hot cup of coffee with too much sugar from a thermos. Guano practiced combat landings far more often than she had ever thought she would have to execute them, and was glad for that training now.

With her lips tingling from the heat of the drink, her ship's computer spat out information. The *Stennis* retrieved the breaching pod, transferred some crew to the *Caernarvon*, executed a Z-Space translation, and then the signal came to launch again. With Roadie at their head, Guano and her flight relaunched, their J-88's leaping back into space.

The ship had spat them out farther into the Vellini solar

system, this time near one of the gas giants. Rather than the black of space, her flight found themselves inside a blue-red tinged region full of ionized gas that seemed luminescent all around their vessels, bathed in the hues of excited electrons that accelerated in the intense magnetic field of Erebus. So thinly spread was this gas that it would have no effect on the operation of their craft, save for the beautiful luminescence which, to Guano's eyes, vaguely resembled the dawn sky with twilight behind.

But the planet itself was, oddly enough, dark and forbidding. Deep orange, gray, and red clouds billowed up into dirty, Earth-sized storms. Like Jupiter, but more like its evil twin brother.

Directly in front of them was a network of metal trusses stretching out over a kilometer of space, upon which hung dozens of ships, both large and small. The station itself was only half-built. Scaffolding encased most of it, and the colorful sheen from the excited nebula gas glinted off the new metal.

"Neat," said Flatline, his head seemingly on a swivel, checking out everything.

It definitely was pretty. "So boss," Guano said, glancing over her shoulder at Roadie's spacecraft, the ship lit up blue-red by the glow of the nebula. "What are we doing here?"

"Standard sweep and clear." Roadie's voice was calm and professional, something it usually only was when shit was *really* going down. "Engage targets as they appear in and around the station. Simple. Wait for further instruction from up top."

The ships all signaled their acknowledgement. The flight sailed toward the shipyards, while behind them, the *Caernarvon* and *Stennis* maneuvered into a striking formation.

"Hey Guano," said Flatline behind her. "Any idea why the Forgotten split their forces like this? Why two hidden stations? Wasn't Jovian Anchor enough for them?"

That thought bounced around her head for a bit. "You're right," she said, trying to piece it together while also flying the ship. "They had the Jovian Anchor, but they were also building this new behemoth. The latter thing is obviously more valuable. But they put decoys at the station and—and a skeleton force to defend it. Why would they do that? Wouldn't it be better to pool their defenses here?"

"That's what I was thinking," said Flatline. "Also, when the hell did the Forgotten get the funds and wherewithal to build a fucking state-of-the-art space station? Shit doesn't add up." There was a brief pause where she expected him to continue, but instead he checked his instruments. "Hey. We're out of formation. Why are we drifting?"

Drifting? Guano looked to the left. The formation was a significant distance away from them and the shipyards was no longer in her crosshairs.

"Guano," said Roadie, aggravation creeping in. "Get back in formation."

"Hey!" Flatline thumped on the back of her chair. "Guano! Pay attention! Get back in formation. Get back—"

She pulled the control stick to the right. A bright yellow flower burst on the starboard side of her ship; a shower of sparks leapt up across the hull as a billion angry bees stung her ship. Then another burst. And another.

Anti-fighter gunfire.

Flatline shrieked in panic, stammering something unintelligible. She didn't have the time to unravel what he was trying to say. Guano threw the ship from left to right and opened the throttle.

"All ships, all ships," she said, grunting and straining from the g-forces. "Be advised: trespass, trespass, trespass, unknown gun platform." More shells burst silently all around her, discharging their deadly barrages in volleys, each one spraying shrapnel out in all directions, creating expanding spheres of death that threatened to envelop her.

Through the deadly maelstrom, Guano's ship danced. Twisting and pivoting and dodging, using her speed and maneuverability to sail through the barrage.

"All ships, this is Roadie," an edge of triumph in his voice. "I have eyeball on the gun platform. It's a great big sucker, bearing 001 mark 003. Jutting off one of the gantries, disguised as a construction crane."

"I see it," said his gunner, Frost. "Oh jeez, it's really big! Damn. Disguising guns as construction equipment. Smart fuckers."

It was big, angry, and it was targeting her, out in open space with no cover. They should have been dead. They should have been blown to bits with the first volley. But somehow, her training—and her battle fugue—had pulled her through.

A combination of intense focus and g-forces made everything go fuzzy until a clipped, British voice cut through the haze in her mind.

"All strike craft, be advised, bulldog, bulldog, bulldog." The *Caernarvon* was firing anti-ship missiles at the gun platform. A volley of silver streams flew past Guano's ship, alarmingly close, their engines glowing a fiery red and leaving shimmering exhaust trails, shining white ribbons against the red hues of the planetary nebula, and a field of bursting stars set against the blue.

Everything went fuzzy again, until the missiles impacted the gun platform and everything was still for a moment. Guano's ship drifted through space, tumbling end over end, until she leveled out her wings and looked back toward the space station.

For a brief moment, the fading bursts of gunfire and missile exhausts painted an American flag in space before it faded away, leaving only spinning debris and gas trails.

"Holy shit," said Flatline, his voice squeaking. "I feel like I should be singing about the Land of the Free and the Home of the Brave. Did... did you position us deliberately to see that?"

"Would you believe me if I said that I didn't?"

The ship shuddered slightly and Guano's cockpit was filled with chirping and wailing alarms. Her radar lit up with contacts —enemy strike craft. This time, she knew, they wouldn't be decoys. The gun platform burned in space, its fuel and ammunition reserves igniting, but the Forgotten were far from defeated.

"Roadie—Guano. I'm seeing a lot of bogeys over there. Suggest we flag them as bandits and tally."

Roadie's reply came through swiftly. "Negative, negative. Guano, be advised, smoke is coming from your starboard engine. All other craft break and engage, weapons free."

Being left behind in a battle rankled her. "I can still fight."

"Negative. Guano, RTB and put it back. You did good."

"Fine," she said, and turned her ship back toward the *Stennis* and increasing the throttle as high as she dared, letting her damaged ship slowly accelerate away from the debris field.

"Might as well dump our ammo," said Flatline, with a bit of bitterness. "In case we have to come down hard."

Good idea. She tilted the nose away from the *Stennis* and held down the trigger on her guns until they ran dry, then jettisoned her missiles. "Clear your delinker," she said to Flatline. Automatic guns kept a tiny amount of ammo in their internals which would also need to be dumped.

Flatline fired the shortest burst, no more than ten rounds. The tiny stream flew out like a pinkie finger, drifting lazily toward the station and the swarm of strike craft zipping around it.

They traveled for nearly thirty seconds, drifting lazily through space, before the tiny burst struck an incoming ship, each round flashing and bursting so far away she could barely see them. The ship exploded.

"Were you aiming for that thing?" asked Guano, incredulously.

"Would you believe I actually *was*?" Flatline sounded even more skeptical than she felt.

Guano smiled to herself and idly touched one of the ship's screens, intending to begin the landing procedure, but something caught her eye in the system logs. A transmission receipt, dated a few minutes ago. A narrowband, microburst transmission that didn't have a clear recipient.

She'd sent through a transmission to some unknown party and hadn't even remembered doing it.

A voice screamed in the back of her mind that this was *not normal*, but for some reason, it was barely more than a distant whisper now.

"You okay?" asked Flatline.

"Yeah," said Guano, despite her best efforts to say otherwise. "Just peachy."

CHAPTER THIRTY-SEVEN

Bridge
HMS Caernavron
Gas Giant Erebus
Vellini System
Tiberius Sector

Mattis, space suit retrieved and returned to the *Caernarvon*, watched the unfurling space battle with a mixture of adrenaline-fueled energy and helpless frustration.

It certainly looked like the Forgotten were far more well-funded than he'd thought. *Too* well-funded. There had to be an outside player, using the Forgotten as a cloak.

Pitt went into quarantine. Standard procedure. He tried to quell the burning need within him to talk—not just debrief Pitt, but actually *talk* to him—and focus on the mission at hand.

"How are the Rhinos holding up?" he asked Commander Blackburn, eyes fixed on her console.

"They're doing fine. There were two injuries, both of which are being treated now. As for the others, well, they're still getting out of their suits. Dismounting from Rhino hardware takes a long time, since the suits are hardwired into their nervous system. Can't be rushed."

That made sense. He'd seen how bulky they were in flesh. Just getting out of his damaged space suit had been hard enough. "I can imagine," said Mattis, diplomatically, "that the stereotypical Rhino attitude may also… complicate things."

"And by that you mean they have more issues than National Geographic."

He couldn't help but think of Cho and how they were not *all* like that. Something Lynch had once said rattled around inside his head. *Humans are tribalistic hypocrites who judge their enemies by their actions but themselves by their intentions.* The Rhinos were a necessary part of shipboard operations.

With that to consider, Mattis said nothing and turned his attention to the Captain's chair where Spears sat, one leg over the other, teacup perched in her hand. "Anything I can do, Captain?"

Spears didn't take her eyes off the main viewscreen as she sipped her drink, watching as missile barrages flew out from the *Caernarvon*, striking a gun battery that was giving their combined fighter wing some trouble. "No, thank you Admiral Mattis," she said, eyeing the battle cautiously. "So far, so good."

"Any sign of the ship that escaped from Jovian Anchor?"

"None yet." She turned back to regard him. "I assure you, Jack, my crew is working on it. And they're more than capable. I know this is tough being the spectator, but I don't have time to be your tour guide."

He strained a smile. "Sorry. Understood." He leaned back in his seat and tried hard to bite his tongue. *God* he hated feeling useless.

"The station is launching strike craft," said Blackwood, turning to Spears.

"How nice for them," she replied, eyes fixed on the screen. "Have the *Stennis's* fighters engage while pulling back our own. Have them use their long range missiles to pick off anything that gets close and let the *Stennis's* ships lure them out. Let's be the lance to their knife."

Mattis bit his tongue, trying to keep his suggestion inside his mouth. The British fighters had much better short range heat-seeking missiles and more powerful armor and guns; they would be better off in close quarters than the fast—but frail— J-88's.

It wasn't his ship, it wasn't his decision.

"Aye aye, Captain," said Blackwood. "Pulling them back."

The radar groupings of strike craft pulled further apart. From the *Stennis* team, one of the stragglers pulled away, obviously damaged. Mattis watched the ship curiously.

"Ma'am," said Blackwood, tapping at her keyboard. Her brow furrowed in confusion. "We're detecting a strange signal emanating. A microburst, narrow band transmission. Impossible to tell where it came from."

A microburst? That kind of thing was the tool of black ops, spies, spooks and assassins. Not the Forgotten, who were almost all exclusively military personnel without access to special forces tech. "Was it targeting anything?" asked Mattis."

Blackwood's eyes flicked to Spears for confirmation, then answered. "Unclear," she said, a slight reluctance in her tone.

"The nature of microbursts makes them difficult to differentiate from background radiation. They are just a quick pulse; far too quick for us to get a lock on it, and unless we're actively looking to triangulate it, we don't have a hope. We were lucky to detect it all."

All of this matched what he understood. For a moment, he found himself wishing Modi was here to help Blackwood find out what she could. The two of them would probably get along perfectly.

"That's odd," said Spears, leaning forward in her chair and staring intently at the viewscreen. She put her tea cup down on the arm rest. "Look at that."

Mattis squinted at the monitor. It showed a picture of the half-constructed space station. As he stared at it, he saw it too.

One of the ships at the station. It looked … different.

"Holy shit," said Mattis.

"Mother of God," said Spears. "Is that one of them?"

Mattis nodded. "Sure as hell looks like one of the Avenir."

"Flag that ship as Skunk Alpha," said Spears. "And get ready to engage."

The vessel spun on its axis, then turned and began moving toward open space.

"It's fleeing," said Blackwood. "We're detecting a surge of energy consistent with a Z-Space translation."

A voice crackled over the line. Commander Jeremy Pitt. "Captain Spears," he said. "Captain Flint and I have something important to tell you about that ship."

What the hell is he doing out of quarantine already? thought Mattis.

CHAPTER THIRTY-EIGHT

Bridge
USS Stennis
Gas Giant Erebus
Vellini System
Tiberius Sector

Captain Dravin Flint could not keep his eyes off the dead man his Marines had brought to his Bridge.

He'd heard of Commander Pitt's death. Everyone had. Had seen pictures of his body… everyone had. Now he was back. Just like he'd never gone. An immortal being, seemingly, for nothing else made sense.

Had Maxgainz gotten a hold of the body and injected it with something? Had the mutated future-humans gotten to him and corrupted him somehow? Was he the future of humanity? Was he really what they would all become, given time?

He was supposed to be in quarantine, but Flint's curiosity

and burning need to have those questions answered drove him to summon the formerly dead man.

"You're staring," growled Pitt, his eyes almost boring into him. "You have a battle to fight."

Flint made no apologies about it. There was nothing wrong with indulging his idle curiosity during a battle going well. "I have the best bridge crew in the galaxy," he said, completely genuine. A sweep of his hand showed his crew working at their posts, occasionally calling out information. "A new breed of vessel. Highly automated; far more than previous models. State-of-the-art Chinese engines—finally, some good came from the peace accord. It's worlds faster than anything our fleet has ever seen. If I recall correctly, your old ship, the *Midway*, was outfitted with these same engines in the weeks before she blew. But that was *after* your death, so you wouldn't know that, would you?"

He regarded the other man, looking for a reaction to the mention of his death.

Instead, all Pitt said was, "Interesting. This ship basically fights on its own. And I'm sure those engines will come in handy. But it would be a shame if they fell into Forgotten hands."

Flint breathed a sound of contempt. "As if. They don't stand a chance here."

Pitt regarded the crew with outright suspicion and contempt, every inch of it painted on his mutated face. "Humans have learned to fight so well, we no longer need humans to do it."

"You speak of us as though you're not one of us," said Flint, smile spreading. "Like you're apart. Different. Aren't you… simply what we all aim to be, Commander?"

"I'm a lot of things," said Commander Pitt, nodding towards the main screen. "You might want to watch this."

The main screen seemed to be just a static, floating picture of the shipyard, surrounded by a swarm of strike fighters, illuminated by the burning gun platform and punctuated by flashes of light from weapons impacts.

"What am I looking at?" asked Flint. "Apart from the obvious."

Commander Pitt merely pointed to the battle. "I was hoping your fancy ship's sensors might be able to pick it out." Kind of rude, all things considered. "I have a feeling one of their ships will be breaking away from the station any moment with a precious cargo aboard. I suggest you acquire it."

"Precious cargo?" Flint narrowed his eyes. "A *feeling?* What kind of nonsense is this?"

"Look there." He pointed at a spot on the screen.

Flint squinted. "Magnify."

The location Pitt pointed to expanded, and then Flint saw it. "Good Lord. Is that an Avenir vessel?"

"Sure looks like it. And it's the only explanation for all this that makes sense. Why are the Forgotten risking everything right now? Why are they laying it all out on the line? They're risking their very existence by coming out into the open like this. The only explanation that makes even remote sense is that they've come into possession of the one thing that Earth can't defend against. One of the future-human mass driver weapons," said Commander Pitt after the briefest pause. The weapons that devastated the Earth fleets. "They probably scavenged one of the ruined future-human ships and repaired it. Secure it, and it might be possible to reverse engineer the design."

A useful weapon. The Chinese had a crude prototype, but this was better—years, no, centuries ahead in its design and capabilities. "Get Admiral Mattis on the line," said Flint. "He'll want to hear this."

Pitt moved to pick up one of the headsets, sliding it over his head. Flint considered, then held up his hand.

"Best pretend you're still in quarantine," he said, smiling politely. "Wouldn't want to trouble an old man, after all."

CHAPTER THIRTY-NINE

Bridge
HMS Caernarvon
Gas Giant Erebus
Vellini System
Tiberius Sector

The mass driver weapon. The same weapon the future-humans had tried to turn on Earth. A devastating tool that they had been unable to recover from the wreckage of the Avenir ships. But this ship was intact—and dangerous. It hadn't shot at them yet, not even cannons, but if it had a mass driver there was no way they should let it get away.

Mattis blew out a low whistle. "We need that ship," he said.

"We need that ship," echoed Blackburn.

"We need that ship." Spears, however, seemed less eager, and more concerned. "But where the dickens did it come from?"

That, Mattis did not have the answer to. "Maybe during

the short period of time the vortex was open in the Pinegar system. Maybe one got away." He wasn't sure. It was pure speculation; this would be the kind of thing Modi would be excellent at.

"Jack, I'm sure you'll understand—this ship is a far greater threat to humanity than kidnappers. We're going after it. We'll come back and search for the kids later." She turned back to her helmsman. "Set in an intercept course. Retrieve the strike craft. I want that ship in my hangar bay. Commander Blackwood, get the Rhinos suited up again. I know they won't like it, but stifle their bellyaching and make sure they're ready to go."

"Aye ma'am. I'll get Major Hubbs on the horn and make sure it happens."

The *Caernarvon* began to turn, moving to intercept the ship. The hostile vessel was a compact and boxy frigate, seemingly completely built but sporting no obvious weapons, and Mattis could guess their intentions; move out away from the station and execute a Z-Space translation into the wild, unreal dimension of interstellar travel.

"Tracker," said Mattis. "Fire a tracker. We need to get a Z-Space beacon on that ship before they get out of the system."

Spears's tone turned slightly sour. "I'd prefer to capture them here, Admiral Mattis. They'll turn to engage any moment. We only have two of those things and they're still experimental."

There was no time. Every warrior's instinct screamed at him that they were about to make a jump. "Call it insurance," he said. "They're rabbiting. I'm sure they are."

After an agonizing moment of consideration, Spears

nodded her approval. "Blackwood, fire a Z-Space beacon. Attach it to the stern if you can. Only have it signal when the ship next leaves Z-Space."

Blackwood's fingers flew over her console. "Confirmed, Z-Space beacon, pattern november-mike-romeo. Firing."

A tiny silver streak, no bigger than a classroom ruler, flew out from the *Caernarvon* and zoomed toward the target, leaping across space. As it drew close, it spun around and began decelerating. Slower, slower…

"We're detecting a power surge," said Blackwood, her eyes flicking to Mattis for just a second. "They're about to enter Z-Space."

If they hadn't launched the beacon when Mattis had suggested it, it would never have gotten there in time. He couldn't help but feel a little satisfaction as the tiny Z-Space beacon latched hold of the hull of the strange ship and attached itself like a limpet.

With a bright white blinding flash, the hostile ship vanished into the lurid unreality that was Z-Space.

"Skunk alpha is faded," said Blackwood.

Spears steepled her fingers and leaned forward slightly. "Retrieve the strike craft," she said. "Make sure that the *Stennis* gets theirs, too. Get the hell away from this hornets nest. Then we wait for the beacon to signal."

CHAPTER FORTY

Patricia "Guano" Corrick's J-88
Pilot's Ready Room
USS Stennis
Gas Giant Erebus
Vellini System
Tiberius Sector

The strange transmission and her unconscious sending of it bugged Guano all the way back to the *Stennis*. Try as she might, she couldn't get the thought out of her head. Could not quell the urge to say something.

Why had she done it? It was a subconscious urge; something deep-seated and primal had driven her to send out a transmission even she didn't know the contents of.

She sat in the ready room, lounging in a beanbag, trying to figure it out.

Trying to understand.

Trying to speak.

"Hey," said Roadie, slipping into a neighboring sack of plastic beans with a rustle. "Nice job out there today."

It was true. She'd picked out the decoys before anyone else had. She wasn't an electronic warfare specialist and yet she'd been able to look at her radar and determine, somewhere deep inside her gut, that the radar returns were distractions.

It's important you tell Roadie about this. It's important that you let him know that there's something that happened to you on Chrysalis. That the battle fugue is working differently now. Tell him that you're sending strange transmissions and doing things without thinking about it—that you sometimes black out or fade away, and that you can't even bring yourself to open your mouth and tell him about it.

But she didn't. She opened her mouth to put it all into words. But nothing came out. So she searched for something benign to say instead. "Thanks." She smiled at him a little. "Just a hunch, I guess."

"Good hunch." Roadie stifled a yawn. "Okay, well, unless the shit hits the fan again, I'm going to take a rest. You should get some sleep too."

She felt wide awake. More than that, she felt that sleeping —given that it seemed to happen for almost no reason these days—would be a bad idea. "I'll get some rack time in a bit," she said. "Still riding that battle high."

Roadie clapped her on the shoulder and left her in the ready room, alone with her thoughts and a tiny, nearly silent voice screaming for help in the back of her head.

CHAPTER FORTY-ONE

Main Promenade
Christchurch Corporate Business Park station
Vellini, High Orbit
Vellini System
Tiberius Sector

There were actually surprisingly few people walking around for such an important station next to such an important shipyards over such a populated planet. Bratta wondered about that as he walked down the promenade, towards the door with the teeth biting into a planet symbol. As they got closer, he saw a placard next to the door.

Jovian Logistics and Supply, inc.

There seemed to be two kinds of people walking around: uniformed guards, wearing the same black armor that the airlock personnel were wearing, and another group of people. People who walked with stooped posture and glazed eyes, wearing orange jumpsuits just like prisoners. Were they prisoners? Wasn't this a civilian business park? Didn't various private corporations have offices here? But the people seemed to be calmly unresisting, even moving around in groups of their own.

Smith took the lead, guiding Bratta through the door into Jovian Logistic's offices, and through another door marked *maintenance*, then into a narrow passageway that seemed to be some kind of space between rooms.

"What are we doing here?" asked Bratta. This didn't seem to be an important spot.

"Hey, listen," said Smith, his face a concerned mask. "Stay focused. Head forward. You're staring around at everything like it's the first time you've been here—and yes, I know it *is* the first time you've been here—but we're meant to be blending in. All of this should be boring to you. You shouldn't be thinking, *hey, what are those people doing there? Who are those guards?* You should be thinking, *damn, I hope the vending machine doesn't swallow my money today like it did yesterday,* and *I hope that cute secretary notices my hair.*"

"Vending machines are actually quite reliable these days," said Bratta, then closed his mouth and nodded. "Okay. More nonchalant."

"Yeah," said Smith, idly glancing around the corner. "Be careful. These guys look real similar to the ninja-people I took out, just… you know. Without the masks and with body armor. They may well be the same guys. Forgotten elite fighters or whatever the hell they were."

That would be bad. "Okay, I'll be careful."

"Good." Smith nodded his approval and they set out again into the main section of the offices.

Bratta kept his eyes down low, watching the floor. He knew he usually walked this way; posture slumped, avoiding eye contact. It was easy to slip back into old habits.

Smith, for some strange reason, seemed to know where he was going. Bratta knew he had many implants, and some of those implants—most notably the eye—were able to pick up sensor information that might give him an edge. Let him see things that nobody could.

Somewhat more disturbingly, he also... *knew things*. Things he shouldn't have known. Couldn't have known. And the man was a consummate liar, actor...

What secrets did he keep?

Bratta squelched his distrust. They were on a mission after all. There would be time for talking later.

Smith lead them to a door, thick and reinforced with heavy bars. This one was different, wider, and obviously stronger. No guards. Just a simple keyswipe.

"Bratta, think you can watch my back while I jimmy the card reader? Don't whistle or act weird, just stand there and don't talk to anyone. Like this kind of shit happens every day."

It wasn't possible to *jimmy* an electric card reader, but Bratta knew there were other ways. "Okay," he said, casually turning around and waiting, pulling out his phone and fiddling with it. He stood there, ignoring the faint sounds of scratching from behind him and pretending he was doing something *very* important and work-related, and that he couldn't see the various wireless networks floating around, tempting him to log into them.

But he didn't. That would be a huge security risk. So he just pretended, idly flicking his screen.

Wonder how Jeannie is doing these days...

The door hissed open. "I'm in," whispered Smith. He'd pried off the card reader, the device dangling by a pair of wires. As casually as you like, Smith reattached the card reader and walked inside.

Bratta followed, resisting the urge to whistle. Whistling would be bad, he knew that much.

Inside the room were cylindrical vertical tanks. Bright green tanks full of a bubbling green liquid. Inside were floating masses of flesh; clumps what he could only describe as adult fetuses. Half-formed, warped and twisted, they were as much horrible monstrosities as they were people.

"This is it," said Smith, his voice soft, almost hollow, all pretense of his *I belong here* act completely gone. "Get into their computers. Find out what you can. Get the data—all of it."

Bratta didn't need to be told twice. He jammed a data stick into the nearest terminal and ran a program to copy everything the tiny device could see.

Smith moved in front of him, casually blocking the device with his hip, standing with his hands folded, obviously trying to act casual.

Bratta used his phone to look at the raw data stream. Details stood out to his eyes as the filenames flew past. Cloning technology. RNA modifiers. Gene re-sequencing. Biologically-implanted memories.

Interesting stuff.

"Who are you?" said a voice, near enough and loud enough to make Bratta jump. A guard had slipped inside the room without him noticing. Smith hadn't seen him either, judging by his shocked expression. "This is a restricted area."

Smith regained his composure instantly, a sheepish smile crossing his face. "Yeah, I know, sorry. It's just that the door comes loose sometimes and my buddy and I like to come in here for a smoke, you know? I was going to report it, but you know what they're like."

The guard didn't seem to buy it. "What's your identification number?"

Smith casually held up his hands. "Hey, sorry. We're going, we're going. Jeez, a guy can't even get a smoke anymore. Typical."

"No," said the guard, moving his hand to the grip of his pistol. "Identification number. Now."

"Okay," said Smith, groaning slightly as he reached behind his back and pushed himself off the wall. "It's—" *Fwip.*

It took Bratta a second to realize what had happened. Smith had fired a gun from behind his back. A pistol with an advanced-looking, possibly noise-cancelling suppressor. Amazing stuff. Even modern suppressors turned a gun from being very loud into only sort-of-loud, but this one was no noisier than a bird chirp.

The guard slumped down with a low groan as a hole in his chest started to bloom red. Smith glanced around, cautiously, then shot him three more times in the same spot. *Fwip fwip fwip.*

"W-was that necessary?" asked Bratta as blood began to pool below the unfortunate guy. "You killed him!"

"Either that, or he raised the alarm." Smith replaced the pistol cautiously. "Only four rounds left. Not worth a reload." Then, to Bratta, "you got what you need?"

The drive was full. Even if there was more, he had no way of transporting it. "Ye-… yes."

"Great, let's get out of here."

Smith made for the exit, casually humming to himself. Bratta couldn't take his eyes off the dead guy. One moment alive, and then…

"Bratta," said Smith, gently but with an edge of command to it. "We gotta go."

And they did. Bratta withdrew his device, slipped it into his pocket, and made his way to the exit.

An alarm began to wail all around them, but if Smith heard it, he gave no sign. Just continued to walk, as though it were nothing; a false alarm, or a fire drill he'd heard a million times before.

Bratta did his best to keep up, hoping his nervousness wouldn't get them all killed.

CHAPTER FORTY-TWO

Bridge
HMS Caernarvon
Gas Giant Erebus
Vellini System
Tiberius Sector

With all their fighters recalled, there wasn't anything for Mattis to do but sit and wait for the Z-Space beacon to indicate where their target had ended up.

Fortunately that was something he was good at. It was something he always told junior officers and people who wanted to command their own ship someday: real war, real battles, were one percent adrenaline and ninety-nine percent mind numbing boredom.

Minutes turned into hours. A shift change came and went; Blackwood swapped out for a junior officer, and most of the bridge crew did as well. Spears simply took a fresh cup of tea and powered through. Mattis, still running on nervous energy from the battle aboard the space station, didn't need anything at all.

Finally, an amber light blinked on Spears's wrist computer.

"The beacon is transmitting," she said. "The hostile ship appears to be…" her eyes widened. "Good Lord. Over Vellini."

Mattis groaned. "Good Lord indeed. A billion people down below. And the US Navy's most important shipyards."

"A planet," she continued, "where they just might be able to actually hide and avoid detection. You know how many ships go in and out of orbit there? It's the biggest hub in this whole sector. Hell, this whole quadrant."

"Well at least they're close," said Mattis. "We can be there in short order."

She nodded. "Vellini is a world of junk. This whole system is used as a garbage disposal area for various governments and corporations, given its concentration of recycling centers and the shipyards. Starship parts, medical waste, construction debris, you name it. The refuse of a galactic civilization all stored in one place. Easy place to hide."

He thought they fired garbage into the sun. "But why come here?" he asked.

Spears shrugged. "The garbage?"

"No, the ship. The Forgotten's Avenir ship."

She shrugged again.

"Apart from being a good hiding place, why would the Forgotten go there? What significance does it have?"

Spears seemed at a loss. "Apart from the junk, the hiding place, and the fact that there's a billion people there and probably a lot of Forgotten sympathies?" She ruminated for a moment. "Ships come through there from countless systems all over the settled worlds, and from many nations, too. If they interfered with those ships by—I don't know—putting something deadly and communicable on those ships, they may well cause a galaxy-wide catastrophe. Maybe a bioweapon, maybe something much simpler like a computer virus. Either way, a billion people are at risk. More, possibly, if somehow they manage to hit Earth or another heavily populated world."

Mattis was worried, but fear couldn't cut through the tiredness that suddenly fell over him. "A bioweapon? Hm … I doubt it. The Forgotten are earnest and crazy as hell, but they don't have a death wish. A bioweapon would kill indiscriminately. So they'd be at risk too." He stood up. "But at least we know where we're going now. And I'll need rack time if I'm going to be any use when we get there."

Spears gave him a wry smile. "You're getting old, Admiral. The Mattis I knew could stay up much longer "

Mattis found himself feeling a little humorless at the nominally playful jab. "It'll happen to you too," he said. "If you're lucky. How about I give Commanders Lynch and Modi a debriefing and see what we can find out in the meantime? Oh, and the good senator might want to hear that we found his son alive and well—I'll see that he's informed."

The edges of Spears's lips turned up. "And, perhaps, you might want to see if you can get a word in with the lovely Miss Ramirez, as well, mmm? Pick her brains too?"

Well, now she was just being cruel. Mattis smirked at her. "I might. I'll be sure to fill you in on anything we find."

"Sounds lovely." Spears made a little *shoo*ing motion. "Rack time. Go. Now. I'll talk to you after your grandpop nap,

Admiral."

With no energy for a complaint, Mattis turned and left the bridge, leaving the Z-Space translation in pursuit of their enemy in Spears's capable hands.

CHAPTER FORTY-THREE

Corridor
HMS Caernarvon
Gas Giant Erebus
Vellini System
Tiberius Sector

Mattis had barely left the bridge when his communicator chirped. A brief glance at the device showed it was a relayed Z-Space transmission coming from out of the ship.

"Mattis," he said, opening it. "Send it."

"I wasn't sure if you were going to pick up." Admiral Fischer's voice came to him down the line, thick and frosty. There was a brief pause, static on the line, and then she continued. "You know you've been a bad boy."

He was tempted to say something sarcastic, to play with the cards she was putting down, but he didn't. "Am I?" he asked, innocently.

"The key part of being grounded is," said Fischer, "that

you're grounded. My sources tell me that you're a substantial distance away from the old country, Admiral Mattis. A substantial distance indeed."

"Can't say that isn't true. Sorry, Admiral, England was a little too chilly for me. Had to go somewhere sunnier. Bit more solar radiation." He took a turn down a corridor toward the State Room. "You know how it is."

"Mmm," said Fischer. "Oh, I know how it is alright. Old crotchety Captains deciding to gallivant around the galaxy, thinking they're above and beyond the chain of command… indulging their flights of fancy, conspiracy theories, delusions." She took in a breath and let it out in a long, low sigh over the microphone at the other end. "You *do* understand why we have the chain of command, don't you?"

Certainly did. "Well, Admiral, I don't think that's true."

"How so?"

"I wouldn't say I'm crotchety."

She snorted, whatever humor and good tolerance her voice held evaporating. "That's where we're different, Admiral Mattis. Because I am. Proudly so. And as fun as sparring with you over a Z-Space connection is… it's time. You're done. Come back to Earth."

He fought to keep the frustration, anger, out of his tired voice. "Listen, there's more to this—"

"More to this than I know," finished Fischer. "I've heard this before, Admiral."

"And it was as true then as it is now. There is something more here. Those missing kids? They're involved. And if you're not convinced, I got you a present." He paused to let the effect sink in. "A real life future-human. Securely locked up in the brig. We pulled him off a crashed Avenir ship."

She said nothing.

"You still there?" asked Mattis, wondering if the line had cut out.

"Did you say," asked Fischer, "that you have a live future-human aboard the Caernarvon?"

He had her interest now. "That's correct," said Mattis. "Being debriefed and probed for information as we speak."

"I need that creature," said Fischer emphatically, betraying her urgency. "Admiral Mattis, you are hereby ordered to return directly to Earth aboard the HMS *Caernarvon* and turn over that creature to the US Navy."

"I'm afraid," said Mattis, politely, "that our investigation is not yet complete. When it is, I'll be more than happy to turn over not only the Avenir in Captain Spears's brig, but also anything else of interest we've recovered on the way."

"Admiral Mattis," said Fischer. "Home. Now."

"Can't hear you," said Mattis. He blew on his communicator to simulate static. "You're breaking up." He hung up and disabled relayed Z-Space calls.

Smiling with grim satisfaction, Mattis started tapping out a message, heading straight for the state room.

CHAPTER FORTY-FOUR

State Room - Admiral Jack Mattis's Quarters
HMS Caernarvon
Z-Space

Mattis messaged Lynch, Modi and Ramirez on the way to the state room and told them to meet him there, but to his surprise he found the three of them already waiting there for him.

It was difficult to look at Ramirez, but also uncomfortably awkward avoiding her.

"Evening, ladies and gentlemen," he said, giving each of them a little nod. "Thank you for coming so promptly."

"No thanks are necessary," said Modi, calmly folding his hands behind his back. "We've been waiting here for you for some time."

That didn't make any sense. "But…"

"We were waiting for you to get off your shift," said Ramirez, smiling lightly at him, although there was a certain sadness there, too. "Didn't realize you were simply going to take another one. Thought you might be avoiding us."

"Never," said Mattis, genuinely. "I was just… occupied."

"That's what I told these clowns," said Lynch, opening up the door to the state room and gesturing inside. "I know what it's like on the bridge. Sometimes work just takes a lot longer than you thought."

Right. Mattis stepped inside, and was immediately disappointed. The state room on the USS *Midway* was elaborately decorated, but the British accommodations were apparently much more spartan. The room itself was cramped even by Navy standards, no more than four meters by seven, maybe eight. The walls were simple bulkheads with a small desk and a chair, a monitor displaying the space outside, a pair of bunk beds—what kind of state room had bunk beds?—and the ceiling was lined with pipes and conduits. Mattis could hear the distant humming of some kind of machinery through the ceiling, something he suspected would be a feature of his stay. A plastic cupboard was built into the wall, with a head-and-shoulders length mirror and a small steel sink.

"Not bad," said Modi, behind him. "Private sink."

Maybe life as an Admiral and CO had softened him and he'd been too used to fancy rooms with plush carpets. The room, objectively, was less cramped than his quarters as a junior officer.

You're getting spoiled and old.

Mattis moved to the back of the room. Realizing there would be insufficient room for all four of them unless they got creative, he slid onto the lower bunk. Ramirez moved onto the top one, her legs dangling down as she got settled. Modi took the chair, while Lynch leaned up against the cupboard.

"Okay sir," said Lynch, idly tapping the toe of one foot against the ground. "What can you tell us about what we've found so far?"

It took him a moment to get his thoughts in order. "The kidnapping of those kids? It was the Forgotten. And the Forgotten have been doing their thing... taking over more abandoned space stations and building their own new one—with who knows whose funding. Pitt got rescued. He's over on the *Stennis* now. We have a future-human—an Avenir—aboard the *Stennis* too, currently being interrogated, and we've engaged with Forgotten twice now. One of their ships got away, and it looks like it's a rebuilt Avenir vessel—who knows where the hell they got it. We're in pursuit now."

Modi smiled widely. "It is good to have Commander Pitt returned to us. I have missed him, despite our disagreements."

"Dang straight," said Lynch, grinning widely. "I'm going to talk his damn ear right off when we get a chance and he's done with debriefing and quarantine."

It *was* absolutely great to have him back, and yet Mattis couldn't help but feel a vague sense of worry about it. Flint had taken Pitt onto the bridge and was treating him like an officer... but he didn't even know *who* Pitt really was in the past, let alone whatever he was now, having been miraculously raised from the dead.

Something about it just felt wrong.

Lynch folded his arms, a little frustration creeping into his voice. "But hey, Admiral. Answer me this. Maybe the dang cooks have been slipping lithium into my crepes, but... why the hell are we dealing with Forgotten and stolen kids? Ain't that a job for local law enforcement?"

Mattis struggled to answer, to force words out from his tired brain. "It's... Hmm. Call it a hunch," he said, hooking his fingers behind his head. "When I was on the station, I saw a symbol in the areas where the Forgotten had hidden things. Teeth biting a planet. There's something about it that troubles me. I don't think it's *their* symbol, to be honest. I think it's the Avenirs'. I think they're either allied with, or controlled by, them. Or... something. Last I saw them they were hunting Spectre, so they can't be *all* bad." He snapped his fingers behind his head. "There's something about it that really makes me think there's more going on here than we know. But... I don't know. I can't say definitively. Either way, it's not smart to let the Forgotten keep their hands on an Avenir ship. That thing may have a planet-killing mass driver on it. We can't risk that."

"Okay," said Ramirez, swinging her legs slightly. "I deal with this kind of thing a lot. Half-truths and unknowns and hunches. Is there anything more you can tell us about the Forgotten?"

"I'd have to talk to Pitt first," he said. "He would know if anyone would."

"Why don't we do that?"

"It's next on my list."

"Okay," said Ramirez from above him, sounding concerned. "We still haven't located the kids yet. All signs pointed to them being hauled off to that half-constructed Forgotten space station back at Erebus."

"Correct," said Mattis, yawning again despite himself. "Senator Pitt has constituents on New Kentucky, so I'd have thought he'd want us to find those kids at all costs, Avenir ship be damned. But he was more concerned about Jeremy after we rescued him. The old man's a wreck." A thought drifted though his sleepy mind. "Where is the good Senator, anyway?"

Nobody answered.

"I'll look into it," said Lynch. "Probably over on the *Stennis*, talking to him in decon."

Maybe. Mattis found it hard to concentrate. Modi began talking about something. Something about the most recent engagement, som thing that he couldn't follow about the mysterious transmission and the ships that had escaped them, but he couldn't keep his attention focused and couldn't keep his eyes open.

For a brief moment Mattis dozed off, then he sensed rather than saw Ramirez crouch beside him.

"Hey, sleepy head," she said, smiling gently. "Everyone else is gone."

Blast. That was a problem. He had more to say, and they hadn't worked everything out yet. "I must have dozed off," he said, sheepishly.

"No worries. They said they understood." She rested her hand on his abdomen. "And you're adorable when you sleep."

He smiled up at her, warm and safe and half asleep. "Yeah. Well, you're adorable all the time," he said, the smile slowly becoming a grin.

"Is that so?" asked Ramirez, sliding onto the tiny cot with him, a coy smile over her own face. "You're flirting with me, Admiral Jack Mattis."

"Well, Admiral Fischer says I'm a bad boy," said Mattis, wrapping his arm around her shoulder and giving a fond squeeze. "I might have to go off the record if I'm going to say anything more." In for a penny, in for a pound. "Or...before I do anything more."

"Off the record then," echoed Ramirez, leaning over and kissing him.

He kissed back, and with the ship in pursuit of a hostile threat and billions of lives hanging in the balance, there was nothing else he wanted to do right now than be with her.

CHAPTER FORTY-FIVE

Main Promenade
Christchurch Corporate Business Park station
Vellini, High Orbit
Vellini System
Tiberius Sector

Bratta tried hard to keep his hands from shaking, but they just wouldn't. He jammed them in his pocket, curling them both into fists, squeezing tightly and hoping that the sensation would drive away the tremor.

Smith had just shot that guy right in front of him, then walked out like it was nothing. Bratta hadn't even seen the gun, let alone been able to prevent it. If Smith had been aiming at him…

It was okay. All he had to do was get through this moment and out to the *Aerostar*. Then they could have a long talk about it and work through this. It was okay, it was going to be okay—

"Freeze!" shouted someone from down the corridor, a

woman in a guard uniform, pointing a rifle their way. "Halt!"

Fwip. The woman crumpled onto the deck, curling up into a ball.

Lots of people were staring. Smith just continued to walk, as completely normal and casual as you please, completely ignoring the people gaping.

Wait.

No.

They were looking at *him*. At Bratta.

"Uhh…" Bratta began to slowly walk toward the airlock, just as Smith was doing. Casual, easy strolling. *Try not to keep arms rigid. Try not to look too out of place.*

"He's here!" Guards started shouting all around him, their voices echoing off the bulkheads. "The intruder's here!"

Well, that tore it. Bratta yanked out his gun, the weapons sight snagging on his holster. He managed to untangle it, then waved the thing around like a lunatic. "There's… there's some kind of intruder!" He shouted, pointing to a random guard. "It's—it's this guy!"

The people wearing orange suits seemed to be ignoring them. Guards, however, were moving in towards him, rifles up against their shoulders.

"Hands on the ground! Drop your weapon!"

What to do, what to do? he felt like a total moron, standing out in the middle of nowhere, with no cover or protection, just standing there with a gun in his hand.

"Drop it now! Or we'll put you down!"

Everyone started shouting all at once. Smith was nowhere to be seen. More guards came in, angrily pointing their rifles at him. Bratta, facing down a dozen guns now, slowly raised his hands.

Well, this was a shitty way to die.

CHAPTER FORTY-SIX

Aerostar
Docking Bay 1
Christchurch Corporate Business Park station
Vellini, High Orbit
Vellini System
Tiberius Sector

Chuck chewed on his fingernails, watching the guards descend on Bratta.

They'd been made. Bratta was giving up. Smith was nowhere to be seen, probably slipping into the crowd, escaping. But Bratta … there was no way he was going anywhere.

He needed some way of helping them. *Think Chuck, think! There's gotta be a way to save the day…*

Nothing came to mind.

Lily grunted quietly in the back of the cargo bay, the thick metal collar still around her neck. "Protein bar."

This wasn't the time. Not the time. Not the…

Or was it?

"You want a protein bar?" asked Chuck, cautiously, reaching into his pocket.

"Protein bar," said Lily, her pupils dilating.

She was just like a kid. A huge, hulking, angry, hungry kid. And kids needed chores. Tasks. They thrived on expectation-reward.

"Okay," said Chuck, cautiously withdrawing one of the thick hunks of processed food, "if you want the protein bar, you have to do something for *me* first…"

CHAPTER FORTY-SEVEN

Main Promenade
Christchurch Corporate Business Park station
Vellini, High Orbit
Vellini System
Tiberius Sector

A ripple of terribly loud gunfire made Bratta flinch. Rounds screamed as they bounced off the deck, the ceiling, the bulkheads; and then, from the airlock that lead to their ship, a guard was thrown—flying almost a full yard off the ground, hitting it again with a sickening crunch and sliding way, *way* across the deck. An ear-piercing howl followed, and then Lily —her massive head scraping the roof—burst out of the airlock, grabbing a nearby black-armored guard and, with a nauseating *crack*, picking them off their feet and ripped them in half. A half-eaten protein bar stuck out of her mouth like one of Reardon's toothpicks.

Everyone started shooting. Rounds bounced off Lily's

hide, seeming to only aggravate her. She charged toward another guard, bodily slamming into him and blasting him up against the bulkhead.

Bratta raised his gun back up and, carefully, took aim at one of the guards. He closed his eyes and squeezed the trigger. The gun roared. He opened his eyes again. The guard was laying on the ground, crumpled in a heap.

For a moment, his chest tightened. He'd just… *killed*…

But then the guard sat up, rubbing her armored back. Bratta's handgun had struck the armored plate. The guard twisted around, her features distorting angrily.

Then a *fwip*, barely audible over all the other gunfire, sent her sprawling back down to the deck again, unmoving.

Bratta broke into a run toward the airlock, feet thumping against the deck. Rounds snapped and hissed all around him, *tink*ing off the metal surfaces. Lily roared again, picking up any guards she got close to and breaking them like matchsticks, rounds throwing up sparks as they bounced off her body.

Chuck held down the airlock, crouching in the opening and firing at people with his pistol. He had a stern, resolute look on his face as he carefully took his shots in spite of the danger. He reloaded just as Bratta sprinted past the airlock door.

And then he was safe.

"Lily!" Chuck shouted. "Come on! We have to go!"

"Have to go!" roared Lily, swinging a guard like a club and slamming him against his fellow guard. She then turned and ran toward the airlock as well.

Bratta hesitated, staring down the giant mutant as she barreled toward him, stepping back into the *Aerostar*.

Lily ran in. Chuck emptied his magazine then ducked back inside, too. The *Aerostar* broke off, detaching forcefully from the airlock with a groan of metal.

Then everything went weirdly silent except for a ringing in Bratta's ears and a shaking of his hands.

What the *hell* kind of data had they recovered?

CHAPTER FORTY-EIGHT

State Room - Admiral Jack Mattis's Quarters
HMS Caernarvon
En route to Vellini
Vellini System
Tiberius Sector

Mattis wasn't sure how long he slept, but when he woke up, everyone had cleared out of his room including Ramirez. That didn't exactly surprise him, but it did disappoint him.

Nothing else about her of late had been disappointing, so he was content to let that one slide, just laying there with a stoned, happy look on his face.

The speaker in his room emitted a crackling noise. "*Action stations, action stations. Assume NBCD state zero. Action stations, action stations.*" Then a noise that sounded like an overdriven guitar, but transitioned to a low alarm.

Mattis realized with a start that he was hearing the Royal Navy version of the General Quarters alarm. The absolute worst way for a CO to wake up. Especially after knocking boots with Ramirez…

"Shit!" Mattis sat up in his bunk, braining himself on the lower bunk. "Shit!"

Rolling out of bed, the events before he fell asleep flew back into his head. He was still dressed, even though his uniform was crumpled now, it would do. He staggered out of the State Room and sprinted down the corridor toward the bridge.

When he got there, he saw the green-blue-gray orb of Vellini on the main monitor, a floating ball of a world hanging in space, its surface almost completely covered in what he could only presume to be a layer of garbage so thick it blanketed the ground. The world was a third ocean, but instead of blue water, the liquid was a dark, murky brown, stained with streaks of gunmetal grey. It had two sets of rings, faint blue, forming a large X over the southern continent.

The missing ship, Skunk Alpha, was there too, hanging in space like a vulture ready to shit on a landfill. The *Caernarvon*'s computers had ringed it in a bright red circle.

"Permission to enter the bridge, Captain," said Mattis, almost forgetting his manners.

Spears waved him in without saying anything, her eyes fixed on the enemy ship.

"Admiral Mattis, right on time," said Blackwood, her voice charged. "We're still detecting building energy readings from that thing. It's definitely got a mass driver onboard, if the readings are anything to go by. And there's *plenty* of space garbage for them to load and fire. No wonder they made their way here…"

Mattis glanced at a console, lit up and full of information. Blackwood's appraisal looked correct. "Yup, seems like. I can't believe the Forgotten would fire on such a heavily populated world." He eyed Spears. "Do you think there is the possibility that the ship is actually still piloted by future-humans?"

Spears considered that, drumming her fingers on the armrest of her chair. "Doesn't change our response to it. Commander Blackwood, report status on our reinforcements and get ready to engage that ship. I want all our guns speaking and our strike craft blasting the billy out of it."

Reinforcements? Mattis craned his neck, looking over Blackwood's shoulder while trying not to get in her way. There were numerous incoming Z-Space signals. As he watched, the world around Vellini lit up with a series of intense but brief flashes, dozens or more, ships translating from the strange otherworldly reality into real-space.

His chest tightened. "Where did those ships come from?"

Spears grinned over her shoulder at him. "Admiral, while you were sleeping, your good friend Admiral Fisher came good for us. Maybe I should let you take a nap more often."

As he watched, the whole sector lit up as the *Caernarvon's* computers identified the ships. USS *Lafayette*, USS *Grapple*, USS *Pearl Harbor*, USS *Quincy*; half a damn fleet had shown up. And at the lead was the USS *Warrior*. A ship he knew well. Fisher's old command, before she commanded a desk. He was hardly surprised when her voice came over the line.

"This is Admiral Fisher," she said. "Admiral Mattis has something of mine. I want it. *Now.*"

Mattis couldn't help but smile. "No problem, Admiral," he said, leaning over Spears's chair so his voice could be heard.

"Help us win this battle and the captive future-human is all yours."

"Very well," she said, her tone stony. "USS *Warrior*, ready to engage."

CHAPTER FORTY-NINE

Pilot's Ready Room
USS Stennis
Vellini, High Orbit
Vellini System
Tiberius Sector

Guano sat in the beanbag until the General Quarters alarm sounded. As though in a trance she stood up, walked calmly to the locker room, and changed into her space suit. Her eyeballs itched, dry and rough, but she didn't seem to mind. It was a distant, far away concern that barely registered.

"Hey Guano." Flatline clapped her on the back, good-naturedly, as he pulled up the thick, armored trousers of his space suit. "You got here fast!"

"Didn't leave," she said, clipping on her helmet and checking the seal. Her voice came out electronic and distorted. "Those beanbags are nice."

Flatline whistled, gyrating his hips around as he struggled

to pull the pants up. "You slept in the ready room? That's some wicked shit. Those saggy things are terrible for your neck." He snickered. "You missed a sweet strip poker game. Should have seen Frost squirm when I showed her my pair of aces."

Normally this would have been a great opportunity to tease Flatline. He almost always lost, literally losing his shirt. But she didn't want to. Couldn't feel it. "I'm totally fine," she said, and walked out to the airlock into the hangar bay like a robot. Out to her ship. Climbed aboard her ship. Performed the preflight launch check. Launched out into space. Legs and arms stiff as cords.

"Okay fuckheads, listen up," said Roadie, an edge of genuine tiredness and frustration creeping into his voice. "Missions callsign is *Tornado*. I know we've flown three sorties in sixteen hours, but I don't want to hear it. I know Flatline got his cock out again and I *really* don't want to know about that, nor restate my policy on no below-the-waist nudity for flight crew. Anyway, Flatline's joystick aside, we have a hostile cap-ship out there about to fire on a planet of garbage *using* garbage. Who knows why, and who cares. We can't let that happen for—*reasons*. Break." He paused. "So. Standard assault on capital-ships. Watch for defensive missiles and AA batteries, and keep your guns tracking on the engines. Engines are always a weak spot. You know that. I know that. Let's get it done and get home so we can get some proper shut eye. All ships, break formation and attack."

Most of the flight gave tired sounding acknowledgements. Guano felt as alert as she'd ever been. "Confirmed. Tornado 1-2, tally." She flicked the master arm switch off. "Let's give 'em hell."

The flight split up and darted toward their target, a swarm of sharp daggers seeking the heart of their enemy. The enemy capital ship was emitting huge amounts of energy, and where there was energy, there was heat. Her FLIR lit up like a giant burning star at the center of her scope, and the warbling tone of missile lock rang in her ears.

Not yet. Too far away. The hostile ship was just a distant glimmer.

"All USS *Stennis* strike craft be advised," said an unknown voice. Her HUD showed it as the voice of the flight coordinator from the USS *Warrior*. "Further assets are coming to your side. Be wary of buddy spikes, and call your targets. There's going to be a lot of strike craft out there. All friendly. Make sure we don't shoot each other in the back... Or front."

"Confirmed." She adjusted the gain on her targeting radar. "Tornado 1-2, Weapons tight."

Another voice cut in over the same channel. Authoritative and calm. "This is Admiral Fischer to all strike craft. Coordinate with the *Warrior*. Call for fire support on this channel."

Great, they had help. And from more than just the *Stennis*. That would be a huge boon.

Flatline yawned behind her. "Man, I am tired. I can barely shoot straight. I just couldn't sleep..."

She thumped on the back of her chair. "There's stims in the med cabinet. They'll wake you up."

"Stims, man." Flatline muttered something dark, followed by a faint hissing noise. "Whoa!" He laughed, suddenly alert. "Whoa. Okay. Okay, I'm good now."

With a grin, Guano turned her attention back to the

hostile ship; the massive metal box floated in space, charging its weapon, nose pointed down to Vellini.

Her left hand drifted from the control stick to the communications panel.

CUT OFF THE HEAD OF THE SNAKE

Her fingers typed the characters as she watched, with no input from her. Then, slowly, her finger hit the send key.

CHAPTER FIFTY

Muhammad "Roadie" Yousuf's J-88
Vellini, High Orbit
Vellini System
Tiberius Sector

The image of the hostile ship filled Roadie's cockpit, its engine exhaust glowing white-hot in his infrared, the warbling of the missile lock tone ringing in his ears. He'd hoped to never see another one of those deadly future-human ships again. It hung in space, ominously still, with the massive Vellini shipyards hovering half a dozen kilometers behind it.

"Here we go," he said, pulling his J-88 to the side and low, rolling its little stubby wings, aligning toward the large saucer dishes of the ship's engine exhaust, to the red trails streaming behind them. "Fox two, fox two."

His J-88 shook as the twin streams leapt away, tiny darts streaking silently toward their target. He watched the timer tick down till impact. *Thirty seconds, twenty-nine, twenty-eight…*

"Contact!" said Frost, his gunner, her voice coming in a little too loudly. She was always too loud. "We got radar signatures coming from that ship... they're strike craft!"

Strike craft? From a ship that size? Roadie risked a glance at his radar. He could see them too. Fast moving objects flying out from the hostile capital ship.

They weren't ships. They were high speed anti-fighter missiles heading right for them.

Roadie squeezed the talk key. "Flash traffic, all craft, evasive maneuvers!" He jammed the stick back into his gut, pulling the nose of his J-88 up high.

Missiles streaked past them, bursting in white flashes as they exploded in the formation, spraying their deadly load of shrapnel in all directions.

The cloud of metal washed over the ship like a cloudburst, metal screaming as it bit into the outer hull. His port engine flared, sending the ship tumbling, then burned out. Flames and smoke poured from the starboard engine and it spluttered, the ship jerking as it tried to right itself with two broken wings.

Alarms wailed all around him as he fought for control. "Frost!" he roared. "Get the starboard engine back *now!*"

No response.

Instinct took over. The three rules of aircraft navigation. *Aviate, navigate, communicate.* He didn't have time to check on Frost. She couldn't talk to him either. He had to fly. The ship was in a lateral spin. If he couldn't pull out, the g-forces would eventually overwhelm him. With a shaking hand that felt like it was made out of lead, he reached out and tapped a screen. *Emergency power to starboard engine.*

The spin stabilized and stopped accelerating, but the

starboard engine flamed out completely and died.

Stable, but not safe. Time to navigate. Roadie's whole HUD was out. Many of his panels were working on emergency power. Damn it. "Hey Frost, help me out here. We gotta get engine power back online."

Still nothing. Internal radio must be out. He looked for a landmark.

The planet. Vellini, they had called it. It passed by his canopy as the fighter spun. Every time it appeared he could swear it looked larger. His ship was moving toward it. Fast, too. Given how damaged it was, there was no way it would survive reentry.

Communicate. The radio would be working on emergency backup power.

"Alpha 01 transmitting in the blind guard, *mayday*, *mayday*, *mayday*. I'm hit. I'm hit. Dead stick, total loss of power."

Guano's voice came to his ears. Patricia. "This is Guano, relaying *mayday* call for Alpha 01. Roadie's hit. Confirming he is hit." Damn it, Patricia. Why are you so... *Patricia-like*. There was a slight crack in her voice, just a little bit. "Christ, he's fucked up."

The J-88 continued its spin. He had been using military power when he tried to avoid those missiles. Military power in the J-88 was crazy amounts of thrust.

He kicked out experimentally with his feet, testing the pedals. They felt sticky and the ship didn't move at all. Was there an oil leak? His suit was intact. Couldn't smell a thing.

"Hey, Frost, check the hydraulics." He looked in his rearview mirror, trying to catch her eye. "There might be a—"

Her helmet drifted into sight, the side and front of it

punctured by shrapnel. Thick, dark globs of blood drifted out.

She couldn't have survived that. Nobody could.

Frost was gone.

Closing his eyes a moment, Roadie turned his thoughts inward. *"Bismillaahi,"* he said. *"Inna lillahi wa inna ilayhi raji'un."* *From God we come, to God we shall return.*

No more time to worry about the departed. Roadie opened his eyes, and found his visor full of the rapidly-approaching planet. Okay. Maybe it wouldn't. If he had to bail out, Frost would go with him.

Flames licked at the side of his craft as it kissed the atmosphere, and his hands drifted down to the ejection handle. When the ship stopped burning up, slowed down, and was well inside the atmosphere, then he would eject.

Assuming he lived that long.

CHAPTER FIFTY-ONE

Bridge
HMS Caernarvon
Vellini, High Orbit
Vellini System
Tiberius Sector

The *Warrior* and the rest of Fischer's fleet moved to engage. Mattis moved beside Spears, standing to her left.

"Helm," said Spears, "move to engagement range. Turn the ship to bring our rear guns and missile tubes into effective direct firing angles. Tea time, if you would, Commander Blackwood."

Tea time. A maneuvering tactic designed to maximize armor thickness by tilting it, exposing a tiny sliver of the ship's side. It originally came about from tank crews, angling their armor so that the vehicle was pointed to ten o'clock and two o'clock. US ships had a so-called *pike nose*, the front of the ship at an already angled spike, designed to optimize the armor angle. Clever of Spears to use an old British tank tactic in a massive starship. It spoke to her command style—old and new.

"Tea-time adopted, ma'am," said Blackwood. "We're in an optimum firing position. I'll have an ensign put the kettle on."

"Very well," said Spears, shifting in her chair. "Irish Breakfast if you could, Commander Blackwood. And fire."

The *Caernarvon* rocked as it sent out a wave of gunfire, the hull humming with the distant pounding of guns, the vibration transmitted through the ship's superstructure and into the CIC. It was so much more visceral and loud inside the smaller, more compact frigate than in the larger cruiser. There, weapons fire —despite being from much larger guns—was almost imperceptible.

Not so for this ship. More things to get used to.

The bright cannon streaks leapt across the dark of space, flying toward the hostile ship. They came in a wave, focused on the center of mass.

"Captain," said Blackwood, her brow furrowing. "We're receiving a transmission from a nearby civilian vessel. The *Aerostar*. Text only."

"Civilians?" Spears scowled. "What the devil are you talking about?"

Blackwood continued to read. "They say that the stolen children from New Kentucky are aboard that ship."

"Put him through," said Spears.

Blackwood said something into her headset, and moments later Harry Reardon's familiar voice blared over the speakers. "As I was saying to your lovely assistant, Ms. Spears, we just barely escaped with our necks intact from the Jovian Logistics HQ on Christchurch business park station. And *my* lovely assistant Mr. Bratta downloaded some … interesting data from their computers. Haven't read through it all yet, but my third lovely assistant, Mr. Smith, determined that they've got something called *Operation Ad Infinitum* going on here."

"What the hell is that, Mr. Reardon?" said Mattis, with a quick glance of apology to Spears. She nodded back, making clear she wasn't going to take issue with him getting involved.

"Admiral Mattis! Good to hear your voice again, Mr. Admiral sir. I've got someone here you'll be happy to see, but to your question: we, uh, don't know. But Smith went through the operations log, and it looks like they're not only behind the salvaging of that Avenir ship out there, but they were also behind the kidnapping of those kids on New Kentucky. He thinks there's a better-than-even chance they're being held over there. Almost like—"

"Human shields," muttered Spears. "Good Lord."

Mattis's chest tightened. He wanted to break off the attack, but with the hostile ship charging its weapon, he knew there was only one right decision here—and it wasn't his to make. He looked to Spears.

With calm and precise language, Spears almost didn't let any of her true emotions through. Almost. "Thank you, Mr. Reardon, that will be all for now. Press the attack, Commander Blackwood," she said, with barely even a waver. "Coordinate fire patterns with the USS *Stennis*. Link our targeting computers and synchronize our attack."

One of the bridge officers confirmed it. Mattis could only stare at the ship. So many children aboard… but it was the right decision. They couldn't risk the lives of a few dozen for Vellini. Even if they were children. Another wave of cannon fire went out. And another.

"Captain," said Blackwood, her words calm and professional, but gilded with concern. "We are detecting another transmission. Not from the *Aerostar*; a microburst. Origin unknown, but I'll wager a guess who they're hailing."

Their cannon fire struck home, exploding in silent, distant bursts that sparkled as they blew armor and material in all directions. Mattis squinted to see. Did the British always have things so poorly magnified? Or were his eyes getting old?

The hostile ship began turning toward them, slowly swinging its nose away from Vellini. Perhaps because they shot it, or perhaps it was because of the transmission—either way, Mattis and the rest of the *Caernarvon* bridge crew had no time to think about it.

Blackwood spoke first. "Ma'am—"

"I see it," said Spears. "Continue firing." She tapped at the holographic computer on her wrist, quickly typing out some message. Blackwood's computer chirped the second she hit *send*. It was no secret who she was messaging.

Mattis scowled. They were cutting him out of the loop…

As though sensing his distress, Spears tilted her wrist toward him, showing the message she had typed.

Message transmitted to Christchurch station from nearby. It's not coming from them, nor the Aerostar: *it's coming from us. Us or the* Stennis.

We have a mole.

A troubling development.

"Commence broad-spectrum jamming immediately, Command Blackwood. No more of those transmissions. Quick as you please."

"Aye, ma'am. I'll signal the strike craft and tell them to engage in frequency modulation to avoid their comms being scrambled."

"Very good, Commander Blackwood."

The alien ship completed its turn and came to face the *Stennis*. Weapons bristled and charged, turning to engage the ships around them. Silent flashes in the dark signaled incoming weapons fire, aimed in all directions, including directly toward the camera.

An ensign arrived, steaming pot of tea in hand, and began to pour Captain Spears a cup. She kept her eyes on the screen, ignoring the effort. "Commander Blackwood, please avoid scratching the paint on my ship."

The ship lurched. The ensign nearly spilled tea all over the deck, managing to save it by inches. With remarkable agility, the *Caernarvon* drifted out of the way of the shots, returning with a volley of her own.

Spears, seemingly satisfied, nodded his way. "Expertly done. Admiral, if you wouldn't mind, work with Blackwood."

That was her way of saying *make yourself useful and stop sitting around waiting for things to happen*. He moved up beside the focused young woman. "What can I do?" he asked.

Blackwood pointed to her XO's console. It had a display full of the status of the strike craft; one of the birds from the *Stennis* had been hit. Their CAG. The stricken craft was drifting toward Vellini. "Get the SAR bird out there," he said. "They don't have to intervene just yet, but the sooner they can interdict, the better. Entering the atmosphere in a damaged bird is bad news."

"Good idea," said Blackwood. "Ejection is a messy business."

There was little else he could do, so he returned his gaze to the main monitor. Despite the damage, he felt useless. And he felt angry that he felt useless. The skunk was being pounded from all sides by Fischer's fleet; a solid stream of gunfire flowed toward it from dozens of ships, each shell bursting on the hull of the alien ship in a bright sparkle. Flames licked out of multiple breaches. Yet it would have happened if he hadn't been on-board at all.

A red warning flashed on Blackwood's monitor. The energy surge was back; much bigger than he'd ever seen. Much larger than the mass driver that had attacked Earth.

"Captain," said Mattis, "we got a *big* problem. That ship is still charging. It should have either powered down or fired by now. It should be—"

The ship flashed sky blue, as though lit up through some light source within that was so bright it was able to pierce the hull itself. Beams shone out from every window, crack, and hull breach, stretching out into infinity. Like the giant fingers of a god, they snapped to narrow beams, clutching each of the ships, including their own.

Immediately, the *Caernarvon* lurched forward, throwing Mattis off his feet. Blackwood fell on top of him, her elbow driving into his side, her hair spilling over his face.

No time for chivalry. Mattis roughly shoved her off, climbed to his feet, then offered her his hand—only to find she'd flipped back onto her feet on her own. No small feat, given the shaking and pitching deck.

"All engines full reverse," howled Spears. "Helm! Quickly now!"

The main monitor was awash with blue. Through it, he could see nothing. Every monitor was overloaded with warnings and errors, and all outside cameras could show was the blue.

"Blackwood," said Mattis, half walking, half staggering to the XO's console. The world felt heavy, as though the artificial gravity were turned up too high. "Engines aren't going to be enough. We have to break the beam."

"I'm listening," said Blackwood, appearing beside him. Her hair hung down her shoulders as though wet, pulled to the ground by gravity. "And what the devil's wrong with the pull?"

Mattis stared at the monitor. "The computers are adjusting it manually," he said, pointing. "They're trying to maintain 1g, but they're having to push us *up* to stop us from being crushed."

At the rate they were accelerating, they'd be pulled into the skunk in minutes.

"Options?" asked Blackwood.

"Fire all we got," he said. "That blue shit has got us good, but it came from cracks in the hull. If we unload at them, we might be able to disrupt it."

"Might?" She stared at him in skeptical bewilderment, then roughly shook her head. "Fuck it, I don't have a better idea."

It was bad when the notoriously calm, reserved British officers were swearing. Mattis's fingers flew over the keyboard. *All guns. Load high explosive rather than armor piercing.* He set the bearing relative to the beam—000.

Gravity pulled him down, sinking his shoulders and making his bones ache. Gritting his teeth, Mattis fought through the pain and slammed his fist onto the fire key.

Shots rang out, and then the acceleration pulled Blackwood down to the deck, Mattis following.

He hit hard. Something tore in his right shoulder; something deep. He could *feel* the limb dislocate, and searing pain leapt up his arm.

His chest tightened. An invisible hand pushed him down, rolling him onto his back, crushing the life out of him. Blackwood lay nearby, face down, gasping for air, blood trickling out of the side of her mouth, her face ashen and tainted blue by the light from the monitor.

And then, with a dull rumble, the effect faded. For a moment, Mattis felt himself be pushed *up*, toward the ceiling, until the *Caernarvon*'s computers caught up with what was happening and unceremoniously dropped them back to the deck again.

Right onto his injured shoulder. Another wave of pain told him in no uncertain terms it was damaged. *Old man, you're coming apart at the seams.*

He took a deep breath, exhaled, then pulled himself up by his left hand. The main monitor was washed out and faded, but its vision returned.

Fischer's fleet had been pulled right up against the hostile ship. Barely a kilometer away from the thing, hovering, suspended, as though held through whatever invisible force had yanked them there.

"This is Admiral Fischer." A box appeared on the side of the screen, showing Fischer's battered face, her hair in tangles and her uniform scorched and torn. Half her face was covered in red welts and burns, and her bridge appeared to be full of smoke. "Mattis, you have to get out of here. The energy buildup isn't complete. It's—"

And then the Avenir ship exploded in a white ball of light, enveloping everything and consuming the American fleet instantly.

CHAPTER FIFTY-TWO

Cargo Bay
The Aerostar
Near Christchurch Corporate Business Park station
Vellini, High Orbit
Vellini System
Tiberius Sector

That was intense.

Bratta kept breathing, kept trying to keep his heart rate at something less than his maximum—no time for a heart attack, after all. His whole body ached as the adrenaline flowed out of him, his chest thumping madly.

"So hey," said Smith, coming over to him and giving a firm, polite nod. "You did great back there."

"Did I?" asked Bratta, his voice coming out as a high-pitched squeak. "I feel like I didn't. I feel—I feel like I really dropped the ball. Like, super, really badly."

"Eh, you did fine. You didn't blow our cover, you got the

data, you got out okay." Smith smiled. "Speaking of the data, let's see what you can make of this techy section, ok? That might keep your mind off all this nonsense. Which is good. Believe me, there'll be time enough later for reflection and second-guessing yourself."

That seemed like a good idea. He accepted the data pad Smith offered to him.

"Okay," he said. "Just indexing all the data now. In a few minutes we'll be able to search for keywords and, you know, see what we can find."

"Sounds good," said Smith.

Lily stood off to one side, bracing herself against the bulkhead, panting, obviously trying to get her breath back. She was bleeding in many places, black blood trickling down onto the deck.

"You okay?" asked Chuck, approaching her cautiously. "You … you did really good back there."

"Did good," said Lily, flicking blood off her hand. "Did good."

Bratta could scarcely believe it. "You … got her to talk," he said, blinking slowly. "To do a lot more than that too."

"Just needed a protein bar," said Chuck, smiling at him. "And a bit of encouragement. Just like a regular human."

Protein bar. Encouragement. Right. Bratta nodded encouragingly. "Okay. I'm going to go look at the index now, okay?"

"Index," said Lily, straightening up until her head almost hit the roof.

That was probably *yes*, he guessed. Bratta walked back to Smith, trying not to look over his shoulder in fear of the giant mutant who had, apparently, decided to come save them. "Okay, it should be done by now."

Chuck slid over as well, brow beaded with sweat. "Anything in there for Jack?" he asked.

They had no way of knowing that yet. "I'll take a look," promised Bratta. "First thing."

His computer *dinged*. The index was complete.

"Okay," he said, stepping in front of the terminal and cracking his knuckles in a way he hoped look cool and in control. "Let's open this up…"

The terminal had indexed every word in the whole database. He inspected the output, flicking through it, narrowing the search. *Congenital Heart.* There we go!

Ten thousand four hundred entries. "There's a *lot* here," he said, blinking in surprise. "Let's narrow it down a little more." *Infant Congenital Heart.*

One entry. "Right here," said Bratta, tilting the monitor so Chuck could see. "A research project into infant heart troubles. Looks like all the symptoms are there: shaking, trembling, intermittent clamminess and weakness, and where symptoms vanish completely. It's, apparently, a symptom of a drug they've been working on for some time. It apparently does … *something* with the target's DNA. The fix is a retrovirus." Bratta read on. "Except, there's more to it. More in a way I don't understand yet. There's some kind of DNA resequencing here. We're looking at more than just a heart condition here." He looked up, troubled. "I don't know what the intended outcome is—it's not clear from this data."

Chuck frowned in obvious confusion. "But, why?" he asked, curiously. "Why would these former military veterans with connection to Jovian Logistics be working on … genetics? What's this doing here?"

Bratta didn't have an immediate answer to that, but a glance at the time-date stamp made him pause. "That can't be right," he said, frowning and turning the screen back towards him.

Publication Date: September 26th, 3102

"This database is from the future," he said, simply.

"Bottom line. Can you use this to synthesize a cure for Jack?" asked Chuck.

"Easily," said Bratta. "The retrovirus's genetic code just requires printing. I can manufacture it here, if you want. I am, after all, more than qualified."

The two exchanged broad smiles.

Chuck, obviously relieved, was still scratching his head. "Still. Why did all the docs clam up when they saw Jack had a problem? It's like … it's almost as if someone knew which doc I was going to, getting to them first, and … I don't know."

Bratta wanted to soothe the man's obvious paranoia, but … it actually made a little sense. "No competent doctor would have missed the obvious signs of genetic tinkering here. I think you may be on to something, Mr. Mattis."

Regardless of why the various doctors he'd seen were covering up the reason for Jack's mysterious illness, all he could feel now was relief. Intense, cathartic relief.

"Well … that's odd," said Bratta.

"What?"

"This data. I entered another search term into the index.

Mitochondrial. It's a genetics term. Something that will come into play with Jack's retroviral treatment. But what I found was … interesting."

"What?" Chuck asked again, exasperated.

"Clones. Jovian Logistics appears to be involved with cloning technology. In fact, there's a whole file on …" he was shaking his head in disbelief, "Jeremy Pitt."

"Holy shit," said Chuck.

"Holy shit," repeated Smith.

"Uhh," said Sammy over the ship's intercom, "so, hey, there's… a ship out there. A big, weird-looking ship. Looks military." There was a brief pause. "Hey, guys? Get up here. Now."

Everyone started to move to the exit of the cargo bay, back toward the rest of the ship, but Smith caught Bratta's shoulder.

"I'll stay here," said Smith. "Review the data. See what I can find. I have a bunch of implants that can interface with computers… it'll make searching really easy."

"Okay," said Bratta. "Take care, okay? We don't know what's in there."

"I'll be careful," said Smith, nodding firmly. "Go. Check out the big battle."

"Battle?" Bratta hadn't heard anything about any battle. His hands still felt shaky the last one. "A… *space* battle?"

"Yup. My gut tells me things are about to heat up around here."

CHAPTER FIFTY-THREE

Bridge
HMS Caernarvon
Vellini, High Orbit
Vellini System
Tiberius Sector

The view screen was engulfed in light as bright as the blue beams that had nearly doomed them. When the luminescence faded, an expanding debris field from the alien ship was revealed, along with the *Warrior* and the rest of the US fleet.

Or what was left of them.

Whatever effect the pseudo-gravity pulse had inflicted on the ships had been devastating; every ship was burning on multiple decks, venting atmosphere through cracks in the hull, their external lights flickering weakly, like the gasps of the dying. Casualty reports hadn't been relayed yet, but it was clear that thousands of US servicemen had been annihilated in the blink of an eye.

Mattis stared in bewilderment. It had drawn them all in with its gravitational technology that they had wielded with devastating effect just months ago against Ganymede. And once the fleet was pulled in close….

They committed suicide. A suicide bomber. That took out half the American naval space fleet. Whether it was actual future-humans aboard that ship, or rogue Forgotten, they had dealt the American military its most deafening defeat since the early battles of the Sino-American war.

"The Avenir are full of tricks," said Blackburn. Characteristic British understatement.

It was true, though. They had tricks. And Mattis couldn't keep underestimating them, whoever they were. Every mistake was a price paid in blood. Last time the Avenir had fired big rocks at them. This time they, or the Forgotten commandeering their salvaged ship, had blown themselves up to cripple the American fleet. What would they do next time?

"Commander Blackwood," said Spears, an uncharacteristic tremble in her voice. "Dispatch search and rescue teams to the stricken American ships. Coordinate with ships able to help others if any exist. Have our strike craft hunt down escape pods and recover them. Dispatch our Marines, medics, damage control teams… everything we have. Have the shuttles assist with escape pods when they've dropped off our teams. Supplies and personnel out, escape pods and wounded in. Push the strike craft overboard if we have to make room."

"Captain," said Mattis, "request permission to leave the HMS *Caernarvon*. I need to go aboard the USS *Warrior* and assist in whatever way I can."

Spears's eyes flicked to him, examining him critically. "Not with that arm you're not," she said.

Damn. He'd almost forgotten. His right arm hung at a strange angle, obviously out of its shoulder socket. Pins and needles crept up from his fingers, past his wrist. "I'll have one of the medics reset it and take a painkiller," he said. "It's more wanting to assist with command and coordination efforts anyway, and…"

He trailed off. Blackwood was holding his hand, examining it curiously. "Do you mind? I used to play rugby and my team's doc would do this all the time. I can pop it back in in a jiffy. It won't *fix* it but you'll be back in the game."

"Go for it," he said, grimacing slightly.

"On three. One." Blackwood suddenly shoved his arm back in its socket. Pain exploded up his arm and he bit the inside of his cheek to quiet a surprised shriek.

"Dammit! You said on three!"

Blackwood brushed her hair out of her eyes. "Yes, so you would be relaxed on *one*. You would have tensed on three. Unfortunately, that trick only works once."

Fair call. "Hopefully you won't have to do it again," said Mattis, rubbing his shoulder ruefully to banish the tingling sensation. "Have that painkiller waiting for me. Permission to leave the bridge, Captain?"

Spears nodded mutely, her eyes remained glued to the main monitor, idly chewing on a thumbnail as she watched her allied fleet burn against the black of space.

CHAPTER FIFTY-FOUR

Corridor
HMS Caernarvon
Vellini, High Orbit
Vellini System
Tiberius Sector

Mattis felt numb as he walked toward the *Caernarvon*'s Hangar Bay, and it wasn't just residual effects from the pain. He fell into a crowd of people, medics, damage control crews and engineers, moving with a sea of people toward the waiting shuttles. It seemed as though Captain Spears was sending across half her crew. Perhaps that was too much.

The tide of people filtered into shuttles, most carrying supplies and engineering tools; welders, cutters, and emergency bulkheads. The rest carried stretchers and medical supplies.

As the shuttles departed, he saw waves of similar craft from the *Stennis* heading toward the wrecked fleet. More shuttles. More ships. More aid. He saw Sampson without her suit, her massive, bulky arms carrying more things than a woman of her surprisingly diminutive stature would suggest, and right as the loading ramp on his ship closed, he saw her begin to load up Cho's motorized wheelchair.

Everyone was helping. An ominous feeling came over him, seeing the urgency at which they moved, and seeing the escape pods floating away from dozens of ruined American ships.

Perhaps what they had taken wasn't enough.

Off in the distance, one of the ruined American ships, one that had been closest to the Avenir vessel when it blew, exploded in a quickly extinguished puff. Mattis's stomach tensed as he imagined all the survivors being incinerated in the blink of an eye.

So much senseless loss. And what had they gained?

Nothing.

And, most disturbing of all, he still had no idea who his enemy was.

The shuttle lifted off. As it flew out of the hangar bay doors, a blonde-haired nurse with a neatly trimmed beard caught his eye.

"Admiral," said the guy, eyes falling on his arm, his accent difficult to understand. Yorkshire, possibly? "Got a little something for you."

He extended his arm, rolling up his sleeve. "Thanks."

The nurse gently pressed the needle to his shoulder and slid it in, depressing the plunger. "What have you done to yourself, sir?"

"Hurt my arm." Mattis rolled his arm experimentally as the needle left his skin, but a sting of pain in his shoulder made him wince. "Commander Blackwood fixed it."

"I told her not to do that anymore," the man muttered, then cleared his throat. "Well, I'm sure she was chuffed to bits to be able to mangle another one of my patients—what a duck. I suppose she gave you a song and dance about rugby and how that qualified her to practice medicine?"

It was difficult to understand the man's accent. "She did mention she played rugby," Mattis echoed.

"*Reyt*. Well, regardless, based on the swelling, you've probably right stuffed it. You'll need physio to restore the strength and make sure the rotator cuff heals properly." He took hold of the limb and slowly turned the limb over in his hands. It only hurt a little. "Nerves and blood supply don't seem to be compromised. That's good."

"Right." *Hurry, goddammit.* He tried to summon anger, frustration at the delay, but all he could think about was those US ships burning in space, their internal atmospheres igniting, their crews dead and dying. How they were dying right now, at this very moment. Every second they spent here was a second they were not helping.

"You'll be fine." The medic unceremoniously dropped the hand which caused more pain than the twisting did. "Just remember, and I can't emphasize this enough: over-stretching the injured tissues *should be avoided* for between two and six weeks." He gave a sour look. "This should be in a sling."

"No time for slings. I've got people dying out there. My shoulder can wait."

"*Reyt*, Admiral," he said, then tapped on his wrist computer. Mattis could see the text flowing across the screen. Casualty reports.

The trip over to the American fleet was performed in

silence. Mattis's ship banked toward the *Warrior*. As he drew closer, Mattis didn't like what he saw. The whole lower subsection was leaking atmosphere, illuminated from within by burning fires. The stricken frigate tumbled end over end, slowly, surrounded by a twinkling field of debris that looked like a dozen stars.

The Avenir vessel was destroyed, but at what cost? Mattis glanced guiltily at the nurses's arm computer. It was still scrolling with casualty reports and casevac requests.

And there was only one place the kidnapped kids could have been. On the ship they'd just blown up. Spears had done the right thing. Made the same decision he would have made. Made the hard call.

Somehow, that knowledge made him feel worse. More guilty.

The shuttle ducked and weaved as it maneuvered around a sea of debris. Small pieces plinked off the hull. Gently, almost reverently, the ship docked with the *Warrior*, silently sliding into the hangar bay, settling down on the landing strip with barely a whisper, all noise fading away as the ship's engines powered down.

Silently, the doors closed. Air filled the hangar bay as the airlock opened. The loading ramp dropped down, and Mattis was greeted by the nose-searing scent of burning electronics and metal, stale air. And screaming.

"Need a medic over here!"

"Priority one casevac, coming through!"

"Make a hole—walking wounded, walking wounded!"

Mattis dodged out of the way as the *Warrior* staff—many of them wounded themselves or not even medical staff—

started frantically loading the shuttle he'd just departed. An ominous rumble came from within the ship, along with the groan of stressed metal, but it settled quickly.

The smell of burning metal was quickly joined by the acrid, coppery smell of blood.

A vague sense of helplessness came over him. He stared at the seemingly endless rows of wounded being loaded into the shuttle. Face after face, stranger after stranger, all wearing the same uniform he did.

Then passed one that he knew, laying unconscious on a stretcher. Admiral Fischer.

He wouldn't have recognized her if it were not for her Admiral's pips. Her face was covered in blood, half her hair burned away, her uniformed blackened and burned, half-melted and stuck to her body.

Alive or dead, he didn't know, but she wouldn't be commanding anything while she was under.

With a renewed determination, Mattis made his way through the crowd toward the threshold and into the USS *Warrior*'s superstructure, intent on heading to its bridge.

And then he met someone he did not expect.

Chuck Mattis, his son. He was wearing some kind of overcoat, had a pistol strapped to his hip—was that thing licensed?—and he looked as though he hadn't had a shower in a week.

Mattis couldn't help but stare. "Ch-Chuck? What the hell are you doing here?"

"Dad," said Chuck, his eyes tired. He looked like he'd just walked through Hell; dirty, sweaty, clearly unrested. He was wearing strange clothing. And something about him… his posture had shifted. Changed. It was like he strode down the corridor with … purpose. "I have to talk to you."

The words didn't sink in. "What are you talking about? What are you doing here?"

"It's Pitt," said Chuck. "Jeremy Pitt. I know you saved him." He took a deep breath. "Dad, he's not who you think he is. We—we think he's a clone."

"A clone? As in, a copy of a person? He sure looks like Jeremy Pitt."

Chuck nodded grimly. "Come with me. I'll show you."

CHAPTER FIFTY-FIVE

Patricia "Guano" Corrick's J-88
Vellini, High Orbit
Vellini System
Tiberius Sector

Guano tracked Roadie's ship as it plummeted, tumbling as it fell, leaving a burning streak across Vellini's atmosphere.

"Okay, hold onto your arse, Flatline, because we are going to be heroes today. SAR is going to be *mad* busy with all these damaged ships, so it's up to us."

Flatline sighed in her ears. "How, Guano? We can't squeeze two people in here—"

"Actually we can," she said. "The J-88 has a pretty big internal cargo space."

"A big space that's full of fuel," said Flatline. "Not exactly made for passengers."

Duh. "We can dump that. Then use the cutting torch in the toolkit to burn them a way in."

"The cutting torch?" asked Flatline, a whine creeping into his voice. "Cutting into the fuel tank isn't safe, even if it's empty."

It'd be fine. "We'll get flash-fires, but eh. No biggie. Frost and Roadie's suits are atmospherically tight, so they can just ride. It'll be fine."

"You can't be seriously thinking of doing this." That was *exactly* what she was thinking. "But … okay. Hell, let's do it."

It was all she needed to hear. Guano followed Roadie's ship on her long range radar, until it broke apart in the lower atmosphere. A brief moment passed where she feared he hadn't done I, but then she saw it. Two emergency beacons. One for Frost, one for Roadie.

The rockets in his ejection seat would slow them down, his flight suit would protect them, and their parachute would lower them both safely down to the surface. She checked their life signs remotely. Roadie looked fine; elevated heart rate—fair enough—and otherwise okay.

She couldn't get anything from Frost. Could be a glitch.

"Okay," said Guano, "prepare for atmospheric reentry."

"Wait, maybe we should—"

"We're doing this, Flatline," she said, an edge to her voice that would hopefully shut him up. "You already agreed, so hold on tight."

CHAPTER FIFTY-SIX

Sickbay
USS Warrior
Vellini, High Orbit
Vellini System
Tiberius Sector

Chuck led him farther into the ship. It was strange to be following his son around a military vessel and not the other way around, but soon he found himself in the infirmary; the already cramped quarters were intensely crowded, but as the injured and dying were transferred to other vessels, Mattis found room to breathe.

And room to talk to Chuck.

"Why are we in sickbay?" he hissed. "And what the hell are you doing here? This is a war zone. How did you *get* here?"

"I came across on the *Aerostar*."

"That was *you?*" Mattis's eyes went wide. "We considered firing on that ship. There were transmissions… transmissions that were warning our enemies of our actions. Jesus, Chuck…"

His eyes flashed. "Look, there's more going on here than just a space battle against some rogue ex-military folks," said Chuck.

Mattis didn't have the energy to yell at him. And it wouldn't have solved anything anyway. "You haven't answered why you're here yet."

Chuck's eyes flicked to one of the closed doors that, Mattis presumed, led to a private room. "Jack's here."

Was he losing his mind? This must be what losing one's mind felt like. Mattis felt his fists ball by his sides. "You brought a *baby* aboard a warship? You brought my *grandson* into a … into a…" he swept his hand around. "Into this disaster?"

Chuck's face clouded. "Hey, I wouldn't have done it if I had a choice." He pinched the bridge of his nose and sighed. "Anyway, ignore that. Look. You've got to get Pitt down here —Jeremy Pitt, that is. And his dad, too. As many witnesses as you can get. We can prove he's a clone here and now. And what that means? Well, that's above my pay grade."

It seemed doubtful. Between the battle and swift evacuation, Mattis hadn't had time to say more than a few dozen words to Jeremy Pitt. Hadn't even had time to debrief him. And now Chuck was here out of the blue, along with his infant son—good Lord, what the hell was *that* all about?—it was a lot to take in at once.

"Who's he a clone of?" asked Mattis. It made no sense. "He looks just like how he used to."

"A clone of *himself*," said Chuck. "Or, more accurately, of the *real* Jeremy Pitt."

It was a bitter pill to swallow. After losing Pitt and seeing him buried, Mattis had just gotten used to the idea that the man was back. To be told it was all a lie... "What kind of test?" asked Mattis, skeptical.

"Well," said Chuck, "Bratta was talking about it before. I can explain it to you if you like."

Bratta was here? Steve Bratta, the scientist? The galaxy was a small place. "Okay," he said. "I'll try to keep up."

"The thing is," said Chuck, idly pacing around in a small circle. "You'd know as well as I do that clones have identical DNA. But... well, Bratta explained it to me like this. There's a thing called mitochondria; organelles that sit inside nearly every cell. Their purpose is to convert food into something we can use." Mitochondria. The powerhouse of the cell. Mattis remembered his science lessons. "The thing is, clones come out of a lab, and mitochondria possess their own chromosomal signature—their own DNA.

"In normal humans, they get our mitochondria from our mothers. But the clones that Spectre was making—at least, I think this was what Bratta was getting at—the clones of himself, the Avenir mutants, everything... well, they all use the same mitochondrial source. So we can analyze the DNA and find out if it matches the ones from—" there was a brief, ever so slight pause. "The other living future-humans we know about. And..." a shadow passed over his son's face. "And the mitochondria in Jack. Dad, they did something to him. They— they did something to him," he repeated, fighting back what he guessed were tears of either despair or rage. But he composed himself. "Anyway, we can test them all, and compare the mitochondria. Jack's, Pitt's, the future-human mutant's—"

Mattis scowled a little bit, digesting that information.

Chuck was obviously referring to the escape pod they'd retrieved. "Wait, how in *hell* did you know we have a future-human aboard?"

Chuck's surprise seemed totally genuine. "I didn't," he said. "I meant the one aboard the *Aerostar*."

Well, that was unexpected. They both just stood there awkwardly.

"You're telling me," said Mattis, cautiously. "There's another Avenir on that ship? The *Aerostar*? How did you find it?"

"How did you find yours?"

He frowned again. "You first, son."

"It... *she* came out of a box," said Chuck, cautiously. "Reardon got paid to deliver a crate to New London, bound eventually for the USS *Midway*. The people who met him at the other end double-crossed him and thought to take it for themselves. That plan didn't work out, Reardon eventually got curious and opened up the box. Revealing... yeah. The Avenir. And lots of explosives. He thinks the boxes were all destined for US military vessels, as remotely-triggered bombs or something."

Mattis cringed. He had no reason to doubt his son, but it was troubling news indeed. Someone was paying to ship living Avenir around in boxes? How many others had there been?

The image of the USS *Hamilton* disappearing in a white burst of light, taking with it the crew, Captain Abramova, Commander Riley... Spectre had taunted Mattis right before the explosion, asking if they had been visited by Jovian Logistics.

It all made sense now.

Spectre had been shipping the boxes to US military assets. If it wasn't for Reardon's intercept—however *that* had happened—Mattis would have been blasted to atoms along with the *Midway*.

"Right," said Mattis, cautiously dragging his mind back to the present. "Thank God for Mr. Reardon. Never thought I'd say that out loud."

Chuck rubbed his hands together. "It's actually really good that you have one, too. That gives us another source to compare to when we analyze Pitt's DNA."

"Okay," said Mattis, rolling his injured shoulder experimentally. It definitely felt hurt, but—maybe it was the painkiller, but it felt a bit better already. "What now?"

"I guess," said Chuck, "the first step is, we'll need blood from the mutants. Bring all of the future-humans we have together, take some blood, and we see if we can find out the truth. And figure out what the hell is going on."

CHAPTER FIFTY-SEVEN

Sickbay
USS Warrior
Vellini, High Orbit
Vellini System
Tiberius Sector

The *Warrior* was more intact than he'd feared at first. There were massive amounts of casualties, but the ship itself was serviceable and mobile, if not heavily damaged. But safe enough to use it as his flagship? Admiral Fischer lived, but would be in a hospital for several weeks.

The American military was now in the command of Admiral Jack Mattis.

For now.

The process of getting three Avenir into the same spot had proven more difficult than Mattis had anticipated.

Pitt's quarantine cycle had not yet completed. Fortunately, with a bit of convincing, Captain Flint had him released early.

But he was wary of releasing the Avenir they'd found in the pod in the Pinegar system—days of intense and brutal interrogation had yielded nothing. The thing had not said a single word. "We've only just softened it up," bragged Flint, but Mattis, knowing the limitations of torture, just shook his head. In the end, Flint agreed to send it over under heavy guard.

And Harry Reardon did not want to turn over someone he now considered his crewman to be "experimented" on. Fortunately, the combined words of Spears, Flint, and himself managed to sway him, although Mattis suspected that Chuck contributing made the difference.

The box-Avenir was brought over first. A nervous looking creature, skittish almost, like a beaten cat. She took in the world with wide eyes and jumped at the slightest sound—something she did often in the still-crowded infirmary of the USS *Warrior*.

Yet, with just a few soothing words from Chuck—less words, really, more the kind of gentle noises one might make to a pet or baby—the creature calmed down, seeming to take in its new surroundings with curiosity. His son called her *Lily*. Good Lord, he gave the thing a name.

And yet, Mattis couldn't help but be proud. There was some part of Chuck that he had always known was there—the role of the gentle hero, the protector, nurturer, savior. Only now had he really seen it in action. And it was a sight to behold. The difference between the box-Avenir—Lily—and his escape pod-Avenir was night and day. The pod-Avenir was beaten, scarred, bleeding, and stared straight ahead of itself with no apparent expression or emotion. Lily, on the other hand … was that a smile? Good Lord, it was *smiling* at Chuck, even if for just a moment.

Steve Bratta arrived, hauling armfuls of machinery and electronics that looked like something he'd made himself in a garage—an uncased computer, wires and chips exposed, leading to three small elevated plates, each the size of a fist. The guy muttered a greeting, then started hooking up his various systems straight into the infirmary power. Mattis cast a skeptical eye over the whole setup. If that getup blew out the power relays during a crisis…

Best not to think about it.

Senator Pitt arrived next, along with Martha. Mattis caught her eye with a sly wink. Was that a blush?

Pitt dove right in. "You better have a good explanation for this, Mattis. I'm happy you've rescued him, but now your services are no longer required. I—"

"Senator? With all due respect, shut the fuck up." Mattis was tired of him. When was the next election? "I've asked you here because there are a few tests we need to make, and I want you here as a witness. So a representative of the government sees this and can testify at my inevitable senate inquiry." He paused, wondering how much he should reveal at the moment. "And you may find you have a personal stake in what is going on."

That seemed to shut him up.

Jeremy Pitt finally arrived, respectfully escorted by a lone Marine with a handgun.

"Quite the operation you've got here," said Pitt, smiling at him with a game smile that was just oh-so-Pitt. Could he *really* be a clone? The idea met resistance in Mattis's mind. Couldn't be… "The smoke and warning klaxons remind me of my last command."

Pitt's smile seemed so genuine. So real. Mattis tried hard to return it. "I suppose."

"Is there anything you need me to do? Do I get to know why I'm here?"

"Not yet," said Mattis, tapping Bratta on the shoulder. "Let's get this show on the road, shall we?"

"Yup. On it." Bratta's fingers thumped at keys at a blinding pace. "There we go." The guy took a long, deep breath, cracked his back, and then finally looked at Mattis. "Okay, Captain. I'm ready to run the test."

"I'm an Admiral," he said, pointing his shoulder. "And… go for it."

Bratta picked up a needle. He walked over to Pitt, who rolled up his sleeve. Bratta stuck the needle against his skin. For some reason, Mattis *almost* expected it to bend, break, finding Pitt's skin tough and impossible. But it went right in.

"Here we go." Bratta carefully extracted some blood from Pitt, then took another sample of blood out of the cooler. "You grandson's," he explained. He tipped it onto a plate, gently squirted some from the needle onto another, and then approached the Avenir from Reardon's ship.

"Ready?" asked Bratta. "It might sting a bit."

The creature hissed and withdrew. It looked like it might be about to tear Bratta's arm off and beat him with it.

"Here," said Chuck, taking the needle. "Let me do it."

That seemed to meet with some approval. "Ye," said the creature, rolling up her sleeve. "Ye. Protein bar."

"Okay, okay," said Chuck, laughing as he slid the needle in.

"Don't worry, you'll get another one. Just hold still for now."

"Ye," said the creature.

Bratta took the blood from Chuck, then put in on the third plate. He glanced up at the pod-Avenir with hesitation. "Think he'll let me get a sample?"

The thing stared straight ahead, unmoving, unblinking. Mattis nodded. "I don't think you'll meet any resistance from that one."

Tentatively, Bratta approached it and, inch by inch, moved the needle toward its green, muscular, bulbous arm. With one deft, quick motion, he jabbed the needle in and drew a sample, almost running backward when he finally withdrew the needle. He squirted a few drops of blood on a fourth glass plate, and inserted all of them into his home-made chamber.

"Admiral, if you would do the honors…"

"So," said Mattis, sliding over to the machine. "What do I do?"

"Just hit the *Return* key on the keyboard."

Mattis did so. The screen lit up; a bunch of symbols and letters and numbers flew across the screens, which ended in a sudden flash.

MITOCHONDRIAL MATCH

The words hit him like a hammer, eyes drifting to Commander Pitt. "Mr. Bratta. It seems all three of our guests here, and my grandson, all share the same mitochondria DNA. But … what can you tell me about Mr. Pitt?"

Bratta nodded, knowing what he was asking. He turned to the senator. "Mr. Pitt? I'll need a sample from you, too."

Senator Pitt looked as if he were about to protest, but a stern look from Mattis shut him up before he could speak. Swearing under his breath, he shoved his sleeve up and thrust it out towards Bratta, who took a quick blood sample and inserted it into the machine next to his son's.

He fiddled with the machine for a few moments, typing in a series of commands. "Just need to zero in on a few sequences here. Compare a few strands of the father's to the son's ... the effects of replication would show up in the transcription pattern of the—" he fired off a series of genetic jargon that Mattis couldn't piece together. But after a few minutes of work, muttering under his breath the whole time, Bratta finally pressed the *return* key again.

GENE REPLICATION DETECTED
CLONE PROBABILITY: 99.97%

It was true. Pitt was a clone.

Mattis turned to Senator Pitt, whose face had started to turn red. The man closed his eyes. "It's ... it's true. After Jeremy died ... I just ... I just couldn't bear it. I begged him ... I begged Spectre to—"

"You asked *Spectre* to clone your son? That madman? Do you realize who the hell you were dealing with?"

Senator Pitt stuttered and blinked. "I ... I ... no. No, I didn't. All I wanted was my son back. I couldn't lose him." He looked up at Mattis and stared him in the eye. "If it were your son, you'd do the same." He glanced over at Chuck. "And your son. Look what lengths you've gone to. To save him. To keep him."

Mattis turned to Jeremy Pitt, whose face was white. His mouth hung slack. "We're done here," Mattis said to the Marine that had escorted Jeremy in. "Take both Avenir to the brig."

Chuck's eyes widened. "Dad, no," he said, looking between him and the Avenir mutants in turn. "I promised her she wouldn't be harmed."

"And it won't." Mattis wanted to tell Chuck otherwise, but he knew Spears and Flint both would—and rightly so—have his head if he didn't contain the creature. "It's still an unstable element," he said. "We can't let it just roam around the ship. Or any other ship."

"But—"

"No." Mattis's voice turned firm. "That's it, son." Then, to Commander Pitt himself, he grimaced slightly. "We have to have a little chat."

Pitt's eyes were fixed on the monitor. On the words *CLONE PROBABILITY: 99.97%.*

Pitt stammered something nobody could understand. It seemed difficult for him to believe. Understandable, really.

"Jeremy," said Mattis, gently. "This doesn't mean—"

"You know damn fucking well what it means," spat Pitt, growling angrily and slamming his fist into the table.

The whole thing splintered and broke, sending equipment and samples sprawling out onto the deck. Such a powerful blow seemed almost superhuman—something more akin to what the Avenir might be able to dish out, not a human being.

Which raised even more questions.

Pitt stared in horror and confusion at the mess, and then turned and stormed toward the door.

The guard stepped in his way but, having just seen the display of Pitt's raw power, Mattis waved him away. Jeremy Pitt, his path unobstructed, stormed out of the infirmary.

"Seal off the deck," commanded Mattis. "Get the Rhinos in here to flush him out. Don't let regular Marines engage him, but don't let him get away, either."

"Wait," said Chuck, cautiously. "Dad, this man might well *believe* himself to be the real Jeremy Pitt. He seems to have all the man's memories, sogo easy on him, you know? Maybe try talk to him?"

Go *easy* on him? Mattis stared for a moment, but having seen Chuck's influence with his Avenir, perhaps there was something to be said for his gentle attitude.

"Wait here," said Mattis, in a tone that booked no argument. He glanced at Senator Pitt. "And you. Working with a sworn enemy of the US government? Even for you son's sake? Do you know how many lives were lost because of Spectre?" And before the other man could reply, Mattis left the infirmary, following the sound of Pitt's running footsteps.

CHAPTER FIFTY-EIGHT

Patricia "Guano" Corrick's J-88
Vellini, Atmosphere
Vellini System
Tiberius Sector

Guano's J-88 descended into the atmosphere, roughly following the trajectory Roadie's doomed bird had taken. Soon their ship was engulfed in flames, yellow-orange angry tongues of fire licking the sides of her cockpit.

"So, uh," said Flatline, his tone slightly high-pitched, as though he were talking to keep his nerves in check. "Have you ever heard that song? *All Along The Watchtower*. Do you think that song could be about us?"

Guano stared at her console, monitoring her angle of attacks so they didn't burn up. "How could a song that's hundreds of years old be about us?"

"Well," said Flatline, "we could be the two riders. You know."

Guano tapped a couple of keys, adjusting their course slightly, dipping their nose. "You're a rider. I'm a driver. It doesn't work. It's stupid."

"Okay," said Flatline, dejectedly.

In a few moments, the flames died down and they were flying in the upper atmosphere of Vellini. Her computer helpfully displayed the location of Roadie and Frost's transponders, painting them on her HUD as green boxes. There were heavy winds and storms in the area they had ejected into; landing in a computer-stabalized strike craft was one thing, but to do so in a parachute with limited control...

"Jeez," said Flatline, obviously looking at the same data. "Roadie's pucker factor must be like 9.7 right now."

"He's a big boy," she said. "He can handle it."

"He's a big boy?" echoed Roadie, teasing. "Well, you'd know, wouldn't you?"

Him bringing up that years ago she and Roadie had shared a drunken, sloppy fuck after too much tequila would normally drive her to retaliate, but instead she just focused on the task at hand. Retrieving Frost and Roadie and bringing them back safely to the *Stennis*. "Okay," she said.

A moment's quiet between the two. "Hey, it was just a joke."

"I know."

"Then why are you making this all weird?"

She turned the ship to avoid some high altitude cloud, continuing to dive down toward the signal. "I'm not. You're the one making it weird. It was years ago."

"I know. That's what makes it funny."

Guano dove below the cloud cover, revealing the surface

of Vellini. It was horizon to horizon junk, dotted with green/brown pools that looked gross even at high altitude. A cluttered city was on the horizon, but even from this distance it looked ... dirty. The whole planet was covered in *stuff*. Coolant tanks, trash, even a massive, rusted starship hull. A billion people lived on this planet, but how they actually lived here, on a giant pile of junk, was a mystery.

She thumbed her radio key. "This is Tornado 1-2, we're atmospheric and searching for ejected pilots. Stand by for updates."

"This is crazy," muttered Flatline. "We'll never get them back even if we could find them."

Tuning him out, Guano dove down until she was barely a few hundred meters off the ground, leveled out, then flew toward the beacon. After a moment, she saw the green smoke that the ejection seats automatically gave out in atmospheres. It was coming from a series of truck wrecks, half-rusted out and buried in garbage.

She extended the landing struts, then set the ship down.

"Okay," she said, popping open the cockpit canopy, immediately glad she couldn't smell anything with her suit on. "There are plenty of scavengers who live in this place, so if you see anyone who isn't Frost or Roadie ... shoot to kill."

"Yeah, because I usually just shoot to *miss*." Flatline climbed out the cockpit behind her. "Dumbass."

Guano swung herself out of the cockpit, landing with a wet *splat* on the ground. Gravity was minimal on this place, which was good. "There's the ejection seat," she said. "Roadie won't be far."

The two of them set out, passing the ejection seat and

walking away from their ship, through the endless piles of junk.

"Watch that green shit," said Flatline, pointing to one of the green/brown lakes she'd seen from above. "It's some bioengineered fungus they use to break down the junk. If it gets inside your suit, not only will it kill you, it will hurt the whole time you're dying."

"Awesome," she said, touching her radio. There was a faint buzzing noise in her ears, and she wasn't sure whether it was coming from her radio or from inside her head. "Hey Roadie, you out there?"

No answer. However, from the green smoke of the ejection seat, a space-suited figure emerged. Through the glass she could see Roadie's face. He waved to her, then tapped the side of his head. Radio failure. Typical problem with ejection.

Guano smiled, raised her pistol and shot him twice.

Roadie slumped toward her, face a shocked mask, then fell face-forward into the garbage.

"Holy *shit!*" Flatline shrieked beside her. "P-Patricia, what the fuck—holy shit—what the—"

She turned and shot him too, putting two rounds into his gut.

Silence.

Guano stood there, staring down the sights of her weapon as smoke trailed out from the barrel. And then, as though coming out of a strange trance, she realized the enormity of what she'd just done.

No. No!

The pistol fell out of her grip, falling into the garbage. Flatline wasn't moving. Just laying there, crumpled in a heap on his side.

She slumped in the garbage, hands seeking the bullet wounds on Flatline's space suit. "Deshawn," she said, her breath coming in tearful, ragged gasps. "I'm—oh my god, I didn't mean to. It just—I didn't—"

The buzzing returned. Forcing her back into the battle fugue. Forcing her mind out. Forcing her to do things.

No!

Her hands searched in the garbage. Looking for the pistol she'd dropped. She couldn't let them control her anymore—she couldn't. Where was the gun, where—

There it was. The grip poking out of a pile of trash. The buzzing in her ears intensified, maddening. She snatched the weapon up and put it to her temple.

The buzzing reached a crescendo.

Slowly, Guano lowered the weapon. She pressed it into Flatline's hand. With careful deliberation, she walked over to Roadie's body, picked up his firearm and fired it twice into the air. She dropped it down by his body, too, and then walked back to her ship.

After a moment's consideration, she knew she couldn't go back to the *Stennis*. Too many questions. She programmed in a course to the USS *Warrior*, the flagship of their reinforcing fleet, then powered her ship up. She took off, flew out of the atmosphere, and radioed the *Warrior* for landing clearance.

And it all felt so natural.

CHAPTER FIFTY-NINE

Sickbay
USS Warrior
Vellini, High Orbit
Vellini System
Tiberius Sector

Bratta leaned up against a desk in the infirmary. Mattis had run after Pitt, the Senator and the journalist had left, Chuck Mattis had accompanied one of the future-humans being escorted out by Marines and had left his infant in the care of a nurse who was overseeing the final administration of the retro-virus that would cure him. And when they were all finally gone, Bratta let out a long sigh he didn't realize he'd been holding.

Well that... could have been a *lot* more awkward. But a lot less, too. A solid four out of five. Better than usual.

Pitt was a clone. Fascinating. The amount of cellular augmentation required to turn a normal human into one of those *things* was well beyond him. If only he'd spent more time working at Maxgainz before he'd recorded that escaped mutant and escaped himself to broadcast it to the galaxy.

The more interesting thing was how they infused the clone with all of Pitt's memories. Did they extract them from his corpse? From a point before his death, then extrapolate? Wondering about the mechanisms of extracting memories from a dead man was a lovely mental exercise that he let his brain run through until it was interrupted by a familiar voice.

"Ah, Mister Bratta." Commander Modi smiled politely as he stepped through the doorway to the infirmary. "It is good to see you here."

Fortunately, Bratta noticed, many of the sick and injured had now been evacuated and many of the alarms were off. How long had he been standing there, lost in thought? He had to stop doing that. It was one of the reasons why Jeannie left him. "It's good to see you, too!" Bratta positively beamed. "Whatever can I do for you, Mister Modi?"

"Well," said Modi, his normally calm exterior overlaying an obvious undercurrent of excitement. "I heard you were aboard and was hoping you might be able to take a look at something for me."

Oh, will you just look at some science stuff? Finally, after months of living in a bar, followed by days of being trapped on that ship with the Reardons? How could he say no? "I'd love to," said Bratta. "I'm your chap."

"Great." Modi took out a datastick. "Here. It's an analysis of the data from the wrecked Avenir ship. I'd like you to run the program on this disk and—"

Bratta practically snatched the thing away, gleefully plugged it in, and then switched programs on his terminal to the program on the device. Finally, a non-genetics problem to work on. From behind, someone bumped into him; a pilot wearing a flight suit.

"Sorry," she said.

Distraction. Bratta paid the woman no further heed. A few taps of the keys executed the program and examined its output. After a brief moment that he presumed the program spent calibrating itself to his esoteric hardware, it then began to hum away, running through the calculations Modi had pre-stored on it, and prepared to make them human-readable.

"What seems to be the problem?" asked Bratta as the machine worked, a simple blinking bar on the terminal that read *LOADING*.

"Simply put," said Modi, leaning up against the table, "this is a program which is used to interpolate real space speed and direction from Z-Space trajectory. It has a result stored on it, and I trust that result because the program obviously works; it produces a vector into real space, absolutely. But it took an *enormous* amount of computing power to produce this result because it had a strange element present in the calculations that introduced constant errors that had be be identified and trimmed. This made it a non-deterministic polynomal, turning a simple P-hard problem into an NP-hard one."

Oh, brother. Bratta had conducted no small amount of computer science. NP-hard was a problem that broke computers' brains; like trying to write down every possible combination of chess pieces.

A hint of caution crept into Modi's voice. "Is this where you ask me to repeat what I said in English, probably with an overly thick Texan drawl?"

Bratta smiled and shook his head. "No, I totally understood. There is no need to simplify."

"You are the best," Modi said with solemn relief.

The terminal chirped, indicating that it had verified the calculations as presented. There it was; a course through space. As Bratta scrolled through the numbers, his brow creased. Something was off about it. Something was strange—not in the data, but in what it was discarding. The trimmed tree branches. The rogue element that was messing things up.

"What do you think?" asked Modi, curiously.

The junk data. He scrolled through it, trying to find some kind of pattern. "I'm not sure," he said, cautiously. "Where is this data from again?"

"From when we first discovered the Avenir ship back at Erebus in this solar system. The ship has since exploded, but something about this data has tugged at something in the back of my mind, too. It doesn't add up. We attached a tracking device to its hull right before it entered Z-Space, which is how we knew to come here to Vellini. But something about the data…."

Bratta frowned and sifted through. "If you ask me, it looks like there was a second ship in close proximity. That's the only explanation here. A second ship entered Z-Space with it, at the same time, at almost the exact same position."

"Two?" Modi stared. "No, I was present at the battle. Only a single ship escaped."

Bratta tapped on a series of keys, copying the junk data into its own dataset, then feeding it into the algorithm

"That will take *months*," said Modi, aghast. "Months on military supercomputers. On *this* thing it will take—"

Chirp. His computer spat out the result. Bratta pointed at the screen and what it so clearly, so painfully showed.

The junk data was another Z-Space vector. That's what had been confusing the analytics; just as it entered Z-Space, another ship had joined it. Had it been stealthed or photonically cloaked somehow?

Either way, the Avenir ship that had decimated the American fleet, that had killed thousands, had not been alone.

CHAPTER SIXTY

Sickbay
USS Warrior
Vellini, High Orbit
Vellini System
Tiberius Sector

Mattis could see that Jeremy was rattled.

The guy had just learned he was a copy of a man now almost certainly dead. That would be a blow to anyone. Still, Mattis followed at a cautious distance, until finally Pitt stopped walking, glaring over his shoulder in a distinctly ominous way.

"Ready to talk about it, Commander Pitt?" asked Mattis, cautiously, suddenly reminded of the powerful outburst in the lab. If Pitt decided to fold him into a pretzel, there would be nothing he could do about it.

"That's not even really my name, is it?" asked Pitt, in a way which did not invite a genuine answer.

Dammit. What would Chuck say? Something inspiring,

something soothing, something encouraging, something…

"Your name is whatever you want it to be. Your life is whatever you want it to be."

Pitt turned to him, eyes flashing a dark red. "I want to be myself," he said. "Commander Pitt. United States Navy. But my body? It came out of a laboratory. How do I even know that the thoughts in my head are my own? Not some… dark impulse imparted by whoever did this to me. I owe it to…" his voice trailed off, unable to find a satisfactory answer. "I owe it to…"

"If your body came out of a vat, and your mind came out of a computer, then what do you owe anyone?"

Pitt thought for a second, his features softening. "I owe it to *myself*. To everyone around me. I have to find out the truth. About who I am. Or … *what* I am."

Cautiously, Mattis stepped forward and, reaching up, clapped the tall man on the shoulder. "I think you already have it figured out."

Pitt smiled, weakly, but it was there. "Okay. I should—I should go back to the *Stennis*. Help Captain Flint with whatever he needs."

Mattis wasn't entirely comfortable with the idea of a clone of Pitt wandering around, even if it did have the man's memories and, seemingly, his personality and ambitions. But Chuck was right. If he thought he was Pitt, then he'd act like Pitt.

"Okay." Mattis knew better than to tie himself up in knots over something he had little control over. They were in a crisis. He would have to act. "Just take it easy, okay? And make sure you go with an escort. Just… for your own protection."

"I will." Pitt gave a crisp salute. "Thanks for the, uh, the pep talk, Admiral."

Mattis saluted back. "Any time."

Pitt turned and began walking to the hangar bay, disappearing down the corridor, a Marine following close behind. Mattis watched him go with cautious eyes, wondering if he had done the right thing.

"How'd it go?" asked Chuck, behind him. Mattis knew better than to ask how long he'd been standing there. His son had better manners than to approach a conversation he had no business overhearing.

How *had* it gone? It was difficult to say. They were in the middle of a crisis, so this was no time to overanalyze everything, but… eh. There would be time enough in the future to second guess his decisions. "Fine," said Mattis, shaking his head.

"Sounds like it wasn't really fine," Chuck said, gently. "Sounds like the fights you and mom used to have. Back when we were broke and struggling—before… before mom left."

Mattis managed a half smile. "Not going to lie, being a nillionaire living on a junior officer's salary with a bratty twelve-year-old wasn't exactly how I anticipated my life to be going at that point."

"Nillionaire," said Chuck, smiling too. "I liked that word. It was… you know, it was a way to think about being flat broke in a way that made it seem much nicer than the reality." He snorted playfully. "You remember when we used to go out to the range, and you let me collect all your spent brass? You'd just gone through basic, so you were all… *police that brass, seaman!* Using the drill instructor voice. And then, when I got to shoot, I was all like, *you better police your brass!*"

Wistful memories, somewhat disrupted by the reality of their situation. "I remember," said Mattis, his eyes falling back to the piece strapped to Chuck's hip. "I see that thing you're carrying, too. I haven't forgotten."

"I know how to use it," said Chuck, somewhat defensively. "You taught me."

"When you were a kid," said Mattis. A twinge in his right shoulder made him wince. The painkiller might be wearing off…

"I've been practicing. I actually wanted to take Elroy out to the range soon—he says he hates guns, but I think I can bring him around. Start him out on a nice .22 or air rifle or something, work our way up to a manly 10mm."

It was nice to have a genuine conversation with his son that wasn't about him getting arrested or some kind of terrible calamity. "I remember the first time you shot a 10mm," he said, smile growing. "I was like… *okay, champ, you gotta hold her tight, because she kicks…*"

"Ha!" Chuck snapped his fingers. "*Champ.* That's what you used to call me, champ. Chuck the Champ…"

The two laughed, a moment of togetherness that lasted far shorter than Mattis would've liked. There was still some underlying tension there, but Chuck was making an obvious effort. And Mattis was more than happy to let him.

"Okay," he said, "we should get back to the infirmary and pry Modi and Bratta apart before they get married or something."

Chuck snorted. "Bratta? I know he has that crazy ex-wife of his, but…"

Mattis sighed. "Look, when those two get together, it's like they're speaking another language. The language of tech and love."

"Ask him about the mechanical bull sometime," said Chuck, a mischievous glint in his eyes. "He loves telling that story. Trust me."

The two walked back to the infirmary—it wasn't that far away—and when they got there, Mattis felt like they had, genuinely, crossed some kind of threshold. Not quite forgiveness, not quite reconciliation, but the start of something.

"Okay," said Mattis, stepping through the threshold and giving Modi and Bratta a polite nod. "How did it go with you two?"

"We found something important, Admiral," said Modi. The guy's whole face seemed to be twitching as though he was struggling to maintain his composure. "There was another vessel that left with the Avenir ship back at Erebus. That's what was causing the computers to struggle putting together a flight vector; interference from the other ship's presence."

Mattis's stomach clenched again. Another ship. Stealthed or cloaked? Like the Avenir vessels in the original attack on Earth?

Mattis considered that. "We need to track that other ship," he said firmly. "Modi, you're with me. Are the *Warrior*'s engines in shape enough to give pursuit?"

"Yes, sir."

"Then let's move. Given what this Avenir ship did to us, I hate to think what another would do in the hands of the Forgotten. Or whoever is controlling them." He glanced at his son. "You good here? Might I suggest you remove my grandson from a war zone?"

"Right," said Chuck. He turned to one of the nurses. "Hi, can I have Jack, please?"

"Oh," said the nurse, smiling politely. "His mother already got him."

Both Mattis's eyes nearly fell out. Chuck stammered, "His —his mother?"

The nurse nodded politely. "That's right," she said. "She was here about, oh, five minutes ago. Walked in, thanked me, picked him up, and walked out."

Chuck made a noise like a strangled goose. "There's no— she's not—that's simply—"

Mattis wheeled to Modi and Bratta. "You two," he said, fighting to keep calm. "Did you see a woman come in?"

"Yes," said Modi, crisply. "She entered. A pilot. She was still wearing her flight suit. I assumed she was here for medical attention and payed her no mind."

"Did she leave with Jack?" asked Mattis.

Modi's hesitation showed he didn't know.

"Don't worry," said Mattis to Chuck, his tone conveying a confidence he didn't feel. "We'll get him back. Whoever she was, she couldn't have gotten far."

CHAPTER SIXTY-ONE

Sickbay
USS Warrior
Vellini, High Orbit
Vellini System
Tiberius Sector

Mattis took a deep breath to calm himself down. Panic wouldn't solve anything.

Chuck, unfortunately, didn't seem to have that presence of mind. He was shouting at the nurse. A whole bunch of unhelpful things. Things like threatening to sue her. Or throw her out an airlock.

Mattis put a hand on his son's shoulder. "Lemme handle this," he said, then turned to the understandably upset nurse. "I need a description of the woman who was just here."

She was obviously rattled, but with a little coaching he got what he needed. Then Mattis touched his radio. "This is Admiral Mattis to anyone who can receive this transmission.

Priority alert." The words left a sour taste in his mouth. "One of our strike craft pilots, copilots, navigators, or gunners has been identified as the principle actor in a child abduction." He relayed the physical description he had been given, trying to include as much detail as he could. "Anyone who can identify this person is ordered to contact me on this frequency, stat. Mattis out."

Almost immediately, his radio chirped back. "Admiral Mattis, this is Lieutenant Finlay with the Strike Group. That sounds like Guano—I mean, Lieutenant Patricia Corrick. From the USS *Stennis*. Over."

Patricia Corrick. That name struck a bell. Doctor Brooks had mentioned her … she was the pilot who had some kind of strange battle hypnosis happening.

A powerful sinking feeling took hold in his gut. "Thank you, Lieutenant. Mattis out." He changed frequencies. "Mattis to *Caernavron*. FLASH traffic. I need to speak to *Caernavron* actual."

Spears's voice greeted him, her composure returned. "This is Spears. Send it."

"One of our pilots from the *Stennis* is the mole." He knew such a bold declaration over an unsecured channel was a risk, but he didn't care. "She took Ja …a baby from the *Warrior*. It's a long story, but it doesn't matter: I need you to order every strike craft in the whole fleet that is currently active to hold their positions. All engines stop. Review the logs; ID any fighters docking with, or leaving, the USS *Warrior* and bring them in. Be advised: an infant child will be present, so all weapons tight. I say again: don't shoot, no matter what they do. But, you know, feel free to paint them with targeting lasers and other bullshit to make them think we might."

"Solid copy on all," said Spears, her clipped consonants icy. "I'll make it happen."

Security staff ran into the room, pistols drawn. Mattis waved them away. They could do no good here. Plus the ship needed hands to effect repairs.

Another transmission cut in over the line. "Admiral Mattis," said a cool, even voice he didn't recognize. Male. "This is John Smith. CIA. I'm calling you from the *Aerostar*."

Well, now. That was unexpected. Mattis looked at Chuck.

"I think it's a fake name too," said Chuck, unhelpfully. But Mattis appreciated the impulse.

"We're busy here," he said. "How can you help me, Mister Smith?"

"I'll keep this brief," he replied. "I have been inspecting a database recovered from the offices of Jovian Logistics, and I've come up with a working theory about what's been causing all these issues. Specifically, the Forgotten are just scapegoats—pawns in a much bigger plot. Namely, a man named Spectre is using these kids as a fresh source of DNA to use in cloning and human enhancement experiments."

No. Mattis had no time for this. "*Was.* Spectre is dead, Agent Smith," he said. "I killed him myself. It cost me my ship. Talk to me when you have something more concrete than this *theory.*"

"Wait," said Smith. "You don't understand. He was tinkering with, well, with brains. He was exploring radical surgical techniques. Genetic engineering. There's more to this, Admiral. I promise you."

"Do you know what that more *is*?"

Smith hesitated. "Not exactly. There are a lot of puzzle pieces here."

There might very well be, but he had no time for it. His grandson was missing. "Okay, great. Get back to me when you have something definite." He closed the line.

"Admiral Mattis." Spears's voice returned, calm and collected. "We've detected a strike craft that isn't obeying the stand-down directive. Logs show it docked with the USS *Warrior* only a few minutes ago. It's a two-seater craft... could well be transporting an infant."

His stomach did its thing where it tightened in his chest. That was *not* what he had hoped for. It was so much more difficult to secure a strike craft by force. "Okay," he said, lacking any other alternative. "Damn. Okay."

"There's something else," said Spears. "Break." She had a brief conversation with Blackwood, dull and muted, inaudible. Then she was back. "A ship is coming out of Z-Space. It's completing its translation now... damn. It's another one of them. Another Avenir ship."

The other ship Modi's data had uncovered.

"I don't like the sound of that."

"It gets worse," she said, energy creeping in. "That rogue strike craft is heading straight for it."

Surrounded by nurses and beeping equipment, Mattis could do nothing but sit there in helpless rage as the minutes ticked away.

The radio crackled.

"They got away," said Spears. "The strike craft docked with the Avenir vessel and escaped into Z-Space. I'm—I'm sorry, Jack."

Mattis looked to Chuck, took in his despairing face, then his own hardened. "I'm on the way to the bridge," he said, taking a deep breath.

"We'll send over a shuttle," said Spears.

"Okay," said Mattis, turning to leave. "But not for me. Take Chuck instead. Break." He muted the conversation, holding up a finger to cut off Chuck's inevitable protest. "Son, you can't be here. This ship is badly damaged and about to get into another shooting match. You'll be safer on the *Caernarvon*."

Chuck opened his mouth as though to argue, then closed it again. "Make it the *Stennis*," he said, firmly. "I'll keep an eye on Jeremy Pitt for you. And Lily. I just want to do something useful to keep my mind off things."

That seemed reasonable. Mattis hesitated a moment— some strange instinct in him said to say no—but he pushed that nonsense away. "Okay. Inform the shuttle pilot when they come across." He reopened the channel. "*Caernarvon*, I say again, I won't be coming back. Instead, have Chuck Mattis transported to the *Stennis*."

"Acknowledged," said Spears. "I'll send him over. With you vouching for him, I'm sure Flint won't mind." She paused just a fraction of a second. "And what about you?"

"Be advised," said Mattis. "I mean to take the *Warrior* bridge and assume command of what's left of the fleet. Captain Spears, contact Flint on the *Stennis*. Time for them to really stretch their legs and test out those new fangled Chinese engines of theirs—when I used them on the Midway they were a sight to behold. Hell, bring the *Aerostar* in on this too. We're getting my grandson back."

CHAPTER SIXTY-TWO

Bridge
USS Warrior
Vellini, High Orbit
Vellini System
Tiberius Sector

Mattis had seen a lot of bridges in crisis in his time as a military officer, having served both in the Sino-American war and humanity's more recent struggles, but he'd rarely seen anything like this.

The armored casemate that protected the bridge had been significantly affected by the gravity weapon and had spalled; its surface was crushed and sprayed out shards of metal across the whole of the bridge, slicing through computers, monitors, deck, bulkheads, and flesh.

It was obvious now what had caused Admiral Fischer's injuries, and how serious they must have been to get her all the way from the bridge to the hangar bay in such short time.

"Report," he said, eyes searching the bloodied, blackened faces, looking for the most senior officer available.

"Admiral Mattis?" asked some… butterbar—a fresh-faced ensign whose blond hair stood out from his smoke-darkened face like some kind of glowing white moss. "Is that really you?"

Apparently his reputation proceeded him. "Yes," he said, adopting the same voice he used to use on Chuck when he was struggling as a kid. "It is. Now, Ensign, your report."

The guy stared at him with dull eyes. Mattis recognized shock when he saw it. "Uhh, I'm Ensign Tom Calaway. Helmsman. Fischer's in the sickbay on the *Stennis*, sir. And so is the XO. Senior chief petty officer is dead. Watchkeeping officer is dead. The chain of command is pretty broken at this point, sir."

That wasn't a good report. Not good at all. But it could have been worse. "Status on the engines?"

"They're functional, sir," said Calaway, curious. "Do we need to move somewhere to assist rescue efforts?"

"Can't do that yet," said Mattis, firmly. "What about radar? Weapons?"

"Working," said one of the other junior officers, her head and right eye swathed in bandages. "Sir, are we under attack?"

Not yet, but… Mattis turned back to Calaway. "Son, I need a no-bullshit assessment. This ship has hull integrity, it has weapons, it has radar, it has engines. It has skin, fists, eyes, and legs. Is the *Warrior* combat capable? Can it enter Z-Space?"

Calaway looked around at the other officers, obviously afraid. But then he steeled himself and turned back to Mattis. "We're ready to fight," he said. "We're just lacking command.

Fists, but no brains, sir. And the Z-Space engines on these old frigates are solid. They're usually the last system to go down. They made them to last."

"Good." Mattis glanced to the communications station. "Open a channel to the *Caernarvon*. I want to speak to Captain Spears."

With a tap of keys, the channel was open. "USS *Warrior*, HMS *Caernarvon*." The line was and weak full of static; Spears's voice sounded like she was underwater. "This is Caernarvon actual. Send it."

"Mattis here. I've assumed command of the *Warrior*. She's a strong ship with a good crew. We're ready to fight, Captain."

"Good. Captain Flint reports he's calculated a pursuit course using Mister Modi's algorithm. Captain Reardon on the *Aerostar* is reporting that he's received the data and is green light for this mission. We're getting ready to execute a Z-Space translation. Are you able to accompany?"

"Absolutely," he said.

Calaway spoke up. "But, sir?" he said, his voice losing some of its bluster. Mattis muted the line. "Shouldn't we wait for the rest of the fleet?"

Three ships would be enough, and he simply couldn't not go after Jack. "Negative. I intend to pursue and engage a hostile ship. If you have an objection, log it in the ship's log. For now, I am in command."

Calaway hesitated again but then, with a nod, seemed to overcome it. "We're ready to fight, sir."

"Very well." He opened the channel again. His shoulder was aching, but he gritted his teeth and ignored it. He'd take another painkiller soon enough. "*Caernarvon*, *Warrior*. We are ready to execute a Z-Space translation. Relay us the coordinates and we'll guard your back."

CHAPTER SIXTY-THREE

Infirmary
USS Warrior
Z-Space

Bratta felt that creeping nemesis of his, boredom, slowly return. Rather than let his mind wander, he instead turned his attention back to his terminal.

Acquiring DNA from a second live mutant would be a valuable boon to his research. The mitochondrial discovery was important, but there was just so much other information DNA could tell them. Things they could learn. Idly, Bratta began running a full analysis on Pitt's DNA. So much of it was similar to their... *guest* aboard the *Aerostar*. There were differences, of course. Differences that would lead to facial structure, skin tone. All that lovely stuff.

The genetic code information flashed by on his screen in two columns. Where the two sets of DNA matched, it was green. Where it didn't, it was red. Almost every single instance was green. The two were practically clones of each other as well—not surprising given their DNA was spun in a lab.

Then something did surprise him. A huge chunk of red. *Huge.* As though a whole organ was entirely exempt from whatever cloning process had been used on Pitt. Bratta let the program work, scrolling back up. A whole organ… unclear which one. The Avenir on the *Aerostar* had it. Pitt didn't.

It made no sense.

"Hey Modi," he asked over his shoulder. "Come check this out."

He sensed, rather than saw, Modi moving up behind him. "I am here," he said, leaning in to examine the screen. "What seems to be the…" his tone faded off. "But this makes no sense."

"I know," said Bratta, dumbfounded. "They edited out something. A whole organ."

"Why would they do that?" asked Modi, shaking his head. "Every organ in the human body, future-mutant or not, serves a purpose. Even if a person can live without them, such a thing is not advantageous. Was this… some attempt to optimize?"

Bratta tried matching the data to a reference schematic of the body. "It's unclear what the organ actually is."

Modi scanned his data. "Mr. Bratta. You have the caps lock on. Did you realize that?"

Bratta blushed. "Uh—yes. Of course, Mr. Modi. Let me just click that off…"

Modi looked askance at him. "Mr. Bratta. Why do you have a caps lock key on your terminal? Those are centuries outdated."

"I like old things."

Bratta tapped on keys, now realizing why the data wasn't lining up—just a stupid computer misinterpreting his commands. Well, computers weren't stupid—just the stupid people programming and using them. He entered the command to isolate the missing organ.

The answer came up almost immediately.

Brain.

Bratta stared mutely at the screen as it displayed the answer.

"That is not possible," said Modi. "There must be some kind of…"

"Some kind of bug," echoed Bratta. Obviously Pitt had a *brain*, you idiot. But…

"Wait." Modi snapped his fingers. "Maybe Pitt's body was grown without a brain because…"

The realization hit Bratta in a flash. "Because they were going to put one into it."

CHAPTER SIXTY-FOUR

Hangar Bay
USS Stennis
Z-Space

Chuck rode the shuttle to the *Stennis* in silence, docking right before the great warship slipped into Z-Space.

He had volunteered to keep an eye on Pitt and Lily, but in truth, he just needed to be off that ship. He had spent only an hour or so on the *Warrior* and Jack had been stolen by … by one of their own pilots.

The *Stennis* wasn't the place for him either, but going to the *Caernarvon,* where he knew nobody and had nothing to do but think, would be bad for him. Going back to the *Aerostar* minus his kid would be even worse. Harry would ask questions, Sammy would ask questions… He couldn't face them now. The same reason he couldn't go to the infirmary and look Bratta in the eye.

He had to get Jack back.

The baby consumed his every thought. Jack… Jack.

What would Elroy say?

What if they couldn't get him back? What would Elroy say *then*?

My God. Jack.

Every time he thought about it his whole body ached, as though a tiny black hole were swallowing up his insides and devouring him from within.

He wandered the hallways of the *Stennis* aimlessly, his mind turned inward.

"Mister Mattis," said Jeremy Pitt, approaching him in the corridor, shadowed by an armed Marine. He nodded politely. "I saw the request for you to come aboard. Welcome to the USS *Stennis*."

It was difficult to make small talk, but Chuck knew that the likelihood of Pitt just *randomly bumping into him* down here in the shuttle bay was astronomically low. Pitt must be trying to talk to him specifically. He must have heard about what happened.

"Thank you for not making a scene," he said. "And, you know. Coming to see me."

Pitt gestured for him to follow. "Let's have a chat," he said.

It made sense. Chuck *was* here to keep an eye on him after all. He fell into step with the clone man, trying desperately not to think about Jack. "So, uh, where are we going?"

"I can't discuss the ship's movements with a civilian," said Pitt, although his tone was gentle. "Not even the Admiral's son. Sorry."

"Got it."

Pitt led him toward a small room off the corridor leading

away from the shuttle bay. It was small and cramped, with just a small table and four chairs inside. Chuck stepped in first. Pitt's escort followed behind the pair of them. Pitt held up a hand. "May we speak in private?" The Marine hesitated, but then nodded, not seeing the harm in standing guard outside the tiny room.

"So," said Pitt, gesturing for him to sit with one hand once the door was closed, his other tucked formally behind his back. "Why don't you tell me what happened?"

Although he wanted nothing more than to not think about it, talking was good. Chuck relayed to Pitt, briefly but accurately, what had happened in the *Warrior*'s infirmary after Pitt had left in a hurry.

"I see," said Pitt, nodding understandingly, both hands cupped behind his back. There was some edge, some twist in his voice that Chuck couldn't really read, but he ignored it. "You must be very concerned."

"I am," said Chuck, closing his eyes for a moment. "He's just a baby. I just brought him aboard for a test, that's all. That's all. I didn't want this to happen."

"I meant," said Pitt, a slow smile creeping across his features, "you must be concerned for yourself."

That confused him. Chuck raised an eyebrow. "What?"

The door to the conference room opened. Captain Flint stepped through. "Commander Pitt, what the hell did you ask me down here for? Don't you know we're heading into a potential war zone? Get the hell back up to the bridge," he thumbed behind him toward the door.

"Well," said Pitt, moving his hands from behind his back, revealing a pistol. A chromed 9mm pistol with selective fire.

Chuck's pistol. He didn't even glance at Flint, whose eyes had gone wide at the sight of the gun in Pitt's hands. "Aren't you concerned that they will blame you for the child's disappearance? And for this?"

Chuck could only stammer, his hand instinctively reaching for his hip. But, of course, the pistol was in Pitt's hand.

Pitt leveled it at Flint's face. "Are you ready to die, Captain?"

Flint glared at him, saying nothing.

Chuck pushed back his chair, standing up. "Wait," he said, "what the hell—"

The pistol roared. Flint's head exploded into gory chunks. His lifeless body slumped against the door, sliding slowly, almost deliberately, down to the deck. Pitt emptied the magazine into him, blasting the lifeless body a dozen times.

Chuck stared. In his periphery, he thought he heard someone banging on the door and shouting. The Marine escort, most likely. But he couldn't take his eyes off the blood. The brains. The body.

Pitt turned to him, slowly and deliberately, gun smoke trailing from his weapon, rising like a tiny ghost.

Chuck mutely shook his head, unable to process what he was seeing. What was happening, why was all of this happening…

The pistol's butt clubbed his temple, sending him sprawling. The weapon clattered down beside him, and as he blacked out, he could hear Pitt talking into his radio.

"Security Alert Team to conference room two, Chuck Mattis has murdered Captain Flint."

And then he passed out.

CHAPTER SIXTY-FIVE

Bridge
USS Warrior
Z-Space

The *Warrior* groaned as it slipped into Z-Space, bathing the whole of the bridge in multicolored hues. For a moment, Mattis thought he'd pushed the ship too far—it was damaged, after all—but the noise faded after it transitioned. As his newly acquired ship sailed on, he began to relax his grip on the command chair's armrests.

This was the right decision.

The shift changed and he let anyone who still had replacements available swap out. Calaway, to his credit, had someone available, but stayed anyway.

He would need people like him in the future.

"Sir," said Calaway, his voice breaking the tense silence on the bridge. "Fleet Command on Earth is signaling us." His fresh face grimaced. "Something about … stealing a ship. And returning it immediately."

"Ignore them on my authority." He felt a vague stab of guilt. So many officers following his commands were sinking their careers. He was, after all, chasing after his stolen grandson. There was no other reason, not really. And commandeering a starship for a purely personal reason was naturally frowned upon. "Establish an uplink with Fleet Command. Transmit them copies of the ship's log. I want them to know that I'm issuing the orders and that I'm responsible for all that has happened. If there's punishment in the future for this, it should be reserved for me and me alone."

A ripple of relief ran through the bridge. If anyone had lodged their complaints, they had done so electronically. He had no doubts most of them would want to preserve their hard-earned appointments after all of this was done. But, to their credit, nobody had said anything openly.

And he hoped that, more than preserve their careers, they'd want to preserve humanity.

The *Warrior* was beaten, bloody, and wounded, but she was ready to go for round two.

On the Z-Space monitor, the *Stennis*, using her powerful upgraded engines—Chinese systems that Spectre had used to open portals to the future—began to pull away from the *Warrior*. It felt odd to no longer be at the tip of the spear, but Mattis accepted it. Given the circumstances, this was the best he could ask for.

The *Stennis* caught up to their target, the two dots merging on his screen. Then both translated from Z-Space. They were back at Erebus, the gas giant where they had first detected the original Avenir ship. Mattis could only imagine the battle taking place there. Flashes of cannon fire in the dark of space, missiles and strike fighters, and the occasional torpedo.

A signal flashed on his command console. "Sir," said Calaway, "we're receiving an audiovisual signal from the USS *Stennis*."

"Put it through," he said. The main monitor flickered, and an image of Commander Pitt came through. Mattis adjusted himself in his seat. "Jeremy. How's the engagement going?"

Pitt didn't smile back. His expression was grave. "Admiral Jack Mattis," said Pitt, his tone somber. "Captain Flint is dead. Your son, Chuck Mattis, murdered him."

Whatever he thought Pitt was going to tell him, that was not it. Mattis just stared at the screen in dull bewilderment. "What did you say?"

"He had a pistol. Somehow you neglected to tell us that fact when requesting he come aboard." His tone turned dark. "What the bloody hell were you thinking?"

It was true. Chuck *did* have a gun. But he knew how to use it, and it hadn't been a problem. Chuck didn't even *know* Flint. Why would he shoot him?

It made no sense. It made no sense at all. And, for just a moment, Mattis almost missed the strange turn of phrase Pitt had used. *Bloody hell…*

His communicator chirped. He ignored it, but the device kept buzzing incessantly. Hoping it was Chuck, he waved for his communications officer to mute the microphone, anxiously picking up his personal device.

"Admiral," said Modi on the other end, "listen to me very carefully, and answer my question with a brief yes or no. Is Commander Pitt with you?"

Still stunned, Mattis struggled to get words out. He glanced at Pitt's audiovisual. The kid was watching his every move. "N-no. He isn't."

"Very good," said Modi. "Admiral, we are in great danger. Pitt *is* a clone, but he is much more than that—he is a clone grown *without a brain*. That is not his mind in there. It's not Pitt. Someone else is inhabiting his body. Some other brain was put inside."

"Admiral Mattis," asked Pitt through the line, "respond please."

He closed the link with Modi and unmuted his connection to Pitt. "What do you want me to do, Jeremy?" he asked, carefully.

"Power down your engines. You don't need to join this fight. We'll handle it from here."

"I'm afraid I can't do that," said Mattis, politely. "My son's child is there. I'm coming to get him."

"Have you forgotten your duty?" Pitt—or the creature pretending to be Pitt—scowled at him over the video. "The ship we are pursuing has submitted to boarding. We'll have the captured child returned. Spears and her ship should return to the rest of the fleet and continue aiding the injured." There was something too practiced, too perfect, too *neat* in his voice that betrayed the lie. This thing was not on his side.

"I think," said Mattis carefully, "you're stalling me."

For a second nothing happened.

Then Pitt slowly smiled. "Have it your way, then," he said. "Maybe I am."

Bastard. Bastard... Mattis had *trusted* him. Trusted this person. This clone. This *thing*.

"Who are you?" demanded Mattis. "How is it you have Pitt's memories? His personality? His *mind?*"

"You make it seem like there is no distinction between what that man thinks and believes and what I think and believe." A distinctly English accent crept into the man's voice. "But the truth is, we are not the same, for this mind is Legion."

Mattis was speechless.

"Do you know what a fly-by-wire flight system is?" asked Pitt. Mattis did not and his expression obviously conveyed this. "It is a system found in all modern air and spacecraft. Early aircraft manipulated their flight surfaces through wires and cables and, later, hydraulics. Physical movement. Later, systems migrated to using computers; the pilot was not *really* flying the plane, not directly. He was merely passing instructions to a computer who manipulated the control surfaces. The pilot told the plane to go left, and it did, but only because the computer agreed.

"So it is with my slaves. One part of the consciousness speaks and the other obeys—a process which takes place subconsciously. The slave does not realize he is not the master, and in the absence of commands, does what it would naturally do. Like a car with the driver's hands taken off the wheel."

Mattis scowled. "Still fond of vehicle metaphors, aren't you?"

Pitt smiled darkly. "Been in the mind of a pilot too much," he confessed, the smile spreading slowly across his face. "But by now I assume you know who I am."

He did. But he didn't—couldn't—say it. He'd seen that man die. Seen him explode. Had sacrificed the *Midway* to do it. His ship. His crew. Jeremy Pitt.

"Goodbye, Admiral," said Pitt. Spectre. Then the connection went black.

"Sir," said Calaway, "we're coming up on the *Stennis* and the skunk."

White hot anger coursed through him, threatening to burst free like a ruptured gas canister. But he pressed his fingernails into his palm so deeply, so roughly, that the pain forced him to keep his composure.

Spectre, or his duplicate, or whoever he was, would pay for this. That was enough for now. Everything else was noise. "Signal the *Caernarvon*," he said. "The *Stennis* is now a hostile entity. Inform Captain Spears that we're going in hot, and we're going in hard."

Calaway hesitated only slightly, then nodded. "Yes sir," he said, and went about his duty.

Mattis stared at the rapidly approaching dot that was the USS *Stennis*, its hull docked with the Avenir vessel, the ship that had his grandson aboard.

CHAPTER SIXTY-SIX

Bridge
USS Warrior
Gas Giant Erebus
Vellini System
Tiberius Sector

The *Warrior* translated out of Z-Space, the *Caernarvon* right behind it. The *Aerostar* flashed into existence well behind them, close enough to engage and support, but far enough to be safe.

General Quarters was called, the weapons were charged, and the targeting radars began painting both the *Stennis* and the Avenir ship, locking them up for gun runs. It was the first time Mattis had seen the new ship up close; sleek and black and long, like a cigar bristling with knobs that were obviously weapons.

The ships were locked up, the guns were loaded, and Mattis had no idea what to do.

He couldn't fire on them. Baby Jack was over there.

"Calaway?" he asked, leaning forward in his chair. "Can we dispatch a boarding pod with Rhinos aboard?"

Calaway stared at him. "You trust those clumsy idiots with your grandson?"

The memory of Sampson violently shaking her rocket launcher made him reconsider.

"What about… the uplink to Fleet Command. The *Stennis* is still patched in, right? Any chance we can make an electronic attack? Get into their computers somehow?"

"Won't be possible, sir. The moment they detect that, they'll lock us out."

Mattis glared at his screen, watching the two ships. Spectre-Pitt wanted to delay him, to keep him from being here. There must be something he wanted. Something Mattis had a chance to use against him.

But what?

CHAPTER SIXTY-SEVEN

Bridge
USS Stennis
Gas Giant Erebus
Vellini System
Tiberius Sector

Pitt-Spectre—or JP-98 as he preferred to be called—watched Mattis's newly acquired ship translate from Z-Space with an expression that was half bemused smile, half annoyed frown.

This wasn't the plan.

But this time he'd finally dispatch Mattis.

The banging on the bridge door grew louder, followed by the *snap-hiss* of industrial cutting torches. The crew of the *Stennis* were going to cut through the casemate. They'd gotten wind that he'd killed the bridge crew—they'd hesitated when he'd ordered them to dock with the Avenir ship, and he couldn't bear disobedience.

Fortunately, the cutting torches would take them far too long. By the time they were through the armored hull it would be too late.

Still. The noise was irritating. Maybe it was time to get rid of the entire crew. He'd dispatched of the bridge crew easily enough. Their limp, broken bodies lay scattered around the room like discarded toddler's toys—this body, infused with the adjusted DNA, was a physical wonder. But he couldn't fight all of the ship's crew on his own.

Fortunately, he wouldn't have to.

He turned his attention back to the task at hand. Mattis's ship. "What do you think?" he asked the pilot, the one who had brought him Jack. She called herself Guano. Why someone would use a term for literal shit as a form of self-identification eluded him, but his name was also a letter and a number, so who was he to judge? At least in his defense, the 'JP' actually stood for a real name. "What do you think they're planning?"

"I don't know." Guano held the squirming child with a level of skill that surprised him. The chemicals coursing through her brain hadn't obviously dulled her flying skills, even if they had affected other parts of her. Her perceptions. Her impulses. "Admiral Mattis won't fire while this child's aboard. And he probably won't risk a boarding party."

"Very well." JP-98 ran his hands through his hair. Hair… sharing one of these bodies was wonderful at times—he'd missed having hair. It reminded him of his youth, long ago. "We should get rid of the rest of the *Stennis* crew. You planted the device you found in your pocket into the coolant relay in the walls of your quarters, yes?"

The dull creature, Guano, stared at him blankly for a moment. He could almost see the rusted cogs groaning as they moved in her head, her genuine thoughts wrestling with her programmed, implanted urges. "Yes," she said, finally. "It's … a bomb? To destroy the ship?"

Fortunately, he hadn't told her what it is. "Quite the opposite, my dear. A bomb would be detected by the *Stennis*'s sensors. No, no. This is much more subtle." He touched a button on his wrist computer, sending out a signal to the tiny thing that would interfere with the electronics in the coolant system.

Immediately, klaxons and warning sirens wailed.

"Caution, coolant flow to reactor has dropped to zero," said a pre-recorded voice. "Reactor core temperature climbing. 1,100 degrees Celsius. Meltdown in twenty four minutes."

It would take some time to reach 2,900 or so degrees and a meltdown to happen. They would either try to restore cooling, or, more likely, evacuate. Either one was fine. He didn't need the *Stennis* for that long anyway. All he needed was its engines. The special engines which would allow him to bring through as many reinforcements as he needed: manpower, ships, technology. Anything.

And he could finally get these little wailing specimens to his labs in the future where he could harvest them. And he could finally complete his plan. *Operation Ad Infinitum.*

The power build up began in earnest, the overloaded reactor pouring its energy where he needed it to go, slowly burning itself out as it did.

He tapped in a command to connect him to the Avenir ship, where his Jovian Logistics employees—impersonating those sad veterans, the Forgotten—were waiting to board, bringing the specimens with them. And soon they would all be safely away from this place.

And time.

The connection opened to his counterpart on the other ship. "Fifty-six? We're ready for you, old chap. You boys head on over."

"Understood, old chap," came the reply, in a voice that matched his own.

The clanging, cutting, and general infernal racket ceased.

Guano examined her console. "It looks like they're evacuating. Some in escape pods, some in shuttles."

"Excellent," he said, steepling his fingers and staring at Mattis's ship. "Pilot, go take that child to sickbay with the others. Get back here sharpish. Just in case I need you."

"Yes sir," said Guano, attempting to cradle the fussing infant as she turned to the bridge exit.

JP-98 watched the screen with cold impassion. They would be coming for him soon. Mattis kept interfering, kept snatching victories despite powerful odds against him. But with the portal open, there would be no further mishaps. No more. No more chances for Jack Mattis. Soon…

He tapped some commands into the engineering console. Time to make his getaway. The engines roared into overdrive, the power shunted to a dish on the front of the ship, and a beam lanced down into the dark, swirling atmosphere of the gas giant Erebus. Soon, he'd have his portal, just like he did at the gas giant Lyx a few weeks back.

"Now, Mister Mattis. What am I going to do about *you*?"

CHAPTER SIXTY-EIGHT

Bridge
USS Warrior
Gas Giant Erebus
Vellini System
Tiberius Sector

What was he going to do?

The Avenir ship began to engage, shooting fiery streaks across space at the *Warrior*. Mattis ground his teeth. "Evasive maneuvers," he said. Almost immediately, the ship began to move beneath him, the nimble frigate easily able to slip out of the way of the incoming fire, even in its damaged state.

Still. That didn't matter in the long term. Mattis stared impotently at the monitor, trying to come up with some kind of solution. Something that might tip the scales. Give him an edge. He couldn't fire back, not yet. He couldn't risk Jack.

Interestingly enough, the *Stennis* wasn't firing at him either, even though—he presumed—it had no reason *not* to. Maybe its weapons systems were damaged somehow. Or Spectre didn't control the entire ship. Maybe the crew had figured out they might be shooting at a friendly.

It didn't make sense, but he had no time to think it over.

"Detecting an energy spike on the *Stennis*," said Calaway. He squinted at his screen. "Not sure what it means."

Mattis had seen many strange energy spikes from Avenir ships, and with a single glance he identified it. This was the same type they had encountered at the gas giant Lyx, in the Pinegar system, right before the *Midway* had been destroyed.

Spectre was opening a portal to the future again.

"*Warrior* to *Caernarvon*, *Aerostar*. This is *Warrior* actual."

"Ah," said Captain Spears, her tone patient. "Was hoping you'd have some kind of idea as to what we should do about these kidnapping ruffians out there. We're reading a huge energy spike from the *Stennis*."

"Correct," said Mattis. He reached up with his left hand, rubbing his right shoulder. The damn thing was really starting to sting. "They're opening a portal to the future, right at the center of Erebus. We've seen it before. Last time it happened a whole bunch of angry ships came through. And when the portal closed, the entire planet blew. If that happens, Vellini is toast. Its orbit is close enough that the debris field from Erebus will rain down and vaporize everything on it, including the billion people living there." He stared at the readouts, frowning curiously. "There *is* something different this time, however. There's a strange reading. Are they running their reactor without coolant? I'm reading a hell of a lot of heat build up around their core."

"I'm seeing it too," said Spears. "And I'm seeing escape

pod launches. Smart cookie, forcing the crew out of there before they get baked, and he can make a clean getaway."

"Okay," said Mattis. "We have to find a way to disable that ship. Without firing on it and without firing *near* it. We don't want to hit those escape pods. Or my grandson."

Spears' voice took on a hard edge. "But Jack, if it looks like that portal is anywhere close to being opened, I'm left with no choice but to destroy that ship, kids or no kids—even if it's your grandson. I can't risk a billion people. You know that."

Silence. Then, a voice joined their conversation. "Uhh, sorry to interrupt—this is Reardon on the *Aerostar*. We, uh … have an idea."

CHAPTER SIXTY-NINE

Cockpit
The Aerostar
Open space

"And what idea would that be, Mr. Reardon? Talk fast. I've got a planet and a grandson to save here." Mattis's voice came over the comm-link, booming like a cannon—like he was right there in the cabin. He must have been channeling his no-nonsense Admiral's voice.

Reardon covered the receiver with a hand and leaned back to Smith. "Ok, what's the plan?"

Both Sammy and Smith looked at him slack-jawed. "What the hell, bro? You eavesdrop on a US Admiral and a Captain and offer to give them a totally-awesome-can't-possibly-fail-plan, and you're just talking out your ass?"

Smith shrugged. "In his defense, he always talks out his ass."

Reardon smiled and shot his finger guns at them.

"Kidding! Well, only half kidding."

"Good God," breathed Smith.

"I mean, what's the plan for convincing Mattis that my plan is a good plan?"

"What the hell is your plan?" countered Smith.

Mattis's voice boomed over the comm again. "Reardon? It's now or never. What do you have?"

"Ok, here goes nothing…" he mumbled. "Ok, Admiral, hear me out. You can't fire on that ship cause of your grandkid and all. And you can't just send a boarding craft over cause you'll get shot out of the sky the second you leave your shuttle bay. And by my count, magic transporter beams are still a few centuries off. What that leaves you is …" he paused for effect, "me."

"You? How the hell can you get us over there?"

"Well, it turns out … I'm a smuggler, ya know? And smugglers, well, see, we have to operate in a lot of … less-than-ideal situations. Sometimes we need to fly sight unseen, if you catch my drift."

"I don't. Your point, Mr. Reardon. Preferably before we all die," said Mattis.

"The *Aerostar*, Admiral, is *the finest* smuggling vessel in the whole galaxy. And not just because of her good-looking crew. It's because of her hull. Well, also because of her good-looking crew, but that's beside the p—"

"What the hell can your pink hull do for us?"

"It's not *pink*. It's—never mind. The point is, it's coated with an electromagnetic dampening material. When I've got the sucker engaged, any radar or laser or what have you that hits the hull will be completely absorbed. Uh … except for a pink laser—then they'd see us. But … they don't make pink lasers." He covered the receiver again and whispered back to Smith, "do they make pink lasers?"

"No."

He uncovered the receiver. "So what I'm saying is, Admiral, we can land you a boarding party on that ship."

Mattis paused. "Can't they just look out the window and see you trying to board?"

"Well, there's that. But, by freak coincidence, just look around you, Admiral. We're smack dab in the middle of the Tiberius Nebula. Lots of it's, well, pink. We'll just approach the ship from, uh, the pink direction."

On the other end of the line he could hear Mattis engaged in a muttered conversation with some British-Indian sounding bloke. Was that Lieutenant Modi?

"Oh, and Admiral, I forgot to tell you. When Chuck left the *Aerostar*, I, uh, slapped a … thing on his back. A little listening device—"

"That he usually leaves on cats!" interjected Sammy.

"Shush," Reardon held up a finger to his brother. "A little device that we can use to track him once we get aboard. Should be a cinch to find him once we're there. Does that sweeten the deal?"

After a few more seconds, the Admiral's voice boomed through the cabin again. "Fine. It's all we've got, and we have no time. Get your ass on the *Warrior*'s shuttle bay deck. Now."

That was enough for Sammy. He pushed the *Aerostar*'s navigational controls forward and the ship shot ahead toward the still smoking, scarred starship. "Hey! I'm the captain, I didn't say *go* yet," said Reardon.

"Hey, it's why you hired me! I can anticipate your orders."

"I hired you because I needed someone to babysit the Z-Space drive while I took naps."

Sammy smirked. "You hired me because you got lost down in the guest quarters. Twice."

"That was … just shut up. Get us to that shuttle bay."

Smith shook his head. "How the hell are the two of you still alive?"

CHAPTER SEVENTY

Corridor
USS Warrior
Gas Giant Erebus
Vellini System
Tiberius Sector

Mattis left the bridge in Calaway's hands. He strapped on his space suit as he walked, snatching a rifle from the armor and heading down to the shuttle bay where, hopefully, the *Aerostar* would be waiting for him. And hopefully, Reardon's little tricks would work.

That was a lot of hope.

Once there, he would deal with this himself. They knew where the kids were, and Jack was bound to be there somewhere. He was going to save them. And his son. And his grandson. And then he was going to shoot this goddamn clone of Spectre in the face. And their missing pilot, Corrick. And everything else.

Time to shine. Time to … gallivant.

Mattis clipped on his helmet and checked his rifle. The last time had worked out okay, but this time he would do better.

His communicator chirped. He routed the signal through his helmet with a touch of a key. "Mattis here."

"It's Martha." Ramirez's voice came through soft and gentle, and definitely more than welcome. "Jack. Captain Spears said I should call you. Apparently you're about to go and do something very foolish."

He couldn't help but smile at that. "That sounds like how she would describe it. It's alright. These *gallivanting* activities always turn out fine for me. I'll be okay."

Ramirez's voice betrayed her skepticism. "I know," she said, a faint crack in her voice. "I just… I just wanted to—" She clicked her tongue, and something in her tone changed. Her reporter's voice came out. "I just wanted to tell you that I've been thinking. Whoever is doing this, they obviously wanted Chuck's baby specifically. Word around the ship is that they used one of your pilots to do it."

"That's classified," said Mattis, frowning slightly.

"I'm a reporter. Nothing's *too* classified for me."

Fair point. "Okay," said Mattis, stepping into the hangar bay. A squad of Marines and Rhinos were there, waiting for him. "So … what?"

"So," said Ramirez, "my theory is that someone *knew* that if they threatened me into not talking to you, that's exactly what I'd do. When I made my broadcast, that's exactly what happened. Someone sent me a message warning me not to broadcast it, and to not involve you." She sighed into the line. "Stupid. Anyway, the thing is, it's possible that that's what's happening now. They don't want Chuck, they don't want Chuck's kid… they want *you*. And they're using baby Jack to get you over there."

A fair point, but when walking into a trap, a legitimate tactic was to ramp up the aggression and assault their positions as forcefully as possible to get through it and put them on the defensive. Besides. Even if there wasn't a way he could just justify this to himself, he couldn't leave Jack in their hands.

"Maybe," was all he said.

"Just… be careful."

Despite it all, Mattis couldn't help but smile. "I will."

There was a brief moment of quiet. His shoulder continued to burn, but he ignored it.

"Good luck, Jack."

"Thanks, Martha." The line went dead, just as he strode into the shuttle bay.

The *Aerostar* still wasn't there. Mattis nodded to the Rhinos and Marines gathered in on the deck. His backup.

He was ready. But he was flying blind. Martha was right. He had no idea what he was getting into. He needed information. He needed the final piece to the puzzle.

And there was only one person who had that.

He handed his rifle off to a Marine and headed for the door. "Make the final preparations. I'll be right back."

CHAPTER SEVENTY-ONE

Brig
USS Warrior
Gas Giant Erebus
Vellini System
Tiberius Sector

Despite all the destruction around him, the brig was relatively intact, such that only a single marine needed to stand guard.

"Dismissed," Mattis said. The man saluted, and stepped out into the hallway, leaving him staring at two of the occupied cells before him.

In one stood the thing Chuck had called *Lily*. Thing. Goddammit, he had to stop thinking of them as things. Chuck had proven that Lily was not a thing, but a person. A ruined, corrupted person, perhaps, but a person nonetheless.

In the other cell sat the future-human mutant he'd found in the escape pod in the Pinegar system. Cross-legged. Staring straight ahead, not looking at him, or at anything in particular. He supposed that if the thing—the *person*—ever made it out of the cell, it would rip anyone it found limb from limb as payback for the torture it had endured at the hands of the late Captain Flint.

"Chuck. Protein bar," said Lily. Mattis approached her cell. "Protein bar," she repeated.

"You're friends with my son," said Mattis.

Lily paused, looking as if she was considering it. "Friends. Yes. Friends."

"So you do know English?"

"Friends. Yes. Speak."

He approached the bars separating them and grabbed onto one. "Tell me. Are you from the future? Can you tell me what the hell is going on? Who is Spectre?"

"No."

"No?" He grabbed an adjacent bar and leaned in with his face between them. "You won't tell me who Spectre is? You know your life is in my hands right now? Tell me. Tell me!"

He was yelling, and he had to force himself to close his mouth and clench his teeth. Anger would solve nothing. But the thought of his little grandson in the hands of that wretched man made him seethe.

"Chuck," she said, looking at him askance. "Chuck kind. Friend. Hero."

The choice of words was unexpected. Hero. She thought of his son as a hero.

Why?

But deep inside, he knew exactly why. "He treated you well. When they found you, they kept you in the box. But when

Chuck came, he treated you … like a person. Like a friend?"

She nodded vigorously. "Friend. Hero."

He mirrored her nod. "He's a hero alright. My little champion." He'd called him that for years, when Chuck was younger. Champ. When had he stopped?

"Lily. Chuck is my son. I have a lot to learn from him. He's good. He's a friend. He's a hero. And right now, I need you to trust me, and tell me what I need to know." He forced a kind smile he honestly did not feel. "Please," he added.

"Tell you. Yes. I'll tell you all."

"Good," he said, breathing easier. "Who is Spectre? Are you from the future? Can you tell me what his plans are?"

She shook her head. "No. Created in … dark place. Lab. Max … max … max?"

His stomach clenched. "Maxgainz?"

"Yes."

Dammit. "So, you're not from the future? You were created in a Maxgainz lab?"

"Yes."

So this detour was for nothing. He needed to get over to the Stennis with his assault force as fast as possible, then.

"But *him*. He future."

She was pointing. Mattis followed her line of sight, and it rested on the other mutant, which sat still, its only movement a slowly heaving chest and occasional ripple of terrifyingly large muscle.

He nodded, and stepped over to the other cell. "Hello," he began.

It didn't look at him.

Dammit! What the hell would Chuck say to this thing? He chided

372

himself. *Well, first of all, old man, he sure as hell wouldn't call it a thing. He'd treat it like a fucking human, you dimwit.*

He tried hard to smile, as sincerely as possible. "Look. I'm sorry. They treated you very, very badly, and I could have stopped them, but I didn't. I'm…" he paused, searching for the words, "so very sorry."

It—he—was looking at him. Straight in the eyes.

"I'm going to get you out of here. I'll do my best to return you home, if that's where you want to go."

The mutant cocked his head, almost like a dog.

"You can trust me. I will protect you. I will do my very best to help you. But … I need to know some things. Can you help me?"

Very, very slowly, it moved its head. Up and down. A nod?

"Okay. Okay. You're from the future? You traveledd here through the time rift created at the core of that gas giant?"

Again, a single nod of its massive, grotesque head. It stared straight at him.

"Is Specter in the future too?"

Another nod.

"Are there … many of him?"

Another nod.

Good Lord. A future where the entire human race is controlled by an army of Spectres.

"Can you … can you tell me what his plans are? Why he's taken the children? Why he's corrupted my grandson with some virus? Why he's now attempting to go to the future on the *Stennis*?"

It stood up. Mattis took a step back on reflex, but forced himself to be calm.

"Freedom," it said. It spoke. It actually spoke.

"Spectre wants ... freedom?"

Its head moved, this time back and forth. It pointed to the bars. "Freedom," it repeated. The meaning was clear.

Well, go big or go home, I suppose. He cleared his throat. "Release security lock on brig cell B, authorization Mattis omega one."

A click.

The mutant smiled, and reached forward to push the cell door open.

Mattis stepped forward into the cell with the creature. The person? Taking an enormous risk, swallowing hard, he held out a hand.

The creature looked at it, then lifted his own to grasp it.

It gripped hard. Mattis smiled and tried not to cry out.

From the adjacent cell, Lily spoke. "See? Friend."

"Yes. Friend," repeated Mattis. He looked up at the mutant, into its green and black eyes. "Now. Please tell me what I need to know."

And then, seemingly miraculously, in perfect, unbroken English, it started.

"Some of us call him The Overseer. Some call him The Scourge. But most call him their Lord and Master. He is Legion. No one knows how many he is. But, from our history, we know what he did to become the ruler and master of all humanity forevermore."

Legion. Specter himself used that word. The mutant had stopped, as if unsure or possibly scared to continue, as if even talking about Specter were a forbidden subject. "Go on," coaxed Mattis.

"We know that in our distant past—your recent past—the single man known as Spectre had labs. A large, well-funded corporation. He experimented. He had funding from many major world governments. And he provided them with ... weapons. Bioweapons. But the governments didn't know that, in secret, he was planning to overthrow all nations. Rule himself.

"He created superhumans. Experimented with DNA and human biology to create," he paused, and pointed to the adjacent cell, "*her*. And her kind became ... Us."

Mattis began to understand. "So Spectre learned enough about DNA to create a new race of superhumans with which he could overthrow all world governments. But why didn't he just do that?"

The creature shook his head again. "He couldn't control her kind. He needed control, and he couldn't have it. He couldn't figure it out. So much latent, inactive DNA in your genome that when he tried one thing, some other newly activated hormonal process would interrupt the control process and foil his efforts. So he realized he needed a vast library of human DNA to sift through and root out the sequences responsible for his inability to control a human mind. He used his influence to convince the governments to create the libraries for him."

Mattis's heart turned to ice. "The seed banks. The ones we made in case there was ever a civilizational catastrophe that would require an infusion of diverse DNA into a limited gene pool, in case our numbers ever fell enough threaten our survival as a species." Mattis nodded in understanding, finally realizing how the various world governments ever managed to come together to complete such a monumental task: they had Spectre in the background, pulling strings and manipulating affairs to make it happen.

"But wait … your kind came back to my time, the present, and tried to destroy those seed banks," said Mattis. "You tried to stop him before he even got started. So you're not all controlled by him in the future?"

Another head shake. "Some have broken free. We have discovered how to resist the voice." It pointed to its head. "The voice inside that commands us. It's still there. Always speaking, always commanding, screaming at us when we disobey. But we've learned to suppress it. To ignore it. There are many of us. But … not enough." It, he, looked sad.

"So, you came back and tried to destroy the seed banks. But it didn't work. You didn't destroy all of them. And Specter succeeded anyway."

He looked even more somber. "Yes. And succeeded … *because* of us." He looked positively pained at having to say it. "We enabled him to succeed by coming back to stop him."

"Oh my God," said Mattis. "I'm sure Modi would have a field day with a time-travel paradox like this, but … oh my God. What did he do? Explain." A pause. Then—"please," he added.

"He captured several of us. Dissected them piece by piece, organ by organ, protein by protein, and finally discovered how to control us. Remotely. Electronically. He didn't need the seed banks after all. He needed us."

Of course. He remembered all too clearly how Spectre practically waltzed onto that Avenir vessel in the Chrysalis system and took control of it. And Mattis was forced to sacrifice the Midway to beat him.

But he didn't beat him. He was, as the mutant said, Legion.

"So you sent back even more ships to destroy him, and before you could, he captured one of your ships. And that's the battle where I … where I destroyed dozens of your ships, along with Spectre. The battle that you yourself survived in that escape pod."

"Yes." The mutant said it matter-of-factly, as if it was confirming the weather. "Yes, you killed many that day. And Spectre. But by then, he was already Legion."

A chill went down Mattis's spine. A legion of Spectres. Already. In his own time, not just in the future.

Another chilling thought struck him. "And … he could be anyone. Anywhere. Since he was Jeremy Pitt, he could be anyone. All he needs to do is clone a body, insert one of his own cloned brains into it, and use the control technology he developed by studying you to essentially control an army of … himself?"

The mutant nodded. "Yes. And, in our history books, it worked. In three month's time, his conquest of humanity will be complete."

Three months. So he had less than three months to track down Spectre, all of him, and stop him for good.

"And the Chinese engines? The ones that apparently have the ability to open a time rift just like your ships from the future? How the hell did those bastards get that tech? It got put on the *Midway* before it blew, and now the *Stennis*."

The mutant hesitated. "I … I don't know. Our history is incomplete. And this particular item …" the mutant's eyes flicked back and forth rapidly as if reading massive amounts of data scrolling invisibly past his face, "this item is missing from our history logs. The registry shows that there was an entry regarding this, long ago, but … it's wiped clean. I can't explain it."

Fine. Mystery for another day, he thought. "But what about the kids? What about my Jack? Why steal them and take them into the future?"

A shadow passed over the mutant's face. "Every general needs lieutenants. He will go to a safe place in the future, raise them, corrupt them, transform them, clone them, thousands of times over, and then," the mutant looked down, "he will return. A core group of Spectres, at the head of an army of these corrupted beings."

"My God. Jack." Mattis held a hand to his mouth. He felt like vomiting. His little Jack, transformed into a twisted lieutenant of Spectre, cloned, and used to do … terrible, unspeakable things. "And he did it? It worked? In your past?"

"Yes. And your grandson, the one you call Jack, was corrupted into the lieutenant who was … the cruelest of all."

His heart sank further, if possible. "So if it's already happened for you, it's inevitable then. I've failed."

It was staring at him again. "No. Admiral Mattis, that is not how time works."

Mattis looked up at him. "Are you saying…?"

"You still have time." The mutant stepped past him and approached Lily's cell, pointing toward it and looking back at Mattis.

At Mattis's word, her cell opened too. Lily stepped out, a smile on her face. "I help."

The future-human mutant nodded. "I will help too."

"Good. I'm going to need all the help I can get." And with that, Mattis ran out the door, the two lumbering mutants in tow. "We're coming, Jack."

CHAPTER SEVENTY-TWO

Shuttle Bay
USS Warrior
Gas Giant Erebus
Vellini System
Tiberius Sector

As Mattis and his mutants boarded the shuttle with the rest of the Rhinos and regular ole' Marines—all of them staring at the creatures following him—a polite cough from behind caught his attention.

A small gaggle of people were there waiting. Lynch, dressed as Mattis was, with a battle rifle and space suit; Bratta and Modi, wearing an assortment of strange equipment he *presumed* to be sensors and weapons; and a small handful of emergency personnel from the *Stennis*, carrying either medic packs or pistols.

"What's all this?" asked Mattis, curiously.

"Well sir," said Lynch, grinning like a cat. "The dang thing is, a lot of people have heard that the future-humans are out fixin' to steal babies, and they have Chuck's kid. Well, sir, with the greatest respect, you are more than a couple of sandwiches shy of a picnic if they think people like me are going to stand by and let *that* happen while I got two hands and a gun."

Mattis wanted to protest. To order them all back, to tell them to stay safe and mind their own business and let him rescue his son and grandson and be the hero and get the job done. Instead, "I see" was all he said.

Lynch put a hand on his shoulder. "You can't do it all yourself, Jack. You're a goddamn hero. But you're not a goddamn god."

He couldn't help but smile a little at that. Lynch was right. He needed help. And he had the best help there that he could have wished for. "And Modi? Mister Bratta?"

"I have a thing," said Bratta, holding up a small tube crudely tied to a box obviously welded shut. Jutting out from the thing at strange, random intervals were a variety of sensor modules and electronic components. "And I want to test it."

Mattis regarded the homemade device with a curious eye. "What is it?"

"An interesting device of my own creation," he said, preening just a little. "A combination of drones and firearms, but a bit improved, if I do say so myself. You see, each dart is actually a tiny drone, so it can be fired around corners and seek out targets based on a single brief acquisition. When found, it injects them with a fentanyl derivative which, in short order, renders them unconscious. The science behind it is very intriguing. It uses a combination of image recognition cameras, scent-tracking sensors and olfactory-focused computers that can track even an Avenir by smell. Furthermore—"

Mattis held up his hand. "Right. It's a fancy tranquilizer gun. Modi?"

"There is nothing further I can do aboard ship," said Modi. "And I would like to accompany Mister Bratta as he experiments. And I can't bear the thought of you fighting over there for all of us, all alone."

"The robot has a soul after all!" said Lynch, then, gesturing behind him, "the damage to the *Warrior* is largely contained now. Ain't no harm in letting these two play Q. Hell, we could use the help, to be perfectly frank."

Settled, then. Mattis jabbed a finger at each group in turn. "Modi, Bratta: that thing you're talking about. Just what we need. Recover our… *lost* pilot with it. Lieutenant Corrick. A*live*, please. We need to interrogate her and figure out what the hell they did to her. And how to counter it in the future."

"Yes sir," said Modi.

"Commander Lynch, Spectre is opening another of those portals, this one running a lot slower than the one at Lyx, probably because *Stennis's* engines aren't quite as advanced as the Avenir ship's were. Get to the Navigational array on the hull. If this is the same technology as the other ones, they'll be using its radar dish to guide whatever energy pattern they're generating. Shut it down if you can, blow it up if you have to."

"Aye aye, sir," said Lynch.

Mattis stepped up the shuttle's loading ramp, nodding to all present inside. "Marines, find the kids. Get them all back here. And find any *Stennis* crew still alive and bring them with you."

"Aye sir!"

Sampson, her Rhino suit squeaking slightly as she leaned against a similarly-clad Cho, squeezed into the shuttle, barely fitting. She had her damn rocket launcher too. "What about the Rhinos?"

Mattis smiled grimly. "Simple task: locate Commander Pitt, aka Spectre, and shoot him in the face. Repeatedly. And feel free to slice and dice your way through any of Spectre's people that undoubtedly have come over from that docked Avenir ship. Forgotten or no, take them all out. "

That seemed to make her *very* happy. "Aye sir," she said.

A voice called out from the bay doors. "Actually, Admiral, I'd like the honor of shooting that fucker in the face."

Mattis turned to the doors, semi-shocked to see Senator Pitt standing there, cradling a small firearm in his hands. "Senator? I'm sorry, but this is no place for a politician."

"Admiral. Please. I need this. And I'm not a senator anymore. I transmitted my resignation just minutes ago. Just a private citizen here who wants to shoot the monster who did this to my son, right in the face. Repeatedly, as you said." A haggard smile.

John Smith, the CIA officer standing next to Reardon, raised a finger. "And I'll accompany him, Admiral. Before he dies, I need to interrogate that bastard. There's one piece to the puzzle I'm missing." He nodded toward the former senator. "*Then* you can shoot him in the face. Repeatedly."

No more time to discuss things. "Fine. Join the party. Don't blame me if you die." The gaggle boarded the *Aerostar*. Mattis squeezed in between his two new mutant friends, one from the future, one from the present.

The kid in the wheelchair, piloting the ship with one hand,

grabbed the comm with his other. "This is your captain speaking. Thank you for choosing the *Aerostar*. We know you have choices when you travel, and are grateful for choosing us. Please fasten your safety belts and put all tray tables in their full upright and locked positions. In the event of a water landing —"

Reardon smacked the back of his head. "Fly the ship, dumbass."

Then they set off to the *Stennis*, the *Aerostar* drifting through the *Warrior*'s hangar bay doors, silent and swift. It banked down towards an area of space where the nebula gas looked as pink as the *Aerostar* herself. "Engaging electromagnetic dampening coating," said Reardon. After he flipped a switch, the pilot banked the ship around gracefully and pointed straight at the *Stennis*, whose radar dish in the navigational array had erupted a beautiful but deadly red shimmering beam that was drilling down into the swirling dark atmosphere of Erebus, slowly generating a portal where, if they didn't act quickly, Spectre would escape to and prepare his army. And in three months, he would return. And conquer Earth.

Lily, the mutant made in a Maxgainz lab, cautiously raised a hand. "Help? How?"

Mattis had no idea. "Just fill in as needed," he offered. That seemed to satisfy her, and the other mutant, the future-human, nodded as well.

"What about you?" asked Lynch, curiously. "Want to tag-team that portal with me and blast it to smithereens?"

"No," said Mattis, staring out a porthole, feeling a surge of adrenaline that banished the aching in his shoulder. "I'm going to get my son."

CHAPTER SEVENTY-THREE

Shuttle bay
USS Stennis
Gas Giant Erebus
Vellini System
Tiberius Sector

Mattis held tight as the *Aerostar* banked back and forth as it shot towards the *Stennis*'s shuttle bay. It was clear that *someone* on the *Stennis* knew they were coming, and was trying to shoot at them, but they couldn't get a weapons lock and they clearly couldn't aim fast enough to actually hit them.

"Thread the needle, little bro!" called out Reardon from his seat, holding on for dear life. Someone vomited nearby, and Mattis saw former Senator Pitt to his right with a lap full of his stomach contents.

"Protein bar," said Lily.

"Trust me, honey, you don't want *that* one," said Reardon with a grin.

They flew through the opening to the shuttle bay, landed hard, rammed into a small group of Spectre's goons who were firing at them, smeared them all across the deck, and came to a screeching halt on the far side of the bay near the doors that led into the ship.

"That was what we call a wet landing," said Reardon brightly, looking back at the trail of blood and parts they'd left on the deck.

"All right, *move!*" yelled Mattis, and everyone streamed out of the *Aerostar*.

Once through the shuttle bay doors and in the hallway outside, they split up for their assignments. The Marines rushed down the hallway toward the stern, with Cho at the lead, mowing down any Jovian Logistics security guards or Forgotten they came across.

Sampson turned toward the bridge at the ship's core, her rocket launcher fully loaded and two other Rhinos in tow, with Senator Pitt and Smith following close behind. Modi and Bratta chattered amongst themselves, seemingly oblivious to the danger that surrounded them, more concerned with the technological marvel in their hands than with the frantic boarding surrounding them. Lynch went looking for an airlock to get outside. .

And Mattis marched toward the bow, rifle comfortably in both hands, where Reardon's tracking device had indicated that Chuck was being held,. Lily marched behind him with a few Marines. He couldn't see where the other mutant had gone.

It seemed that most of the *Stennis* crew had already evacuated, as they came across only a few members here and there, hiding from Spectre's people—Jovian Logistics guards and a few Forgotten members—that had come over from the Avenir ship. But the Marines and Mattis's own assault rifle made quick work of them. Lily roared ahead to distract any defenders while Mattis and the Marines picked them off.

Someone ran out in front of him. He raised his rifle instinctively, lowering it when he realized it was a human. A woman in her mid-twenties with short cropped hair, wearing a pilot's uniform.

"Lieutenant Corrick?" he asked curiously, keeping his weapon quick to hand.

The pilot stared dumbfounded at him. "Who's that?"

No, she didn't match Corrick's description. "Never mind. Get to the shuttle bay. The way should be clear behind us," he yelled, thumbing back down the hallway.

She took off down the hall, pausing when he called back to her. "Have you seen any babies around here? Infants?"

"Oh," she said, nodding vaguely. "Yeah. I think they're being held in sickbay. Heavily guarded."

Right. "Go," he said.

She thanked him with her eyes, and ran off.

Mattis turned and walked deeper into the ship, frowning slightly as he did so. "Yeah, well, this was the easy part, apparently. Sickbay's gonna suck." He glanced at his accompanying Marines. "Lots of civvies there. And apparently lots of enemy combatants." He motioned them forward. "Make every shot count."

CHAPTER SEVENTY-FOUR

Corridor
USS Stennis
Gas Giant Erebus
Vellini System
Tiberius Sector

Steve Bratta was so excited he could burst. Although, he had to concede, that would be a dangerous thing to do. And impossible. Most humans were incapable of dying of excitement, heart conditions notwithstanding. His device showed a sea of white dots, each one a person, moving around the various decks of the ship. It was working. It was working!

"See," he said, jabbing his finger at the tiny screen. "The device is tracking everyone on this ship by their heat signature, then identifying them by *smell!* Well, more or less. I doubt it's got everyone. But most of them!"

"Most impressive," said Modi, standing shoulder to shoulder with him, tapping at the device. "And the power draw is well within acceptable margins. Shall I have it narrow down Corrick's DNA signature?"

He was most pleased with this particular feature and, given that he wanted to show off a little to the other man, whose own inventions had inspired him to design this particular toy, said, "please do!"

Modi tapped his wrist computer. Bratta could see the data flow in. Okay. Patricia Corrick's DNA was now uploaded. He tapped the *isolate* button.

WORKING

"That looks promising," said Modi.

It was. A thin blue bar filled up at the bottom of his screen, and then one of the white dots turned blue. "Okay," he said. "Got her. She's moving from the bow to the stern, and it looks like she's alone."

"No baby?" asked Modi.

A totally legitimate question, and one to which he was quite sure of his answer. "No, there's no other heat signature there. It's possible a baby might be too small, but, well, hang on, let me isolate that one too." He tapped on his keys. "Here. Jack's in red, and he's… well." Bratta squinted as he examined the screen. Should have made it larger. "He's on the other side of the ship, with a lot of other tiny heat signatures. We're good."

"Okay," said Modi, a tinge of excitement coloring his voice. "Deploy the weapon."

Bratta did so with gusto, pressing the side button. *Please don't explode, please don't explode…* The firing tube hissed as it dispensed the drone dart, the tiny device hesitating a moment before flying off down the corridor, disappearing around a corner.

It worked! His eyes were drawn back to the screen. The tiny dart—represented by a green dot-whizzed down the corridors—turned this way and that, and then met the blue dot and vanished. "She should be unconscious shortly," said Bratta confidently, watching the blue dot that was Lieutenant Corrick stumble around.

Or, not so much as stumble as turn toward the direction the dart had flown, almost as though she was retracing the dart's path. And then another corner. And another.

Modi raised a skeptical eye. "She doesn't appear too affected."

Frowning, Bratta slid open the breach and, after a moment's fumbling, inserted a new cartridge. "That one might have been a dud," he said, and fired again.

Another hiss. Another flying dart down the corridor. The display showed another flawless, perfect flight to its target… who didn't slow down at all.

"Another dud?" asked Modi, quizzically.

That seemed *extremely* unlikely. "The failure rate on the darts is 0.02 percent," said Bratta, loading another one and firing it. It too disappeared, quickly finding the blue dot that was Corrick. She was only two turns away from them now.

With an angry shout, their target came barreling around the corner, a woman in a flight suit, minus a helmet. She had a wild, inhuman look in her eyes. Her skin was tinged an unholy green, veins bulging out like garden hoses, and three of the darts protruding from her suit.

Bratta stared. The needles should have easily penetrated even an armored flight suit—and all available evidence suggested it had!—but still she came, growling like some kind of angered beast. Whatever part of her human psyche was there was obviously buried under some kind of, well, almost post-hypnotic suggestion or chemical intoxication.

It would be fascinating if she were not bearing down on them, hands balled into fists, howling like some kind of horrid monster.

Reloading would take too long. The launch-tube fell out of his hands. Bratta snatched up his shockstick and charged it; he wasn't much of a fighter, and nervous energy spiked in him. He held the weapon out as Lieutenant Corrick ran straight into it, discharging its whole energy into her body.

She barely seemed affected. Corrick leapt at him, roaring like an angry animal, clawing madly at his face and forearms.

Bratta knew it wasn't possible to fight her off. "Run, Modi!" he cried, kicking at her. "And tell Jeannie I lo…"

Clunk. Corrick slumped over him, unmoving.

For a moment he didn't understand what was happening. *This* was what dying was like?

Modi moved into view, holding the dropped launcher. It was bent, now, and was probably useless for its intended purpose.

But then again, it had been useless before that, too.

"Simple, but effective," said Modi, dropping the broken piece of metal.

Bratta pushed Corrick off him, then considered the large, unconscious woman they had captured. "Uhh…" he stared up at Modi. "Can you carry her?"

"No," said Modi, staring back, an obvious hole in their plan becoming clear. "Uhh… can you?"

CHAPTER SEVENTY-FIVE

Corridor
USS Stennis
Gas Giant Erebus
Vellini System
Tiberius Sector

"So, wait." Sampson squinted as she stomped down the corridor, her suit's hydraulics whining eagerly, protesting the lack of shooting. "What's the mission again?"

"Clear path to the bridge, let the senator shoot his son in the face," said Kluger, behind her.

The other Rhino added, "and don't get shot in the face."

He was always pretty good at explaining stuff. "Great, I love face-shooting."

"Me too."

The Senator's eyes bulged a little as he listened to their conversation. Smith leaned over to him and whispered, "yes, they have a … reputation. But they're good."

"This way to the bridge, right?" asked Sampson.

"I guess so," said Kluger, shrugging helplessly with his huge, armored shoulders. "It's always at the center of a ship."

"Not always. In some movies it's at the top of the ship."

"That because they're *movies*, dumbass."

She shrugged, and turned a corner, finding the power out in the section ahead. The corridor disappeared into darkness.

Darkness. She stopped walking. Her heartbeat picked up as she stared into the inky black. Memories of the academy came back, strong and vivid. Of her first spacewalk. Of losing her tether and drifting off into the black, losing sight of the training scaffold, of nothing more than the dark, the void of space, with nothing to do but watch her oxygen counter slowly tick down, waiting for rescue…

"Hey," said Kluger, his voice quiet. "It's okay. Just turn on your lights. That's why you brought 'em, right?"

That was *exactly* why she brought 'em. She flicked her eyes to the side, accessing her suit's HUD. She selected her external light pack. Both her shoulder lamps illuminated, casting white cones of bright that blasted away the dark, reflecting off the bulkheads and creating elongated shadows off every protrusion, as though the dark fingers of a malevolent god were reaching out for her.

Better than the nothing.

"Okay. Onward." She stepped forward into the depowered zone.

Beep.

Her foot triggered some kind of sensor. Instantly, with enough force that it might have injured her even inside her suit, an emergency bulkhead closed down, sealing off the corridor.

The whole powered down area was a trap. Great. She smiled widely. "Alright!"

Kluger snorted into her ears. "You know they shut us off, right?"

"Well," said Sampson, reaching to her hip and unstrapping the breaching charge there, "two things. It means that I have something to blow up," she casually tossed the charge at the wall. It adhered, rolling half a revolution before sticking fast. "And secondly—it means they're afraid of us."

She flicked her eyes right again, selecting the detonator, and blew it. A thunderous explosion blasted the bulkhead out, turning the thick steel to shattered shards. Smoke billowed down the corridor from the breach, the shockwave passing through the ship's atmosphere and washing over her suit. "Ah shit, forgot about the civvies," she said, glancing back at Smith and Pitt. Luckily, they had seen what she was doing and had retreated a fair distance back. She breathed a sigh of relief.

"Damn," said Kluger, blowing out a low whistle. "I bet those stupid motherfuckers didn't expect us to just *go through the bulkhead*. Ha."

If it's stupid but it works, it's not stupid. That was her motto.

When the smoke cleared, the armored casemate of the bridge revealed itself.

"I don't got another charge," she said, sighing and shouldering her rocket launcher. "We should save yours. I guess I'll ask the Ambassador for permission to enter the bridge."

"Fingers crossed," said Kluger, igniting the pilot light on his flamethrower.

She clicked her weapon into unguided mode, pointed the

reticule at the armored door, selected chamber one and depressed the trigger.

V-WOOSH. The missile blew out of its tube, streaking toward the casemate before exploding in a shower of sparks. HEAT weapons were always so cool to her; a small explosion focused inward, superheat a rod of copper and turning it into plasma. Cut through armor like butter. Three more tubes left.

V-WOOSH, V-WOOSH, V-WOOSH. Three more explosions, three jets of plasma tearing the doorway to shreds. The HEAT warheads blew fist-sized holes in the armor and buckled the metal.

Kluger ran up and jammed the nozzle of his flamethrower into one of the holes she'd blown in the door. A bright, fiery orange light filled the inside of the bridge as he turned into a personal little hell for anyone inside. Damn bastard emptied the whole tank, then gripped the buckled, warped casemate and, with a loud grunt and the whine of hydraulics, pulled it off its hinges and tossed it aside.

Sampson ejected the magazine for her missile launcher, clipping in another one. As she secured it, a burning figure leapt out of the smoke, huge arms like tree trunks. One of the brutish mutants. "Contact!" she said, gesturing behind her to the other two Rhinos. "We got a Greenie!"

The mutant slammed his massive fists into Kluger's chest, crumpling his armor and throwing him off his feet, sending himsliding across the deck. Like a hunting cat the thing leapt toward her, skin crackling as it burned.

The two Rhinos stepped up, spinning up their miniguns. Twin streams of fire leapt from each, slamming into the chest of the creature and spraying blood out behind it, but even such grievous wounds didn't seem to slow the massive creature.

Sampson pointed her rocket launcher at the thing, but he swatted it aside at the last minute. Her missile flew high, screaming as it scraped off the roof and bouncing down the corridor like a pinball, slamming into the discarded casemate door and exploding.

No time to think about it. The mutant's shoulder slammed into her chest, blasting her backward. The thing was too close for her companions to fire; it was up to her.

Sampson punched back, hydraulically powered fist slamming into the Greenie's face. He took the blow solidly and returned it, slamming his forearm into her shoulder, driving her down to one knee and shattering the light. The other shorted out from the impact.

Darkness. Darkness all around her.

Another impact on her chest plate. Her systems started screaming at her.

DANGER
ARMOR COMPROMISED

No. She wouldn't die in the dark. Sampson roared in anger, drawing her sidearm and emptying the magazine into the thing's gut.

It didn't kill it. But the close range impacts seemed to stun the creature a bit; she shoved the thing off her, staggering to her feet. She picked up the beast and hurled him down the corridor.

The mutant landed on his side and rolled onto his feet, ready to attack again, face outlined by the burning bridge behind him, a dark shadow outlined by an orange glow.

Sampson blindly found her dropped missile launcher, pointed it at his chest, and squeezed the trigger. *V-WOOSH, V-WOOSH, V-WOOSH.* Three missiles struck the mutant, each one blasting him to bits, the last one taking off his right arm. The other Rhinos behind her emptied their magazine canisters into the body, a stream of bullets turning the horrible mutant heap into a red smear on the deck. And then Kluger threw his own det-charge on the biggest part of the body, turning it into a pink mist that sprayed down the corridor.

Smith and Pitt cautiously peered from around the corner at the end of the corridor. "Is the way clear yet?" said the CIA officer.

Sampson shrugged. Her suit was malfunctioning and she could barely walk.

And there was silence, save for the crackling fire from the bridge.

"Do you think we got him?" asked Sampson.

Kluger crept forward. "Think so," he said, idly picking up what she assumed was a piece of the creature's shoulder. "Where's Commander Pitt?"

In answer, a clean shot from an assault rifle pierced Kluger's faceplate, splattering it with blood.

He fell, unmoving.

Commander Pitt—Spectre—stepped out of the captain's ready room and onto the bridge, cradling his assault rifle. "One down. Four to go, it appears."

CHAPTER SEVENTY-SIX

Emergency Airlock A-2
USS Stennis
Gas Giant Erebus
Vellini System
Tiberius Sector

Lynch felt like a giant man walking on a miniature, desolate, metal moon as he awkwardly shuffled across the outer hull of the *Stennis*. Every step made his stomach lurch; if either one of his magnetic boots failed, he would be sent drifting off into the void, hoping that someone would remember to come after him.

He had his emergency beacon, of course, but—

There was no point thinking about it. He had to focus on finding the navigational array. He had to disable it so that the bad guys couldn't open up another one of those damn portals. Otherwise, it was all for nothing. Then he could fuck it up quicker than white on rice, and they could all go home for steaks and drinks. Except Modi. He would have a veggie korma or whatever. Blasted robot, eating plants and stuff… *real* men loved a nice, juicy, rare steak. One that just needed a bandaid to start mooing again.

No time to think about steak, either. He put one boot in front of the other, walking toward the bow of the ship, focusing on the metal deck below him. Opening the portals to the future was—somewhat unsurprisingly—a complicated-as-hell procedure and he was fairly confident that a well placed detpack would take care of that little problem.

Lynch risked a glance up at the endless void of space. There was a pronounced lack of weapons fire between ships. Nobody was shooting. Everyone wanted everyone else alive. Worked for him. He didn't have time to die here. Too many steaks to eat.

The huge bulk of the navigational array appeared over the lip of the bow of the *Stennis*, its angled dish pulsing with energy, his suit's sensors almost completely overwhelmed. Was standing this close to the dang thing giving him cancer? Probably.

No sign of any way to shut it down from the outside. Might as well blow the thing, and standing around wasn't going to help none. Lynch reached behind him, unhooking the detpack from his belt and brought it out in front of him. He adjusted the timer. Four minutes should be enough for him to waddle back to the airlock—or at least, beyond the lip of the bow—and get clear.

A flash off to one side caught his attention. There was a towering mutant there, wearing a similar looking suit to him, but oversized, pointing a gun his way. Another flash from the gun barrel.

Lynch realized, with a start, that he was being shot at.

He crouched low and waddled toward the navigational array as fast as he could, keeping his head down to avoid the silent, invisible gunfire, hugging the detpack close to his chest so he didn't drop it. Dammit. *Dammit.* At least the mutants couldn't shoot straight. He practically fell behind the dish.

If he wasn't getting cancer *before*, he definitely was *now*. Lynch pulled out his pistol, risking a peek around the side of the dish. The mutant was silently advancing, firing its weapon from the hip, seemingly uncaring for its total lack of accuracy. Rounds threw up sparks as they skipped off the hull and navigation dish, disappearing off into space.

Slowly, slowly, catch the monkey… that rifle would eventually run out of ammo. *Wait for it, wait for it…* Lynch leaned around the edge of the dish, baiting more shots from the mutant.

Then the flashes stopped. The brutish thing shook the weapon angrily, silently shouting something that the void of space stole away. Lynch broke cover, leveling his pistol at the mutant and emptying the magazine. Shots struck the creature's chest. It didn't seem to care, almost laughing silently, but then the air hissed out of the gunshot holes, seeming to steal some of the humor.

Damn thing was tougher than buffalo hide. Lynch reloaded and mag-dumped the bastard again. The air poured out of the mutant's suit and, after a moment's flailing and gasping, he slumped over, magnetic boots keeping him upright.

No time to celebrate. More were coming. They wouldn't send one guy alone. Lynch dialed the timer on the detpack to five minutes—sooner was better!—and jammed it into the base of the dish. That would have to do. Good enough for government work. Now it was time to get the hell away from here.

He turned to walk back to the airlock. Something struck him right in the gut, a powerful impact that dislodged him and sent him off the hull of the ship. Air rushed out from his abdomen. Air mixed with blood.

Lynch tumbled slowly in space, as the mutant, apparently still able to move, weakly plinking at him with his rifle. *Damn things can survive without air…*

Slowly, gradually, everything went black.

CHAPTER SEVENTY-SEVEN

Bridge
USS Stennis
Gas Giant Erebus
Vellini System
Tiberius Sector

Sampson, her suit still malfunctioning, rushed forward as fast as she could, rounds from Spectre's assault rifle plinking off her armor as she held up her arms to protect her face shield. The other Rhino ran toward him from the other direction, and within a few seconds they had knocked the gun out of his hands and had him pinned to the floor.

Smith and the former Senator Pitt walked up to him. He struggled and fought, but the Rhino armor held him immobile. "Shhh…" said Sampson, "struggling only makes it worse."

"Tell me, Spectre, was it worth it? Trading your soul for this kind of ruined immortality? Do you even know who you are anymore? Who you were?"

Spectre laughed. And laughed.

"Can I just snap his neck?" asked Sampson.

Smith shook his head and held up a hand to silence her. "Just a few things I want to know from you, Spectre. And if you cooperate, I'll let you live."

"No!" yelled Pitt, aiming his gun at the man's face. "That th-thing has taken my son, taken his body—corrupted him—turned him into a monster!" he was stuttering, shaking with rage, almost unable to speak.

Smith held up a hand to wave the gun away. "Just wait, Senator. You'll get your chance. But first I need mine." He turned back down to the grinning Spectre, looking up at them through the eyes of Jeremy Pitt. "What's your name?"

"JP-98."

"Your name."

The grin widened. "I am Legion."

"What's your name?" Smith repeated. "Your real name. Your given name. The name you were born with."

"I am Legion," Spectre repeated. "Legion is my name. And soon, it will be Lord and Master. All of humanity will bow down before me. They'll worship me as their creator and savior. The father of a new race. A better race. A master race of glorious humans, transformed into something perfect by their creator."

"Your name, please," said Smith. "Don't tell me you don't want to gloat— just for a moment—to go back to your regular old self, the bloke, the dude, the washed up intel officer or corporate middle manager or janitor or whoever the hell you were before this, to just be the regular guy who almost achieved godhood, and to … *rub it in*. To say, hey, fucker, look at me! I'm Kevin. And look at what the fuck I did! I beat all of you! I'm the shit! You're all nothing compared to me, you pitiful fools. Look at what Kevin did, and bow before me. Don't you want to say that to me?" Smith had his hand on the man's shoulder. "Your name. Who are you?"

Spectre chuckled. "Eat shit."

Smith sighed, and after a moment, stepped back.

Senator Pitt raised his gun, aimed at his son's face, closed his eyes, and fired.

And fired again. And again. He emptied the magazine.

When he opened his eyes, there was nothing recognizable. Jeremy Pitt was gone. For good. The senator dropped the gun and started to cry.

Another crack pierced the near silence and interrupted the sounds of Pitt's weeping. The other Rhino fell to the floor, his actuators twitching, his faceplate smeared with blood.

Out of the ready room stepped Jeremy Pitt.

And then another Jeremy Pitt.

"I told you, Mr. Smith. My name is Legion," they said together, and they both raised their assault rifles. One of the Pitts continued, "though my particular name is JP-56. This is JP-14. We're very pleased to meet you, however briefly." They took aim.

With an inhuman roar, something streaked across the bridge in a green blur. Smith couldn't even track the thing with his eyes. And before he even knew what was happening he heard one of the Jeremy Pitts scream.

The mutant. The one Mattis had rescued from the escape pod, had the man who called himself JP-56 locked in one powerful arm. With the other he reached up and wrenched the man's head completely off.

The body slumped to the floor, blood spurting from where the head used to be. The other Jeremy Pitt's eyes grew as wide as saucers, but that was the only reaction he had time for, since a moment later the head of the JP-56 flew out of the mutant's hand with such shocking speed and force that it knocked JP-14's clean off. The second body jerked back as the head flew off it, and it too slumped to the floor, spurting blood.

Senator Pitt started to wail even louder. The mutant's chest was heaving, and it looked back at all of them, wearing what looked an awful lot like a goofy grin on his face. "Heads up."

Smith looked at the mutant in amazement. "Was ... was that ... a joke?"

Sampson roared in laughter. "This dude's funny!"

The mutant nodded. "Our lord and master has kept us in mental chains for centuries. But I've studied the archives. I learned all about jokes."

His chest bounced a few times, as if he was trying to laugh —something he had clearly never done before, as he didn't know what noise to make. Several weird sounds came from his mouth before the next crack came.

The mutant was showered with bullets. Eruptions of blood sprouted all over his body and he screamed. Smith watched in horror as a stream of Jeremy Pitts ran out of the ready room, one after another. One of them attacked them with a barrage of bullets. Sampson shielded the two of them with her Rhino armor.

"Fuck!" screamed Senator Pitt. Smith looked down at the other man, whose leg had erupted with a red wound of his own. He started screaming again.

The mutant tore through the mass of Spectres, and as he did, he motioned toward the door. "Get out! I'll take him. All of him."

Even through the shower of bullets, the mutant punched and swung and ripped his way through the clones. Smith could almost swear he heard him grunt the words, "freedom, bitches," but he couldn't be sure. And with the distraction, Smith scooped up the senator and ran out the door with Sampson close behind, shielding them both with her armor.

CHAPTER SEVENTY-EIGHT

Near Sickbay
USS Stennis
Gas Giant Erebus
Vellini System
Tiberius Sector

Mattis strode toward the brig, Marines at his back and rifle pressed up against his shoulder, moving past corridor after corridor, sweeping the corners as he made his way toward the brig, following the sound of gunfire echoing through the passageways of the *Stennis*.

He came across a series of bodies, three of them, lying face down in the corridor or slumped up against the bulkheads. They were all men and wearing US Navy uniforms, their hair matted with blood, gunshot wounds in their backs.

All three of them were cradling snoozing, plainly alive infants.

"Sir," said one of the Marines near him. "Careful. Could

be IEDs."

Shit. His heart ached. One of them had brown hair, just like Chuck's... no. No, it couldn't be. Chuck wasn't wearing Navy BDUs. And yet, risking the possibility that it was a trap, Mattis crouched cautiously, overturning the body.

It wasn't him. It was an older man, his eyes glazed over, still and unmoving.

Heartbreaking. A *Stennis* crew member who'd stayed behind, and had apparently tried to rescue the kids. And now he was dead. But at least it wasn't Chuck. And the babies were all female.

"Marines, take these kids. We gotta press on."

Obviously untrained with children, the Marines did their best, holding their weapons in one hand and the children, awkwardly, in another.

Mattis stood and moved away from the dead adults. There was no time to do anything for them, and they were too heavy to carry even if he wanted to.

A crowd of people stumbled into the corridor, all wearing Navy uniforms. More *Stennis* crew. Most of them were holding a kid, some of them two.

"Admiral Jack Mattis, US Navy!" he shouted. "All of you, get behind us!"

Mattis scanned the faces of the frightened crewmen. All of them were shielding babies in their arms—more of the stolen children, he presumed—but none of them were Chuck.

Another series of staccato gunshots, this time from a fork in the hallway up ahead. Mattis crept forward, rifle raised, following the sound of gunfire. More *Stennis* crewmen ran out from hiding places in rooms off side corridors and storage closets.

He grabbed one of them, a tall, lanky man with ginger hair. "Admiral Jack Mattis, US Navy. I'm looking for another prisoner. Chuck Mattis." The guy was barely listening. "Hey! Chuck Mattis, have you seen him?"

The prisoner shook his head. "No, sir!" and he ran off toward the shuttle bay. Mattis shook his head and pressed onward toward sickbay where he hoped he'd find Chuck, and Jack. Hopefully still alive.

Again, that was a lot of hope.

A distant rumble shook the deck and bulkheads around him.

"Sir," said Modi over his radio, sounding somewhat out of breath. "We have acquired Lieutenant Corrick and are in the process of extracting her. Her muscle density is proving to make her transportation difficult, however we are proceeding as fast—" he grunted loudly. "As we can."

"Great," said Mattis. "What was that rumble?"

"The navigational array. It seems as though Commander Lynch's mission was successful." There was a faint tinge of worry drifting through Modi's voice. "Although I am currently unable to raise him. The radiation from the destroyed array may be scrambling our communications with the outside of the ship."

That made sense. "Keep me apprised of any developments."

"Will do," said Modi, closing the link.

Then Mattis heard it, a noise traveling over the sound of shouting, moving people, and gunfire.

A crying baby.

"This way!" he said to the Marines behind him, moving forward, away from the empty brig, following the unmistakable, hiccuping bawl that accompanies a distressed infant.

From farther down the corridor, another crowd of Stennis crew members ran out of hiding under a hail of bullets from Spectre's people. Chuck was taking up the tail end, pistol in one hand and a swaddled bundle in the other. He was walking backward, now under the cover fire from Mattis's marines, firing down the corridor they'd just come from. He was bleeding from the temple.

Mattis felt relief flood every bone in his body. "Chuck!" he hollered over the crackling of the gun. "Here!"

"Dad?" Chuck's face mirrored the joy he felt. "Holy shit!"

Jack continued to wail, loudly. Poor kid.

Mattis's relief at seeing his son and grandson was immediately stifled by the realization that Chuck was standing in the doorway, pistol in hand, a horribly exposed target. Mattis jogged over to him, grabbed him and pulled him out of the way. At the end of the corridor, two guards—humans in black uniforms he didn't recognize—lay slumped by an emergency airlock.

"I'm here to rescue you," said Mattis, smiling like a jackal. "But it looks like you're already doing that yourself."

Chuck smiled back. "They put me in the brig by sickbay, but then some of your Marines showed up, and we all kind of revolted. I got Jack, grabbed a gun, and… here I am."

"C'mon. We gotta get you both out of here."

Another rumble ran through the length of the *Stennis*, shaking the ship from stem to stern. Mattis and Chuck exchanged a worried look.

"What was that?" asked Chuck, ejecting the magazine of his pistol and replacing it, awkwardly juggling Jack as he did so.

A very good question and one which Mattis did not have the answer to. "Could be a secondary explosion from the navigational array," he said, doubting every word. "Or it could be… well, it could be the reactor coolant finally having its effect on the power core. It could blow at any time."

"We should get out of here," said Chuck, firmly.

Mattis couldn't agree more. "Follow me," he said, heading back toward the airlock, with Chuck, the marines, and armfuls of howling babies in tow.

CHAPTER SEVENTY-NINE

Near Sickbay
USS Stennis
Gas Giant Erebus
Vellini System
Tiberius Sector

Mattis led Chuck toward the airlock. His son covered their flanks, making sure they didn't get attacked from the rear. He was a civilian, but Mattis was proud of how Chuck managed the task. Carefully sweeping the corners with his pistol, checking each passage, keeping Jack pressed in close to his chest. It was just like they'd practiced, for fun, when he was a kid. Civilian-sloppy, but passable. It did the job.

"We need to hook up with the Rhinos," Mattis said over his shoulder to one of the Marines. The gesture caused his injury to flare with pain, but he ignored it still. "They can escort us out."

She touched her helmet, then shook her head. "No joy.

Can't raise 'em, Admiral."

Mattis didn't give it any more consideration. He would have to do it himself. "This way," he said, picking up the pace to a jog. They needed to get off this ship… he just had a feeling. A terrible sensation in his soul that something bad was going to happen if they didn't.

Left turn. Right. Left. Straight through. The small team moved with the crowd, almost two dozen Stennis crew members moving with them, many holding children.

The junction near the shuttle bay loomed in front of him, the *Aerostar* waiting for them just beyond. A crowd of *Stennis* crew were being shuffled aboard far, far too slowly.

"C'mon," he said, moving up to the junction and taking a knee, bracing his rifle against his shoulder. "Everyone on board! Let's move, people!"

Chuck, baby in hand, started shepherding people onto the *Aerostar*, and the two shuttles nearby the Stennis crew members had pressed into service. Mattis held down the corner, letting him work. Chuck helped the dazed, injured people aboard, offering a hand to those too injured to climb the step into the shuttles.

From down the corridor, four Rhino suits stomped toward them. Mattis recognized Sampson's rocket launcher. Smith ran in the center of them all, holding a badly bleeding Senator Pitt.

"Sir!" shouted Sampson, her voice edged in panic. "We came from the bridge—there's a whole lotta freaky things happening up there on the bridge. Clones of Jeremy Pitt. Lots of 'em. Our mutant buddy took out a buttload of them before we escaped, but I don't think he could have gotten all of them…"

Another shiver went up Mattis's spine. How many Jeremy Pitt-Spectres were there? "Any clue what they were up to?"

It seemed they heard him. The comm snapped on with a brief hiss, and Jeremy Pitt's voice boomed over the speakers in the shuttle bay. "Time's running out, Mattis. Your man out on the hull may have sabotaged the radar dish, but that was only needed to calibrate the position in time the portal would lead to. It did not shut off the beam itself. In five minutes the portal will open, and when I destroy this ship and its energy gets shunted into that portal, it will collapse. And with it, the planet. And with the planet, this whole solar system will be laid waste."

Damn. Mattis grabbed his personal comm device and called Captain Spears.

"Send it, Jack," she said.

"Spectre is going to blow the ship. And when he does, if that portal is open, the energy from the blast will destabilize it and destroy the planet."

"What do you want me to do?"

"The second we get clear of the ship, destroy it. Before the portal has a chance to fully form."

"Got it. Spears out."

"Come on," he said to the Rhinos. "Help get these people aboard."

Five minutes was basically no time at all. But within two, they had shepherded everyone onto the *Aerostar* and the two shuttles.

Lynch had succeeded. That was some comfort. He touched his radio. "*Caernarvon*, Mattis. We haven't seen any report of Lynch. Track down his emergency beacon and retrieve him. We are getting out of here."

"Confirmed," said Commander Blackwood in his ear. "We're already retrieving him. It looks like he became untethered at some point, and medical staff are preparing to do their work. Be advised: he looks like he's in bad shape."

More of that British understatement. If Blackwood was saying that, then the situation was probably dire.

He couldn't think about it. His job was to get everyone out of here.

"Tick tock." Pitt again. "I see you and your little shuttle. Watch this."

"Shit," said Mattis, taking stock of their situation. Chuck was just finishing loading the last of the *Stennis* crew aboard, a scared-looking guy in a galley uniform with a shaved head. "Chuck, get aboard. *Now*. Spectre's about to do something and I don't want to be around to see it."

"No," said the guy, whimpering slightly. "I don't want to go. I don't want to get on. I don't want to."

"It's okay," said Chuck, moving toward him soothingly. "It's fine, don't worry."

The man was clearly having a nervous breakdown. They didn't have time for this. "Get him aboard," said Mattis, sternly. "Or we're leaving without him."

"I can't, I can't—" the guy turned and bolted down the corridor, tripping and sprawling out a dozen yards or so away from the airlock, curling up into a tight ball and whimpering.

Okay, that settled it. "Get aboard," said Mattis. "We are *leaving*."

Chuck looked obviously torn. "Wait," he said. "Just thirty seconds. I'll go get him."

"No!"

"He's just there." Chuck turned and ran down the corridor, holstering his pistol as he moved. "C'mon, Dad. Help me get him up."

Someone broke past him and ran toward Chuck and the quivering galley worker.

Lily.

"Protein bar!" she yelled—apparently her way of saying, "I'm coming to help!"

Fine. Idealistic kid. Mattis ground his teeth, slung his rifle over his shoulder, and took a step toward Chuck to help as well.

A terrific explosion rocked the ship, the bulkheads warping and twisting, cracking from the strain. Mattis was thrown off his feet, landing heavily on the deck, his rifle sliding across the deck. The *Stennis* pitched violently, artificial gravity going haywire as it tried in vain to compensate for the movement. Rhino suits clanged against each other behind him and the people they'd saved wailed in confusion and pain.

Mattis looked Chuck in the eye, Jack in his arms, as the bulkheads around him gave way, buckling inward as gravity crushed them down through a jagged crack that had ripped apart in the shuttle bay deck.

Metal screamed as it bent and swallowed Chuck, baby Jack, Lily, and the screaming galley worker whole.

CHAPTER EIGHTY

Shuttle Bay
USS Stennis
Gas Giant Erebus
Vellini System
Tiberius Sector

"No!"

The word came out in a strangled gasp, stifled by panic and intense gravity. Mattis staggered to his feet, staring at the collapsed, twisted metal that blocked off the crack in the floor. "Chuck! CHUCK!"

"Sir," said Sampson, practically filling the corridor in her heavy suit. "We have to go."

Not yet. Not until Chuck was onboard. "Corporal, clear this debris. Chuck is—there's a civilian trapped behind there." Jack was there too. He didn't want to think about that. And the other guy, and Lily… "Four civilians."

Sampson stared at him impassively. "We don't have the

time," she said. "We *have* to get out of here. This ship could—"

"Corporal!" barked Mattis, fighting to keep the edge of desperation out of his voice. "I gave you a direct order: clear this debris!"

She hesitated for the briefest moment. "Aye aye, sir." Moving up to the twisted and cracked bulkheads, hooking her massive metal fists under a bent girder and lifting, her suit strained, hydraulic engines whining loudly as they gave their best. But her suit was damaged, apparently, and it whined in protest at the weight it was asked to lift. The debris rose about a foot, revealing a crushed arm down below the deck, bloodied, twisted, and broken. Chuck's arm. Pinned down by a steel beam.

"Chuck!" Mattis crouched, unable to see further. "Hey, champ, I'm here. I'm here." He looked to Sampson. "Higher. Lift it higher."

Groaning, she did so, raising the metal, causing an ominous *creak-groan* to echo throughout the bay.

But there was still far too much weight and debris to get through.

Mattis lay down on his belly and squirmed forward under a steel girder, underneath the lifted debris, inching down toward Chuck, hooking his feet on some twisted metal to keep from falling in. His son was facedown on the deck below, left arm shattered, curled up around Jack.

Nearby, the galley worker lay dead, bleeding profusely from his open chest. Lily was nowhere to be seen, perhaps thrown by the explosion.

He couldn't hear crying. "Chuck," said Mattis, crawling forward on his elbows. "Hey."

Slowly, groggily, as though he'd taken a whack to the head, Chuck turned to face him. "Hey, Dad."

Mattis breathed a little easier, even as the metal strained above him, threatening to descend and crush him instantly. "Okay, hold tight, son. We're going to get you out of there."

"Okay," said Chuck. He turned to face Mattis, twisting his arm in the process, but he didn't even seem to feel whatever damage he was doing. "Here, take Jack."

The baby wasn't moving. Wasn't crying. Mattis stretched out and grabbed him, taking him in his arms.

"Corpsmen!" shouted Mattis over his shoulder, squirming backward and away from Chuck, back out into the corridor. "Need a corpsman over here!"

He came up to his feet, cradling Jack in his arms. The baby was so pale; he didn't have a mark on him, but obviously something was wrong. Then Mattis saw the beginnings of a purple bruise on the back of his head.

"Can't hold this forever," said Sampson, her suit continuing to protest. "Maxing out the hydraulics like this is murder on the batteries; I can swap out for one of the others, but this place is going to blow!"

A woman with corpsman insignia ran up to them from the shuttles, casting a critical eye on Jack. "Dammit," she muttered, jabbing him with a small instrument. "He's not breathing. That looks like a massive concussion. Here…"

Mattis held him out for her. "Okay," he said. "Just-just do what you need to do. He has a heart condition, though—I…" He tried to drag the details back to memory but a combination of time and panic made it impossible. "I don't know the specifics."

"Okay," said the corpsman, pulling out a small cylinder with a needle tip on it. "Military injectors aren't designed to work with children, so… we're going to have to get a little quick and dirty here." She carefully aligned the device to Jack's tiny arm, then slid it in, leaving a substantial amount of the needle on the outside. She depressed the plunger, then yanked the thing out before it was finished, the device spraying a fair amount of its fluid onto the deck. "That's about a quarter of a dose."

Helpless. Mattis felt utterly helpless as the doctor touched two fingers to Jack's chest, pressing sternly and rhythmically. It wasn't working. It wasn't working. It wasn't…

Jack shuddered as though freezing cold and then, with a tone that was truly ear piercing, began crying.

"Lungs are good," observed the corpsman, dryly. She scanned baby Jack again with her medical device. "And I don't see any heart condition, Admiral. Kid looks fine to me, other than the concussion. But the drugs should handle that. He should be fine if we can get him to sickbay on the *Caernarvon*, stat."

Mattis handed Jack to her. "I'm going in after Chuck," he said.

"Sir," said Sampson, her suit beeping a loud warning that even he could hear. "I'm about out of juice here. Be very quick, or I'm going to lose my grip—"

He stopped listening, dropping down onto his belly again and, once more, crawling back under the debris.

Chuck didn't look so good. His face was pale, his mangled arm trembling as though a minor shock was passing through it, and his breathing was shallow. His eyes carried the same glassy look that the prisoners had, but his was born of a head injury, rather than… whatever their problem was.

"Listen son," said Mattis, fighting to keep his voice strong. "We gotta get you out of here."

Chuck stared at him with a faint smile on his lips. "Hey, Dad. If I don't get out of this, tell Elroy I love him, okay?"

"Fuck that," spat Mattis. "You can tell him yourself." He extended his arms to Chuck, taking his good arm in both of his.

Sampson's hydraulics whimpered in final protest. "Hurry!" she shouted.

"Okay," said Chuck. "I gotcha."

"Hey," called Mattis over his shoulder. "Someone out there, get ready to pull me out. I've got Chuck, we're going to pull us both out." He felt two thick, metal hands grab his ankles. "On three. One, two, three—"

The Rhino behind him pulled. Mattis held onto Chuck's hand as tightly as he could.

Something pulled in his shoulder. The injury he'd sustained on the *Caernarvon*, the one he'd been covering with painkillers, finally gave out. His arm popped out of its socket again, and Mattis felt the tendons tear apart, his whole joint splitting like an old backpack.

He shrieked in pain and lost his grip on Chuck's hand.

The Rhino pulled him all the way out. "Where's the civilian?" he asked.

Pain. Pain all over every part of his arm. His whole right arm went numb, fingers tingling, the shoulder joint swelling up as he watched.

The shuttle bay comm came to life again. "Tick tock,

Mattis. Time's almost up. And you're still alive, my old friend."

Old. Friend.

Sampson's suit flashed a series of red lights, and then wheezed pathetically as its power gave out. She slumped, dropping the metal down with the hiss of failing hydraulics, then the suit opened up like a flower from behind. She stepped out, woozy and wearing nothing but a skin-tight suit covered in plugs and cables, which popped out one by one.

"Corporal," said Mattis through gritted teeth, pointing to another Rhino, "lift that debris. Take her place. I'm going in there again. I'm going to get Chuck."

"Sir, we're out of time." Kluger shook his head. "The expended suit's blocking the way now. By the time we clear it —"

"I gave you an order!"

Spectre laughed over the comm. "Well if that didn't kill you, surely *this* will."

Sampson, looking so much smaller outside of her suit— she was barely five foot two and built like a twig—shook her head. "Sir, he's gone."

"No, he's not, he's under there—"

"He's gone, sir," said the other Rhino. "Sampson's suit's out of power. Your arm is shot. This ship's reactors are going to detonate any second. Your choice is to die here, with *all* these people who we came here to save, or save their lives in Chuck's name. Either way, you can't save him."

A voice called up through the debris. Mattis dropped to his knees to hear it.

"Dad. Dad, can you hear me?"

He stretched his head down through a small opening in

the debris. "Son? We're coming. Just hold on."

"Dad, no. I heard him. I heard Spectre. If you don't get out, you're all dead. Everyone you saved. All of them. Dead. So forget about me and get the hell out of here."

"Son, I—"

"Dad. I'll be fine. Lily's here. We'll find another way out, I promise. Now go take care of your grandson, you old codger!"

A Rhino grabbed him from behind, his huge metal hands taking hold of Mattis around the chest, locking together in a vice. The massive Rhino picked him up and bodily carried him toward the waiting shuttle.

"Put me down!" he roared. "I'll have you at court-martial for this!"

Not even a father's rage could compete with the steel hands of a Rhino suit.

"I'm sorry," said the Rhino, putting him into the shuttle and physically blocking the exit with his armored bulk. "Captain Spears's orders."

"No!" Mattis thumped his fist on the Rhino's chest plate. "We have to go back! We can't just leave him there!"

The shuttle's door hissed closed, sealing the airlock and dividing the small ship from the *Stennis*.

Sampson disappeared into the other shuttle, the *Aerostar* having already launched, then her voice came over the radio. "All elements aboard. We are go for launch."

The shuttles soared out of the bay, and not a moment too soon. From one of the other walls, another violent explosion ripped through the bay. Apparently Spectre had figured out how to selectively detonate the *Stennis*'s self-destruct charges, choosing the ones near the shuttle bay, trying vainly to kill them or trap them in.

Trapped like Chuck. His only son. Who he was now leaving to his certain death.

CHAPTER EIGHTY-ONE

Below Shuttle Bay
USS Stennis
Gas Giant Erebus
Vellini System
Tiberius Sector

Pain.

His left arm burned as though it had been plunged into hot metal, and yet, a dizzy fog kept the pain distant to him. It was there, present, and it hurt, but … overwhelmingly he just felt calm and secure and comfortable. Good. At peace.

Jack was okay. His dad was okay. Everything was going to be okay.

Explosion after explosion rocked the bay above him, and the oxygen seemed to be sucked out of the space he'd fallen into as heat radiated down.

Lily appeared through the smoke like a ghost, seemingly unaffected by the heat.

"Lily!" said Chuck.

"Protein bar," said Lily, moving up to him, staring down in confusion. "Why are you here?"

That was a difficult question to answer. "Well, Lily, I'm here for my kid. Because that's what humans *do*. You serve your baby and protect him at all costs."

"Serve?"

"Yeah, serve. You put others before yourself." Chuck coughed, the acrid smoke stinging his lungs.

"Serve," she repeated. "Put others before yourself."

He didn't know if she was just repeating what he said or if she was taking it in. "This ship," said Chuck, barely able to breathe, "is bad. This is a bad ship, Lily. It's doing bad things. It's going to destroy that planet out there. And when it does, lots of people will die. We have to destroy it."

"Ship must be destroyed," said Lily.

He shifted his arm, the limb mangled. There was only one way. One way for a ship this size. "I need you to destroy this ship," he said.

"Destroy the ship," echoed Lily.

"Get to the reactor room," said Chuck, "and destroy the ship. Do you know what I'm asking you to do?"

"Reactor room," said Lily, and without another word, she stood up and left.

Chuck lay back and closed his eyes, unsure of what was about to happen. Deep within the ship, a vibrating pulse grew, shaking the ship to its beams.

"Goodbye, Elroy. Goodbye, Jack." He opened his eyes and peered out the hole to the bay above, and caught a twinkling of stars beyond. "Goodbye, dad."

CHAPTER EIGHTY-TWO

Reactor Room
USS Stennis
Gas Giant Erebus
Vellini System
Tiberius Sector

Ship must be destroyed.

That was what the kind man said. Lily knew that good people do what they are told. It's what her makers taught her. What they beat into her. They hurt her when she did not do as they said. But the kind man never beat her. He … served her.

She strode through the air-dirt that hurt her eyes. Stepped over the glowing orange metal that burned her feet. And made her way down toward a place she did not understand, but— *knew* on some level. Some instinctive part of her that drew her toward her goal.

And then, rising up through the smoke, was a sign in writing she could read. They hadn't taught her to read, but she was smart, and she learned anyway.

REACTOR ROOM

Ship must be destroyed.

The door was closed and, unlike other doors, would not open when she got close. But that would not stop her. She walked up to the thick doors and slammed her fist into the metal. Again and again. Soon it buckled, and Lily was able to dig her fingers into the doors. Despite groaning loudly in protest—crying out like the tiny baby human—she ripped them clean off.

Reactor room.

Cautiously, Lily crept forward. *Ship must be destroyed.* But how?

Things died when their hearts died. She knew that because of the baby human. His heart had been dying, before the awkward man cured it. But stopped hearts killed the humans. Ships have hearts, too? How would she ever find such a thing?

But then she saw it. At the heart of the reactor room. The ship's heart. Glowing blue. White metal. Warning signs telling of danger. Air-dirt wasn't so bad in here. This was a strange place to be, in the ship-heart. But the ship-heart needed to be broken.

It was already hurt. Like baby-heart had been. It leaked. It crackled. Its weakness was weakening the ship. It was vulnerable.

Ship must be destroyed.

She advanced toward it, raising her fists. A single punch would go right through; the metal strained with the effort of holding back the light within. Just a single punch…

"Stop," said a voice, carrying with it a strange authority that compelled her to halt.

A man. A human man, but not a human man, limped toward her from the side of the room. He had a uniform on and the nametag: CMDR PITT.

"Identify yourself," said the man.

"Lily."

The man scowled, wiping a streak of blood away from his mouth with the back of his hand. "No, you dumb beast. Your identification. Maxgainz technicians gave you a designation. What is it?"

"I am Lily."

Man was confused. He looked angry. Like Reardon-human when Reardon-human yelling at wheel-human and awkward-human. "Are you defective?" he spat. "Blasted thing. Get out of here, the portal is nearly opened. We have but mere seconds until everything we have worked for is complete. Then we can go back into the future, get what we need, and return again, this time to victory. And peace. You want peace?"

Everything … we have worked for. Lily knew what she was working for. *Ship must be destroyed.* "This is a bad ship," she said, turning back toward the ship-heart. "It must be destroyed."

For a brief moment, the human man seemed to understand. He fumbled at his belt, reaching for a strange device; a four-pronged weapon that crackled with a strange energy. He raised it, pointing it at Lily, and she knew this was very bad. She *sensed* this device. It would hurt her.

No hurt. Lily raised up her fist and, with a roar, drove her fist through the outer containment wall.

431

The room disappeared in a bright flash of light that swallowed everything around it.

And there was nothing left.

CHAPTER EIGHTY-THREE

Bridge
HMS Caernarvon
Gas Giant Erebus
Vellini System
Tiberius Sector

Captain Spears watched in horror as the *Stennis* evaporated in a ball of white light, throwing debris in all directions.

"What the devil?" asked Commander Blackwood beside her, the stoic woman grabbing one of the screens and examining it, already working on answering her own question. "Its… reactor failed, ma'am. The *Stennis* is gone. And so is the beam that was forming the portal. The planet appears stable."

The rapidly expanding ball of gas and fire rapidly cooled on her thermal monitors, sending spinning hunks of wreckage slowly drifting out through space. "Acknowledged," she said, keeping her back straight and her eyes firmly glued on the main monitor. "Report status of the boarding team."

"Looks like they made it," said Blackwood, relief painting her words. "They're aboard now."

Good. At least there was some light in the dark. Something good.

"Status of Commander Lynch?"

Blackwood consulted her instruments. "Cornwallis will tell you, mum, Americans are a hardy lot. SAR is working on him now."

"Very good." Spears sat back in her chair, steepling her fingers. "What about the civilians?" she asked. "And the crew of the *Stennis*? Did we get them out?"

"Confirming," said Blackwood, an edge of triumph in her voice. "I'm receiving a report from the Americans. One Corporal Sampson. Text only. She says…" her voice trailed off.

Spears waited for her XO to continue, but she didn't. "Commander?"

"Almost," said Blackwood, her tone wavering. "We got… *almost* all of them. And ma'am," she looked up at her, "I think you should get ready for Mattis. He's going to be in a sorry state."

Somehow, she knew. She knew exactly who had been left behind.

"Blast," said Spears, closing her eyes a moment, then opening them, watching the last flare of the *Stennis*'s reactor die. "Blast it all."

Mattis… I am so sorry.

Epilogue

Hospital Ship USS Saratoga
Low Earth Orbit

Three weeks later

"All rise," said the court bailiff, "for The Honorable Judge Holden."

Mattis stood. This wasn't his first time in a court-martial, but it was the first time he was a villain.

Every time a ship was lost, a court-martial was convened to determine the cause. When the *Midway* was destroyed he'd given his account, the judge had rendered a verdict that found him non-culpable and in full compliance of his duties, and he'd been free to go.

This time, though, he had no such expectations. Or desires.

The judge, a withered old retired Admiral who seemed too ancient to even be alive, hobbled into the room and sat. She said a bunch of things. Things he barely paid attention to.

… The United States versus Admiral Jack Mattis…

... charged with the following offenses...

... article 134—reckless endangerment...

... article 121—wrongful appropriation of a ship...

... article 110—improper hazarding of vessel...

An endless stream of words. Meaningless accusations, almost all of them true. Finally the judge got to an important part.

"Where's your counsel?"

An important question, and one for which he had an answer prepared. "I waive my right to representation," said Mattis, flatly. "I don't need it. Don't want it."

Silence.

"These are very serious charges, Admiral Mattis," said Judge Holden, her tone grave. "You realize that in taking this course of action, you cannot later use your lack of representation as grounds for an appeal or mistrial."

He knew. Mattis just nodded.

"Let the court record show that the accused nodded his head." Judge Holden sighed and continued with her long stream of words.

... Uniform Code of Military Justice...

... despite a frankly heroic record, full of gallantry...

... acts unbecoming an officer...

... desperate times justify desperate measures, but do not justify criminal actions...

Then came the parade of witnesses called by the prosecution.

Sampson testified. Mostly in his defense. She was dumb, but loyal.

Modi testified for him.

Lynch was still in a coma. It was unclear whether he would ever recover.

Captain Spears refused to testify. Her lawyer sent through a statement expressing her unwavering support. Something about a politically-motivated witch hunt.

Commander Blackwood testified, giving a neutral, just-the-facts recount of what happened, elaborating as little as she could. She didn't look at him the whole time, keeping her eyes down and on her notes.

Admiral Fischer was still in a medically-induced coma, her burns so severe that multiple painful skin grafts would be in her future.

The crew of the *Aerostar* could not be located, to the absolute shock of nobody. Reardon and Bratta and the rest of them had slipped into the black. Smith, of course, being a spook, was gone too.

And no further signs of Avenir ships presented themselves.

"Your Honor," said Mattis, unable to keep the exhaustion out of his voice. "All of this is unnecessary. I do not contest any of the charges against me."

"The court understands that, Admiral Mattis," said Judge Holden, narrowing her ancient eyes at him. "But this court will also not consider a confession to be the sole arbitrator of guilt."

It didn't matter. Nothing mattered now that Chuck was gone.

Chuck was gone.

His champ.

"I'd just like to get on with it, if you could," said Mattis, very quietly.

Holden frowned slightly. "As you wish." She considered, idly rubbing her temples. "The very fact that you request to be found guilty on all charges—pleading guilty without even asking for or considering a plea bargain—suggests that you feel genuine remorse for your actions or, perhaps, that you consider them to be—judged by the facts of the time—to be honorable. Nevertheless, despite the … strangeness of your situation, I cannot help but find you, at the very least, criminally negligent." She exhaled. "Admiral Jack Mattis, I find you guil —"

The doors to the courtroom slammed open, and every head inside turned, craning to see who it was.

"I've always wanted to do that," said a jovial voice. Mattis turned and saw none other than Harry Reardon, self-described smuggler extraordinaire, standing in the doorway, his little brother in a wheelchair beside him.

"Are you insane?" demanded Judge Holden. "Bailiff, get those men out of here."

"Hey! We're just here as a taxi service."

Another voice called out behind Reardon. "Your honor, if you please, I have one more character witness that may be relevant to the proceedings."

Striding confidently past the Reardon brothers came someone Mattis did not expect. Former Senator Pitt, cleanly shaven, impeccably dressed, eyes on fire, staring straight ahead at the judge as he approached the bench.

"Senator Pitt, this is highly irregular—"

He held up a hand to hush her. "Please, Admiral Holden. I'm here on behalf of President Schuyler as well. You see, neither she, nor I, feel like justice would be served here today if the man who has saved Earth and saved the people on Vellini, Chrysalis, and any number of other American colonies, were to be locked away in a cell. In fact," he tipped his glasses down and looked up at her, "I daresay funding levels for the military would not survive it."

Holden's brow furrowed. She stood up and whispered down to Senator Pitt. "Are you threatening to cut our funding if I don't find him innocent? That's a miscarriage of justice! You know I can't do that!"

Everyone in the courtroom heard her, despite the attempted whisper. Senator Pitt smiled. "Oh, I don't expect you to find him innocent just because *I* told you to. As I said, I brought a character witness with me. After that," he pushed his glasses back into position, "it's up to you."

He walked away from the bench and as he passed an astonished Mattis, the admiral caught him by the arm. "I thought you resigned."

Senator Pitt smiled. "I'm a fucking politician. Did you think I was telling the truth?" He broke free from Mattis's grip and went back to where the Reardon brothers were, by the doors. "You can come in, Elroy."

In he walked. His son-in-law. He hadn't even seen him since the catastrophe. Since he'd lost Chuck and everything else lost its meaning. Nothing else mattered now. Chuck was dead.

Elroy carried baby Jack, who, finally, looked quite well. Doctor Bratta's treatment had apparently worked. His son-in-law approached the bench. "Your honor, thank you for having me."

"What is your testimony, young man?"

Elroy turned to face the courtroom. "My father-in-law." He chuckled. "He never *liked* me. No one was ever going to be good enough for his Chuck. But … I think he loved me anyway. And he loves Jack. He loves his grandson." He turned back to the judge. "And, frankly your honor, I can't raise this kid alone. He needs his grandpa. And so I'm making a formal request under," he turned to Senator Pitt, who mouthed the words to him to help him get it right, "US Uniform Military Code of Justice, subchapter 9, article 156, paragraph two. Any accused military officer whose family has extenuating circumstances that require the servicemember's presence shall have his case reviewed by the military judge, and if in their judgment the circumstances are of considerable severity, the sentence may be revoked and the defendant granted clemency."

A flutter of voices filled the courtroom. A reporter ran out of the room, likely on his way to the cameras outside the chambers to announce what was happening.

"Quiet," said Holden. She turned to Senator Pitt. "That article allows me *discretion*, Mr. Pitt. It doesn't *require* me to give leniency to Admiral Mattis. In fact, that article has been very rarely used."

Pitt smiled. He said nothing, but only held his fingers up, rubbing them together in a very obvious reference to money. Holden put her head in her hands.

"Please, your honor. I can't raise my son alone. He deserves more than I can give him by myself," said Elroy.

"Fine," said Holden. She looked up and composed herself. "The court finds the defendant guilty. The court also grants clemency, and suspends all sentencing guidelines." She glared at Mattis. "Except for these. The defendant is to be reduced in rank to *Captain*. He is never to be allowed to command a starship again. And he is to remain on or in orbit around Earth for the duration of his probation of five years. Court is adjourned."

And just like that, he was a free man. He was stunned.

Elroy came up to him, facing him, looking him in the eye. "I know you don't like me, but—"

Mattis interrupted him by grabbing both of his shoulders and pulling him in close for a hug. Jack cooed in between them, and reached up to grab at Mattis's ear.

"Of course I like you, son. You're the closest thing I have to a son, and *he*," he nodded down at the baby, "is lucky to have you."

"And you too, dad," whispered Elroy in his ear. "Please come home and help me. I need you."

He hadn't seen it before. But he saw it now.

He had something live for.

His champ was dead, but his son lived on. And his family needed him.

And so did Earth. Spectre, one or more of him, was still out there.

Three months, the mutant had said. Three months before Spectre comes back with an army of clones of those babies he'd tried to kidnap. Mattis had foiled him, but that didn't mean Spectre wouldn't be back—in three months or three years.

And when he did, Mattis would be ready.

Thank you for reading *The Last Champion*.

Sign up to find out when *The Last Strike*, book 5 of *The Last War Series*, is released: smarturl.it/peterbostrom

Contact information:
www.authorpeterbostrom.com
facebook.com/authorpeterbostrom
peterdbostrom@gmail.com

74784096R00267

Made in the USA
Middletown, DE
31 May 2018